Praise for Carter Quinn's

VANISHED

" *Vanished* is not a rollercoaster of emotion. It is a slow downward spiral into oblivion. You experience every gut wrenching second with Henry. You experience the confusion, the fear, the loss, the hope, everything. In the end, I was bawling my eyes out. I was making myself dizzy crying so hard for Henry and Tom. I can't remember a book affecting me so deeply."

–Prism Book Alliance

"For such a short story, so much happens. There is no time to get settled, there are no "down" spots; *Vanished* keeps going until the very end. As the story comes to a close there is one last zinger. I was left speechless, which doesn't happen very often when it comes to books."

–MANtastic Fiction

"This story has just blown me away, chewed me up, spat me out and left me physically and emotionally drained. It's not very often that I read a story that gets me sobbing buckets, but this one did it!"

–Sinfully Gay Romance Book Reviews

"There is a lot of punch packed into this short story. It is suspenseful and thrilling and a real page turner."

– The Blogger Girls

"Life is a collection of important moments strung together by time. Carter Quinn offers us glimpses of those moments between Henry and Tom, scattered throughout Henry's search for his husband. It's beautiful and heartbreaking and hopeful and tragic all in one. This is one emotional story, guys."

–JK Hogan Books

"Carter Quinn, you packed so much into this story, but the best you gave the reader are the feelings you draw out of us. It is the thought that a loved one could in a moment of time be gone, poof into thin air. It is the feeling of helplessness. Henry is so off kilter, so lost as is the reader. Where is Tom MacKinnon?"

– The Paranormal Romance Guild

Praise for Carter Quinn's
VANISHED 2

"I felt Henry's emotions rolling off the page as if I were experiencing everything he was. ...On a final note, this is an amazing series that no one should miss. A highly recommended story."

–The Novel Approach Reviews

"These books are compelling and thrilling, full of twists and turns and jaw-dropping realizations. ...I highly, highly recommended this book."

–Reviews by Jessewave

"Holy Moly! Carter Quinn is writing a mystery worthy of the best in the genre. ...I am going to say that this story is beautifully written, beautifully constructed and beautifully told. When you combine a master story teller with a master writer, what do you have? Artistry."

–It's About the Book

"The fantastic writing style of Carter Quinn in this book for me is perfect, sits well with me and fits me like a glove. Writing I can truly wrap myself up in and get completely lost in for a few wonderful and memorable hours.

–Sinfully Gay Romance Reviews

"This is a fantastically woven story that took me a bit by surprise and left me breathless and wanting to jump right into the next one."

–The Blogger Girls

"Our author plays the reader like he would a violin, twisting and turning the strings slowly killing us and Henry's hopes that Tom is somewhere alive."

–The Paranormal Romance Guild

Praise for Carter Quinn's

VANISHED 3

"This was a riveting story and I highly recommend it."

–Gay Book Reviews

"I have never been so pleased to get my hands on a book in my life. ...Could I have guessed the final outcome? Absolutely no way."

–Sinfully Gay Romance Reviews

"And the resolution is exciting, suspenseful, creative, and really rewarding. ...I don't want to give anything away because this is such an amazing suspense story and it is so cleverly done."

–Joyfully Jay

"...it has everything. There's a huge mystery. There are smoking hot private investigators, and plenty of action. Captivating."

–It's About the Book

"It is exciting and heart wrenching. Quinn kept me turning the pages. ...Seriously, you will not want to miss this series but have some tissues handy."

–Prism Book Alliance

"I'm gobsmacked! ...I won't give spoilers away, I never do, so all I'll say is this was an edge of your seat, hang on for your life conclusion to an already powerful, emotional story. ...Go. Read. It. Now."

– The Novel Approach

"This entire story was riveting and heartbreaking, beautiful and heartwarming. It was unique and exciting and kept me on the edge of my seat. ...It was amazing."

– The Blogger Girls

VANISHED

The Complete Trilogy

CARTER QUINN

Carter Quinn Books

Carter Quinn Books
carterquinnbooks@gmail.com
www.carterquinnbooks.com

Book Layout ©2013 BookDesignTemplates.com
Cover design by Scott J. Latimer, SJL Graphics, LLC

Vanished: The Complete Trilogy/ Carter Quinn. -- 1st ed.
ISBN: 978-0-9907732-6-9
Ebook ISBN: 978-0-9907732-7-6

DEDICATION

For my Dad.
Finally, one you could have read,
Pops, I'm sorry I didn't get it done in time. Love you.

ACKNOWLEDGMENTS

I'd like to thank my beta readers, Aniko, Kristen, Lara, Whitney, and Marie Sexton. Your feedback was invaluable.

As always, a huge thank you to Marilyn for always cheering me on, even when I'm beyond a shadow of a doubt positive that the whole thing sucks rocks.

And to you, the reader, I offer my biggest thanks. Without you, I couldn't do the one thing I've wanted to do since I was ten years old.

AUTHOR'S NOTE

Some of you may know I wrote this book so that I'd have something my Dad would feel comfortable reading. Don't get me wrong. He was always supportive of me and my writing. I didn't encourage him to read the previous two books because, frankly, the thought of my dad reading the things Riley got up to with those other guys kinda gave me the heebie-jeebies.

I failed.

Dad passed away July 30. I didn't complete the ugly first draft until August 8. I'd like to think it doesn't matter that he didn't get to read it, but it does. But what also matters is that I know he loved the concept. At least I gave him that.

What I'm trying to say is, don't take time for granted. We all have a finite amount of it. Live, laugh, and love while you can. Dad set a great example for those who loved him. He did all three of those things as hard as he could.

I love you, Pops. Rest easy.

CARTER QUINN BOOKS
More than just friction fiction.
carterquinnbooks.com

ONE

I forced my eyes open to confront another Monday and immediately regretted it. I couldn't remember why I had allowed Tom to get me tanked on wine on a Sunday night, but I was sure this hangover was going to linger longer in my memory. Every cell of my body hurt, my stomach churned, and my brain pounded against its cage with fury.

I stifled a groan, rolled onto my side and reached for my husband, finding only cool, empty sheets. Behind closed lids, I rolled my eyes and then regretted that too. Even after all the wine we'd consumed the night before, he was already out for his morning run. I would never understand how, after an evening dedicated to drinking every last fermented grape in the house, he could possibly commit to all that bouncing around—and then actually do it without hurling into the bushes. But come six o'clock every weekday morning, rain or shine, hangover or no, he set off for his run. Not that I didn't enjoy the benefits of his dedication. Just over twenty-one years after we'd first met, Tom was still the most desirable man I knew.

I crept out of bed and cast one last, yearning glance back at it. Instead of crawling back in and sleeping away my hangover like I ached to do, I straightened the covers enough to make the bed presentable. Making it properly required more energy than I could muster.

I stumbled into the adjoining bathroom and caught sight of myself in the mirror. "God, Henry, you look as bad as you feel," I grumbled. After downing a glass of water and a few pills to battle my headache, I began my morning routine: shave, shower, and then breakfast for both of us.

Friday had been incredibly hectic at work and Monday, being Monday, promised to be the same or worse. It was always that way at the end of a fiscal quarter. My team invariably spent days explaining to the brass just how so many of their supposedly brilliant decisions had caused a financial loss to the company, Excellere Global. Somehow, even with all our explanations, dire warnings, and unheeded advice, that list of bad choices grew longer each time. This quarter's loss was the seventh consecutive and one of the largest in the company's 117-year history, second only to the one after the financial meltdown of 2008. It was my job to fling logical explanations and recovery recommendations at the blank wall of corporate honchos and hope one of them stuck. None would. They never did.

Tom still hadn't returned by the time I'd finished eating, which wasn't altogether unusual for him. His architecture firm in the North Panhandle district—NoPa, for short—was close enough to our Ashbury Heights neighborhood that he could start to work later than me. Some mornings when he was back in time and wanted to get an early start on the workday, we'd enjoy the five minute walk together to the corner of Frederick & Masonic. There I would give him a kiss goodbye before dashing over to Cole & Carl to catch the N line to the Financial District, while Tom continued his walk up to Grove Street.

Some mornings he met his best friend, Jamie, and they ran Buena Vista Park together. The one time I'd gone there with him, I had been so unnerved by the recycled headstones lining the paths as rain gutters that Tom had never asked me to go there again. Most mornings he ran alone in Golden Gate Park. Occasionally he would get caught up talking to the old woman who tended the flowerbeds in the Queen Wilhelmina Tulip Garden. He probably knew more about her and her family than I did about his.

Matthew and Althea MacKinnon still hated me and my presence in Tom's life. Although they were usually on their best behavior in their son's presence, they were passive aggressive enough to show it whenever

Tom stepped out of the room. It didn't matter to them that I had loved their only child faithfully and to the best of my ability for twenty-one years. It didn't matter that because of that love we had adopted CJ, providing them with their only grandson. It only mattered that I wasn't the woman they had always envisioned their son marrying. I'd long ago given up trying to win them over.

To his credit, Tom wasn't oblivious to his parents' behavior. He'd spoken to them repeatedly over the years. They would do better for a short period before falling back into their old habits. I tolerated it because Tom loved them and I loved him. He didn't ask me to spend any more time around them than necessary, and I didn't try to keep them apart. I would never make him choose between us. Thankfully, they loved CJ as much as any grandparents could.

I put Tom's breakfast in the oven and left him a note on the entry table so he'd find it as soon as he got home. I always hated leaving the house without telling him I loved him, but sometimes a note had to suffice.

"LISTEN, PHIL, I understand what you're saying, but that's just not the way the numbers play out." I clasped my hands behind my back to stop from clenching them into fists. We'd been talking in circles for over an hour and I was sick to death of it. Phil Jenkins, the vice president of online sales, had made his case for reduced pricing on the company's various websites. I had countered with reasons against it in several different ways, but he wasn't absorbing my words through that thick skull of his. He was determined to carry out Excellere CEO Ossi Aaltonen's dream, come hell or high water. Aaltonen was determined to reverse engineer the company into a pale imitation of Amazon, that much had been evident for years. He would fail. That had been evident just as long.

"Let's take this from the abstract and into specifics, okay?"

He rolled his eyes but nodded. Some days tried my patience more than others. This one found it guilty of being on a very short leash.

"Aright. Let's take the new signature refrigerator for example. What is the retail on it?"

"It retails for $4299.99, but—"

I cut him off. "I know. We never sell it for that. Doesn't matter." I wrote the number on the whiteboard and again two feet to the right. Above the left number I wrote "in store" and above the right, I wrote "online," for the benefit of the slower brains in the room. "What's cost on it?"

"Eighteen forty-nine thirty-seven," Joe Hoopes answered. I was never sure what his job title would be from one quarter to the next, but his actual job remained the same: to purchase refrigeration appliances from the vendors. I liked him. He'd jumped on my train of thought as soon as it left the station, but he didn't have the right title, so the seven-figure earners in the room ignored him just like they did me.

"Can someone do the math for me here?" I asked as I wrote the numbers on the board.

"Your difference is $2450.62," Joe supplied again.

I continued drawing pretty numbers on the board as I explained again that reducing online pricing versus in-store pricing only served to reduce revenue, which, in turn, reduced profit. Considering the reason for these meetings was the extreme loss of profit this quarter, one would think the opinions of the CPAs would carry more weight. One would think. One would be wrong. "So after figuring all overhead in each sales stream, and without taking any discounts, the difference between revenue generated online versus in-store with the same exact selling price is six hundred dollars."

I thought I had seen light bulbs go off above some heads as I walked them through the process, but I was wrong. Blank faces stared back at me, waiting for me to put more color in the drawing or something. "Joe?" I asked, praying he could put it into words small enough these people would understand.

"If we offer a lower price online than we do in the store, we reduce profits."

"Yes! Thank you! Ladies and gentlemen, in a time when profit margins are slim, the easiest way to fatten them up again is to keep the online pricing the same as or higher than the in-store pricing, especially since we honor online pricing in-store when asked."

"But if we sell more units online, we'll get that back," Phil argued.

Joe shoved the paperwork in front of him off the table. "I'm done. Good luck, Henry. I have another meeting in ten minutes." He rushed out the door with only one guilty glance back at me.

If I could have run out with him, I would have. Instead I turned to Phil. "You haven't been in retail long, have you, Phil?"

He regarded me quizzically. "I've been with Excellere for about eight months."

"And before that?"

"Before that I was in the healthcare industry."

I nodded. "I see." I had to get out of there before I did something in appropriate like take Phil's temperature anally with the whiteboard marker. I clapped my hands. "Excellent meeting everyone. Thank you for your time."

I DIDN'T get a break from the meetings and ass-chewings until almost two o'clock, and no one around me was the better for it. Once, when we'd first started dating, Tom had seen me overly hungry and dubbed that crabby version of me Mr. Crankypants. It wasn't funny, but it was damn appropriate. So I was extremely happy to walk into my office and see an Apple-Manchego Panini and small Cobb salad waiting on my desk. I poked my head back into the reception area and gave my personal assistant, Trevor, a huge smile. "You're an angel."

He pointed in the direction of my office and scowled. "Don't talk to me until after you've eaten."

I laughed and sought out my desk, my mouth watering in anticipation. I took one apple- and cheese-seasoned bite and luxuriated in the incredible mix of flavors. I swallowed and greedily took another bite before checking my phone. No messages or missed calls from Tom.

I shrugged away my disappointment. Perhaps his day had been as insane as mine. I dashed off a quick text saying I hoped he had a good day and reminding him I was stopping for Thai takeout on the way home. I signed off with the little heart emoticon and laughed at myself for my sentimentality after all our years together.

The coming Thursday was our twenty-first and sixth anniversaries. We'd married legally on July 17, 2008, during that brief but wonderful June to November window when California first allowed civil marriage to same-sex couples. I leaned back in the chair, closed my eyes, and allowed myself to remember the best day of my life.

Our wedding day dawned cool and overcast in Napa at six o'clock on the dot. I awoke snuggled against Tom, my head on his shoulder, an arm thrown across his chiseled chest, a leg draped across his thighs. He snuffled away in sleep, oblivious to the upwelling of emotion that instantly inundated me. I pressed a kiss to his skin and closed my eyes.

It was fifteen years to the exact date that Tom first said he loved me. We'd been together about three and a half months when he surprised me with an electric lantern-lit picnic on the beach. I'd already decided he was the love of my life; I was just waiting for him to catch up. I'd teased him about choosing a picnic date.

"Thank you for bringing me here."

He pecked my lips and took the basket from my hands. "Of course. Now make yourself comfortable and let's see what's in this thing."

I looked at him sideways. "You didn't pack it yourself?"

He laughed. "Do I look like the kind of guy who'd own a picnic basket like this?" He gestured to the sturdy wicker thing like he'd never seen one before.

I grinned at him. "Actually, yeah. You do."

"Shut up." He opened the basket and started digging around inside, carefully avoiding my gaze. The pleased smile on his lips and the rosy glow staining his cheeks gave him away.

"It's yours, isn't it?"

"Shut up."

He was so cute when he was embarrassed. "How many other guys have you taken on picnics? Is this a regular routine for you?"

I had meant it as a joke, so the storm on his face surprised me. "I've never brought anyone else here, ever."

The sea breeze had ruffled his perfectly styled hair, so I figured it was okay to touch. I threaded my fingers through his curls and brought his forehead to mine. "I was only teasing, Tommy. It's okay. I'm not jealous."

He pulled back and studied my eyes. "What if I want you to be?"

The turnaround was sudden enough to throw me off. "What?"

"What if I want you to be jealous? What if I said—" He sighed and pulled me down onto the blankets with him. We settled Indian-style, our knees lightly touching. He took both of my hands in his, stroking them gently with his thumbs. "I had this elaborate seduction scene set up in my head, but that isn't really the way I want to do this." A line formed between his eyebrows as he contemplated his next words. "You spilling coffee on me was the best thing that ever happened to me." He winked and I chuckled, still embarrassed at my clumsiness. "Asking you out..." He shook his head and grinned. "Smartest thing I ever did, no question. It's crazy to think how much my life has changed in the three months we've been dating. I don't want it to stop, Henry. I only want it to change and grow and get better."

He tugged one hand away and scrubbed it down his face. "I'm screwing this all up. What I'm trying to say is that I don't want you to see anyone else. I don't think you are; I think you made that decision on your own, but now I'm saying I want to be certain. I want us to be exclusive." He cupped my chin, his thumb tracing the slight cleft there. My breath caught at the intensity in his eyes. He started speaking again, his words coming faster, almost panicky. "I love you, Henry. You don't have to say it back, but I needed you to know. I want this to be just us and I want to see where the future can take us, together."

If my body had wings, I would have taken flight and danced across the pre-sunset sky. I laughed, relieved he wasn't breaking up with me, excited and scared that he had said the words. I flung my arms around him with enough force we tumbled back onto the blanket. I breathed in his sweet scent, the linen of his suit coarse against my cheek. "I love you too," I whispered into his neck.

Beneath me, Tom stretched exaggeratedly and pressed a kiss to the top of my head. "I love you even more now, you know," he said in that sleep-hoarse voice I loved so much.

I turned my head to smile up at him. "More now than when?"

"More than when I first told you. More than yesterday. More than a minute ago when I woke up to find you daydreaming with that goofy smile on your face."

My tear ducts threatened to spill over. "How did you know what I was thinking about?"

"Because I know you, barista. You're the most sentimental person I've ever met. It only makes sense that on the morning of our wedding you'd be thinking about that night." He leaned up and kissed me. "I've been thinking about it for days. It was a great night," he whispered.

"It was," I agreed. "Who would have thought then that we'd end up here?"

He rolled me onto my back and ducked his head to nibble on my neck. I laughed and tilted my head to give him better access. "I knew it," he said between tiny bites. "I was never letting you get away, even if it meant I'd run the risk of getting burned by coffee every single day for the rest of my life."

I laughed and pinched his bare ass under the satin sheet, earning a yelp in return. "Keep talking. The deed isn't done yet."

He grinned at me. "Yes it is. It was done years ago. I have the ink to prove it."

I caressed the tattoo on his left inner biceps as his hand began to slide up my thigh. "Now who's the sentimental one?"

In answer, he bit my shoulder, and then rolled away and off the bed.

I took in the sight of his naked and aroused body. I didn't know or care if my love for him colored my perception, but Tom MacKinnon at thirty-seven was infinitely sexier than Tom MacKinnon at twenty-three—and that younger version had been able to get me from zero to sixty in thirty seconds flat. "You're not going to take advantage of me one last time before I'm an old married guy?"

He yanked open the sheers shielding the French doors leading to our third floor balcony. From our room we had a terrific view of the vineyard, but I knew he wasn't looking there. Far beyond the vast expanse of grape vines, our hill rose in the distance. It was our special place, our escape from the complexities of dealing with Tom's parents. Once, right after college, I'd laughingly wrestled Tom to the ground to stop him from carving our initials into the ancient blue oak tree that stood apart from its brothers near the crest of the rise. We'd made love under the boundless azure sky and a secret adventure had been born. After that, we made a point to spend time at that hill each time we visited Lasthenia Valley Vineyard and Villa Dimitri. After we adopted CJ we sometimes took him along with us, meaning we had to play by PG rules, but we didn't mind. We knew why we were there, and that was enough.

Tom threw open the doors and turned back to me as the cool, crisp air rushed by him. I felt his heated gaze slide along my naked body. "As long as you're sure your fiancé won't find out about it."

"I won't tell him if you won't."

"In that case, prepare to be ravaged." I laughed as he took a running leap onto the bed.

Several hours later, as we stood together fifty feet from the top of the hill, I could still feel him in me. "One last time" had turned to twice. The first had been rough and fun, filled with laughter and dirty talk as we pretended to be clandestine lovers enjoying a final romp. The second time had been just for us, a slow, sensual love making without games, just savoring the emotion of the day. After fifteen years and one son, our relationship would finally be recognized as equal and valid. Even Matthew and Althea's silent disapproval couldn't take that away from us. In 1993, the idea would have been ludicrous. Yet there we were, about to walk up the hill to our small group of witnesses and pledge ourselves to one another as legally married husbands.

Tom took my hand in his big, rough one, the prearranged signal that we were ready. Katie started to sing Westlife's "To Be Loved" a cappella. Our friend Chloe, who had been with me that fateful day I'd met Tom, was acting as our officiant. She stood smiling under our blue oak tree with CJ, who looked dapper in his first tuxedo.

Shaun, my best friend since college, stood next to Jamie, who gazed lovingly upon his wife as she sang. My dad, Martin, tried to covertly swipe a tear from his cheek. Even Matthew and Althea wore genuine smiles. As we started up the hill, I squeezed Tom's hand and tried to hold back tears of joy. I shouldn't have been emotional as I was. In theory, we weren't undergoing any fundamental change. Our relationship would be the same as it always had been. We were only making it legal. But somehow, knowing we were seconds away from pledging to love and care for one another forever in front of our family and friends—something I hadn't even realized I was missing until marriage equality started marching through the states—made my heart almost burst with love.

We stopped before CJ and Chloe. We both gave her a kiss on the cheek and then held out a hand to our son. He looked at us curiously, but turned to join us and took our hands. I didn't know how we looked to our guests, but standing in a small U in front of Chloe, joined at the hands to the two men I would love forever, I wouldn't have had it any other way.

Chloe had encouraged us to write our own vows, but I wasn't even sure I could get through the two "I do's," much less be able to speak coherently. In the end, we'd decided to go with the traditional promises, tweaked to allow for two husbands, and added a third one. By the time Tom slid the ring across my knuckle, I was a complete wreck. I'd never been so happy, so filled with his love, or as confident in our future as I was at that moment. When it was my turn to slide his ring on, my hands trembled so much he used both of his to steady them, giving me a moment to pull myself together.

"And now for my favorite part," Chloe said. Tom and I grinned at each other's tear-stained faces and looked down at our son. It sent a pang through my heart to realize we wouldn't have to look down at him much longer. At thirteen, the top of his head already reached our shoulders. "Christian James," Chloe intoned, "do you consent to this marriage between Henry and Tom?"

CJ nodded quickly.

"And do you take these two men to be your fathers? To love, honor, and obey them for as long as you all should live?"

I could see the confusion on his face, then the quirk of his mouth as he fought against denying he'd ever obey us, but mostly I saw how much he had grown from that scared, discarded nine-year-old boy we'd first met four years earlier. I was so proud of him. I'd never imagined or believed how much I could love a child before he came along, but my love for him was limitless and unconditional. He looked at each of us before, with a trembling lower lip, he finally answered, "I do."

"Thomas Matthew and Henry Jasper, do you both promise to be the best fathers you can be to Christian James? To love him and honor him, to teach him and learn from him, and to seek to understand him for all the days of your lives?"

Tom's "Always," and my "I do," crashed over each other as we raced to hug and kiss our son. I heard someone laugh in the peanut gallery just as someone blew his nose.

Chloe waited until we had resumed our positions, then straightened her back and said proudly, "Ladies and gentlemen, may I present for the first time as a *legally married couple*, Mr. Thomas MacKinnon and Mr. Henry Cooley, with their son Mr. Christian James Cooley-MacKinnon."

"Wait," Tom objected. "Don't I get to kiss my husband?"

Chloe smirked. "Like you haven't done that enough in the last fifteen years?" She gestured at me. "Okay, fine. Have that first legal kiss. Just remember there are children and old people present."

"So extra tongue then?" Tom asked, already reaching for the back of my head.

"Of course!" Chloe agreed with a laugh.

When I looked into Tom's eyes as he leaned in to kiss me, all the teasing was gone, replaced with such a look of unending love, I was sure

I would drown in it happily for the rest of my life. And when he kissed me, it was as sweet and tender and full of promise as that one on the beach after he'd first said he loved me.

THE HOUSE was dark and quiet when I got home. I set the bag of takeout on the mail table by the door and shed my suit jacket with relief. The fewer things I had to remind me of another Miserable Monday at work the better. I made a quick dash to the bedroom to change out of the suit. Instead of shredding it into a million pieces like I desperately wanted to, I hung it in the closet like a good boy. I tossed my dress shirt, undershirt, and socks haphazardly into the hamper. I put on my favorite pair of soft, well-worn jeans and a ratty old t-shirt that I was surprised Tom hadn't thrown out yet. As the family laundry guru, he was also the final arbiter of what was still worth the effort to launder and what was to be sacrificed to the clothing gods. Some items were lucky enough to be reincarnated as cleaning rags, others just disappeared forever. I knew this t-shirt's days were numbered, so I was determined to enjoy it as often as I could before its day of reckoning.

Much more comfortable in my sloppy clothes, I returned to the living room to retrieve the takeout. As I lifted it from the table, my peripheral vision caught a sheet of paper floating to the floor. I picked it up. It was my note to Tom from this morning. I frowned at it as I turned it over and inspected the blank back side. I was surprised to see Tom hadn't left a message in return.

I checked the time on my watch. 6:33 p.m. I was slightly late getting home, the side jaunt to the Thai place having added a few minutes to the trip, but it was even later for Tom. Although he often left for work after I did, he frequently beat me home. On the average traffic day, the walk from his Grove Street office took ten minutes less than my commute from the Financial District.

I put the takeout on the kitchen counter, pulled out my cell, and speed dialed his number. As the phone rang in my ear, I checked the oven. Tom's breakfast sat untouched exactly where I'd left it. I was reaching for the plate when the call finally connected. Instead of Tom's soothing baritone, I heard a computerized voice.

"We're sorry. You have reached a number that has been disconnected or is no longer in service. If you feel you have reached this recording in error, please check the number and try your call again."

I sighed and cancelled the call. It seemed that any time Tom ventured outside the NoPa/Haight/Buena Vista Park area and our Ashbury Heights neighborhood, his phone had a hard time deciphering signal. The recording I usually got was that he was outside the calling area, but sometimes the provider's wires got even more crossed than usual and I heard the 'no longer in service' message. I checked the text messages. The ones I'd sent him earlier in the day had been marked undelivered with the same error code I'd reached when I'd tried to call him: number no longer in service.

I scraped Tom's neglected breakfast into the trash and felt the familiar pang of mourning for Boston. I wondered if maybe we shouldn't start thinking about getting another dog. Boston had been gone for three years and I still missed him like crazy. I knew no other dog could ever replace him, but I also missed his silly antics and his constant demands for attention. I almost missed finding bits of kibble "buried" in out of the way corners and under his doggie beds.

I put the plate in the sink and ran some water over it, deciding I'd wash it when I did the dinner plates. Looking at the takeout, I was hesitant to put Tom's dinner in the refrigerator, but I didn't know how much longer he would be working. I pulled a bowl out of the cupboard and filled it with my Pad Kee Mow. If he wasn't home by the time I finished eating, his food would go into the fridge. It was a comfortable compromise. He'd probably walk through the door any minute anyway.

I settled on the couch and clicked on what I still called the boob tube. Although the television itself no longer had a picture tube, once it was turned on, there were no limits to the number of boobs I could see, in any form of the definition. I channel surfed until I came across the opening scenes of *Thor: The Dark World.* I smiled and set down the remote. I'd always been a sucker for superhero movies, and I couldn't deny there was something decidedly homoerotic about the interplay between Chris Hemsworth and Tom Hiddleston as Thor and Loki. Maybe it was a figment of my imagination, but judging by the fact that a fan-made poster depicting Thor embracing Loki was mistakenly used by a Shanghai cinema to promote the movie, it wasn't just my mind that went there.

I allowed myself to get pulled into the movie. It was only when the credits scrolled across the screen that I noticed I'd long since finished eating. I glanced out the big picture window to the darkening world outside and wondered again what was keeping my husband. Eight thirty was late, but not late enough to really worry. He could have spent most of the day visiting clients outside of his offices in NoPa and then become mesmerized by his creative process when he got back to the office.

I was a numbers man, safe and happy in a world of right and wrong, always answerable equations, but Tom had that creative mind that I didn't understand. I'd seen him get lost for hours in a project, only stopping to eat because I forced him to. It made him happy and drove us both crazy, but it also made him the man I had loved for almost half my life.

If he was back at the office, and if he had any charge left on his phone, he should be able to receive my call. I carried my dishes into the kitchen and tried him again. A ping of concern skittered around my brain when I reached the same error message. I knew there was no point in dialing the office number because it would go directly to a machine, so I didn't even try. For the first time all day, I felt uneasy. I tried to rationalize that it didn't mean anything was wrong. Even though we had the same phone in different colors, Tom's cell service was notoriously unreliable, always had been, while mine never was, except sometimes when we were together. I had teased him about being part magnet for years.

I washed my dishes, put Tom's dinner in the refrigerator, and poured a glass of wine. On my way back to the living room I surreptitiously grabbed the bottle and brought it with me. No sense having trips to the kitchen interfere with the buzz I was planning to help me forget Miserable Monday.

TWO

I awoke bleary-eyed once again, fragmented memories of disquieting dreams disappearing into the mists of my mind. I rolled over to find Tom's side of the bed cold and empty for the second straight morning. The lack of imprint on the soft surface of the pillowcase told me he hadn't been to bed while I slept. I crawled from the bed and peeked into the living room and kitchen, neither of which bore traces of his presence. I yawned and absent-mindedly scratched my bare chest as I wandered around the rooms. Nothing there indicated he'd come and gone as I'd dreamt restlessly.

It had been several months since he had pulled an all-nighter. I tried to remember if he'd talked about being on deadline with a project, but nothing came to me. We talked to each other about work all the time, as all old married couples did, but unless he had secured an exciting new project, it was mostly the usual mindless bitching and complaining. I wondered when we'd each lost enthusiasm for our jobs and begun going about them by rote. In fairness, I disliked my job much more than Tom did his, but some days I could see the strain on his face and in the way he set his shoulders.

We weren't poor by any means and we splurged on ourselves and CJ perhaps more than we should. Even with the nest egg we'd managed to scrape together and the remainder of Tom's trust fund, retirement was still at least fifteen years away. San Francisco was not an inexpensive city to live in. Putting CJ through a private arts high school and helping him pay for CalArts hadn't helped grow our savings any faster, but that was a sacrifice we were both happy to make.

The idea of being unhappy in my job that long was suddenly unbearable. If either or both of us were going to change jobs or careers, we needed to do it soon. Employers weren't excited by seasoned forty-somethings when they could pay blank slate twenty-year-olds half what Tom or I would cost. If we waited much longer those same prospective employers would see us a liability because of our nearness to retirement. There was also Tom's partnership in the firm to consider. It was all too much to contemplate that early in the morning.

In the bedroom, I disconnected my mobile from the charger and dialed Tom's cell again without much hope. As expected, the number was no longer in service. It took considerable willpower to tamp down my frustration. I plugged in the phone again and sighed. As much as I teased Tom about being part magnet, I really needed our service provider to unfuck their shit. I just wanted to hear Tom's voice, to be sure he was okay. It was still too early to call his office, but not for the caffeine infusion I desperately needed.

In the kitchen again I ladled the ground beans into the filter, smiling faintly as I remembered that it was coffee that had brought us together. Much to Tom's continuing dismay I still wasn't a coffee snob, even after so many years under his influence. Regular drip Folgers was sufficient for me. Listening to my beloved husband order at Starbucks was like listening to an ingredient list for a chemical weapon. The occasional sip of his favored concoctions did nothing to disprove that theory. As much as I enjoyed the taste of my boring old brew, I also liked that Folgers had been started in the city we loved and had called home since a year after he graduated college. I worked approximately two blocks from the beautiful old building that was once the company's headquarters and was currently part of the University of San Francisco.

I watched the drips turn into a steady fragrant brown stream into the carafe and fought with myself. I was starting to worry about Tom, but I attributed it to a bad day and less than stellar sleep. He was a big boy; this wasn't the first time he'd spent the night in the office at crunch time. Pushing away from the counter, I forced myself to go about my morning routine and tried to tell myself nothing was wrong.

TUESDAY TURNED into a clone of Monday, filled with more meetings and increasingly obstinate but slightly panicked executives trying desperately to understand why this quarter's losses were so extreme. My team and I were far too astute to explain the real reason: the CEO-slash-largest shareholder was a self-involved ass whose only desire was to increase his personal wealth, the health or longevity of the company be damned.

Ossi Aaltonen was, after all, a hedge fund manager who had made billions before purchasing the company I had given my best years to. He was like a child with severe Attention Deficit Disorder, always flitting from one expensive idea to another, yet giving none of those ideas time to actually work before reversing course with the next. It was maddening. To make matters worse, he continued to populate the executive ranks with people who had no history or experience in the world of retail. People like Phil Jenkins whose background was in healthcare, or, more accurately, medical device sales to hospitals.

Ossi was reportedly a smart man, but everyone hated working for him. We all knew the company was worth more to him dead than alive. It was just a question of when he'd pull the plug instead of pretending to care about fixing what he'd broken.

I always wondered how three months of losses managed to sneak up on the executives. It wasn't like the company lost three-quarters of a billion dollars overnight and suddenly everyone was surprised. No, it took genuine planning and great effort, not to mention a sustained failure to achieve sales goals—which were reported every damn day—to add up to a $769 million loss. Yet the executives were genuinely shocked—*shocked*—to hear to it. Every damn time. In reality, it was as *shocking* as Christmas—the quarterly earnings reports happened the same times every year. I could practically hear their mental calculators tabulating their bonuses even as they suggested layoffs and reductions in hourly payroll. God forbid they lose even a fraction of their seven- or eight-figure salaries.

Thankfully for my mental health and continued gainful employment, I was finally able to break away from the madness just after noon.

"Lunch is on your desk, boss," Trevor said as I walked into his area.

"You're too good to me, kid."

He looked up from his computer and frowned at me. "Let me guess, you've been biting your tongue all morning?"

I laughed. "I might have even drawn blood a time or two."

He shook his head. "Why doesn't he just sell the damn company instead of running it into the ground?"

I leaned a hip against his desk and smiled sadly. "His latest decision is to sell it off piece by fucking piece to raise cash." The company owned several coveted, exclusive brands, from clothing to insurance to household appliances and hardware to automotive parts and service. Each on its own would fetch in the mid to high nine figures. But once those sales were realized, the money would go right into an ever-quickening whirlpool of loss and debt.

Trevor leaned back in his chair, the disbelief written across his face like a bold marker, and considered that for a moment. "And what happens when there's nothing left to sell?"

I winked at him. "Damn good question, Watson. Damn good question." I rapped my knuckles on his desk and walked into my office. The kid was far too intelligent to be wasting his time at this company, but I was damn glad to have him looking after me. He was the best personal assistant I'd had in years, anticipating my needs sometimes before I did and having the solution—or the lunch, more often than not—ready when I was. His work was always error-free and on time.

Trevor had ordered me a ham and cheese melt and an orzo pasta salad with chopped pistachios and grilled pineapple. I ate greedily while surfing the business news sites on the internet. Even news that one of our major competitors had released its earnings report with actual, honest to god earnings couldn't keep my mind from wandering to Tom.

A quick glance at my phone revealed no incoming messages or calls from him.

The article about Hathaway Consolidated's earnings report continued to fascinate me so I only half paid attention to scrolling to Tom's work number and pressing send.

"Thank you for calling Hardwick Architecture. How may I direct your call?" a perky female voice answered.

"Tom MacKinnon, please," I muttered distractedly. I frowned as I brought up an email from Ossi Aaltonen outlining his plan for divesting divisions and closing underperforming stores.

"I'm sorry, sir?" she queried in a perplexed voice.

"I'd like to speak to Tom MacKinnon, please." Of our twenty-two hundred locations, dearest Ossi wanted to close fully a quarter, 553 stores.

"I'm not familiar with that name sir. Can you tell me in which department he works?"

That caught my wandering attention. "He's a Senior Vice President in charge of the tall buildings practice." I didn't often call the main number for Tom's office, but I'd never had this sort of trouble with the receptionists before. I closed out of the email in disgust, more puzzled than annoyed by the receptionist's twenty questions.

"Do you mean Tim McKinley? He's our Founding Partner."

I frowned and looked at the dark screen of my phone. Damn thing never stayed lit when I needed it to. "This is Hardwick Architecture, correct?"

"Yes, sir."

I shook my head as if the muddle was within mine and not hers. "Tom MacKinnon has been with your firm for sixteen years and a Senior Vice President for almost ten. May I speak with him, please?"

"I apologize, sir," the receptionist said, sounding as confused as I felt. "I've only been here a few days and my trainer is at lunch, but I don't see a listing for Mr. MacKinnon. Is there anyone else who can assist you? Human resources, perhaps?"

"Fine, yes. Put me through to Mr. McKinley, please." The name meant almost nothing to me, but then I forgot names like Catholics forgot their sins. Nevertheless it was clear the receptionist and I were going to continue dancing in circles if I didn't get past her somehow. And I would be damned if she'd condemn me to human resources hell. That was where hope and phone calls went to die a slow and painful death. With luck, this McKinley could transfer me to Tom. I nervously tapped a pen on my desk as I waited for the call to connect.

"Tim McKinley," a gruff baritone announced in my ear. His voice sounded as if he had just put out his last cigarette a second before answering the phone. I half expected to hear him exhale the smoke over the phone.

"Mr. McKinley, this is Henry Cooley from Excellere Global. I'm trying to reach my husband, Tom MacKinnon, but your new receptionist doesn't seem to know who he is. I was hoping you could transfer me to him."

I held my breath as the silence lengthened. I could almost imagine him in another time, sitting at his desk in a darkly paneled office sucking on a Lucky Strike, a blue cloud of smoke surrounding him like a carcinogenic aura.

"Never heard of him."

I sighed, feeling blood rush to my face. "With all due respect, Mr. McKinley, Tom's been a Senior VP with Hardwick going on ten years. Your new receptionist claimed she didn't see him on the phone list and now you're saying you've never heard of him? I don't understand what's going on there today, but I'd like to speak with my husband."

"I'm sure you would, Mr. Cooley, but no one named Tom MacKinnon has ever worked here. I should know. I'm one of the founding partners."

I heard his words, even understood their individual meanings, but they didn't make sense in a sentence. "I'm sorry, could you repeat that?"

"No Tom MacKinnon has ever worked for Hardwick Architecture," he repeated.

The ground seemed to open below me, leaving me dangling in midair like some Wile E Coyote-type character. "I don't—I don't understand.

Tom's worked there for sixteen years. I've been to holiday parties at your office. Mrs. Dunning asked for my strawberry cream pie cannoli recipe last year!"

I dimly heard the man laugh. "Iris does love her sweets. It sounds like your young man has some explaining to do."

"That's why I'm calling. He hasn't come home for two days. I thought maybe he was on deadline with a project."

"Well that's mighty unfortunate. I hope he's alright. I don't know what else to tell you, Mr. Cooley. I know every associate and partner in this firm, past and present, and I know that no one by that name has ever worked for Hardwick Architecture. Now if you'll excuse me, I need to get to a meeting."

"Of course. I apologize for disrupting your day. Thank you, sir." I blindly set the phone on my desk. My mind replayed the hundreds of times Tom and I had started the walk to work together. I would leave him at Frederick to get to the metro station and he would continue walking up Masonic to Grove and over to Hardwick's offices. It was one of the best things about living where we did. His commute was walkable while mine was a half hour to forty-five minutes by bus and streetcar, depending on the route I took and when I left.

I didn't understand. It did not compute.

I shook my head to clear the galloping crazies. The old man had to be wrong.

THREE

I didn't have time to dwell on the weirdness that was my phone call to Hardwick. Almost as soon as I set down my cell phone my office phone started screaming. My presence was required in an impromptu meeting on the 37th floor, the executive suites.

Three hours later I exited the conference room off the CEO's office having neither said a word nor been asked a question. That was the way of things with this guy. Ossi Aaltonen wanted—usually demanded—everyone's attention, no matter what more pressing business we could have been tending to while he essentially talked his way to a self-created orgasm describing his own brilliance. I knew the people in the field, as we called them—those who were paid hourly and worked in the actual stores—hated him with a passion. What I'd only just begun to realize was how much those of us in the corporate offices hated him as much as we feared him.

I took the express elevator to the ground level and walked out onto the cacophonous beauty of another San Francisco afternoon. I loved this city and I adored my little corner of the Financial District. I breathed in the scent of hydrangeas and assorted flowery goodness from the gazebo florist as I walked by. Climbing the terraced gardens to the second tier of benches, I listened for the distinctive sounds of the California line cable cars, the rumble of their weight on the tracks, the squeal of their brakes, and the clang of their bells. The familiarity of the plaza calmed me, the ebb and flow of fellow professionals going about their business, more often than ever on telephones securely held to their ears, of tourists marveling at the beauty of the skyscrapers, taking photos with the same types of phones the others were using for business.

About half way through the meeting with Aaltonen, I'd been able to take a small sigh of relief, and I had Iris Dunning's love of strawberry cream pie cannoli to thank for it. I kept returning to that moment in my conversation with Tim McKinley. He hadn't seemed at all surprised that I'd mentioned Mrs. Dunning's name. In fact, he'd sounded like someone who was fondly indulgent of her and her sweet tooth. That one morsel of information helped me remember. Late last year Tom told me that Tim McKinley had been diagnosed with the early stages of dementia. The partners had decided, out of kindness, to continue letting him work his own little corner of the building since he wasn't a danger or a hindrance yet. I hadn't recalled McKinley's name during the conversation because I was so caught up with him not knowing who Tom was. The receptionist wouldn't necessarily know about McKinley's dementia since she was new, which was exactly why she didn't know who Tom was. That was the only explanation—at least it was the only explanation that made sense.

I sat on one of the cushions and speed dialed Tom's cell again. It took considerable self-control not to hurl my own phone when the same 'no longer in service' message played in my ear for the umpteenth time. I pressed the icon for internet, typed in a search for the mobile provider's known outages, and then waited an inordinately long time for the browser to display an answer. Unhelpfully, the only reported disruptions in service were on the Peninsula, not in the City.

I scrolled through my contacts to Jamie's number and pressed send. If Tom had talked to anyone lately it would be Jamie.

He sounded harried when he finally picked up after four rings. "Hello?"

"Hey, Jamie. It's Henry. Listen, I can't get ahold of Tom. I was wondering if you'd heard from him lately."

A thundering silence reigned on the line for so long I almost thought the connection had been dropped. "Are you kidding me right now? I don't have time for this, Henry. Katie's in labor. We're on the way to the hospital now."

"Oh! Oh my gosh! Okay, I'll let you go. Text us when the baby gets here. Good luck!" I knew Jamie and Katie were excited to add another baby to their family. They already had a daughter so they were hoping for a boy this time. The thought of a brand new baby in our midst made me smile. Jamie and Katie were great parents, and Tom and I were eager to spoil other people's kids now that our own was grown and gone from the nest.

The baby didn't distract me for long though. My thoughts kept returning to my husband and that persistent message when I dialed his number. I had grown accustomed to the other one, the one telling me the party I was trying to reach was outside the calling area and to try back again later. The constant repetition of the 'no longer in service' message felt wrong. The more I turned the situation over in my mind the more concerned I became. Jamie was in the middle of a crisis, so I couldn't expect to get any answers from him, but I couldn't imagine him not calling Tom to tell him Katie was in labor. Wouldn't Jamie have said if he hadn't been able to get through to Tom? Those two talked throughout the workday almost as much as Tom talked to me. It was a wonder my dear husband got any work done at all. And that reminded me of Tim McKinley's declaration that Tom had never worked for his firm.

I knew without question that McKinley was mistaken. It was only natural that I took care of the bills considering I was the accountant in the house. Before direct deposit of payroll became commonplace, Tom duly handed over his paper paycheck from Hardwick Architecture every month like clockwork. Even now a line item on the bank statement indicated a deposit from Hardwick each month.

Annoyed and worried, and annoyed that I was worried, I tried Tom's cell again. The same error message gloated in my ear. I growled my frustration and rose from the bench. If I had to walk my happy ass up to goddamn Hardwick Architecture myself, I was going to get answers. And I was going to tell my beloved in no uncertain terms that we were both too old for this crap. He would leave the overnighters to the interns and associates. He was a senior partner, for the love of Pete. He should be home with his husband in the evenings like all good middle-aged men who weren't in the throes of a mid-life crisis.

But what if he wasn't at Hardwick? What if I couldn't get past the receptionist? We usually exchanged phone calls at least twice a day and text conversations were sometimes an all-day project. So why hadn't he called me from a landline if he couldn't use his cell phone? Did that mean he wasn't at the office? Had he even made it there from his run Monday morning? Would anyone have called me to check on him if he missed a day?

I knew I was beginning to panic, but I couldn't stop it. Tom and I had seen an article online a few months ago about a woman who'd died alone at home. They didn't find her until six years later. All her bills were on auto-pay, her lights on timers, and she was known to travel a lot for her job. The neighbors hadn't thought a thing about never seeing her come or go. We'd talked about how horrifying and sad that was. We'd wondered aloud how someone could just vanish one day and never be missed. And here I was, blithely going on about my day while I hadn't seen or heard from my husband in almost forty-eight hours.

No, no, no.

I called Shaun while I practically ran to the Embarcadero Station.

"Hankster!" His cheery voice cut through my troubled thoughts. "What's up, big man?"

That was almost enough to make me break into hysterical laughter. He and Tom were both multiple inches taller than me, but the one time we'd had to scrap to get out of a potential gay bashing situation, I'd proven to be tougher than either of them. Shaun had burst loose with the appellation that night and had used it whenever he felt like ever since. I pushed the memories away as the rising acid levels in my stomach reminded me of my present reality. The loud racket on his end of the line was almost deafening so I shouted to be heard. "Shaun, Tom's missing."

"What? Who?"

"Tom! My husband!"

Suddenly the noise died. I assumed he had stepped into his office. "Very funny, Henry." Shaun voice had lost all levity, which meant he was actually paying attention.

I stopped several feet from the entrance to the station so as not to impose my conversation on my fellow travelers. "I'm not kidding, Shaun. I haven't seen him since we went to bed Sunday night."

I could practically hear the rocks being ground to sand in my friend's brain. "Okay," he drew the word out to several more syllables than it should have naturally. "Have you tried to call him?"

"Yes, of course! I keep getting a recording telling me the line is no longer in service. And when I called his office Tim McKinley, the old man with dementia, tried to tell me Tom had never worked there. I mean, I know that's not true, but I'm starting to freak out."

"Calm down. We'll figure it out. Where are you?"

"Still downtown. I'm on my way to Hardwick to see if he's there. I'm just waiting for the KT. But what if he isn't there, Shaun? What if he's hurt? What if he was mugged and he's in the hospital somewhere and no one knows who he is?" I felt the icy grip of terror around my heart for the first time. I quickly descended into the station, navigated the turnstiles, and rushed to the platform. I needed to get home now.

"Whoa, whoa, whoa," Shaun yelled in my ear. "Slow down. Listen, you just need to keep your shit together for a little while longer. You're in no state to go by Tom's office. Go straight home and I'll meet you there. No more bad thoughts, okay?"

I closed my eyes and tried for a centering breath but all I got was a lungful of fine Metro station air. I coughed a few times the clear it out. My eyes burned as I envisioned standing over an unconscious Tom lying in a hospital bed.

"Hank!"

"Yeah?"

"Focus. Get your ass home. Do not pass go. Do not go to Hardwick. Do not have bad thoughts. I'll be there as soon as I can."

I nodded even though he couldn't see me. "Okay. Here comes the KT."

"Good, I'm right behind you."

I released another long breath grateful to know Shaun still had my back after all these years.

AGREEING NOT to have bad thoughts was a lot easier than not actually having them. By the time Shaun banged on my door forty five minutes later, my mind had put on a horror show for me. There was Tom, mugged, bleeding, and unconscious, in the bushes beside the jogging trail in Golden Gate Park. There he was, hit by a car as he crossed Chain of Lakes Drive. The driver didn't stop and there was Tom, lying dead in those same bushes. Next he was in a hospital somewhere, a John Doe because he had no identification. Then, perhaps worst, he was wandering around the bowels of the city in a daze without a clue who or where he was. When Shaun's knock interrupted a bizarre mental aerial shot of Tom's lifeless body washing ashore on Ocean Beach, I decided I'd never watch another suspense movie or read another thriller again so long as Tom came home safe.

I flipped the locks and pulled the door open to find Shaun on the stoop, still dressed in his suit, but with his tie loosened and askew. The top two buttons of his shirt were undone, exposing the golden skin beneath it. Normally I would have given him a hard time for his disheveled appearance, but I was too frightened and relieved to do anything but pull him into a hug. I spoke into his shoulder. "I'm so glad to see you. Thanks for coming."

He returned the hug, adding several pats on the back, before holding me at arm's length by the shoulders. He looked into my eyes for a long moment as if trying to pull all the information he needed through them. He grabbed me by the forearm and led me into the living room, practically pushing me onto the sofa. He sat in the wingback chair across the coffee table from me. "What's going on, Henry?"

I stared at him for a moment, not even sure where to start. It was all so surreal. One moment my husband was here and the next he was gone. How did that even happen? I boiled it all down into its simplest form: "I can't find Tom." My chin quivered momentarily as my mind flashed to those horrifying scenes again, but I stopped it with determination. I couldn't fall apart now. "Should I call CJ?"

Shaun frowned. "Before we make any decisions, I need you to start from the beginning. Walk me through it."

I nodded. It was almost like I was trapped inside a dream. Nothing seemed real, normal. This couldn't possibly be my life. Any minute, I would wake up in bed next to Tom and this would all fade away. "He was gone when I woke up yesterday morning. I've—"

"What about Sunday," Shaun interrupted.

"What about it?"

"Was he here then?"

"Of course he was."

He frowned again. "What did you do Sunday?"

"Jesus, Shaun! What difference does it make? He was here then!" I stood and started to pace. "I should be out there looking for him instead of sitting here playing twenty questions with you."

Shaun watched me for a silent moment before he stood. "Sit down, Henry. I'm going to get you a glass of water and a Valium, and then I want you to tell me about Sunday."

"I need to—"

"Henry!" Shaun's voice was sharp, a tone he hadn't used with me since college when he'd helped me keep it together when my brother died. "Sit down and do as I say. You won't do Tom any good if you lose it now."

Chastened, I sat quietly back on the sofa and Shaun moved into the kitchen. "Oh, hey, Jamie and Katie are about to have their baby," I called to him as the happy thought bubbled to the surface among all the decidedly not happy ones.

He stopped fussing with the ice. "Really? I thought they just had one."

I smoothed my hands over my jeans. "No, they only have Maya. She's almost three." My knees bounced with nervous energy. We were wasting valuable time. I didn't know what the statistics regarding missing people were, but I was sure that the sooner police and friends were actively searching for them, the better the outcome. I needed to get out there and look for my husband. But first I should call the police and report him missing, maybe even call the hospitals while I waited for the police to arrive. I wondered if that forty-eight hour delay requirement for reporting someone missing was a television plot device or if it was real. Just the idea that I would soon know the answer to that question caused my mind to spin and my knees to bounce faster.

"Don't they have a boy, too?"

It took a moment to zone back in on the topic of Shaun's question. "You must be thinking of someone else."

Shaun walked back into the living room and offered me the glass of ice water and the pill. He watched me swallow it before he answered. "I suppose I could be, but it just seems like Katie's been pregnant forever." He moved over to the bar and poured himself a few fingers of his favorite bourbon. As often as Shaun was over to visit, Tom insisted that we keep a bottle or two for him since neither of us liked bourbon and he wasn't a fan of wine. He shed his suit jacket, draped it across the other wingback chair, and rolled his shirtsleeves two turns before resuming his seat across from me. He took a long swallow of the booze and gestured for me to begin. "Tell me about Sunday."

I took another sip of the water, allowing an ice cube to slip into my mouth. I smothered a grin, thinking how Tom always liked those hot summer days when I used ice to cool him down and turn him on. I chewed the half-moon shaped cube slowly as I pieced together the scattered memories of Sunday.

"We slept in like we always do on Sundays. I woke up first and made breakfast. I think it was French toast, but I can't remember for sure. It was just another morning. I wasn't paying attention. I didn't know I would have to.

"After breakfast we cleaned the house and walked up to Coffee to the People. I had a Chocolate to the People and Tom had something I couldn't replicate on pain of death. We both ordered a dessert and read for a while. It was nice. Very relaxing."

I watched Shaun lean forward, elbows on knees and steeple his hands below his chin. He had long, graceful fingers. The middle ones tapped away at each other, betraying his impatience.

I shrugged and set my water glass carefully on a coaster on the coffee table. "I don't know, Shaun. It was a normal day. We did normal Sunday things." *We made love.* "We made dinner. We watched a movie, drank a couple of bottles of wine and went to bed. He got up for his run on Monday and I haven't seen him since." That tremor of alarm raced down my spine again. I really needed to be out hunting for him instead of wasting time not telling Shaun that Tom and I had had incredible sex on Sunday afternoon.

"Did you see or hear him leave Monday morning?"

I shook my head and finally felt the soothing properties of the Valium roll through my body. "I rarely hear him leave unless I'm having trouble sleeping." I smiled faintly. "The wine pretty much made sure that wasn't the case."

"So you don't know for sure when he left." Shaun's tone made it almost an accusatory statement, not a question. "He could have gone any time after you went to sleep."

My sluggish brain finally grasped his meaning. "He didn't leave me, Shaun," I snapped. "He had no reason to. We're about to celebrate our anniversary!"

"I know."

"Go look if you don't believe me! All of his things are right where he left them!"

"I believe you."

I launched myself from the couch and pointed at him, jabbing the empty air as I made my case. "Then what the hell is wrong with you? My husband is missing! We need to be out there searching for him. He could be hurt or dying while I'm sitting here answering questions that don't goddamn matter. I haven't even called the police yet!" As suddenly as it came, the anger evaporated, leaving me without steam or even hope. I collapsed back onto the couch and covered my face with my hands. "You're supposed to be my friend, Shaun. I called you for help, not accusations."

"I'm trying to help, Hank," he answered quietly. "I really am."

I took a deep breath around my hands and sent them through my hair as I exhaled, struggling to gather tiny bits of composure as I did so. "I know. I'm just scared."

Shaun offered a half smile. "I am too. I've never been in this situation before."

My chin wobbled again. "Me neither. And I keep hoping this is all a bad dream but I can't seem to wake up." Remembering a scene from that werewolf television show made for viewers almost half my age, but that I was highly addicted to anyway, I spread my fingers and counted them: still five, so not a dream. I snatched my glass from the coffee table and rose again. "I'm going to go splash some water on my face. Can you call the police while I do that? From what I've seen on the television, they're going to want to come and get a photo and ask me all the same questions you just did, but it'll probably take forever for them to get here. I'd like to at least get that ball rolling. Then when I get back we can start calling hospitals and homeless shelters to see if he's been seen at any of them."

"Absolutely."

I smiled a thanks at him, dropped my glass off at the kitchen counter, and headed for the master bath. I was on the cusp of losing the tenuous grasp on my self-control and I didn't want to do that in front of Shaun. At least alone in the bathroom, the tears threatening to burst from my eyes would be camouflaged by the water also running down my face.

INSIDE THE master bath, I stared at my reflection as the water ran wastefully in the sink. My mind churned like the Pope himself was waiting for butter. I tried to recall the last conversation Tom and I had but it kept getting lost behind a hazy alcoholic fog. We rarely drank more than two glasses of wine each per night. I still couldn't piece together why we'd thought it was a good idea to have two full bottles—especially on a Sunday night. Were we celebrating? I couldn't remember. I couldn't remember anything of value at all!

Angry and frustrated I leaned forward and slapped cold water on my face. The memory tore through the soft gray matter of my brain like a poisoned arrow and I gasped. I shot upright so quickly I lost my balance and stumbled back against the wall. The horror of that distant memory was clearly revealed on the face in the mirror. "Oh shit," I whispered. My mirror image agreed.

It couldn't be happening again, could it?

No. It was impossible. Well, it wasn't *impossible*; it just didn't make any sense.

And it had been two days. Surely I would have—but *I* wouldn't, would I? And they wouldn't tell me, even if—

Stop. Just stop it.

My eyes stayed locked on those of my mirrored self as we both shook our head slowly. It may not make sense. It may sound paranoid, but that didn't keep it from being possible. I took a deep breath and splashed more water on my face. I had to tell Shaun. I had to tell the police. And I had to go see Tom's parents.

FOUR

The thick carpet in the bedroom muffled the sound of my unintentionally silent approach to the living room. Out of long habit, I stopped a few feet out of the room when I heard Shaun's voice. I wasn't trying to eavesdrop; I was merely being polite by giving him his privacy. He sounded agitated, but if he was talking to the police, that would make sense. Something—a television show or a newspaper article—had given me the impression that missing persons reports were not high on their priority list.

"—completely freaking out. I mean we're talking full-on crisis mode." He was silent as he listened. "And how am I supposed to do that?" More silence. "He's my friend, man. I don't want to hurt hi—."

I frowned and took two steps forward as Shaun pinched off mid-word. I could see his back now. He had one hand on the phone at his ear and the other buried deep in his thick dark hair, gripping it hard. "Yeah, alright, fine." I watched him cancel the call with a thumb tap on the screen. "Thanks for nothing, Jamie, ya piece of shit."

What the hell was that about? Before I could decipher what I'd just overheard, Shaun started to turn in my direction. I quickly took four steps back out of his line of sight. I stumbled back into the bedroom and leaned against the wall, face in hands, as I struggled to pair that conversation with any logical explanation. It didn't have to be about me or Tom, but that was the only thing that fit. I was definitely in full-on crisis mode.

Shaun and Jamie had known each other since shortly after Tom and I had met. We'd introduced them in hopes that they would become great friends and hardly notice that Tom and I were spending almost all of our available free time together. They'd made friends, but it was soon clear that without Tom and me as a bonding agent, they couldn't have cared less. Nothing had changed over the years, so I didn't understand why Shaun had called Jamie now. Besides which, shouldn't Jamie have been in the delivery room with Katie?

I exhaled and told myself to calm down. My paranoia—if that's what the revelation in the bathroom had been—was spreading. Until Shaun said or did something *to me*, he was still the same person he'd been ten minutes before—my best friend aside from Tom.

Instead of going right back into the living room, I detoured into the kitchen to make coffee. If I was going to drive to Tom's parents' house and back, I'd need the caffeine boost. When the coffee started streaming into the carafe, I stepped back into the living room. Shaun's back was to me as he poured himself another drink. I called his name softly so he wouldn't spill the liquor.

He spun around and smiled slightly. "Hey. Feeling any better?"

I grimaced. "Not really. Listen, I—I need to tell you something." I gestured to the chair he'd sat in earlier and waited for him to sit again before I took my place on the couch opposite him. I didn't know where to begin. It was a topic Tom refused to talk about. He didn't want any of our friends to know about it because he feared the way they'd look at him after they found out. It had taken two years of dating before he told me. I'd been spooked, I couldn't deny it. But we had managed to make it through and grow stronger because Tom no longer had a secret he couldn't share with the most important person in his world. And I could finally quit wondering what he wasn't telling me. I'd thought he'd been cheating. If only it were something that simple. And now I had to betray his confidence and tell my friend my husband's deepest secret in hopes of helping him. The worst part was I wasn't even sure if telling Shaun would make any difference, so I might be divulging Tom's secret for nothing. I had no proof my theory was right—and I wouldn't until I'd talked to Tom's parents.

"Henry?"

I looked up into Shaun's worried green eyes and realized I'd lost myself in my thoughts. "Sorry." I sighed, wishing there was a way around this confession and knowing there wasn't. "In the bathroom I remembered something that may or may not be important—well, it's important, but I don't know—shit." I buried my face in my hands, trying to control my breathing. I could feel the anxiety rising. I couldn't do this. If I gave voice to Tom's past, it was like making it real and dragging it into the present. I felt the tears of fear sting the backs of my eyelids.

I jumped up from the couch and practically ran into the kitchen. My hands shook as I took the coffee carafe from the machine. I big splash leapt over the edge of the cup onto the countertop. A small sob tore from my throat as I slammed the carafe back down on its holder. My husband was missing and I was sitting here safe and sound in our home about to reveal his most painful memory and darkest secret instead of being out there scouring the city trying to find him. Angrily, I yanked a paper towel from the roll hanging under the counter, sending the entire roll and its dispenser careening to the floor, crashing my coffee and the broken shards of its cup all over the room in the process. "Fuck!" I shouted.

I tensed as Shaun's hands closed over my shoulders. "Go sit down, Hank." His sympathetic voice came from behind me. "I'll take care of it."

"I can do it."

"Yes, you can, but you're not going to." He turned me around and gently urged me forward. "Go. I'll be in after I finish here."

I was falling apart in fast forward. I wouldn't be any use to anyone soon. I made my way back to the couch and collapsed onto it in a heap of misery. Where was Tom? What if I was right? What if—*No. Stop. You don't know anything yet. Keep your shit together a little while longer.* I fidgeted nervously with the tassel on the throw pillow—the ugliest throw pillow in the known universe, according to Tom. The sage green thing with an embroidered palm tree didn't go with anything else in the room, but when I'd seen it I couldn't pass it up. I didn't know why it spoke to me then and I still didn't, but it had been worth each of the eleven dollars I'd spent on it.

Shaun came back in the room, offering me a fresh mug of coffee. "I hope you made decaf," he teased with a half smile.

I accepted the cup and stared at him in mock shock. "You dare speak such words in Tom MacKinnon's house?"

His smile stretched into a full grin. "I should be careful of the blasphemy, huh?"

"At the very least. Just because he isn't here doesn't mean he won't smite you."

Shaun laughed and held out his other hand. "I brought you another Valium, too. I figured it couldn't hurt. You're awfully damn close to spinning out."

I gratefully took the pill and swallowed it with the coffee as Shaun resumed his seat in the wingback chair. "I forgot to ask. Did you call the police for me?"

His mouth quirked up on one side. "I did better than that. I called Mary Beth Daly. Do you remember her? Christine's sister?"

I groaned. "Christine? Wow. How could I possibly forget?"

Shaun laughed. "Hey, she was a good time."

"Yes," I agreed. "Had by all."

He shrugged, his smile growing mischievous. "She would have given you a ride, too, bro, but you had to be all monogamous and stuff."

I arched a brow. "First, don't ever say 'bro' again. Second, I'm gay, not bi. Third, I'm married. Fourth, if I recall correctly, she wanted to watch you and me fuck—which, for the record, just no—and then she said she'd only join in if we 'pleased' her."

Shaun's face scrunched. "Oh yeah, there was that. If it makes you feel any better, Mary Beth is the polar opposite of her sister. And she's a good cop, too."

"Is she even old enough to be a cop?"

"Hank, the Shaun O'Malley Identity Crisis was ten years ago. Mary Beth must be in her mid-twenties by now."

I groaned. "Jesus, we're getting old."

"You might be," Shaun agreed, pity dripping from his every word. "But I'm still young and spry."

"No actual young person would ever use the word 'spry' to describe himself."

"Shut up. The point is, Mary Beth said she'd be here in—" he rotated his wrist to see his watch "—about half an hour."

I nodded. Thanks to Shaun's presence, I could handle that. He was starting to do his thing: distract me, keep me from freaking right the fuck out. His unflappability was one of the first things I'd learned to appreciate about him all those years ago in college. I couldn't count the number of times he'd yanked me back from the edge about one class or another, yet he'd never seemed anything but calm and in complete control. Nothing ruffled his feathers except someone messing with me or someone else he cared about. He'd been a life saver when my brother committed suicide during my junior year at USC. And when things were tough with Tom, I always knew I could count on Shaun to listen, sidetrack me with something silly, and then send me back home with my head on straight. "Tomwaskidnappedwhenhewassixteen." I said it in a rush, just to get the words out. I didn't know if they were individually distinguishable, but if I was going to break my husband's trust, I wasn't going to fuck around with it.

"What?"

I dropped my forehead into my hands, unable to look at my best friend. "He didn't want anyone to know. We've only ever talked about it a couple of times. I agreed to never bring it up again." I looked up at Shaun then, fear for Tom wracking my body. He was staring at me like I'd suddenly sprouted another head. "What if—what if they've done it again?"

"You're serious?"

His question was like a slap to the face. "Why the hell would I joke about something like that?"

"Why didn't you tell me?"

"I just told you Tom didn't want anyone to know."

Shaun inhaled deeply. "I need a drink."

I pointed to the one on the table next to him and fought back the tears of panic and desperation. I watched Shaun drain his drink in one long swallow. He shoved out of his chair and stalked to the bar, where he poured three generous fingers into his glass. He guzzled half of it before he turned around and spoke again.

"You're completely serious about all this, aren't you? You honestly have no idea where Tom is. And this—this kidnapping thing, that actually happened."

I stared at him in disbelief. "Did you think I just wanted your company or something?" I shouted, hurt to discover he hadn't believed me from the start. "Yes of course I'm serious. I haven't seen Tom since Sunday night and I'm scared to death."

"Why was he kidnapped?"

"Who the hell knows? It was the 80s. People were hijacking airliners and cruise ships, for fuck sake. Why not kidnap the only son of the CEO of the largest oil company in North America?"

Shaun's eyes bugged. "I thought his dad made wines or something."

"He does now. As soon as they got Tom back, his dad resigned and they bought the vineyard. Matthew thought if they disappeared from public life, they'd be off the radar. So he bought a huge property and surrounded it with a wall and several dozen cameras and in-house security. For almost five years Tom had bodyguards following him around, keeping him safe. He finally convinced his dad to get rid of them when he was in college." Suddenly a new thought slammed so hard into my brain all sound ceased and my vision turned white. I reached for the table to steady myself. "Oh, Jesus. CJ." My vision slowly cleared and I stared at Shaun wildly. "What if they go after our son?" I turned to run for the bedroom where my phone was charging, but Shaun's grip on my arm swung me around.

"Do not call that boy, Hank. Do not upset him for nothing. Send him a casual text asking how he's doing. If he doesn't answer soon, we'll have

Mary Beth try to get the local PD to send someone by for a welfare check."

I swallowed hard, fresh tears burning. "I don't know what I'll do if something happens to either one of them, Shaun."

Shaun nodded sadly and wrapped me in a hug. "I know, buddy," he whispered into my hair.

I STARED hard at the phone willing it to ring or chirp or vibrate off the table, anything to let me know CJ was safe. If I didn't get an answer to my text soon, I was going to go stark raving mad. As if daring me to lose my sanity, the damn thing lay there completely dormant.

"Henry." It was said gently, but it had the force of a shotgun blast against my raw nerves.

I looked up at Mary Beth sitting in the chair next to Shaun's, her SFPD uniform still incongruous with my memory of a bubbly but ultimately innocent teenager. I tried to offer a smile but the effort was too much. Between my emotional and physical exhaustion, I was lucky to be coherent at all. And CJ not answering my text message wasn't helping anything. "I'm sorry. I zoned out for a minute."

Mary Beth's smile even reached her eyes. I almost envied her that ability. "It's okay, Henry. I know this is a difficult situation for you. I just want to make sure I have everything correct here. Do you mind if I repeat some of it back to you?"

I nodded and glanced at the phone again. Still nothing. Mary Beth had been here for almost twenty minutes and I'd messaged CJ at least fifteen minutes before that. I knew he was a typical college sophomore with plenty of friends and a very active social life, but shouldn't he be studying on a Tuesday night? If he wasn't, then he damn well should be and I'd be sure to tell him that. He was an incredibly talented and intelligent young man, but CalArts had chewed up and spit out more than one talented and gifted person in its long and distinguished history. As soon as I thought it, I realized his summer term had already ended, so he was either working or playing. Like his dad, he did both with equal determination.

Shaun's hand closed over the phone on the table and my gaze shot to his. "I'm going to take this out back and call CJ," he said. "Relax and concentrate on verifying the information Mary Beth has, okay?" He didn't wait for my approval; he simply scooped up the phone and headed through the kitchen and out into the back yard. I watched him go with rising anxiety. I needed to hear my son's voice or at least see his words on the screen before I could feel sure he was safe.

When Shaun had disappeared from sight, I turned my attention back to Mary Beth. "I'm really sorry. This whole thing has me freaked out. I don't understand what's going on. This isn't my life. People don't just disappear, do they?"

Mary Beth grimaced. "Unfortunately, sometimes they do. But let's not worry about anyone else. Let's make sure we find Tom and return him home safely." She turned back pages in her memo notebook and began to recite the information I'd given her earlier. Thomas Matthew MacKinnon was 43, six feet three, approximately two hundred twenty pounds, with short brown hair greying slightly at the temples, and green eyes. He didn't wear glasses, had no known medical conditions, and had a tiny and very pale birthmark in the shape of an inverted triangle on his right shoulder blade. He also had one tattoo, two interlocking infinity symbols on the inside of his left biceps.

She'd seemed confused by the tattoo description earlier, so I'd shown her my matching one, and she'd taken a photo of it with her phone. Tom and I had gotten identical infinity symbols to celebrate our tenth anniversary as a couple and added a smaller, interlocking one when we'd adopted CJ a few years later. It was our way of proving to him that we were a family forever, no matter who had given birth to him.

Mary Beth's blue eyes drilled into me. "This next set of questions is going to be uncomfortable. They're very personal, but it's important that you be completely honest. If you keep anything from me at all, our chances of finding Tom diminish significantly. If there's something you think Tom wouldn't want us to know, then it's probably something we should know. Don't think of it as disclosing his secrets. Think of it as helping to find him. Do you understand?"

I nodded, knowing I had no choice but to betray Tom's trust again. Somehow without even realizing it, I'd managed to convince myself that the past was repeating itself. I didn't know who had taken Tom or why, but I had little doubt he'd been kidnapped again. I glanced towards the back door once more, hoping against hope that the bastards hadn't gone after CJ too.

"Has there been any discord in your relationship with Tom lately? Any reason why he would want to take a few days away?"

I shook my head. "No. We're fine." I waved her words away like gnats. "Listen, before you go any further, I need to tell you something." I took a deep breath to fortify my nerves. It was easier to say the words this time, perhaps because informing Mary Beth might actually be forward motion, whereas confessing to Shaun felt like telling tales out of school. I was so tired of sitting here doing nothing yet expecting something to happen. It was pretty clear I wasn't going to wake up from this nightmare any time soon, so I needed to do what I could to move things along. "In 1987, when Tom was sixteen, he went on vacation to Europe with his parents, Matthew and Althea. They did the usual tour of the capitals: London, Paris, Berlin. Back then Matthew was the CEO of Cladis Petroleum. At the time, Cladis was the largest oil company in North America."

"Wow."

"Don't be too impressed. The guy's still a dick. No, that's not fair. He's a dick to me. He's mostly a good father and grandfather."

Mary Beth's eyebrow quirked in curiosity.

I rolled my eyes. "I've been with Tom for twenty-one years and they still hate it."

Mary Beth offered a sympathetic smile. "So much for the 'it's just a phase' theory."

I grimaced. "No kidding. The point is that on the way home from their tour, they made a last-minute stop in Rome so Matthew could attend a meeting with some representatives of a Kuwaiti oil company. It turns out the whole thing was a trick." I pressed my hands together to stop their shaking. "When Tom and Althea went out to tour the Pantheon, they were kidnapped by terrorists."

I expected Mary Beth to gasp or clutch her non-existent pearls or something, but she showed no reaction other than continued curiosity. I glanced towards the back door one more time and quickly continued my story. Shaun didn't need to know the few gory details I knew. It was more than enough that he was even aware Tom's kidnapping had happened.

"Like I said, Tom doesn't like to talk about it so I don't have a lot of details. Matthew was somehow able to keep it out of the press. Only one short article in a Roman newspaper mentioned it, and it only referred to an unnamed American teenager. That was easier to accomplish in the days before internet, I suppose. Anyway, all Tom has ever said is that the kidnappers roughed up Althea and sent her back as a warning. They contacted Matthew the next day and demanded an obscene amount of money for Tom's safe return."

I shrugged. "I'm sure there was more to it than that. They must have wanted something out of Cladis too, but that's never been discussed. Matthew was able to get the money and five days later they dumped Tom on the banks of the Tiber River thirty or so miles outside of Rome. They'd knocked him around a bit because he resisted every time they tried to get him to do anything, but they hadn't beaten him. They'd fed him and allowed him water and, uhm, ya know, personal relief. Tom never, ever talks about the other details. I have no idea if they kept him bound or blindfolded or anything like that. He sometimes has nightmares, but he won't talk about those either. As soon as they got back to the States, Matthew resigned from Cladis and bought the vineyard in Napa. And since then, the whole family has pretended it never happened."

Mary Beth's eyes had taken on the glazed expression I'd expected. I attempted an apologetic smile. "You can see why he didn't want anyone to know."

She nodded. "I don't even know what to say to that. It's incredible that he escaped alive." Her brows knit together in a deep frown. "You don't think they've come after him again now, do you?"

I made a helpless gesture. "I don't know what to think, but I feel like it's a possibility." It was too much to say aloud that I believed it. I was afraid it would make it true if I actually said it.

"Henry, almost thirty years seems like an awfully long time to wait to kidnap him again. What value could he possibly have now? His father isn't even in the oil business anymore. That terrorist group probably isn't even around now."

I nodded again. It felt like that was all I did anymore. "I understand it doesn't seem logical, but there is no reason for Tom to have disappeared voluntarily. We're happy. We have a good life, a nice home, and a fantastic son. He loves his work, even if he doesn't always love his job, if that makes sense. There have been no traumatic occurrences in our lives. Our finances are stable. Our health is good. His parents are healthy and a pain in the ass, but that's nothing new."

I'd detached a bit from my emotions telling Mary Beth about Tom's kidnapping, but listing the good fortunes of our life together brought me back into their grip. My voice shook and my eyes burned as I continued. "I don't understand. I've woken up next to this man every morning and gone to bed with him every night for almost half my life. Now I don't know where he is and it's killing me inside. There is no me without him." Tears finally spilled down my cheeks. "Please help me find him, Mary Beth."

She sniffled quietly and packed away her notebook and pen without looking up. A moment later, she stood and offered me a tremulous smile and an outstretched hand. "I promise we'll do everything we can."

We both looked up as Shaun entered the room, a happy grin on his face. "CJ was at the movies with some people named Sophia and Dylan. His phone was on silent so he didn't get your message until they left the cinema. He's fine. I didn't tell him anything, just suggested he hang out with his friends the rest of the night."

I slumped with relief. At least my son was safe. What that meant for his dad, I didn't know, but I allowed myself to be a little more hopeful. "Thank you, Shaun."

Mary Beth moved away from her chair. "I'm glad to hear your son's okay, Henry. I'll go down to the station and get this entered into NCIC and the California DOJ databases. From here your case will be assigned to a detective. Given the potential that Tom hasn't walked away voluntarily, he or she will be in touch soon, but it may still take a day or two." She placed her hand on my forearm and reached up to gently kiss my cheek. "I know it's going to sound trite, but try not to worry too much, and don't do anything that'll put yourself in harm's way. There's every possibility that if Tom's injured, he's just lost in the system."

"Thank you, Mary Beth." I took an uneven breath and let it out slowly. "I hope it's something that simple."

She squeezed my forearm again. "Me too. Just in case, I'm going to flag this as suspicious circumstances to speed things along. Go ahead and call the hospitals and homeless shelters first. Your instincts were right; those are great places to start your own searches. Good luck."

Shaun offered her his arm. "I'll walk you to your car."

I watched them go and then grabbed Mary Beth's mostly untouched coffee and carried it in to the sink. I poured it down the drain and rinsed the mug, going over the conversation again in my mind. Did I leave out anything important? Had I stressed anything too much? Did I inadvertently give them any false leads? Mary Beth had seemed to take the revelation of Tom's earlier kidnapping seriously, but was I wrong to have given her the information? Was she right that it seemed implausible? What if they pursued that angle and there was nothing to it?

What if? What if? What if? I was so tired of the questions!

I needed answers and there was one place I hoped to find them.

The living room was still empty when I reentered it. Mildly surprised, I walked over to the window and peered out into the night. Lit by the street light a few yards away, Mary Beth and Shaun stood close together engaged in conversation. I watched them, thinking of the somewhat flighty teenage girl I used to know compared to the controlled, competent policewoman she'd grown into. Suddenly her posture tensed and her arms flew out in the usual "what the hell?" gesture. I couldn't hear what she said, but the finger she shoved in Shaun's face left no doubt that she was unhappy about something and was letting him know it. Shaun glanced at the window for a brief moment before he turned back to Mary Beth. He gently touched her shoulder but she shrugged him off. He spoke quietly for a moment before she climbed into a little red Honda coupe and sped off. Shaun waited until her taillights were out of sight before looking back up at me. His shoulders seemed to slump as he trudged down the sidewalk and up the stairs to the house.

I was so consumed with starting the next step that I didn't even care what their row was about. He'd probably asked her out and she'd given him what for because he'd already dated—well, slept with—her sister.

"I'm going to Matthew and Althea's," I said as soon as he'd closed the door behind him. "Are you coming with me?"

FIVE

I listened to the sound of the road passing under us for several miles, wondering what sort of reception I would find in Napa in the middle of the night, at least by MacKinnon standards. After Shaun had agreed to accompany me, I'd tried to call their landline again while he went into the garage to check the oil and tire pressure on the Jeep. I was somewhat surprised to have the call answered by an automated voice repeating the number I'd dialed and instructing me to leave a message. It was better than the 'no longer in service' message I'd received earlier, but still frustrating.

Once upon a time I'd been in possession of Matthew and Althea's cell phone numbers, but over the years I'd stopped transferring them to new phones. I'd only had them for emergency purposes anyway. If a true emergency had ever popped up where I needed to be the one to contact them instead of Tom doing it, I was sure one of the household staff would be more than happy to run after their employers and tell them the news. I not only didn't need their cell numbers, I didn't want them.

I knew CJ kept in close contact with his grandparents, but even as a youngster he was aware of the way they treated me, so he had gradually stopped sharing stories about them with me unless it was necessary information. I'd been surprised and suspicious happy when they had immediately welcomed our son into the family. I had pegged them as the types that would never forget to subtly remind him that he was adopted and, therefore, inferior. Somehow our little 10-year-old, blond-haired, brown-eyed bundle of energy, resentment, and distrust had worked his way right into their hearts. That had shown me that Matthew and Althea really did possess the things. I'd never been sure.

Shaun and I had finally managed to leave the house shortly after nine, so best case scenario had us arriving at Matthew and Althea's front door around 10:30. I hadn't been exaggerating when I'd told Mary Beth that Tom's parents still disliked me after all this time. I knew for a fact they held out hope that Tom would wake up one day and declare he had been straight all along and that I had tricked or drugged or worked witchcraft on him from the moment we met.

If my theory was correct and Tom had been kidnapped again and the MacKinnons had been informed, I knew they would see my presence as an annoying distraction. They certainly wouldn't want me hovering around until Tom was returned to us. But if I brought news that their only son had once again disappeared and that there was no news from kidnappers yet, I was practically guaranteed hostile treatment. Even Shaun's presence wouldn't alter their attitudes much. They might try to disguise their hatred in some cutesy passive aggressive speeches and behaviors, but Shaun wouldn't be fooled any more than I would be.

Shaun's sudden laugh broke the quiet in the Jeep. I flipped him off without a qualm. I knew it meant he'd looked over and caught me concentrating intently on my thumbs doing circles around each other in my lap. "I'll never understand you." He was still laughing at me.

I sighed and risked a quick glance over at him out of the corner of my eye. Under no circumstances was I moving my head. "What? You mean why do I live on a peninsula if I'm petrified of bridges?" I swallowed hard as the Jeep swayed slightly with the motion of the bridge. Other people had assured me that I couldn't possibly feel the movement of the bridge unless the winds were much stronger than they were at the moment, but I disagreed heartily. Even if it was just my imagination, I felt the damn thing move. And I didn't like it. I pulled on the shoulder strap to check the seatbelt's connection. It held firm and I breathed slightly easier, but not enough to look anywhere other than at my lap.

"That is what I mean right now, yes."

I pointed out the window at the bridge in question. "It isn't the bridges I dislike so much as the going over them. As long as I'm not on them, I think they're quite beautiful, this one especially."

"Yes, I've heard that about this one," he deadpanned.

"Shut up and drive. I don't have many neuroses, leave me this one."

"Henry, it's the Golden Gate Bridge. It's one of mankind's wonders. Look up! Look around! Enjoy it!"

I rolled my eyes and concentrated harder on my thumbs as the bridge moved again. "It's dark out. What am I supposed to see in the middle of the bridge in the middle of the night that I can't see once we get back on solid ground?"

"The bridge, man! Have you ever watched the bridge as you went across it? It's amazing any time, but it's especially beautiful at night."

I sighed. "It's a bridge, Shaun. Only this one moves. Can you just hurry up and get to the other side? I promise I'll appreciate it from afar."

Shaun laughed again and patted my shoulder condescendingly. If I hadn't known him for twenty-some years and if we hadn't been on a bridge, I would have punched him.

My phobia of bridges didn't include all of them. I was fine with normal zip-across-a-river type bridges. But when it came to the ones I called super-bridges or the steel-framed incarnations of evil, double-decker bridges, I was forced to concentrate on breathing and not looking outside the cabin of the vehicle or face a panic attack. Tom had convinced me to take the Bay Bridge route to Napa exactly once. I was ready to jump out of the car and off the bridge by the time we'd made it half way across. It was a miracle I survived the entire expanse. I'd made him take me back home across the Golden Gate Bridge. It wasn't my favorite alternative because of the way it moved and swayed with the wind, regardless of what other people thought, but at least I wasn't constantly worried an upper deck would come crashing down on me.

"Tell me about meeting Tom for the first time."

"It's only a four minute trip across this stupid thing," I huffed. "I don't think I need distraction therapy."

"Maybe not, but this is going to be a long trip. And since your taste in music is atrocious, we can't turn on the radio. I might as well have your voice droning on and on to keep me awake."

"Why are we friends again?"

"Because you couldn't have survived college without me, and by the time we graduated, you'd become dependent upon my incredibly charming and, need I say, very humble personality."

"Yes, that must be it," I agreed with as much sarcasm as I could muster. Unfortunately he was mostly correct about everything but his humility—and my taste in music. "By the way, I'm not the one with every Lionel Richie CD ever produced."

"You're proving your point. Lionel Richie is a god."

I scoffed. "You were dropped on your head as a child one too many times."

He reached into the console between us and brought out the first CD his fingers ran across. He glanced at it, made a disgusted noise, and threw it on my lap. "Explain that, O Arbiter of Good Taste."

Britney Spears, *Blackout.* Shit. Why did he have to pick that one? "It's CJ's?"

"Bullshit."

I laughed and tossed the disc into the back seat. We'd successfully crossed the bridge so I allowed myself to relax and look around, not that I could see a lot in the darkness. "Fine. It's mine. I liked 'Gimme More' so I bought the thing."

"Sad, man, just sad." He sounded disappointed, but I couldn't tell if it was *in* me or *for* me. "At least Lionel Richie doesn't lip sync."

"God I wish he would—and use someone else's voice to do it."

"Oh, that was uncalled for!" He shoved me playfully.

I brought my best affronted queen voice out of the closet. "I'm gonna hit you one more time if you don't watch the road, bitch."

He laughed so hard that I thought we were in mortal danger for a moment, but he managed to get himself under control before he hit anyone.

As the miles passed and my mind raced, the quiet in the Jeep grew oppressive. "You really don't remember how Tom and I met?"

Shaun chuckled. "I knew you wouldn't be able to resist."

"Hey, it's me or Britney Spears. Your choice."

"In that case, I'm all ears. Pray tell how you and our fair Thomas met. I vaguely remember it had something to do with coffee."

I couldn't stop the smile at the memory. "Actually, I'm surprised you weren't there. You must've been in class or something." I didn't really know how to begin a story he'd heard a hundred or more times since it happened, so I lowered the seatback two notches and tried my best Sophia Petrillo. "Picture it: USC, April, 1993. Chloe and I decided to have lunch on campus for some strange reason so we popped over to the Law School Café to scope out potential future husbands." I laughed at our youthful naiveté. Neither of us had had a prayer in hell of catching a law student's attention, but that hadn't deterred us. "I don't really remember what happened, but I know I was ahead of her in line. I was talking and not paying attention—"

"Shocking," Shaun interjected helpfully.

"—and the next thing I knew I'd turned around to tell her something and collided with a wall of man. I think my coffee got crushed between us because we were both doused in scalding hot liquid. I was mortified. I think my embarrassment burned more than the coffee, especially when I got a good look at who I'd bumped into."

Shaun laughed. "I remember Chloe telling me that part. Angels got their wings, choirs sang, sins were forgiven all over the land, and our little Henry Cooley fell in love at first splatter."

I grinned out the window so Shaun wouldn't see how dreamy the expression on my face must have been. "Well it wasn't quite that dramatic."

"Man, you were already head over heels for the guy by the time you got home. That much I do remember."

Heat raced to my cheeks and the blissful feeling washed through me again as it did every time I remembered the first time I beheld Tom MacKinnon's amazing green eyes. They were flecked with blue. It was the first time I'd seen green eyes not flecked with brown. It almost hurt to look away from them.

While I'd been paralyzed by embarrassment and lust, Tom had taken control of the situation. He hadn't screamed or yelled at me as I'd expected. Instead, he'd gasped as the coffee burned, then grabbed his shirt away from his body—and laughed. He'd actually laughed. Then he'd asked if I was okay. Chloe had been quick to bring us a pile of completely unhelpful napkins, but once Tom was assured I was okay—Chloe had tactfully smacked me upside the head to get me to react in the affirmative to his question—he'd gestured to the gym bag slung over his shoulder and said he'd be right back.

"I couldn't believe it," I told Shaun. "The hottest guy I'd ever seen and I'd practically thrown coffee at him."

"And yourself, for that matter."

"Would you shut up?"

Shaun laughed. "Hey, it worked, didn't it? I'm jealous. If I tried that with a woman I'd get slapped. You got a husband out of the deal."

I sighed like a lovesick teenager. "Yeah, I did. Anyway, I couldn't believe it when he came looking for me after he'd changed. Holy buckets, I'd never seen someone so sexy that close up before."

Tom had waved from across the cafe, carefully winding his way through the tables. "Hey, barista," he called from a few tables away, flashing a smile that stilled my breath. My cheeks flamed. Chloe quickly grabbed my refilled coffee cup and slid it away from me, keeping a protective hand over the lid. I shot her a glare, but she just smiled back at me with a "don't screw this up" twitch of her eyes.

To my surprise, Tom sank into the empty seat at our table. Clad in a tank top and shorts, he'd revealed more silky smooth skin than I had a right to dream of seeing. He'd thrust his hand out to Chloe. "I'm Tom MacKinnon. Nice to meet you."

Chloe's flirtatious laugh grated on my last functional nerve. "Chloe Seabrook. The pleasure's mine. I hope you aren't hurt too badly."

Tom smiled at her. "Nope. No worse for wear." He turned to me and I would swear until I went to my grave that his smile and his voice deepened, just for me. "Tom MacKinnon," he repeated, offering his hand.

I'd read enough fiction to hear about an electric charge passing between two people when two future lovers first meet. I'd thought it was literary nonsense until I'd slid my hand into Tom's grip. It was like time screeched to a halt for a nanosecond and no one noticed but me. I drank in those beautiful eyes of his again and knew my world had changed somehow. "H-Henry Cooley," I somehow stuttered. "I'm so sorry about earlier. I don't make it a habit to throw coffee on hot guys—oh Jesus." My gaze dropped to the table and I quickly pulled my hand from his. "I'm sorry. I didn't mean to say that."

He laughed and patted my shoulder. "I promise I'll only be offended if you didn't mean the hot part."

I stared at him in surprise. "No, no I definitely meant the hot part."

Tom grinned. "In that case, would you like to have dinner with me sometime?"

I blinked several times, sure I'd suffered a series of synaptic misfires that made it sound like he had asked me "On a date?"

He shrugged. "Yeah, sure, if you want to get formal."

"He'd love to," Chloe interrupted, surely saving me from another embarrassment. She quickly scribbled something on one of the seventy thousand napkins she'd brought to the table and gave it to him. "That's his phone number."

"Very efficient." Tom smiled at her again and motioned for a napkin of his own. Chloe handed it to him along with her pen. He scribbled something and passed it over to me. "Here are my digits, Henry. I'll be home after six tonight. Would it be okay to call you then?"

I swallowed hard and nodded. "Yeah, that would be great."

"Okay then." Tom grinned at me again and stood. "Since I'm dressed for it now, I have no excuse not to go to the gym. It was nice meeting you both." He shook Chloe's hand again, sweetly bussing her cheek. He gripped my hand and winked. "I'll talk to you later tonight, barista. Have a great afternoon." And then I watched his ass in those tight shorts as he sashayed out of the café.

I was so caught up in the memory that Shaun's laugh startled me. "After all that, I still can't believe you made him wait to have sex."

"Are you kidding? I was intimidated by his body. I used the time to work on my own. I didn't want him to be disappointed when I finally got naked in front of him. Plus, it was sort of a test. I didn't want to be just another roll in the hay."

"I still say that's the cutest story I've ever heard. If Chloe hadn't backed up every word of it, I never would have believed it."

"You just wish you had a story that cute to tell."

Shaun scoffed. "I'm allergic to cute."

I doubted that was true, but I sometimes wondered what had stopped my best friend from settling down with some nice girl. There had been plenty of them over the years, but they never stuck around for long.

As Shaun took the exit off the 101 onto California 37, the sweet memory faded and reality crashed back down around me. The swift change in emotions left me gasping. I brought my seat upright again. Where was Tom? And what, if anything, did his parents know about his current whereabouts? What hell on earth was I about to subject myself to? I fished my cell phone out of my pocket and dashed off a quick message to CJ. Just in case something happened—and because something clearly already had—I needed my son to know I loved him.

A few moments later my phone buzzed in response. I was sure he probably communicated with his friends in abbreviated text speech, but when he'd first started texting me I'd told him I was too old to learn a new language, so his messages to me were almost always in full sentences. *Love you too, Pops.* My heart swelled. He was such a great kid. His dad and I were lucky to have him in our lives. I hoped we found Tom before we had to tell CJ about his disappearance. I'd do anything to keep that kid from more pain.

I tapped out another message and the response came just as quickly. *What movie? I'm roughing it at Aunt Chloe's this week, remember? She barely has internet. No cable.*

I glanced quickly at and away from Shaun as my heartbeat kicked into overdrive. *Didn't you tell Uncle Shaun you were at a movie tonight?* I texted back.

His response seemed to take forever. *Haven't talked to Uncle Shaun in weeks. What's going on?*

Oh Jesus, Mary and Joseph, what the hell *was* going on? Quickly, I typed that I must have misunderstood and that everything was fine, reminding him again that I loved him. With my son taken care of, I needed to decide how to confront Shaun without killing us both. What the hell was he playing at? Could he have something to do with Tom's disappearance? Was it possible the man I'd known and loved like a brother since I was eighteen was actually a danger to me and my family?

"Stop the truck." I spoke before my thoughts coalesced. I only knew I couldn't be in this Jeep anymore. I couldn't sit next to my lying piece of shit of a best friend anymore.

"What's wrong? Are you going to be sick?" The concern in his voice made my stomach clench. How long had he been lying to me?

I couldn't breathe. I unhooked the seatbelt and reached for the door handle. "Stop the fucking truck! Right now!"

"Jesus, Henry. Okay. Let me find a spot to pull off."

As soon as the Jeep stopped I was out of my seat, doubled over with my hands on my knees, taking huge gulps of the cool July night air. Shaun stepped around the front of the vehicle, full of concerned questions about my health. I didn't pause to think if it was a good idea, I just let fly with a left hook that caught him square in the jaw. Unprepared, he hit the deck like a sack of potatoes while I cradled my aching hand and swore up a blue streak. I'd never struck anyone in anger in my life. But no one had tried to steal my life before either. Tom and CJ were definitely my life. Without them I was nothing.

"What the fuck was that for?" Shaun thundered from his sprawled position on the ground.

I rounded on him in fury. "How long have you been lying to me? What the hell is going on? What have you done with Tom?"

"What are you talking about? I'm not the one who lost Tom."

He started to get up but my finger in his face stopped him. “Stay the fuck down or I swear to god I'll put you down there again.” He held up his hands in the classic surrender pose and I stepped back to catch my breath and, hopefully, some sanity. “I just texted CJ. He said he didn’t go to a movie tonight. He also said he hasn't spoken to you in weeks.”

Shaun shrugged. “Well he probably didn't realize he was talking to me earlier. I used your phone, remember? When I went outside to try to get ahold of him he responded to your text. He said he was fine. I said something like ‘okay just checking’ and left it at that so I didn’t freak him out. I knew you would need more, so I made up with the movie story to calm you down.”

“Why would you do that? And why the hell should I believe a word you say?”

“Check your damn messages and see for yourself!” he shouted.

“You didn’t actually talk to him?”

“No!” I saw him struggle to calm himself. When he had, he continued in a normal tone. “You had texted him so that’s how he responded. I didn’t want to call him back and upset him without a solid reason. We don’t know anything yet. Look, I'm your best friend, Hank. I love that boy just as much as you do. I’ve never lied to you before and I didn’t do it this time to hurt you.”

His words ricocheted off something in my brain, something that I couldn’t quite remember. I stared into his eyes and thought I found truth but I couldn’t be sure, and I wouldn’t be sure until we found Tom. It almost seemed like Shaun had his own agenda, but I couldn’t figure out what it could possibly be.

Through narrowed eyes I divided my attention between verifying his story against my message history and watching as my former best friend slowly climbed to his feet. He wiggled his jaw uncomfortably a couple of times and I directed my smirk to the ground. It was good to know I could handle him if I needed to.

“I did what I thought was best at the time, Hank. I’m sorry it upset you. I knew you were worried about CJ on top of everything else. I just wanted to take that one fear away. I was wrong. I apologize.”

The messages were there, just as he said they'd be. I pushed a few more buttons and pulled up the call log. "Why did you call Jamie?"

He exhaled the sigh of the deeply oppressed. "I wanted to see if he'd heard from Tom and to check on how the labor was progressing. Since there was nothing new to report on either front, I didn't say anything. I didn't want to add to your worries. It's the same reason I made up the story about the movie. I'm only trying to help, Hank."

My anger deflated and a renewed fear for Tom rushed in to take its place. Shaun had made a huge mistake and I didn't completely trust him anymore, but I still needed him. "Fine," I said. "I'll accept your apology this time. But if you ever lie to me again, we're done. I will leave you on the side of the road if I have to."

Shaun nodded and held out his hand for me to shake. When I took it he pulled me into a hug. "Fair enough," he said into my ear. "But if you ever hit me again, you'll be the one picking yourself up off the ground."

I nodded and pounded his back in understanding.

He stepped back and looked me over from head to toe. "Now if you're done being a drama queen, we have an appointment with your in-laws to keep."

I expelled a breath of disgust at the idea. "Let's get on with it. The sooner we get there, the sooner I can get Tom back."

Shaun frowned for a moment. "Answer me when we get back on the road, but I'm wondering why you've decided Tom was kidnapped again. I mean he's a great guy, but what possible value could he have to the bad guys now? This isn't the 80's and Matthew isn't in the oil business anymore. I don't understand why you're convinced."

When we had settled back in the Jeep, I confessed. "Hardwick likes to keep a low profile, hence the relatively modest offices in NoPa, but the truth is it's a huge and influential company. It has several deals to build skyscrapers in China and Dubai. If any—let's call them 'nefarious' organizations— wanted to delay or destroy or otherwise sabotage those buildings, Tom, as the Senior VP of the tall buildings business, would have access to the plans and construction contracts." I sighed and confessed a deeper truth, one that hurt to the core. "But honestly, I have no reason to believe he's been kidnapped again. I just need to cling to something that makes sense, even if it's completely unlikely. Even if it leads me on a wild goose chase to Mama and Papa Evil's house. I need to believe he didn't leave me by choice."

Shaun's hand found mine on my thigh and squeezed it before letting go. I flinched because it was still sore from punching him. "He didn't. No matter what else you may believe about me now, believe me when I say there is no way in hell that man left you by choice."

It shouldn't have reassured me, but it did.

WE CONTINUED the drive in silence but this time it was uncomfortable. Regardless of the words we'd shared, neither Shaun nor I were ready to forgive the other yet. He'd lied to my face without a justifiable reason. Why couldn't he just say "Hey, Henry, CJ texted that he's okay"? Because I wouldn't have left it alone. He was right. I would have pestered him for more information and then been pissed he didn't have any. But if he knew me as well as he should have by now, he wouldn't have let it go at that. He would have asked for more from CJ, some clarification that it was actually him on the other end of that text message and not a kidnapper playing it cool.

It was all so circular. I didn't know a goddamn thing and it was killing me. At least now I knew for certain my son was safe. I'd had an actual conversation with him. The comment about "roughing it" at Chloe's convinced me. She lived in Idyllwild, which probably felt like the ends of the earth to my city kid. But where the hell was Tom? Was he out there somewhere wounded? Had he really been kidnapped? Had he left me? Of all the available alternatives, that one hurt the worst, because that one I had no explanation why and no way of knowing how to fix it. I banged my head against the headrest until I felt Shaun's hand on the back of my head keeping it from making contact.

"Stop it, Hank." Shaun's tone was soothing. It made me want to curl up against him and beg him to make everything okay again. Instead, I leaned forward and scrubbed my hands across my face, letting out a frustrated growl as I did it.

"Do you know you're the only one who's ever called me Hank?"

"I hadn't until you mentioned it. Are you gonna tell me twenty years later that it bothers you?"

"No, not at all. It just seems weird that no one else has ever done it. Tom calls me Henry or barista or honey, but never Hank."

Shaun laughed. "He still calls you barista?"

I shrugged. "Usually when he's horny."

Shaun swerved the Jeep dramatically. "Whoa, son, too much information!"

I backhanded his shoulder. "As if I haven't heard worse from you."

"Totally different. I'm hot."

"Meh. You're okay."

"Dude, you've lusted after me since the day we met. Don't even try to deny it."

I looked at him until he glanced my way, just to make the point. "Shaun, if I'd wanted you, I would have had you. And I would've rocked your world."

His chuckle sounded a little nervous. It made me smile. "Dream on, son, dream on." I let him stew on that for a while. Eventually he asked, "So what do other people call you?"

"Most people just call me Henry. My dad used to call me lots of things, but mostly Zeke."

"Why Zeke?"

"I have no idea. When I was little I thought he was just being mean, you know, like he couldn't remember my name. But now I see that it was his way of showing affection."

"Did you learn that because of CJ?"

I chuckled. "Man, I've learned so many things because of that kid; but yeah, that was one of them. I think I have about a hundred nicknames for him."

"Do you remember when we went skiing in Tahoe in February? You and CJ and I flew up early and Tom was going to come meet us on Saturday."

None of that made sense. "What? When was that?"

"In February. The three of us went up on Wednesday but Tom couldn't join us until Saturday because of some big contract at work. You don't remember?"

"I don't remember that at all." He must have been confused. Not only did I not ski, I despised the cold weather. That was why I lived in California. "Are you sure it was me and Tom and not some other couple?"

"Hmm, I don't think so. Where did you and Tom spend Valentine's Day this year?"

That was a silly question. We'd spent it in the same place for the last ten years. "We went to LA like always. We had dinner on the beach in Malibu, went to a Kings game, and spent the night at the Ritz-Carlton."

"Okay. So...do you ever call CJ 'Zeke'?"

He changed the subject so fast my mind did a spin-o-rama of its own. "Uhm, yeah, sometimes. It seemed like the thing to do. Why are you asking about Valentine's Day?"

"Well you know me, Hank. As the perpetual bachelor of the group, it's my least favorite day of the year, so I try to spend it sloshed out of my gourd. It just seemed to me like we'd spent the week before that snowkiting at Boca Reservoir. Maybe it was just something I thought we could do, but we never did."

"Snowkiting? I don't think I even want to know what that is."

"It's an absolute blast." He chuckled. "I'm not sure you're coordinated enough to pull it off though. You'd probably find the only tree in the area and get your kite stuck in it."

"You're such a prick."

SIX

Eventually even Shaun's inane banter couldn't keep us from arriving at our destination. As he pulled up to the gated entrance, I fished the gate code out of the glove box. "Welcome to Villa Dimitri," I sneered.

The pretentious name Althea had bestowed upon their house and its one hundred acres, including the sixty-five acre Lasthenia Valley Vineyard, was a nod to her maiden name, Dimitriou. Her father had been an up and coming Greek shipping tycoon trying desperately to become the next Aristotle Onassis. Unfortunately for Georgios Dimitriou, he was also a close friend of the King. In 1967, a military coup toppled the monarchy. The hostile new government seized and nationalized the Dimitriou family's businesses and real estate holdings. Althea had been seventeen when the family had hastily fled Greece just hours after the Royal Family departed for exile in Italy. Three years later she had married the ambitious Matthew MacKinnon, whose family was well-bred but of considerably reduced means, as one would put it politely. Tom had been born in January of the next year. Many had viewed the marriage as a different kind of coup for Matthew, considering Papa Dimitriou had managed to keep most of his modest fortune safe in banks located in Switzerland and Luxembourg.

I handed Shaun the paper with the code on it and gave him a shortened version of the reason behind the property's name. I was gratified when it elicited a similar response from him. I took a deep breath as we passed through the slowly opening gates. I needed to get my emotions under control before I confronted the MacKinnons, but the closer we got to a possible answer to Tom's disappearance, the antsier I became. I'd already punched someone in anger in the past hour. I couldn't be positive it wouldn't happen again if I discovered they were withholding information from me out of spite.

"Are you really sure you want to do this, Hank?"

I looked at him quizzically. "I have to find out if they know something. And if they don't, I owe it to them to let them know Tom's missing. I really can't see any way out of it."

In the green glow of the dashboard lights, I saw his nod and the frown that followed. He grabbed the cold dregs of his coffee out of the cup holder and downed them before handing me the empty paper cup. As I placed it in the trash bag I kept behind the passenger seat, he spoke again. "We should plan another snowkiting trip for the winter. We can go somewhere other than Tahoe, but I think we need to make some more good memories. CJ had such a great time last time."

"What the hell are you talking about?" I was growing exasperated with his fixation on this snowkiting, whatever the hell that was.

"We did go snowkiting in February, Henry. You and me and CJ. We went to Boca Reservoir and spent two days snowkiting and one day skiing at Squaw Valley."

I laughed. "You're losing your mind, buddy. There's no way in hell you'd ever get me on a set of skis. You know how much I hate the snow."

Shaun cringed. "You love your son more than you hate snow. CJ convinced you to try the snowkiting since it was on a flat surface and nowhere near as dangerous as downhill can be. He even got you to put on a snowboard."

My heartbeat kicked up and my grip tightened on the armrest. "Why do you keep talking about this like it actually happened?"

"I'm just trying to get you to remember."

"I can't remember something I didn't do. You're starting to wig me out. Stop it."

Shaun drummed his thumbs on the steering wheel. "I'm sorry. I didn't mean to upset you."

He sounded contrite, but I was already angry, which was not a good thing when a confrontation with Matthew and Althea loomed less than five minutes away. "Well for not trying, you're doing a damn good job. I have more important things to concentrate on right now than goddamn skiing. Just give me some time to find my calm place before I have to see Matthew and Althea."

He held up his hands in surrender momentarily before navigating around a curve in the long approach to the house. As the main house came into view, I was disappointed to see the windows were dark and unwelcoming. The Mediterranean-style home was huge and beautiful, and Althea's flair for the dramatic made it look even more impressive. In addition to expansive landscaping, every ten feet around the perimeter of the home, hidden lights bathed the pale stucco walls in an ethereal glow. Unlike the camera-monitored walls around the entire estate, the lighting had been one of the few security measures I'd approved of when Tom brought me to his parents' home the very first time. As practical as they were, they also served to personalize the place, to make it more of a home instead of just a credit card depot. From our position in front of the house I couldn't see the pool area, but I would have bet money the underwater lights were on, lending shimmering, serene splendor to the courtyard.

Shaun was silent as he pulled the Jeep to a stop in front of the main entrance. His nervousness flooded over me, adding to my own. As many times as I'd been to this house over the last twenty years, no one but Tom had ever made me feel particularly welcome. I was keenly aware of his absence next to me. It wasn't the first time I'd come here without him; I'd done it often to pick up CJ when Tom couldn't get away from work to accompany me. Those times Althea or one of the household staff had met me at the door with CJ and his belongings and we'd simply climbed back in the vehicle for the return trip, CJ chattering happily beside me about all the wonderful things he and Papa had done in the vineyard or the cookies he'd been able to help Mrs. Danforth make in the kitchen. Althea was a loving grandmother, but her idea of cuddling her grandson was little more than swimming laps beside him in the pool or setting up a miniature easel near hers so CJ could practice with his watercolors as she painted with oils. The MacKinnon home was filled with Althea's paintings of scenes from her native country. As much as she clearly missed Greece, she'd refused to ever return and forbade Tom from visiting as well. She'd been convinced his life would be in danger if he stepped foot on Greek soil, something I had long ago chalked up to bitterness about her family's exile.

Shaun sighed heavily next to me as I stared intently at the house. The answers to Tom's disappearance might be right on the other side of those heavy oak doors. Now that we were so close to finding out if Tom had been kidnapped, I was paralyzed with fear. I needed to know, but the possibilities petrified me. What if he hadn't been kidnapped? What if he'd simply vanished? What if he was wandering around the city with amnesia? What if...what if he really had left me? The last thought knifed through my heart. I couldn't think of a single reason why he would leave, but the fact remained that he was gone.

"Are you ready?" Shaun asked.

I shook my head, still glaring at the doors. I wasn't ready. I might never be ready. No matter what answers I found on the other side of those big double doors, my life would never be the same. I pulled on the Jeep's door handle. "Let's do this," I answered with as much bravado as I could muster. Judging by the tremble in my voice, it wasn't very much.

The motion sensors kicked on the porch light as I approached, startling me. I must have made a nervous sound, because suddenly Shaun's hand was on the small of my back, lending comfort while still propelling me forward. I pressed the doorbell and waited impatiently, trying to identify flowers and plants in the landscaping to keep my mind from pondering all the "what if" questions that filled it. Considering I barely knew a dandelion from a hydrangea, it wasn't much help.

The sound of locks popping brought my attention back to the doors. Eloise, the elderly maid who had been in the MacKinnons' employ since long before I arrived on the scene, pulled open the door in full uniform. I would have been surprised had I not known that every time someone approached the gate, it sent a signal to the cell phone she carried at all times.

She seemed surprised to see me but recovered quickly. "Mr. Henry, the family isn't in residence at this time."

I slumped in dejection. Despite the fact no one had answered the house phone, I hadn't anticipated that the MacKinnons might not be home. While I was fumbling with some sort of way forward, Shaun came to the rescue.

"We urgently need to speak with Mr. or Mrs. MacKinnon, but Henry can't seem to find their telephone numbers. Would it be possible to either come in and call them or for you to give us their numbers?"

The question seemed to flummox Eloise. She stood in the doorway blinking at us for several moments. I was sure she was about to close the door in our faces and possibly even call security to have us removed. "Eloise, please," I implored. "Tom's missing and I need to find out if Matthew and Althea have heard from him."

She recoiled and straightened as if I had slapped her across the face. "I beg your pardon?"

"I can't find Tom. He hasn't been home since Sunday. I'm worried and I'm hoping Matthew and Althea had heard from him."

Eloise's previously open but confused face closed off with a sneer. "What a hateful thing to say, Henry Cooley! You should be ashamed of yourself!" Faster than should be possible for a woman her age, she reached out and slapped my face.

I was too shocked to do anything other than slowly bring my hand to my face and stare at her. *What the hell?*

Her voice was shaky with emotion when she spoke again. "If this is your idea of a joke, it's not funny."

I glanced at Shaun, who looked anything but surprised by the abrupt change in Eloise's attitude. He gazed back at me with eyes full of sadness and regret. Perhaps he was embarrassed to have witnessed it.

"It's no joke, Eloise," I said. "Tom is missing."

"I'm not an idiot, Henry Cooley," she spat. "Master Tom is dead. Now what are you really doing here?"

I stared at her in shock. *Master Tom is dead. Master Tom is dead.* The phrase ping ponged around my brain but refused to compute. It wasn't possible. I would know. I would feel it. I couldn't have spent almost every day of the last twenty-one years loving Tom and being loved by him and not know if he was gone. No, no, no. it wasn't possible. "I need to speak with Matthew or Althea, Eloise. Please."

She shook her graying head firmly. "No. Absolutely not. I don't know what's wrong with you, Mr. Henry, but until you've got control of yourself, I will not subject Mr. Matthew and Mrs. Althea to such nonsense."

Shaun cleared his throat uncomfortably and addressed Eloise. "Henry doesn't remember Tom's death."

I vaguely registered Eloise's gasp as I swung on my best friend. "What the hell are you talking about?"

"Hank, Tom died in February. I've been trying to get you to remember."

The buzzing in my ears exploded exponentially and my knees threatened to buckle. Bile raced from my stomach to lodge in my throat. "You're lying!" I accused. Tears sprang to my eyes as every fear I'd suppressed since I realized Tom had vanished rushed forward to strangle me. I stumbled against a pillar for support, hands on my knees, gasping for breath. I couldn't begin to wrap my mind around why Shaun and Eloise would say such a horrible, hurtful lie. Tom was at home with me on Sunday. What they were saying wasn't possible. It wasn't. It just wasn't.

Shaun tried to place a hand on my shoulder but I batted it away and stood upright again, backing down the steps away from both of them. The roar in my ears increased as blackness crowded my vision.

The last thing I remembered was repeating, "You're lying. You're lying."

SEVEN

My forehead slamming into the Jeep's passenger window woke me with a start. I bolted upright in the seat, looking frantically around. The overwhelming darkness was broken only by the green glow of the dashboard lights illuminating Shaun as he drove us into the night. I was confused and groggy with a bitch of a headache. The jostling of the Jeep down the bumpy ass trail wasn't helping any of those things. It took a second to figure out why I was in a vehicle in the middle of the night with Shaun. I had fainted in the middle of Matthew and Althea's driveway because—*No!*

As soon as the memory flooded my consciousness, I scrambled for the door handle.

"Whoa, whoa, whoa." Shaun stopped me with a quick flip of the locks and a restraining arm across my shoulders. "We're almost there. Just hang on."

"Don't fucking touch me," I spat, shoving his arm away. "Stop the goddamn car." I had to get away from him and his betrayal. I couldn't believe he would lie about Tom to my face, especially after playing the concerned best friend all night. It reminded me what a liar he was. First about CJ and then about Tom. Had he always been like this? How had I never seen it? How had Tom never seen it?

"I'll stop in a minute. We're almost there."

"We're almost where, Shaun? Where are you taking me?" I suddenly recalled the half-heard phone conversation with Jamie from earlier in the evening and the blood turned cold in my veins. “What have you done with Tom? What were you talking to Jamie about?”

“If you can just be patient for two more minutes, I’ll explain everything.” He was trying for a calming tone, but it only served to set my nerves jangling even more.

“Where the hell are we going?” The real question, the one I couldn’t bring myself to voice, was if he and Jamie were responsible for Tom's disappearance, if they had kidnapped him. My mind couldn’t come up with any possible reasons why they would do it, but then again, nothing made sense now. Why did Eloise think Tom was dead? And why had Shaun said he’d died in February when he’d just been with me three days ago. My emotions were ajumble. The only one I could get a firm grip on was anger—and I wasn’t about to let go of it. “Answer me, dammit!”

Shaun growled, his first sign of frustration since I’d called him earlier in the night. “Alright, fine. I’ve been trying to ease you into this all night, but you’re obviously going to make me do it the hard way. I don’t want to. You’re my best friend, Hank. I hate that I have to hurt you.”

Fear shivered down my spine. “You said that earlier. On the phone.”

He scoffed. “I was talking to Jamie, trying to figure out the best way to get you to remember, but as usual, he wasn’t worth a damn. The only thing he could say was that if I flat out told you, you wouldn’t believe me. So I tried to get you to remember on your own. I didn’t count on Eloise.”

“Just tell me what you have to tell me, Shaun. I’m a big boy. I can take it.”

“See, that’s the thing. I’m not sure you can. I thought you were doing okay. I mean the first couple of months were incredibly hard for you and CJ, but you seemed to be dealing with everything and were finally bouncing back. Then I got your phone call today and I knew I was wrong. I should have been paying more attention. I’m sorry I failed you.”

“Shaun! Stop beating around the bush.” What I really wanted was for him to shut up and never talk again. With each word he uttered, my shoulders tightened and my stomach churned. I still wasn't sure where he was going with his story, but I knew it couldn't be anywhere good.

"I didn't think it would do any harm to take you up to the house. Since you said no one was answering the phone, I assumed that meant no one would answer the door. I was wrong. I'm sorry about that, too. I should have just brought you here in the first place."

I finally looked out into the darkness as Shaun pulled the Jeep to a stop near the top of a hill. I knew it well. It was *our* hill. There was our tree. The one Tom and I had made love under countless times. The one we'd been married under. But why were we here?

Shaun looked around for a moment before maneuvering the Jeep to a different angle. My breath caught in my chest when the headlights illuminated a dark granite gravestone a few yards away.

No! No! NO!

My brain screamed even as I wordlessly scrambled away, hampered by the seatbelt keeping me imprisoned in my seat. Shaun's hand clamped down firmly on my shoulder.

"Easy, easy. You've been here before. It's okay. I've got you."

I forced myself to turn away from the taunting marker and meet Shaun's gaze. I couldn't speak; I could barely keep myself from straining to break free again.

"Hank, are you listening?"

Desperately I shook my head in the negative. I didn't want to see. I didn't want to hear. I didn't want to know. It wasn't possible. It wasn't real.

"Do you want to get out and see it or do you want to sit here and talk?"

"I want you to make it go away," I whispered.

He offered a half smile. "I wish more than anything that I could do that for you." His hand left me as he turned to look out the windshield. I missed the warm comfort of his touch even though it wasn't his touch I craved at the moment.

I followed his gaze back across the dashboard, silently praying I would see only a favorite old tree and an empty night. But there it was, the black granite stone shining in the cool bluish glow of the headlights. As much as I fought the compulsion, the stone seemed to draw me to it. I carefully unbuckled the seatbelt and flipped the lock on the door. I took a deep breath before stepping out into the brisk July night. Legs that felt suddenly unfamiliar propelled me shakily toward the sleek marker. My breaths came shallower with each step. Before I could make out the engraved lettering I noticed it was a double marker, built for a couple, but only one half of it had been completely filled out. I heard Shaun's steps behind me, undoubtedly making sure I didn't make a run for it.

I stopped next to the dark marker and fell to my knees in the grass. My fingertips ran over the rough top before sliding down the smoothly polished surface, the pads hovering above the deep carvings. The words swam before my eyes as the tears fell freely.

Thomas Matthew MacKinnon

10 January 1971 – 8 February 2014

Beloved Son, Husband, & Father

Engraved between his space and mine was an interlocked pair of infinity symbols with the words *Married 17 July 2008.* The right hand side of the stone showed my name and birth date.

There was no denying it. Tom was gone. But how had I forgotten? How had it happened? How could I possibly carry on without him? Unashamedly I allowed the tears to progress to weeping and on to wracking sobs. I'd never felt more alone or lonely than at that moment.

"He's not supposed to be buried! Why is he buried?" I pulled at the grass and sank my fingers into the dry dirt, digging frantically. "He didn't want to be buried!" I had to get him out of there! Shaun's strong hands clamped down on my arms and dragged me away. I screamed and kicked out, trying to get away, but he held fast.

He spun me around and I sank into his waiting embrace, too tired, too alone to fight. "He didn't want to be buried," I bawled. "He wanted to be cremated. We both did."

"I know," Shaun whispered.

For a long time he simply held me, rocking us gently, and stroking my back until eventually I had the sobs under control. I turned back to the granite monument to my husband and knelt down to press my face to the smooth, cold surface, allowing myself to imagine it was him. It took all my self-control to stop myself from digging away the dirt until I was with him once more.

"How?" I whispered.

"It was an accident," Shaun began. "You and CJ and I were skiing at Boca Reservoir. We'd already moved to Squaw Valley so we'd be ready when he got there."

"He couldn't get away early," I interjected, remembering his story from earlier more than the actual event.

"No. He had some contract he had to get the finishing touches on before the weekend, so the three of us went up on Wednesday. He was on his way to meet us on Saturday. It was snowy up in the mountains."

He paused, waiting for me to fill in more blanks, I suppose, but I didn't have anything to put there. "I can't remember," I confessed as more tears came.

He squeezed my shoulder. "It's okay; you'll get there. Tom was on a steep decline. A fuel tanker behind him lost control when one of its chains broke. He was heading for one of the sand traps for runaways but Tom somehow got in his way. I'm not sure how or why, but they exploded on impact."

Sobs wracked my body again at his words. Such a horrible ending to an incredibly loving life. It wasn't fair.

"They...."

Shaun's hesitation made me look back at him. I swiped tears off my eyelashes with my knuckles so I could see him clearly. "They what?"

"I'm so sorry, Hank, but you need to know." He cringed noticeably. "It's why he was buried instead of being cremated." He paused again, swallowed hard, and blinked several times at the night sky, perhaps keeping his own tears at bay. His voice was unsteady when he continued. "They had to identify him through dental records."

"Oh god," I wailed. I pressed my face against the cold granite, wishing with everything in me that I could have given my life for Tom. He was by far the better of the two of us. He was a better man, a better father, a better son. He should have been the one to survive, not me. I wasn't even strong enough to remember he'd died. How could I possibly be a good enough father to our son?

"You and Matthew agreed that to cremate him after he died in a fire was too unseemly. You compromised by burying him here, with the stipulation that you be placed beside him when your time comes. Matthew pulled some strings with the state to make it happen."

I shook my head. I couldn't hear any more. It was too much. Even as Shaun tried to fill me with information, I felt the will to live draining from me and into Tom's grave. I just wanted to be with him. It was all I'd ever wanted. I didn't have any idea how to function without him. For half my life, my every thought, every breath, every action had been intertwined with and dependent upon his. I had no desire to change that. "I can't do this, Shaun. I can't live without him."

"Of course you can."

"I don't *want to* then."

"I know, buddy, but you have to. You have CJ to think about. Where would he be if he lost both of his fathers?"

How had CJ gotten through losing Tom in the first place? And why the hell couldn't I remember everything? "How could I forget this, Shaun? Tom was everything to me. What kind of sick mind forgets his own husband's death?"

"It's not your fault, Hank. There may be five stages of grief, but we don't all go through them in order or in a specific amount of time. Sometimes we get stuck. In your case, I'd say you got stuck in denial. Your identity is so tied up in being Tom's husband that without him you sort of lost your way." He patted my back. "But you're back now and I intend to make sure you stay here. Your son needs you. *I* need you."

A new, unrelated thought slammed into my brain. "Oh my god! Shaun, we filed a false police report!"

He squeezed my shoulder again and offered a sad half smile. "What kind of fool do you take me for? I asked Mary Beth to come over and take the report because you needed to give it, but I told her the truth before she left. That's why she was so pissed at me."

"I wondered what that was about. I figured you'd asked her out or something."

"Nah, that would just be weird considering my history with Christine."

"True," I agreed, turning back to caress Tom's cold headstone again. I wished I could kiss him just one more time, wrap my arms around him and breathe in his scent. Just one more time. Or a hundred more times. It didn't matter how many; it would never be enough. I was on the verge of crying again, but this time I needed to do it alone. "Can you give me some time with him, please?"

Shaun nodded and got to his feet. "Absolutely. Take all the time you need."

I lay down atop the manicured grass covering my husband's grave and wept, for him, for us, for CJ, for me.

EPILOGUE

I awoke bleary eyed and exhausted. Out of habit, I rolled over to cuddle with Tom, but he wasn't there. My husband would never be in our bed again. I would only ever be greeted by cold sheets and an empty spot where my love should be. I caressed his pillow as if it were his face and let my tears come. They were never far away now.

It had been three weeks since Shaun had shown me Tom's grave. Three weeks of fresh grief, as powerful and debilitating as if he had only just gone. My heart was in pieces. I had no idea how I'd made it through the first time, although given my recent break with reality, it was clear that I really hadn't. The thought of losing my mind again scared me almost as much as the thought of living without Tom. For almost half my life he'd been my reason for getting up in the morning and for going to bed at night—and sometimes in the middle of the afternoon. Now our cozy little family of three was missing its biggest component, the one that pumped life and love into CJ and me, and I had no concept of how to compensate for that.

CJ had come home to visit and check on me after Shaun told him what happened. I had tried to shield him from the true depths of my grief, but he was too much his father's son to let me deal with it alone. Much like we had done when Tom had died—I wanted to say "for the first time" because, for me, he had died twice—our son and I had sat on the couch together, flipping through old photo albums, sharing stories, and crying together.

He was a rock, my CJ, much like his father. I wasn't entirely convinced I wouldn't have another grief-induced breakdown, but I was trying to do things differently in order to prevent it. He helped me start to pack away some of his dad's personal items, his clothes and toiletries and business papers, something I had failed to do in February. One afternoon when I couldn't stand the pain anymore, CJ had led me to my bedroom and held me until the tears finally lulled me to sleep.

After that unstoppable moment of weakness, I'd tried my damnedest to pull myself together. I could let CJ see my pain at the loss of my husband, his dad, but he would also see me fighting to come back, to be the father he needed me to be. I never wanted him to think of me as too weak to lean on. He still had one dad left and I was determined to be the best one I could be.

He'd left after five days and, as much as it hurt to admit it, I was glad to see him go. He had his own life and he needed to live it. Our family was proof that one never knew how much time was left. I encouraged him not to waste a minute on regrets or indecision or fear, but to face them head on with the knowledge that he would get through to the other side, even if he didn't like the answers or consequences of his decisions. And I would be there to help him in any way I could. I entreated him to find someone to love as much as his father and I had loved—and would always love—each other.

Shaun had arranged for me to take some time off work. After the way I'd treated him during my grief-induced insanity, it was a testament to our true friendship that he hadn't written me off. He'd been with me as much as he could in his free time. In fact, it was due to his incessant caretaking that I had agreed to see a grief specialist. I'd pushed out my first appointment for another week because I needed to be able to talk about Tom and my brief encounter with the crazies without breaking down. I didn't know if I'd be there by the time the appointment came, but I was trying.

When the first tears of the morning finally dried up, I placed a kiss to Tom's pillow and braced myself against the thought that soon I would have to give up the practice. His scent no longer lingered in the soft cotton, but I was still able to call it to mind in those moments. I climbed out of bed, determined to face my first day back at work like any sane person would—with dread and a heavy heart.

I skipped making breakfast, as I had since CJ returned to Los Angeles. It was too much trouble to go to for one person. Besides which, sitting alone at the breakfast table only gave me more time to soak in the quiet of the house and feel the loneliness seep into me. Instead, I left for work early, catching the 37 bus and the M Line, arriving well before eight o'clock.

Surprisingly, my assistant, Trevor, was in the office before me. I was grateful to see him before I saw anyone else. There was something comforting about having my work day battle buddy be the first person I saw. He greeted me with a huge smile and a handshake.

"It's good to have you back, bossman. The natives are getting restless," he confided.

I rolled my eyes. "When aren't they? What's happening now?"

"You haven't seen the paper today?"

"Nope. I was trying to keep the stress away as long as possible."

"Understood. But you're back now, so brace yourself." Trevor followed me into my office with the morning's *Examiner*. He opened to the front page of the business section and tossed it on my desk. *Excellere Global Sells Canadian Division to DWP Corp* screamed the headline.

My mouth dropped open and I stared at Trevor in disbelief. DWP Corporation. Dimitriou. *Althea Dimitriou MacKinnon.* Dimitriou World Petroleum. How the hell had I forgotten that? Matthew and Althea MacKinnon had partnered with Qatari and Emirati billionaires and gone back into the oil business shortly before Tom's death. "What the hell?"

Trevor nodded. "My response exactly. Why would they want anything Excellere has to offer, much less in Canada?"

"I—I don't know." I couldn't make sense of it on any logical level. Excellere was a retail conglomerate offering products used in and around the home. What possible association could any of that have to an oil company?

The phone in my pocket trilled, making both of us jump. As I dug the phone free, Trevor made his escape, closing my office door behind him. Still trying to figure out the connection between Ossi Aaltonen, Matthew and Althea MacKinnon, and Middle Eastern sheiks, I didn't even glance at the caller ID.

"Cooley," I answered.

"Henry." The connection was good but the voice was hoarse and weak. *Tom.* "Help me."

To be continued...

VANISHED 2

DEDICATION

For Mom.
Thank you for always being there for me.
I love you.

ACKNOWLEDGEMENTS

I'd like to thank my beta readers. Your feedback was invaluable.

As always, a huge thank you to Marilyn. That last brain-storming session means V3 will kick ass!

A huge thank you to my sisters and my Mom for supporting me. I love you.

As always, I offer my biggest thanks to the readers. Without you, I'd be just another guy hearing voices in my head. You've let me exchange the tinfoil hat for a pen. I'm forever grateful.

Massive thanks to Rick Johnson of Rick Johnson & Associates in Denver. I think I changed every single thing about this book after we talked, but I appreciate you taking the time to help the ranting writer figure it all out. Any mistakes I have or will make are completely my own and should not reflect on Rick

ONE

I stared at the phone held in my trembling hands. I desperately wanted to hit the call back button, to hear Tom's voice again. If he was in a safe spot, maybe he could give me more details so I could find him. But if he wasn't—if he'd disconnected the call because he was in danger and about to be discovered—calling him back could be the kiss of death. It didn't matter, though, because no matter how much I might try, I couldn't call back an unknown number.

I tossed the phone on the desk as tremors wracked my body. Henry. Help me. Tom's voice echoed in my brain, growing more anxious and frantic with each repeat. I gripped my head with both hands, pushing as hard as I could to make it stop. To make everything stop.

I couldn't deal with this. I couldn't. Not on my first day back to work of all days. And how fucking selfish was that? Tom was out there somewhere, desperate for my help.

Except he wasn't. He couldn't be. He was dead.

I knew that. I *remembered* that now.

Oh god, I'm losing my mind. Again. I wanted to cry or to cry out, but I could do neither. I thumped my head with the heel of my hand and prayed for sanity to return. I couldn't lose it again. I had CJ to think about. He'd already lost one father to death. How could I put him through losing the other to Crazytown?

I doubled over, putting my head between my knees, cupping the back of it with my hands. The nauseated feeling retreated enough that I could concentrate on controlling my breathing. In. Out. Slow. In. Out. Calm. In. Out. Peace. In. Out. Serenity. In. Out. Insanity.

I fled the office and raced across the hall, punching the button for the down elevator. The walls and uncertainty closed in on me. I was heading for an epic panic attack. The only thing that would ward it off or lessen its impact was being outside where I could feel the breeze on my face, smell something other than stale office building air. But to do that I had to confine myself in the narrow space of an elevator.

When it finally arrived it was blessedly empty. I collapsed against the corner walls, barely able to keep my feet under me. Come on, come on, come on! *Henry. Help me.* I bit back tears, unwilling to explain them if I encountered someone I knew. But then everyone had probably heard the rumors anyway. *Henry Cooley drove the coach round the bend at full gallop. Couldn't face the reality of his husband dying in a car wreck, so he booked a one-way trip to the loony bin.*

All of which was technically true, but I knew it now. I was back in touch with sanity. I'd been to our tree. I'd seen his grave. I remembered bits and pieces of his funeral. I remembered our son being beside himself with grief. I remembered holding him tight as he cried his soul out in front of his family and our closest friends.

The elevator coughed me out on the ground level and I raced for the outside. I took heaving gulps of air, jamming my fingers through my hair. I squeezed my head once more as hard as I could, trying to force it to make sense again, terrified that it never would. Sobs wracked my body as I collapsed onto the terraced garden structure. Was I going crazy again? Had that really been Tom's voice begging for my help? Had I been right all along? Was he really kidnapped?

No. No. Tom was dead. It was a fact.

Wasn't it?

I WANDERED up and down California Street for an hour trying to make sense of what had happened. Like a madman, I kept repeating the call over again in my head. I had no question it was Tom's voice. I'd lived with it and loved with it for more than twenty years. I knew my husband's voice, and that was definitely him on the phone.

I wanted to call Shaun and share the news with him, but I also knew that was a stupid thing to do. I had no proof it had happened aside from the blocked call notation on my received calls list. Shaun would see it as a reaction to going back to work too soon, to not completely grieving Tom's loss, maybe even to slipping back into denial.

I was sitting on a bench halfway down the block, fighting against more tears when I felt a hand on my shoulder. I jerked around to find Trevor standing over me, his face so full of concern that it instantly triggered my guilt response.

"Hey. Are you okay?"

I swallowed and closed my eyes for a brief moment. "Not really, but I will be."

"Do you want to come back to the office, or do you need to go home? I can tell everyone I gave you something rotten for breakfast for leaving me alone for so long."

After everything my morning had entailed, I needed the laugh. "You'd like that, wouldn't you? Be the big hero who actually intentionally poisoned the boss."

He grinned. "You wouldn't believe the elaborate plans some people come up with in the breakroom."

I got to my feet and walked beside him back in the direction of the office. "I bet I would. Wait. How many plans do you have?"

"I'm afraid I can't divulge corporate secrets, boss."

Despite my best attempt at pushing the phone call out of my head, I couldn't focus on work. I opened spreadsheet after spreadsheet but the comfort I usually found in the numbers wouldn't come. They had kept me calm and sane my entire life—although I supposed I should stop using words like 'sanity' where I was concerned. Regardless, I loved the logic of numbers. They always added up unless there was a mistake, and if a mistake existed, there were proven solutions to finding it. Most of the time I enjoyed the chase of tracking down the problem. It was like a game and I was damn good at it. But today those Arabic numerals may as well have been Egyptian hieroglyphs for all the sense they made. I couldn't even enter data correctly.

I tried a couple of tasks I would have normally assigned Trevor, just to get my brain used to working again. Instead of a nice, steady stream of numbers, I ended up with a bizarre column of typos. I chucked a foam hockey puck at the wall and closed the program.

Henry. Help me.

I couldn't get the voice out of my head. I'd never been able to deny Tom anything, especially when he specifically asked for something. But this? This was out of my realm. I didn't have the first clue how to help him. Worse, I didn't even know for sure if he was really still alive for me to help. My life had turned into something out of *The Twilight Zone*.

I typed Tom's name into the search engine on my web browser but hesitated over the Enter key. I knew what I would find: his obituary, articles about his death, articles about the awards he'd received, probably even our wedding announcement if I went back far enough. There would undoubtedly be photos of a smiling Tom, alive, captured in a split second for all time. Seeing those scared me the most.

I could still see him in my mind's eye, moving around the house, laughing while he gave me a hard time, staring down at me with lust-blown pupils, the proudest man in the room at CJ's high school graduation, overcome with grief at our dog, Boston's, death. I dreaded the day those memories started to fade. I was afraid that the photos the internet had collected would somehow superimpose themselves over my memories. Instead of the almost tangible video in my head, he'd be reduced to a series of two-dimensional still shots that didn't capture the essence of him at all. I needed to remember him as more than a grainy newsprint photograph. Even the collection at home weren't enough. The man had never taken a bad picture, something I envied because I swore the only good ones I took were for our engagement announcement and at our wedding. He had always disagreed, but that was his job as the man who loved me.

I closed my eyes, took a bracing breath, and hit Enter. I let the air out of my lungs slowly and opened my eyes. As expected, there were several links to articles about Tom's death. Car wrecks with death and fire tended to make the news. I clicked the first link.

> *The California Highway Patrol says a 43-year-old San Francisco man was killed in a fiery, high-speed accident on Interstate 80 yesterday.*
>
> *Officials say the driver of a Jeep Grand Cherokee was heading eastbound on Lincoln Highway about 10 miles west of Soda Springs when he was struck from behind by a runaway tractor-trailer.*
>
> *The impact caused the Jeep to leave the roadway, roll over, and burst into flames, trapping the driver, who died in the crash.*
>
> *The identity of the driver has not yet been released, but sources say he was an architect with a San Francisco firm and was on his way to a family vacation at the time of his death.*
>
> *Officers say there was no evidence drugs or alcohol were a factor in the accident.*

The screen blurred as water filled my eyes. I recalled in vivid detail every moment of my conversation with the local police informing me of Tom's death. The young deputy had tried to be delicate and compassionate, but that kind of news can't ever be given easily or received well. Or at least it hadn't been by me. I was lucky CJ hadn't been with me. Shaun was, though, and he'd been able to placate the officer and control my hysteria.

I had wanted to go to the crash site immediately. If only I could see it, I could make it not true. I could tell them they'd made a mistake, that it wasn't Tom's Jeep. Of course none of that was possible. It *had* been Tom's Jeep. He had died there. Alone. I could only hope and pray the rollover had killed him before the fire could torture him to death.

The deputy had assured me Tom had died instantly. A lifetime of growing up around paramedics meant I knew that was something they were supposed to say, regardless of the truth. It wasn't until CJ and

Shaun and I had finally asked to see Tom's body that we'd been told he'd been burned beyond recognition.

But had he? His voice on the phone would say otherwise. Unless, of course, I'd imagined it. If I could forget he'd died once—and not just for a few minutes, but for days—what was stopping me from imagining a phone call?

And if it was him? My heart squeezed in my chest at the thought. There wasn't a damn thing I could do about it. I wouldn't have the first clue where to start looking for him. Matthew and Althea either hadn't gotten the same phone call—and why would he call them when he needed me?—or they were keeping it to themselves.

Henry. Help me.

The words haunted me. I was terrified for him. I wanted nothing more than to hold him in my arms and tell him everything would be okay. I'd move mountains if only I had one more clue. But I needed more than a plea for help to be able to that.

My breath shuddered in my chest. I blinked the water off my lashes. I'd had enough. I wasn't going to cry again, not at work anyway. I'd done nothing but relive my grief for the last three weeks, since the moment Shaun caught Tom's headstone in the Jeep's headlights. It was time to man up. Clicking the hateful little X to close the browser gave me a demented sort of pleasure. That was me: moving forward, one click at a time.

EVEN ONE of the longest and hottest showers of my life couldn't melt away the filth of the day. The emotional residue of the phone call wouldn't wash off. Not until I knew for sure it wasn't really Tom on the other end of the line. Intellectually I knew it couldn't be him, but that truth didn't stop my heart from yearning for its own. Tom was the love of my life. Losing him so unexpectedly, so cruelly somehow made his death worse than if we'd grown old and feeble together.

I prepared and ate dinner slowly. Try as I might to keep my mind off Tom's voice on the call, I couldn't stop analyzing it. Did he sound frightened? Relieved? Injured? Exhausted? Was there any background noise I could identify? My emotions swirled the whirlpool, one tiny nudge from going down and being lost forever.

It was almost a relief to pull open the front door and see Shaun standing there with a goofy grin and a bottle of wine. I smiled back and let him in, guilt slamming through me when I made the split-second decision not to tell him about the call. It wasn't like I had proof beyond the blocked call listing anyway.

Shaun stepped into the house. "I thought I'd see how your day went." He raised the bottle. "And because it *was* your first day back, I figured you could use this either way."

I laughed and grabbed the bottle, reaching over to bring my best friend into a hug. "Let's just say I remember now why our wine collection never got very big. That place drives me to drink."

I had actually resisted the urge to have a glass since I'd been home, but now I had an excuse not to. I made for the bar in the living room. "Would you like some?"

Shaun scoffed. "When have I ever drunk rotten grapes? I'm driving so I'll settle for water."

I grabbed a bottle from the mini fridge under the bar and tossed it to him before turning back to open the wine. It smelled delicious. For a man who preferred the hard stuff, Shaun sure knew how to buy great wine.

"So how was it?" he asked from across the room.

I glanced up and did a double take. He'd made himself comfortable on the couch, managing to look relaxed and in control at the same time. Sometimes it surprised me that this confident, handsome man was the adult version of the smooth-talking kid I'd met in college. Like Paul Newman, he seemed to get better looking with age. It crossed my mind again what a shame it was that he'd never found a lover for life, as Whitney Houston had once sung.

I sipped the wine. I couldn't tell fruity notes from woodsy undertones—and I couldn't give a damn less—but I knew what I liked. And I liked this a lot. "It was good to see Trevor and a few others," I answered as I sat across from Shaun in one of Tom's favorite wingback chairs. "It felt like I'd been away a lot longer than a couple of weeks. It was hard to get back in the swing of things. I do remember I hate Ossi."

Shaun laughed, having heard more than one story about the much-hated CEO of Excellere Global. "Finish him!" he growled menacingly.

I groaned.

"Ossi," he explained slowly. "The Finn. ...Finish...him."

"Your puns suck. And I know you were going for a *Mortal Kombat* vibe anyway."

He flipped me off. "Why don't you just quit? Tom left you enough money you'll never have to work again. Hagatha and Ziggy—" I chuckled at his new pet names for my in-laws "—gave CJ access to his college trust fund, so you don't have to worry about that anymore. You could live the good life. Reap the benefits of the hard work you've put in since you were sixteen."

"And what would I do with myself all day? I'd go mad rattling around this place." I cringed at just how close to recent memory that last sentence was.

"You can do all sorts of things—and don't quiz me on them because I'm winging this right now. The point is you've hated that job for years. So take the opportunity. Be daring. Do the one thing you've always wanted to do but you never would because it sounded too crazy."

My mind was a blank slate. "I have no idea what that would be. I've always wanted to work with numbers. They make sense."

Shaun shook his head. "You're exasperating. Tomorrow I'm having Starla make reservations for us to spend a week in Hawaii. We'll go snorkeling and hiking and just soak up the sun between swims. You'll love it."

I laughed. "You're crazy. We can't do that." Trevor would kill me for abandoning him again so soon.

"Why not?"

"We have jobs and responsibilities—and—and—"

"So quit. I'm the boss. I do what I say. And I say we're going to Hawaii." He stood and brushed his shirt down his flat abdomen. "But right now I have to go."

"Hot date?" I teased. I started to get up but he waved me off. He leaned over and gave me an awkward hug.

"Entertaining conversation, incredible sex. What more could I ask for?"

"Long term potential?" I worried about my friend. Women had come and gone with the seasons his entire adult life, but he'd never let one really get to know him. We were getting to the age he needed to put away the playboy ways and find someone he could grow old with.

He ruffled my hair in that annoying way he'd had for twenty years. "Not a chance." He grinned and tipped an imaginary hat. "I'll see you later. Give our conversation some thought. I'll have Starla call Trevor."

Moments later he was gone and I was alone, just me and a hundred-dollar bottle of rotten grapes. I set the glass aside and shuffled into the bedroom I'd shared with Tom for so many—far too few—years. I pulled open his closet door and blocked out the emptiness of it by concentrating on the last two items to occupy the space. I'd kept my favorite pieces of Tom's wardrobe, the two items I most associated with him. They were his favorites, too; he wore them all the time. I took the Hardwick Architecture-emblazoned leather bomber jacket from its hanger and wrapped it around my shoulders. I stroked the sleeve, remembering Tom's excitement the day he brought it home. He'd been brimming with pride and happiness because a client had given it to him in recognition of how hard he'd worked on their project.

I buried my face in the grey-brown button down shirt, the royal blue and maroon checks swimming together before I closed my eyes. I inhaled deeply and pretended the shirt still smelled of Tom. In truth, his scent had faded from almost everything by the time I came back from Crazytown. But here in my possibly-not-dead-after-all husband's closet I could pretend I still had a tangible connection with him.

I wished more than anything that I had something more substantial to hold onto. Something with weight and bulk and warmth I could wrap my arms around and feel safe and loved because, more than anything, I felt like this closet: achingly empty except for a few wisps of memory.

TWO

It was only Thursday of my first week back to work and it was already the second day in a row I was late. I had no one to blame but myself, a realization that only served to irritate me more. I'd never been one to give in to laziness or procrastination, but for the first time in my life, I had to force myself to get ready for work.

Tuesday had seen the first round of pink slips go out around the company, the legacy of the company's seventh consecutive quarterly loss. I was grateful I didn't have to lay off anyone personally—that nasty business occurred in the field, in the stores that were already struggling to staff adequately on lightened payroll dollars, not within eyesight of the cushy executive tower at 101 California.

My phone rang as I climbed the stairs out of Embarcadero Station. I dug it from my pocket and dragged my finger across the screen without looking. "Hey, Trev. I know I—"

"Henry. Help me."

The voice brought me up short. *Oh god.* "Tom! Where are you?" I shouted into the phone as people slammed into my back because of my sudden stop. "Tom!" I yanked the phone from my ear as the silence lengthened.

He'd already disconnected. "Shit. Shit! *Fuck!*"

I moved to next to the wall and brought up my recent calls list. There it was, just like last time. Unknown Caller. Goddammit! I wanted to throw a tantrum like a three year old denied chocolate, but I pushed my rage and frustration down like a good repressed adult male.

I pocketed the phone and resumed my walk to work, trying not to think of all the horrific things that could be happening to Tom at that very moment, which brought me back to the questions of who had him and why. I'd let Shaun convince me Tom had died in the accident, but these phone calls were proof that he hadn't. Weren't they? Who would go through the trouble of faking his death? If they wanted him that badly, why wouldn't they just take him? Was it because they were afraid a missing person's report would bring too much publicity? Tom's parents had been important once—as opposed to self-important always. The press would probably run wild with a story like this.

I didn't realize I'd made it to my building and gotten in the elevator until I saw Trevor's worried face as the doors opened on my floor. He held the corner of an envelope to his lips, tapping it against them nervously. It was a tick he'd mostly conquered, but it resurfaced when he was feeling extreme stress.

"Oh, thank Cher, you're finally here," he gushed, grabbing my arm as I stepped out of the lift.

I reluctantly pulled my brain from thoughts of Tom to focus on my young assistant. "Sorry I'm late. What's wrong?"

Trevor looked both ways down the hall before moving a step closer to me, speaking in a hushed tone. "First, Ossi has called another damn meeting for the senior accounting staff. You have ten minutes to get to Zelda." All of Ossi's favorite conference rooms were named after video games, something else that made me despise him. Trevor looked around again, his face pinching even more.

Great. Just what I needed. Ossi this early in the work day. What fresh hell was he cooking up today? "Okay, what's second?"

Trevor searched my eyes before continuing. "You've received a package." He indicated the envelope he held. "It's a gift, Henry."

I frowned. "From whom?" It wasn't my birthday or any other gift-giving holiday.

"It's from Tom."

"What?!" The volume and tone of my voice caused coworkers and strangers in the hallway to turn and gape at us. I composed myself and half-whispered, "What are you talking about?"

Trevor cringed. "I wasn't sure what to do. I didn't want you to be blindsided—but I guess I just did that, didn't I?"

"Yeah, you kinda did." I strode swiftly to my office, leaving Trevor to bring up the rear. I swung open my office door and stopped in my tracks for the second time in ten minutes. On my desk sat a fairly shallow rectangular box gaily wrapped in baby blue paper decorated with silver swirls and topped with a big white bow.

"It came in a regular box," Trevor explained from behind me. "That's what I found when I opened it. I only opened the card because I thought it might have been misdirected. I know your special days, Henry, and this isn't one of them. I'm sorry if I overstepped."

I tore my eyes from the box to look at Trevor. The poor kid looked miserable. "You didn't do anything wrong."

I held my hand out for the envelope and he quickly handed it over. I ripped the paper to get to the card. It was a traditional anniversary variety. My knees weakened as I opened it. The inside was blank except for Tom's handwriting:

Henry,

Now that our relationship is officially old enough to drink, we should have something special to do the honors from. I love you more than ever. Happy 21st Anniversary.

Forever

Tom

It almost made sense. Our anniversary was twenty-one days ago. But Tom had been long gone by then—either by kidnapping or death, depending on who I believed. I crossed the room to stand behind my desk, never taking my eyes off the box. I set the card aside. With trembling fingers, I pulled the blue paper off the gift, revealing a black velvety box. I glanced up at Trevor who stared at the box with such an anxious expression I almost felt sorry for him.

I took a bracing breath and worked the top off the box. Inside, nestled in more velvet, this time of a brilliant blue, were two wine glasses. I carefully removed one by the stem, holding it up so Trevor could see it too. I rotated it between my fingers until the design etched into the crystal came into view. My eyes slammed closed as pain lanced through my heart. I swayed on my feet, crashing a hand down on the desk to catch myself.

It was our tattoos. The interlocking infinity symbols Tom and I and CJ all sported on the inner side of our left bicep, the declaration that we were one—one couple, one family unit—forever and always.

Which was a nice fucking sentiment until one of us died—or was kidnapped.

The ache of Tom's loss, renewed by this gift, turned swiftly to anger. It couldn't be a coincidence that I got another one of those phone calls and this gift within minutes of each other. Someone was trying to tell me something, I just couldn't figure out what the hell it was.

I put the glass back in the box and closed the lid, brushing my fingers lightly over the black velvet, sadness still echoing through me. I sank into my chair and put the box in the bottom drawer of my desk. I didn't have time to think about all of this right now, but I did still have Trevor. I looked up at him.

"Call the store these came from and find out everything you can about the order. When was it placed, who paid for it, why they just delivered it now, etc., etc." I scrubbed a hand over my face. "I have to get to Ossi's meeting. We'll figure all this out later, right?"

Trevor nodded, looking more like himself now that he had been assigned a task. "Right, boss. I'm on it." He offered a half smile laced with guilt and walked out to his work station, tactfully closing the office door behind him.

I stared at the bottom drawer of my desk but didn't open it. I was in a frightening mental place, half convinced my dead husband was sending me gifts, and almost equally persuaded he was actually kidnapped and calling, begging for my help. And underlying both of those fears was the terror that I was teetering on the edge of a glorious return to Crazytown—and all it would take was the tiniest of nudges to send me there permanently.

If it had been anyone else's voice but Tom's, I would have chalked it up to someone making cruel prank calls. But who would do that and why? And how could they have possibly gotten Tom's voice? It wasn't any crazier than the other ideas, but I dismissed it anyway.

I LET the hot water of the shower rain down on my shoulders until it started to cool, which, unfortunately, was before it had beat the tension out of them. Reluctantly, I stopped the water and started drying off. Today would have been a great time to have that hot tub Tom and I had talked about getting for a couple of years. The day hadn't improved after getting Tom's belated anniversary present. Ossi's meeting had been another in a long line of listening to him expound about his pipe dreams for turning Excellere Global into a newer, better Amazon.com. He'd had yet another brilliant way to accomplish that goal today, and he wouldn't hear a single objection the senior accounting team raised—which we did, quickly and in great numbers, because we could all see that the only way he could accomplish his goal would be to bankrupt the company so completely it would have to be sold for scrap. But in Ossi's world reality didn't exist if it clashed with his vision.

Back in my office after two wasted hours, Trevor filled me in on his phone calls with the wine glass vendor. Tom had stopped there in late December and commissioned these pieces, asking that they be delivered to my office on our anniversary. Since I'd been on leave that day, they'd tried back once a week until I returned to work. So no mystery or clue there. Tom had paid for them in January when they'd sent him a sample. It was almost a relief to know Tom had ordered them so long before our actual anniversary. That was the kind of guy he was. He had usually finished his Christmas shopping by April, while I rushed to finish before

Black Friday. No way was I going into a store by choice between Thanksgiving and New Year's.

The remainder of the day had passed with only a minor headache and a few confusing miscalculations that Trevor and I worked together to solve. Now that I was home and showered, my only plans involved a book, a bottle of wine, some Patsy Cline, and the Thai food I'd brought home.

In the bedroom, I dressed in a pair of running shorts and the shredded remains of my last favorite t-shirt. On an impulse, I grabbed Tom's cologne from atop the dresser. If I was going to salute our marriage with the wine glasses he'd commissioned for that purpose, it would only be fitting that the room smelled like him, at least that way I could pretend like he was taking part in it.

I sprayed the Cerruti Image around the living room, giving myself a comforting reminder of what the house had smelled like before Tom left for work and as soon as he arrived back home. He'd fallen in love with the scent when it came out in '98 and rarely deviated from it. I smiled, wondering how many bottles he'd gone through in sixteen years.

Putting the bottle back on his dresser, I noticed Tom's closet door was ajar. I must have forgotten to latch it after I'd been in there Monday. Either that or the house had settled again and the door had slid open. Almost sheepishly, I opened the door enough to spray one good squirt in there before I closed it again, this time making sure it latched.

In the kitchen, I quickly washed the new glasses and uncorked a bottle of red. I poured a glass and sipped it, staring at Tom's empty one on the counter. On impulse, I filled it, too, and carried both of them into the living room.

I placed his glass on the coffee table and then stretched out on the couch, closed my eyes, and let myself remember our wedding day. By that time we'd long considered ourselves married, but somehow having the state validate and sanction what we'd known in our hearts for fifteen years had made our relationship more real, more precious. Having our son, CJ, join in our vows had only sweetened the already perfect day.

That night, we'd driven down the coast to the spot where Tom had first told me he loved me. Like that night, we'd shared a lantern-lit picnic on the beach. And like that night, we'd made love there with the sound of the surf drowning our cries and gasps.

Tears slid slowly down my cheeks. I missed him with every cell in my body. I missed his touch. I missed the sound of his voice. I missed the smell of him on our sheets. I missed his cooking and his laughter. I even missed the messes he so often left around the house. But most of all I missed his whispers of "I love you, barista." Being alone after so many years was heartbreaking in its loneliness.

I swiped the tears from my face and set my glass down beside his. I picked up his glass and gestured a salute. "Wherever you are, Tom, I hope you know I love you to the moon and back."

THREE

I stumbled to the door, bleary-eyed and grumpy. The bedside clock had said eight a.m.—on a Saturday. I knew of only two people who would be pounding on my front door at that hour, and both of them had a key, so the incessant knocking was a nasty ploy to get me out of bed and moving. My son wasn't devious enough to do that.

"I'm coming, Shaun," I croaked when he banged on the door again. I stumbled the last few feet and yanked the door open to a barrage of sunlight. I recoiled like it would burn me. I wasn't hungover, I just hated mornings. And I especially hated uninvited, unexpected guests in the mornings.

"How did you know it was me?" he asked with a disgustingly huge grin for such an ungodly hour.

"Because you're the only one who would take pleasure in forcing me out of bed before dawn on a weekend," I grumbled. "You didn't even bring me coffee?"

He grinned again and handed over his cup. "The sun's been up for hours, Hank. You can have a sip, but that's it. I figured we'd hit up Coffee to the People on the way."

I swallowed down the coffee and felt my brain become slightly more human. "On the way where?"

"We're playing tourist today." He practically bounced on the balls of his feet. If he'd been a puppy, he might have wet the rug in his excitement.

"No, we are not." I headed for the kitchen and the coffeemaker, but I hadn't made it ten steps before Shaun's hands on my shoulders forced me in the direction of the bedroom.

"Yes, we are. You need to get out and do something mindless and fun. What's more mindless than a tourist?"

"My best friend at ungodly o'clock in the morning?" I let him push me into the bedroom.

He had the temerity to laugh. "There, there. You'll feel better after a shower. You'll probably smell better, too."

"Fuck off, Shaun." Petulantly, I sat on the bed. Mornings really were my least favorite part of the day, especially on the weekends when I should have been able to sleep through most of those hours.

Shaun hauled me into the adjoining bathroom by the earlobe and started the water in the shower. "Don't make me get in there with you. You know I'll do it."

"And would you give me a happy ending to my shower, too?" I taunted, reluctantly stripping off my sleep pants.

He grinned. "There's only one way to find out. Now are you going to do this the hard way or the easy way?"

"You watch too much bad detective television," I grumbled. There was no use arguing with him, so I adjusted the water temperature to my liking. I turned back to see him leaning against the counter watching me with the same quirk of his lips. "Do you mind?"

"Nope. Not a bit."

I shrugged. "Fine." I doffed my boxer briefs, making sure he got a good look at the boys before I stepped into the shower and closed the semi-opaque door. Shaun really was the strangest straight guy I'd ever encountered. He'd always been comfortable around naked men, gay, straight, or any of the other seven thousand sexualities I was just learning about. His nonchalance must have had something to do with having played basketball and lacrosse in high school.

He'd never acted the least bit uneasy about my sex life, even before Tom. He could joke around about gay sex and was more than happy to flirt back with any of the guys who bothered to flirt with him. Everyone knew he was an open-minded straight guy, so they didn't try too hard or waste too much of their valuable cruising time trying to land him. Tom had suggested on occasion that the guys wouldn't have to try all that hard to actually get Shaun to experiment, but I always shut down that avenue of conversation before it got started. The last thing I wanted to picture was Shaun with another guy. It was bad enough he liked to entertain me with stories of his female conquests.

I showered quickly, knowing that Shaun was likely to cause all sorts of havoc if I didn't. Once he set his mind to doing something, it was all systems go until the task had been accomplished. It appeared that today I was his task of choice.

I was mildly surprised not to find him still standing there waiting when I finally turned off the water. I dried off, wrapped the towel around my waist, brushed my teeth, added deodorant, skipped shaving, and went back to the bedroom—where I found Shaun on his back, spread out crosswise and snoring lightly on the bed.

I rolled my eyes at his dorktitude. I loved the guy, I really did, even when he was annoying as hell. I walked around the corner of the bed and pinched his nipple. He practically jumped from the bed, insisting, "I'm awake. I'm awake."

I laughed and pointed at him until he snatched my towel, wound it up in the blink of an eye, and snapped me with it. "Ouch!" I yelled. "You bastard, that's going to leave a welt!" I rubbed my sore ass and gave him a dirty look.

It was his turn to laugh as he tossed the towel on the bed. "Man, this is just like college. You, naked as the day you were born; me, taking full advantage of your carelessness. You'd think you'd have learned to keep a grip on your towel by now."

"Yeah, well, Tom didn't have a habit of snapping me with it. He must have missed that part of How to Be an Asshole Jock class." My ass really did sting. And it probably would leave a welt. And Trevor would look at me strangely when I sat on the other cheek all day Monday.

Shaun pouted. "Aww, poor baby. See what you've been missing?" He picked up the towel and took it back into the bathroom, talking the whole time. "I figured we'd start at Coffee to the People—I think I told you that—and then we'd just do stupid stuff all day. Have you ever been to the top of Coit Tower? The views are amazing. I took a date there once. After hours, of course. One of the security guys owed me a favor. Got the best head of my life looking out those windows."

I dressed while he regaled me with snippets of his sex life. He never indulged in a full story, just these little tidbits. He was far more adventurous than I'd ever been, but then I'd met Tom so young, I hadn't had time to sleep my way through half the men on campus. Tom and I had created our own adventures in the safety of our relationship.

Times had changed so much in twenty-some years. I wouldn't even know where to start looking for someone if I wanted to. I'd read that gay bars were closing at alarming numbers because people skipped the getting to know each other part and went right to hookups arranged through some apps on their phones. Seemed an awfully cold way to go about it to me, mercenary would be the word I'd use if someone asked me. I wondered if that was where Shaun met his partners. Did women really put themselves out there like that?

Shaun walked back into the bedroom just as I finished the last button on my shirt. He gave a low wolf whistle. "Slick," he complimented.

I frowned and looked down at myself. I was wearing casual shorts and an untucked, plaid, button-down shirt. The shorts were sort of a coral hue and the shirt was white and blue, which was definitely more color than I usually wore to the office, but weekends were mine. I could be the Hank I wanted to be instead of Henry Cooley of Excellere Global. "Is it okay? Do I need to change something?"

Shaun rolled his eyes. "Yes," he said, advancing on me. He reached up and unfastened the first button below the collar. He tugged on the material at my shoulders, spreading the opening to show off a bit more of my smooth skin. "Perfect." He patted my chest and winked. He spun on his heel and walked into the living room, already planning aloud his order at the coffee shop.

I refastened the button and followed silently.

WE LEFT his car at my house because public parking in the City was either impossible to find or impossible to afford. We'd donned our shades against the bright summer sunlight and strolled, unhurried, to the coffee shop. Shaun chattered nonstop the entire way. I only paid enough attention to grunt when necessary. My mind kept drifting back to Tom. I was getting nervous about basically ignoring the two phone calls I'd received from him. Or from someone with his voice. As much as I wanted to believe he wasn't dead, I'd seen the grave. I remembered the authorities telling me he hadn't made it. CJ and Shaun had described the funeral, small bits of which I recalled. It annoyed me that my entire memory of the events surrounding Tom's death hadn't come back to me immediately. Instead, I seemed to recall bits at a time that needed to be pieced together with what I already remembered.

The peaceful stroll was a relaxing change of pace. It was only my first weekend after being back to work, but I already remembered how much I required that time off to recharge and recuperate. Shaun chattered on endlessly and I wondered if I should give serious thought to his suggestion that I quit Excellere. There was no question how much I hated it. The only question was what I was going to do about it.

Shaun paused in front of the window of the coffee house, turning to me with a frown. He unfastened the top button on my shirt again. "It's the weekend, Hank. Stop being such a stick in the mud."

I rolled my eyes and followed him into the building.

"Henry!" Kris, the manager, immediately stopped what she was doing and rushed over to give me a hug. "I've missed you! Where have you been?"

I hugged her back and waved at Tiffany and Linc over her shoulder. They kept working with their customers but smiled and waved, calling out an enthusiastic greeting. "I hadn't realized it had been so long," I told Kris. I couldn't remember how long it had been before my excursion to Insanityville, but I hadn't been to the shop since. Coffee to the People had been Tom's favorite coffee house in the neighborhood. When he was alive, we'd practically been fixtures there every Saturday or Sunday morning for years.

"It's been at least six months," Kris complained. She faked a slap to my chest. "We thought you'd deserted us for some other caffeine emporium." She smiled and hugged me again. "It's good to see you." She pulled back, her face falling serious. "I was so sorry to hear about Tom. You know how much we all love you guys around here. It's just such a shame. Are you getting along okay?"

I nodded and tried for a smile. "I'm doing alright now. It was rough for a while."

"I'll bet it was," she empathized, hooking her arm in mine to lead me to Tom's and my usual table. How many puzzles had we put together on top of this scarred Formica? Dozens. Possibly a hundred. It was Tom's favorite way of relaxing on a Sunday morning. Some people read the paper, Tom put together puzzles. It didn't matter the picture or how many pieces, he loved them all. "Tom was a special man," Kris continued as Shaun stepped up and took a seat across the table from me. She pointed at him. "I remember you've been in here with the guys before, but I can't remember your name. Iced mint matcha mocha latte, right?"

Shaun flashed his most charming grin. "That's right. I need to come here more often. I'm Shaun."

Kris tittered her approval. "You do that, Shaun, and make sure you bring this one with you." She turned back to me. "Do you want your usual, honey?"

I blinked stupidly up at her, suddenly unable to recall what that would be. "That would be great," I answered for lack of a better idea.

"I wondered if you'd been here lately," Shaun said as Kris scurried off to fetch our orders.

I shrugged and got up to pull an easy puzzle down from the shelf on the wall a few feet away. "You know Tom was the one with the fancy coffee fetish," I explained on my way back. "Give it to me black and strong and I'm happy."

Shaun laughed. "Careful who you say that to. Someone might take it as your taste in men."

I laughed and chucked a packet of sugar at him. "You seem stuck on sex today, buddy. What's the matter, didn't your date give it up the other night?"

He flashed that charming smile again. "Oh, look. A puzzle."

I laughed again. "You're such a tease."

He eyed me again, his expression conveying a message too subtle for me to understand, even though it was clear that I should. "I never tease about what I really want. You know that."

I ignored whatever he was trying to tell me and started picking out side pieces. We'd managed three sides and were working on fitting together the fourth when Tiffany arrived with our orders.

"I brought two of the breakfast burritos with bacon and avocado," she said to Shaun. "I wasn't sure if you liked them, but I took a chance."

He beamed a smile at her. "It looks fantastic! Thank you."

It looked good enough my stomach took that time to growl loudly.

Tiffany laughed. "Someone's belly remembers this place anyway. We really did miss you and Tom, Henry. Please don't be a stranger just because you like plain old boring coffee. You know we don't judge around here. I mean, we judge and we judge hard," she winked, "but not about that."

"Thanks, Tiff. I promise I'll come around more often." It was nice to know I'd been missed, even without Tom. Coffee to the People had always been like an eclectic extended family. Each of the workers and the clientele were somehow on one fringe of society or another, from the new hippies to the tech geeks and everyone in between. It was a judgment-free zone so long as you respected everyone else's right to self-expression and happiness. It was a microscopic scale of what I imagined the 1960s had been like. Sometimes I wished I'd been around to see that decade.

Tiffany's hand landed on my shoulder as she leaned forward to whisper in my ear. "Linc took Tom's death really hard. Would you mind saying something to him before you leave?"

I offered her a quivery smile. "I guess he's lost his mentor, hasn't he?"

She nodded. "He's more determined than ever to make it into architecture school. Says he wants to finish what Tom started."

I swallowed around the enormous lump in my throat. "That's really great," I choked out. "I'll be sure to talk to him before we leave."

"Thanks, hon," she said, patting my shoulder.

I blew out a deep sigh, avoiding Shaun's attempt at eye contact. Tom's and my lives had been so completely intertwined for so long, it would be a long time before I didn't run into this at every corner. He never met a stranger and he rarely found someone who didn't fall for him in one way or another. It was strange that we'd ended up together, since I rarely had much use for the majority of humanity. It was another of those wonderful differences that had drawn us together. He'd made me learn to appreciate people on an individual level, and I'd helped him learn he didn't have to be surrounded by masses of them to be happy.

"You okay?" Shaun asked, taking another sip of his mocha matchya whatever.

I pursed my lips and blinked away the sting from my eyes. "Peachy. Let's get this puzzle together so we can start being tourists."

He laughed. "You think it's a horrible idea."

I shook my head and swallowed a mouthful of coffee. "So long as you don't use it as a guided tour of places you've had sex, it might actually be fun."

Shaun frowned. "Shit. We might just have to spend the day at your house. Oh wait."

I gaped at him. "You did not!"

"Oh, I did. I *totally* did."

I laughed. "You're such a bastard."

"You love me," he teased.

I shook my head, not wanting to know any more details than that, and turned my attention back to the puzzle. "I *something* you, that's for sure."

When we'd finished our sandwiches, I grabbed the plates and took them over to where Linc leaned against the counter, looking miserable. He was a bit of an enigma to me, but Tom had taken to him immediately.

He had a broad, handsome face, a thick head of ginger hair styled fashionably, and the grace of a natural athlete. Not to mention that he filled out the front and back of a pair of jeans like a porn star. It didn't matter how often I saw him in the shop, he never seemed to feel completely at ease.

He straightened when I approached, plastering the fakest smile I'd ever seen on his face. He reached out to take the plates. "Thanks, Henry. I should have been paying more attention. You didn't need to bring them up here."

"It's okay." I cleared my throat, suddenly unsure of the words to use. Linc had been one of Tom's pet projects at the coffee shop. As soon as he'd found out Linc was interested in architecture, he'd taken every opportunity to talk to him about it, to give him the encouragement it was so obvious he didn't get from anyone else. "Look, Linc, Tiffany told me you took Tom's death hard. I don't know if it means much coming from me, but I want you to know he was very proud of you."

Linc's eyes immediately filled. He blinked valiantly, but one tear escaped to roll down his cheek. He swiped it away almost violently. "He was the only one who ever believed in me," he said in a choked whisper. He cleared his throat, his voice coming out slightly stronger but still as heavy with emotion. "It's so hard to believe he's gone. Every time something good happens at school, I can't wait to tell him. And then I remember and it hurts again."

I put a comforting hand on his wrist. "I know exactly how that feels."

He stared at my hand for a moment, then stepped back from the counter. I hadn't considered he might have an aversion to touch. I put my hand back at my side. "I'm glad you're continuing your studies. If you ever need anything, please don't be afraid to ask. I'm no good with three-dimensional stuff, but I'm great with numbers, if that's any help."

Linc nodded, a flood of color rushing to his cheeks. "Thanks, Henry." His Adam's apple bobbed. "I should get back to work. Don't be a stranger, okay?"

I watched him disappear through the doors into the kitchen and sighed. Kids like Linc reminded me again how lucky I'd had it growing up. We may not have had much, especially considering the sort of wealth Tom grew up with, but we rarely went hungry and I always had my parents to look out for and support me. I wondered if Linc had anyone to lean on or if he'd accept it if anyone offered him a shoulder.

THE ROAR of the boat's engine reverberated through me, filling me with an almost childlike glee. I turned to Shaun and laughed. "I haven't been on a tour of the Bay since CJ was little."

He grinned back, tossing more bread crumbs to the birds. "It's still fun, isn't it?"

"It is!" I much preferred seeing the Golden Gate and Bay Bridges from the safety of a boat than from a vehicle going over them. The tour of Alcatraz had reminded me of its sad and painful past. It seemed silly that I could live in this city, which had such an incredibly rich history, and forget about it as I went along my daily routine. I needed to pay more attention to the people and things around me and less to myself. Maybe that was a lesson all of humanity could learn, but I could definitely start with myself.

We reached the dock and slowly disembarked with all the real tourists. We were closing in on the end of the day, judging by how low the sun hung in the western sky, but we'd had a surprisingly good time. We'd gone to Coit Tower and marveled at the view of the city we were privileged enough to call home. We'd found and taken pictures of each other on the bench near the Filbert Steps with the small plaque that quoted the famous line from *The Wizard of Oz* about not being in Kansas anymore, not that either of us had ever been to Kansas. We'd wandered the Castro and had a drink in more than a few bars. And we'd paid a moment of silent respect to Harvey Milk outside his old camera shop. We'd wondered aloud how different our city and the country would have been if Dan White hadn't killed him.

We'd ridden the Powell & Hyde line cable cars from the turnaround at Powell & Market all the way to Beach Street and Fisherman's Wharf, where we'd lost hours poking through every single shop on Pier 39.

"Let's walk along the Marina Green. Then we can sit on the beach for a little bit before we stop for dinner and drinks at Ghirardelli Square," Shaun suggested in my ear.

I nodded in agreement. A walk along the beach seemed like the perfect end to the perfect day.

Fifteen minutes later we had our toes in the cold sand. I let out a sigh of contentment as we walked along, side by side. Shaun threw his arm around my shoulders and half-hugged me. "You seem happy," he said.

I smiled and draped my arm around his waist, returning the hug. "I am happy. This is great therapy."

He grinned. "Just wait 'til I get you to Hawaii! You'll be doing the hula in no time."

I laughed and shoved him away. "Not in your dreams, O'Malley."

He wagged his eyebrows. "I have very funny dreams. Ooh! Look!" He pointed to a group of teenagers or college kids flying a kite about a hundred yards ahead and took off at a sprint. It was like a scene straight out of *Tales of the City* as he paid them off with what I suspected was a joint or two in exchange for the kite.

I shook my head and laughed again. He was such a kid, even at forty-three. I fished my phone from my pocket and snapped pictures of him trying to get the kite in the air. He seemed to be having a much tougher time of it than the others had.

As I focused it for another shot, the phone rang, scaring the daylights out of me. I stopped in my tracks as my entire body seized with tension. I turned it to view the screen. *Incoming Call... Unknown*

"You don't get to do this to me today," I yelled as I heaved the thing, unanswered, into the Bay. I regretted it as soon as it hit the water. What if CJ needed me? What if Tom said something new this time? What if? What if?

I stood for a minute, waiting for the waves to bring the thing back to me, but it didn't happen. Maybe they knew something I didn't.

I turned to see Shaun running through the surf, the kite high in the air, trailing behind him. He grinned triumphantly and let out an excited, "Woohoo!"

The stress of the phone call started to melt away in the face of his exuberance. "I need booze!" I shouted and jogged over to take control of the kite.

Fuck the phone.

I FUMBLED my way through the front door and into the house, happily exhausted and more than a little buzzed. I waved sloppily at Shaun in the cab and watched as it sped away. Spending time with my best friend doing mindless touristy things had been the perfect cure for what ailed me, despite the phone call from Tom.

I pulled my brain away from that dangerous place. There was no use thinking about it. I couldn't do a damn thing to help him unless or until he said something other than "help me." If he really wanted my help, he was going to have to cough up some damn information. Stupid bastard. I couldn't read his goddamn mind. We'd been over and over that countless times in our years together. Figures he'd conveniently forget that little tidbit now. Not that he didn't have other things on his mind. Like survival or escape. Or fucking with his widower's mind.

I shook my cloudy head, apologizing to Tom mentally for getting mad at him. None of this was his fault. He hadn't asked to be kidnapped—or killed or whatever the hell was going on.

I stumbled into the kitchen without turning on lights. What I really needed was a gigantic bottle of water and a couple of pain relievers before all the beer Shaun had poured down my throat turned into a raging hangover. Not the ideal way to spend a Sunday, especially when I had work to catch up on already.

I grabbed a bottle of water from the refrigerator and headed back into the living room. I'd just plopped onto the couch when the streak of light leaking under the door to the garage caught my gaze. I frowned, trying to remember the last time I'd been in there. I hadn't used the Jeep all week, since I went directly to work and back on mass transit.

I pushed off the couch and wobbled unsteadily over to the door. Yanking it open, I inspected the room for anything out of place without actually taking the two steps down into it. I wasn't sure I'd be able to navigate them again, so I stayed put. Nothing looked out of place.

Tom was meticulous about everything having a home and being in it if he wasn't working on something. He'd even been kind—or condescending—enough to paint outlines on the pegboard for each tool, so I'd know exactly where it went. Helpful since I always forgot where I got it by the time I was done using it. Condescending because, really?

All tools were present and accounted for, and still as Greek to me as the language. Numbers. Numbers made sense no matter what. Thirteen different tools for doing the same thing didn't make sense. But that was Tom's world. He loved his tools.

I sighed, flipped off the light, and closed the door. Maybe Shaun had gone in there for something while I was in the shower. That would explain the light. His favorite position for humans and light switches was always turned on. I stifled a drunken giggle at the thought.

"It's definitely time for bed, old man," I said aloud. "You're getting as bad as he is."

I swiped the bottle from where I'd left it on the coffee table and headed for my bedroom and the cold, empty bed that awaited me there. I blinked at the sting in my eyes and forced myself to concentrate on my bedtime routine. Teeth. Face. Sleep pants. If I didn't think any further ahead than ten seconds, I could pretend for another few minutes that I wasn't alone and lonely. At least that's what I told myself.

FOUR

I have a theory," Trevor announced early Monday morning.

I'd just spent an hour at my cellular provider's store getting a new phone to replace the one I'd so stupidly thrown into the Bay. Luckily I'd set the old one to back-up to the cloud every twelve hours, so all my information was available for a quick and easy download that was neither quick nor easy. After that I wasn't sure I was up for an early-morning theoretical discussion, but, because it was Trevor, I smiled up at him and put my pencil down, giving him my full attention. "What's that?"

"I've been stuck on why your in-laws bought part of Excellere."

"In Canada," I finished for him.

He made a face. "Yeah, that's the part that kept throwing me off. I mean, why Canada? Anyway, I think I've figured it out."

I leaned back in my seat, enjoying the show. Trevor was a pretty good boy-detective when he set his mind to it. On previous occasions he'd found information I'd sworn had been deliberately and completely destroyed years earlier. "Do tell."

He perched on the edge of the seat in front of my desk, his hands folded over the portfolio in his lap. "You know how Kroger has put gas pumps in front of some of their grocery stores?"

"Yeah. You get a discount on the gas price if you buy a certain dollar amount of groceries. What's that have to do with Matthew and Althea?"

"That's what they're going to do. All the properties they purchased in Canada were standalone buildings. They're going to put fuel pumps in the parking lot of these stores, that way they have their fingers in every stage of the process. From import to refining to retail."

I smiled sadly. "That's great, except they don't have a refinery."

He pulled a sheet of paper from the folder and handed it to me. "Oh yes they do. In Regina. Purchased eleven months ago, with a capacity of 200,000 barrels per day. And they've put in an application with the US government to build a new one in Oregon."

I skimmed the short news story about the MacKinnons' purchase of the refinery in Saskatchewan. "I'll be goddamned." I looked up at him. "They're taking this seriously. What the hell are they doing?"

Trevor shook his head. "I don't know. They seem a bit on the geriatric side to be launching an oil empire, if you ask me."

"I agree, but that's exactly what they're doing." I chewed on my bottom lip. "The only question is why."

"You know them better than I do. I can't answer that. Maybe they're building it for CJ?"

I scoffed. "CJ's an environmentalist and an artist. He'd be pissed if he knew they were doing this crap again. The winery is one thing, it's farming of a sort. Plundering the earth of its natural resources and sending it out into the atmosphere to poison us all is a whole different thing." I collapsed back against my chair again. "I'm even more baffled than I was before."

Trevor offered me a sympathetic look. "Sorry about that, boss. I can do some more digging."

I considered his offer. On one hand, Ossi would have a fit if he knew Trevor was looking into something personal on company time. On the other hand, I didn't give a single shit what Ossi thought. I nodded to Trevor. "Keep it on the QT, but go ahead. I'd like to see how long they've been planning this. It just doesn't make sense. They're almost in their seventies. Why bother getting back in the game now? Especially now that Tom's gone—not that he would have taken over an oil company anyway. Where do you think CJ got his environmentalist tendencies?"

Trevor smiled. "CJ's a smart kid. He would have come up with those on his own."

I grinned, always the proud parent. "You're right. Okay, so any new Excellere business?"

Trevor scoffed, a habit he had picked up from me. "Not today, thank Cher. All's quiet from the Throne Room."

I laughed. "Be careful who you talk like that around. Ossi has moles, you know."

He rolled his eyes. "I know every one of them, too. Don't worry about me, boss. I got it covered." He grinned and went back to his work area.

I picked up the paper he'd given me and studied it again. Matthew and Althea controlling all aspects of the gasoline supply line, even if it was just a little percentage of the whole, was not good for anyone.

I INHALED deeply through my nose and closed my eyes at the familiar scent. Home finally smelled like home again. It had to be a figment of my imagination, but I'd have sworn the fragrance of Tom's coffee lingered in the air. I hadn't realized how much I missed it until now. I cast my eyes to the ceiling and gave him a wink up in heaven, acknowledging the message. "I miss you, babe."

Instead of gripping my heart with the loss of him, the scent filled me with gratitude for all the time we'd had together. Twenty plus years of love and lust and arguing and laughing and raising an incredible son. So many people never got that. I was grateful for the love Tom had lavished on me and CJ.

I smiled and set down my briefcase by the door, knowing I had no intention of opening it again until I was back in the office. At this point I carried it only for the sake of appearances. In the bedroom I changed from the suit into comfy clothes, considering my options for the night's entertainment. Monday night television was sketchy at best. I didn't feel like going out.

Decision made, I went to the kitchen to prepare a huge salad for dinner. Dried cranberries, sunflower seeds, bell peppers in a variety of colors, bacon pieces, and all the usual suspects. It would be simple but filling, and at least marginally good for me, depending on how much dressing I used.

I laughed at the memory of Tom's teasing. “Would you like a little salad with your dressing?” he would ask.

“Only if I have to,” I would answer, upending the bottle even further.

The scent of his coffee was even stronger in the kitchen, almost as if in answer to the memory. I smiled for no reason except that my life finally felt right. There was still a Tom-shaped hole, but it didn’t throb with pain for the first time in months.

I ripped the top off the new package of dried cranberries and stopped short, my hand hovering over the trash can, the plastic still gripped in my suddenly shaking fingers. I shook my head and blinked before looking into the garbage again.

There on the top, for all the world to see, was a tiny filter and grounds that could only have come from Tom's machine—a machine I had never used.

I jerked my head up and quickly scanned the room, expecting the intruder to be waiting with an axe or gun or some other deadly instrument now that I’d discovered evidence of his existence. The room looked just as it had before my heart stopped beating.

I put the plastic piece on the counter next to the trash can and tip-toed over to the coffee machine. It was still warm. Swallowing down a sickening combination of fear and rage, I moved silently from the kitchen into the living room. Nothing was out of place, no one was lurking in the very few shadows.

I grabbed CJ's baseball bat from the entry closet and made my way across the living room to his bedroom. It had been closed off since I’d washed his bedding after he left a couple of weeks earlier.

Hearing every tick and tweak of the house, I eased his door open. The bedroom and closet were as empty as the other two rooms.

By the time I got to the bathroom between the bedrooms, I couldn’t hear anything over the rush of blood in my head. I gripped one side of the shower curtain and yanked it open, baseball bat at the ready. Clean tiles greeted me with a mocking gleam.

I swallowed hard and headed for the master, Tom's and my sanctuary against the world. Immediately I noticed Tom's closet door was slightly ajar again. My eyes narrowed in rage as I stared at the gap between the door and the wall as I eased along the wall behind me to check the bathroom. Keeping half my attention on Tom's closet, I glanced into the bathroom. Thanks to open sightlines, I could tell it was also empty of intruders.

I quickly checked my own closet, knowing what I'd find there—nothing but far too many clothes.

In through the nose, out through the mouth. In through the nose, out through the mouth. I repeated the mantra as I crossed the room to Tom's closet. I yanked the door open with a shout, preparing to swing the bat down on someone's head, but again, I was greeted by nothing but air.

I took a moment to slump against the door, already half convinced I'd imagined the whole thing. I glanced into the closet once more and swung the bat with as much force as I could manage.

I pulled the wood from the shattered plaster and lath with an animal cry. No one was there now, but some one sure as fuck had been. The leather jacket Tom had been so proud of was gone.

FIVE

The ride to work Tuesday morning tried every ounce of my precious little patience. All around me people were chatting at the tops of their lungs or just being general jerks of humanity. I wasn't in the mood. To say that I'd spent a restless night would be like saying the sun was slightly warm. I woke at every creak and crack of the house, at every slam of a car door, at every whisper of wind buffeting the house. I finally gave up trying to sleep at four-thirty and cracked open the briefcase I'd sworn I wasn't going to touch. As soon as I settled on the couch with work, I was out cold. The blaring alarm clock in the bedroom woke me at six.

As soon as I awoke, I checked every door and window lock a third time—having checked them twice once I discovered Tom's jacket missing—and settled into a nice hot shower. The billowing steam obscured my view of the doorway, so I washed quickly, dressed, and left for work in a world-class foul mood.

I'd debated calling the police and/or Shaun after I'd realized someone had broken into my home, but ultimately decided against it. There wasn't anything they could do. Dust for prints, maybe, but what good would that do? If they found out about my recent parting of ways with sanity, they'd just write me off anyway. And if they didn't find out about that, it still wouldn't be a high priority for them. *Lock your doors and windows, sir.* So someone had stolen a dead guy's jacket, big deal.

Except it was a big deal to me. It was a huge fucking deal to me. Not only had someone taken one of Tom's favorite pieces, but now I felt violated in my own home. Someone I had not authorized to be there had riffled through our things, felt safe and secure enough to make himself a treat from Tom's coffee machine for god's sake, and decided to steal a piece of our lives.

Dodging idiots on the sidewalk, I pulled my ringing phone from the pocket of my slacks, in no mood to broker fools. I barked my last name, ready to tear someone a new asshole. It wasn't even eight o'clock yet.

"Henry. Help me."

"Tom!" I shouted. "Tell me where you are!"

Silence answered my demand, just as it had every previous time. I swore under my breath and pinched my eyes shut. Somebody was going to pay dearly for this bullshit. If someone had Tom, I would kill them myself. If this was some jackass' idea of a joke, well, they'd better run really goddamn fast.

I shook with rage as I punched the elevator button for the thirty-third floor. Impulsively I also jabbed the tenth floor button, right next to the small brass plaque reading Deveraux Investigations, a listing I'd probably seen seven dozen times, but one that had never registered until now.

People crowded around me much too close for my comfort that morning. Usually I could endure elevator rides with only a modicum of unease, but in my heightened emotional state, I wanted nothing more than to get away from them. As usual, they studied the floor or the ceiling or their portable electronic device of choice. I studied their freakishly mirrored reflection on the doors, waiting for one of them to make a move of some kind. I didn't know who had been in the house or what they wanted besides a hot drink and a leather damn jacket, but I wasn't letting my guard down just yet.

The doors finally slid open on the tenth floor with an obnoxious beep and I burst out of the elevator, turning to see who would follow me. When no one did, I managed to calm enough to take in my surroundings. The building-required plaque on the doors of the office suite to the left subtly announced my destination. I approached the desk, where a Doris

Roberts-type woman stood guard, naturally. How very *Remington Steele*, I thought with an edge of mania.

"I'd like to see your best detective, please," I informed her, trying desperately to keep the edge of crazy out of my voice.

"Of course you would, doll. Everyone does."

I grasped for the remaining shards of my sanity, squeezed my eyes shut tightly, and counted to five in my head. I opened my eyes to see Doris gazing back at me with a contemplative expression. "It's important to me that I see him as soon as possible."

She must have seen something in my face that led her to believe I wasn't here for something so trivial as a cheating spouse or a background check. "I'll see that he makes time for you, Mister...?"

"Cooley. Henry Cooley. And thank you."

She smiled wanly and typed into her computer, then gestured to the row of seating against the wall. "Make yourself comfortable, Mr. Cooley. Dev's with another client so it'll be a little while."

I swallowed hard and nodded in understanding. Luckily it was early enough in the day the waiting area was empty. Or was it always like that? How much business could a private investigator have in the financial hub of the city? Obviously quite a bit or he wouldn't be able to afford these digs.

I FIDGETED uncontrollably, my jerky movements betraying my nervousness. It was probably nothing the man across the desk had never seen before, but I felt ridiculous in the truest sense of the word. Was this what my life had come to?

If I'd have given a private detective any thought at all, I would have expected to find myself in some seedy building in the Tenderloin, with moldy carpets, crumbling brick, and quite probably the twin stenches of stale piss and yesterday's whiskey. Wasn't that how most films and novels portrayed the offices of a swaggering, butch, alcoholic PI? Discovering an investigation firm only a few floors below my own workplace had startled me. To be sitting in one of that firm's offices was surreal.

Waiting and waiting in the outer office, I'd worked myself up to the verge of tears, terrified of talking about it, yet desperate to get it all out. The phone call. Tom's voice. His words. The break in. The theft.

I checked the incoming call log on my phone one more time. It was the only proof I wasn't going crazy again. Unless the unknown number listings in my call log weren't really there. Was I seeing things? Was I sliding off the deep end again? If I was or wasn't, how would I know? How could I prove I was sane when I felt anything but? A missing jacket wouldn't help my cause any. Missing meant I could have made it up in Crazytown.

The man across the desk cleared his throat. My every single emotion fled with the sound. I felt nothing but emptiness. Like those first days after Shaun made me remember. My movements ceased abruptly and I stared back at the clean-shaven stranger who watched me with a mostly bored expression. He was as out of place in my private detective fantasy as the office in which we sat. I appreciated the scent of his spicy, expensive cologne that bore no resemblance to stale whiskey. He wore a conservative but flattering grey suit, a deep blue dress shirt, and a tie that coordinated perfectly. He was younger and better-looking than me, which probably helped considerably in his line of work. People tended to trust youth and good looks. He could probably charm secrets out of anyone if he tried hard enough. Aside from the boredom in his eyes, I would have thought him a regular businessman like a thousand others who walked around this building every day. Then again, maybe that was what we all looked like to outsiders.

"Would you care to tell me why you're here, Mr. Cooley?"

I blanched at the use of my name. We'd been introduced when he called me back to his office, but I couldn't remember his name for the life of me. "I—my husband called." I didn't know when I'd decided to begin at the beginning, but it was a very bad place to start.

"Is that a bad thing?"

"He's dead." I flinched at the words. They felt harsh and abrupt, even if they were true. At least they had been until that first phone call a week ago. I'd visited Tom's grave twice since my little reconnect with reality. I knew every engraving and feature on the headstone. I could probably draw the pattern of the grass that grew on his grave. Yet I'd heard his voice, pleading for my help.

I pushed the button to illuminate the phone log again. It was still there, taunting me.

The detective leaned forward, suddenly a lot less bored. "I'm sorry. Could you repeat that?"

I stood abruptly. "No. This is a mistake. I'm sorry." I lurched out of the office, almost running. I couldn't escape the voice in my head—Tom's voice, pleading for help. The phone call repeated on an endless loop, growing more accusatory each time, like he knew I'd given up on him. Like he knew I'd accepted he was dead just because people said it was true.

"MR. COOLEY?"

The sound of my name alarmed me enough to look up. The detective. I hastily wiped the evidence of tears from my face. I was surprised he had followed me all the way outside. Surprised and instantly pissed off. Why was everyone playing games with me? I stared at him wordlessly.

The man sighed, hiked his pants legs and climbed up to sit beside me. I hadn't even noticed I'd climbed to my usual perch at the top of the seating-slash-garden structure. "Mr. Cooley, you're obviously upset. I don't usually follow potential clients once they've run out of my office, but I thought you might be down here clearing your head."

I nodded, waiting for him to finish whatever he had to say.

"You said your husband called you?"

"Y—yes." I hated the weakness in my voice. Hated that the mere mention of Tom brought the voice on the calls back to my consciousness.

"But you also stated he's deceased, did I get that right?"

"Yes." My vision wavered with an onslaught of fresh tears. I blinked them back and concentrated on regulating my breathing. Focusing on something other than the pain helped push the need to cry back where it belonged.

The detective paused. "Do you have any reason to believe that's not your husband's voice or that he might not be deceased?"

"No. I mean, I don't know." I ran my fingers over my forehead in frustration. "I'm not the world's most reliable witness, Mr...?"

"Deveraux. Blaine Deveraux."

"Mr. Deveraux. I apologize. I knew that. I'm not quite myself at the moment." I cleared my throat as I gathered my thoughts. "I had a...break with reality a few weeks back. I woke up one morning and just forgot that Tom was dead. I thought he'd gone out for a run." My chin quivered as the shame of that weakness and the memory of that fear for his safety pushed forward, still as fresh as if they'd happened an hour ago. I fought to stay in the moment. "Suffice it to say I remember now that he died in a car accident in February. I've been dealing with grieving him again." I laughed uncomfortably. "This is actually only my second week back at work. The calls started on my first day back."

"How many people knew that?"

"Knew what?"

"That it was your first day back to work?"

I frowned. "I don't know. Anyone who works with me. Trevor, my assistant. Shaun, my best friend. CJ, my son."

I could see the gears turning behind his brown eyes, but I had no clue what they were telling him. Hell, I didn't know what to think about anything. My whole world was upside down yet again. I could only imagine what Shaun would think about the whole thing. He'd probably be here in less than five minutes with a court order to put me in a padded room, safely away from all sharp objects and anything electronic. I wondered, perversely, if I'd get crayons.

"Has it been just the one call?"

I swallowed. "No. There have been four or five. They're recorded in my call log."

Deveraux's eyes narrowed as he took in that information. "I'm going to suggest you download an app for your phone to record your incoming phone calls, so we'll have documentation when this person calls again. You should set it to record all of them by default. You can go back and delete conversations you don't want to keep."

I stared at him in disbelief. Dread twined around my chest, constricting my lungs. "You don't think it's Tom, do you?"

Deveraux shrugged. "I don't know, but it's better to be on the safe side. If you have a recording, we can have it analyzed and possibly trace it back to the source. Was the call from a blocked number?"

I blinked. He'd gone from zero to sixty in less time than I'd gone from crazy to sane to crazy again. "Yes. The first time I wanted to call back but I was afraid. I didn't want to take the chance of alerting the people who—" I stopped short. Deveraux didn't need to hear my circular thinking, if I could even call it that. "But you can't call back a blocked number. Wait, does this mean you're taking me on as a client? Do I even have a case?"

The way Deveraux smiled made it clear he knew I needed him to draw me pictures. Finger paints, anyone? "You have someone calling you with your deceased husband's voice and you wonder if you have a case? The only real question is who's doing it and why."

"That's two questions."

He waved the objection away. "Eh, usually when we find out who's behind a situation, they're more than willing to cop to the why. Let me see your phone."

I handed it over.

"Is this last received call the one?"

"Yes."

He copied dates and times I'd received blocked calls into his own phone before turning to mine and downloading an application from the Play Store. He made a few modifications to the program's preferences, then added himself to my contacts list, and handed the phone back to me. "Call me when you have a recording and we can go from there."

I hesitated to bring it up, but I knew it was important. It was possibly the most important piece of the puzzle. "There's more."

"Go ahead."

"Someone's been in my house. Last night when I got home, I started making dinner and I saw in the trash a filter and coffee grounds can that could only have come from Tom's machine. He's—he *was*—a coffee fanatic. The more complex and exotic the flavors, the better. I've never used his machine, ever. It's too complicated. I just like plain black stuff." I paused to stop the spew of unnecessary words. "When I checked the machine it was still warm, so I might have interrupted whoever it was."

"Did he or she leave a dirty coffee cup behind?"

For the first time I realized they hadn't. "No. I didn't even notice that. I was so preoccupied by the jacket."

"What jacket?"

I explained the significance of Tom's leather jacket and how I'd kept only it and one shirt in Tom's closet. Now the jacket was gone.

"Did you file a police report?"

I shook my head. "It didn't seem important for just a jacket." I sighed heavily. "Look, I'm just a few weeks back from Insanityville, as I said. The last thing I need is for the cops to find out about that and decide I've gone nutso again."

Deveraux rolled his shoulders under his expensive suit jacket. "I understand, but you really should have reported it. They may have been able to lift fingerprints from the coffee machine or some other surface. At the very least it would have put it on the record." He pursed his lips. "Is this the first time you noticed something amiss in the house?"

I frowned. Was it? It was so hard to remember. Except.... "No. A couple of days ago I found the garage light on for no reason. And a few days before that, Tom's closet door was open—but I might have just forgotten to latch it the last time I was in there."

"I doubt it, Mr. Cooley. In my professional opinion, you have a stalker. Now, it remains to be seen if that person is the same one who's making the phone calls. We'll have to figure that out later. Either way, you have yourself a dangerous situation. Stalkers escalate. If he was in your husband's closet last week and he's now comfortable enough to steal an item big enough to be noticed *and* use your husband's coffeemaker, he's assuming ownership of Tom's things, which may lead him to become confrontational very soon. I'm going to advise you to change all the locks and have cameras and an alarm system installed immediately. Today if possible."

I stared at him in disbelief. "Is that really necessary? I mean, it was just a jacket. It only had sentimental value."

"And now it has sentimental value to your stalker. Who knows what other trophies he'll come after? Not to put too fine a point on it, but one of those may be your head. Literally or figuratively."

"Jesus." I let the idea sink into my brain and shivered in the suddenly-chilled air.

"Stalkers are not to be taken lightly. Any number of celebrities could tell you that. Most average people don't think they could be the target of one of these sickos, but actually the average person is the one who winds up dead most often. We don't have the ability to pay for around-the-clock security like celebrities do."

I nodded. "I understand. Thank you, Mr. Deveraux."

"Everyone calls me Dev." He got to his feet and offered his hand.

I stood and shook his hand. "Dev. What if...." I rolled my eyes, certain the words would make me sound foolish at best, delusional at worst.

"What if he's really alive?"

The air escaped my lungs in relief that I didn't have to say the words I'd been trying to deny were possible. "Yes."

My new friend pulled a face. "It seems unlikely that would be the case considering the length of time since his disappearance. You said February, right?"

"Yes, February eighth."

"It's August twelfth now. If he were taken for ransom, they would have made contact within the first few hours. I assume that didn't happen?"

I shook my head. "No. We—*I*—don't have that kind of money anyway. If someone was looking for ransom, they'd contact his parents."

"Should I know his parents?"

"Probably not. Matthew and Althea MacKinnon."

He made a note on his phone but otherwise betrayed nothing. "Is there any reason he would have been taken hostage?"

This was so bizarre. We were right back to where we'd been the night Shaun came over to help me figure it all out. I waved a hand impatiently. "No, I mean, not really. Tom is—*was*—an architect. He headed up his firm's tall buildings section, but that seems like a stretch. No pun intended."

Dev pulled out his phone again. "Okay, I'm going to need his full name, date of birth, and social security number. I'll do a little digging and see what I come up with."

I recited Tom's information as Dev typed it into his phone.

When he was finished, he looked up at me and smiled warmly. "Don't worry. We'll get to the bottom of this. In the meantime, your job is to get that alarm system and cameras. Then go about your life normally but safely. I know that sounds impossible, but it's the best thing you can do." He nodded at the building where we both had offices. "Go back to work. Let your mind concentrate on other things for a while. I'll be in touch."

"IN MY office," I barked as I walked past Trevor's desk. I slung my suit jacket over the back of my chair and collapsed into it. The full impact of my conversation with Dev pulled me down hard. How the hell had my life abruptly become so complicated? I was just a regular guy living a normal life. Suddenly my possibly-not-dead husband was calling me asking for help. Or it could be my shiny new stalker playing tricks on me. I rubbed my temples but the stress headache I'd felt building in the elevator ride up had already taken hold.

Trevor closed the door behind him and took a seat across the desk from me. "Are you alright? Have I done something?"

I waved his concerns away with a flick of my wrist. "No, no. You're perfect, as always." I dug in my desk drawer for the bottle of ibuprofen, poured five into my palm, and dry swallowed them.

"It grosses me out every time you do that," Trevor confessed with a shudder. "I keep expecting one to get lodged in your throat. And then I'd have to do CPR on you and, as pretty as you are, you don't pay me enough for that."

I laughed for the first time in what seemed like forever. "Watch it or I'll stop chasing you around my desk."

Trevor grinned. "Aw, now how can I catch you if you don't chase me?"

"So that's your angle. I'll have to remember that." I blew out a breath and leaned my forearms on the desk. "I need you to work your magic today. Someone broke into my house last night. I need an alarm system and cameras installed by the time I get home today." I grimaced. "I don't know how much it'll cost or where you'll find someone on such short notice, but I'll pay whatever it takes."

Trevor's expression had turned from focused to concerned as soon as I uttered the words "broke into my house." "Are you alright? Were you home? Did they take anything?" He held up a hand. "Sorry, none of my business."

"No, it's okay." I shrugged. "Whoever it was took something of Tom's that I'd been saving for sentimental reasons. It might get him a couple of dollars at the pawn shop, but Dev doesn't think that's why he took it."

"Dev?"

"Blaine Deveraux."

Trevor's eyes widened. "The hunky detective from the tenth floor?"

I chuckled. "Really? That's what you're getting from this conversation?"

He scoffed. "Please, I practically already have the stuff installed. My brother owns a security company and he owes me a favor. It'll be done by two. He's going to have questions about specifics like silent versus disorienting alarms, how many hours of footage you want stored from the cameras, if you want them inside or just outside."

"You know me. Answer those questions like I would."

He nodded. "Got it. I'm really sorry this happened."

"Me too," I admitted. I resettled in my chair, leaning back to cup my aching forehead. "Have you received any unusual phone calls or visitors? Any strange packages besides the wine glasses? Has anyone been asking more questions about me than usual?"

"Nnnno." He prolonged the consonant as he thought. "Shaun has called a couple of times for general status reports. I've told him you're doing fine. I didn't think that was a big deal; I know how close you two are. But other than that, the only unusual occurrence was the delivery of the wine glasses. And you know I thought that was weird. I'm sure I would have noticed anything else."

"I'm sure you would have. If anything changes, let me know as soon as possible."

"Will do. Is that all? I should call Tristan so I can get him started on your house."

I sighed. "I'm not looking forward to living in Fort Knox, but yes, that's all. And tell him how much I appreciate his help."

"Absolutely." He was already dialing his cell before he crossed the threshold.

Shaun checking up on me didn't surprise me. He was sort of a mother hen that way. He'd claimed me that year of college and seemed to have me under his wing in one way or another since then. He was the best friend a guy could ask for. But now I wasn't sure I trusted him as completely as I always had. The way he'd lied to me about having a conversation with CJ the night he'd driven me to Matthew and Althea's still stung. And why hadn't he just flat out told me Tom was dead instead of staging an elaborate charade where I was suddenly supposed to remember on my own. He'd even brought Mary Beth into it, without her knowledge or consent, to take a fake missing persons statement from me. As far as I knew she was still pissed at him for that. Why shouldn't I be?

Some doubt had kept me from telling him about the phone calls. That same internal warning suggested I shouldn't inform him of the break in either. Before Tom's death, I'd trusted Shaun fully. After his actions during my Crazytown stint, I couldn't make that same statement. I still loved him to death, but I didn't trust him with my life anymore. Not completely anyway.

Trevor knocked on the door and stuck his head in. "Hey, Tristan needs someone to be there while he does the installation. Do you want to work from home, or do you want me to babysit him? Fair warning: it's going to be noisy and annoying. Sort of like being here."

"You make it sound so enticing." I shook my head. "If you don't mind, I'll let you supervise. I should pretend like I work here."

"Good enough," he said, coming into the office.

I dug my keys out and handed them to him. "If you have any questions about camera placement, you should ask Dev on your way out."

Trevor grinned. "You know, I suddenly do."

I laughed. "Just don't make it too obvious you're lusting over him, huh? I think he's straight."

Trevor rolled his eyes. "He ain't straight. Not completely anyway. But I'll be good. I'm your representative on a business matter. See? I know my place."

"Good boy."

MY FINGERS trembled as I dialed Matthew MacKinnon's number. It wouldn't have been a fun conversation with someone I liked, let alone with someone who had no use for my continued existence. Still I needed answers only he could give me. I used the code words Tom had established with Matthew to actually get him on the phone. His secretaries were remarkably determined walls of obfuscation without them. He'd probably recruited them from the Stasi after the Berlin Wall fell. No one got through to Matthew unless he wanted them to—and he never wanted me to, unless I was calling regarding CJ or Tom.

"What can I do for you, Henry?" Matthew inquired coldly.

"Matthew, do you have a security detail for CJ?" I asked without preamble. Might as well start with the easy stuff first.

"Why would you think that?"

I rolled my eyes. "Can't you just answer the question?"

"I thought I had. Was that all you wanted? I have more important things to do than play word games with you."

"Alright. Well then, have they reported anything unusual? Has anyone been following him or has he deviated from his normal routines in any way?"

"If I had that sort of information, Henry, I wouldn't share it with you. So far as I know from CJ, he's doing fine."

"Yes, that's what he tells me too. But things have gotten weird here. So you'll understand if I'm looking for a more concrete answer. We both want him safe. I just want to know he is."

"He's fine. There's nothing unusual, no new faces are hanging around. Is that what you wanted to know?"

Some of the tension dissipated from my shoulders. "Yes, thank you."

"Will that be all, or are you going to ask about his sex life next?"

"Oh please tell me you don't know details—wait, I don't want the answer to that." I shuddered at the thought of the reports Tom's detail had probably provided Matthew when I'd first started dating his son. We were game for anything, anywhere, anytime. The follies of youth became the sweet memories of the middle-aged.

Matthew laughed lightly. It had been years since I'd heard that sound. It made me just as uncomfortable as it always did. "Let's say he's of a higher moral caliber than you were at his age."

Of course. The inevitable jab at how inferior I was to their beloved Tom. I should have expected it. "Matthew, how certain are you that it's Tom buried in that grave under our tree?"

Even over the phone I heard his chair hit the wall behind him as he leapt to his feet. "What the hell are you talking about? Of course that's Tom! Do you think I would let some stranger be buried on my property?

Are you on drugs? Or have you lost your mind again? Don't think I didn't hear about that, you pathetic excuse for—"

"Yeah, yeah. Listen, I need to know you saw the dental comparisons. I need to know beyond a shadow of a doubt it's Tom buried under that tree. I've been getting phone calls, Matthew. It's his voice asking me to help him. If there's even a slight chance that isn't him in that grave, I need to know."

"I will not stand here and listen to this—this—*blasphemy!* Your reckless lifestyle killed my son long before his time and now he's buried on his family's—on *my*—land where he belongs!"

"And you saw the tests?"

"Henry—"

"Answer the question, Matthew!" I shouted. "Did you see the fucking tests or not?"

"No. Hugh Lowe took care of that gruesome detail."

That wasn't the answer I wanted to hear. With everything in me I'd hoped that Matthew had seen those comparisons, not to be cruel to a grieving old man, but because then I could be sure. Instead, he'd left possibly the most important moment in his life—and mine—to an eighty-year-old lawyer whose head was so far up Matthew's ass he couldn't find his way out with a map and a flashlight. "Then you'll have no objection when I have the grave exhumed and the remains DNA tested."

I could practically feel the heat of Matthew's outraged breath on my face. "What?! I will not! You will not disturb my son's final resting place! You killed him once, I'll not have you doing it again! What the hell is wrong with you? I should have you committed!"

I slumped in my chair. Having me committed might not be such a bad idea. I was *so* tired of feeling like I was going insane again. I closed my eyes and squeezed my temples. "I guess I'll see you in court then. Thank you for the information, Matthew. Please keep CJ safe." Before he could react with more bombast, I disconnected the call.

I rubbed my forehead for a few minutes before picking up the phone again. This time I dialed an old attorney friend I hadn't talked to in months.

As soon as he answered, I launched into the request before I could talk myself out of it. "Justin, I need to exhume Tom's grave, and I need you to do it quickly."

SIX

Wednesday dawned cold and rainy, a perfect match for my mood. I downed two cups of coffee watching the rain from the back porch before I even contemplated the shower. Trevor's brother had the cameras installed inside and out and the alarm system wired and ready for my password input before I arrived home from work Tuesday afternoon. It would take some getting used to, but if it kept little thieving bastards out of my house, it would be worth the expense and intrusion. The system was even set up to immediately dial my cell and the police if it was tripped. I couldn't have asked for more—except maybe not needing it at all.

The phone was ringing on its charger when I stepped out of the shower. I grabbed a towel and jogged to answer it.

"Henry. Help me."

"Who is this?" I shouted into the phone. "Why do you keep fucking with me? Leave me alone!"

I chucked the thing across the room, charger cord and all, and sat hard on the bed, realizing that for the first time I'd given up hope that it could really be Tom on the other end. It was always the same words, always in the same tone of voice. The real question was when had Tom said those words all in a row? Had he been tortured by someone? He hadn't sounded winded or in pain. He'd sounded hoarse and maybe a little bit weak. But maybe he'd always sounded like that on the phone and I'd never noticed? It had been more than six months since I'd had a conversation with him. I could still hear his voice in my head, but I couldn't be sure how accurate it was. I closed the mental door on that heartbreaking thought.

Shit!

Dev needed the phone in one piece to analyze the recording. I rushed over to where it had landed on the floor after bouncing off the wall. Thankfully the protective case had done its job. The screen was intact and working fine.

I tossed it on the bed and finished drying myself.

I dressed in a rush, foregoing breakfast in order to get to Dev as quickly as possible. The recording didn't have a shelf life, but I wanted the mystery solved as quickly as possible. I was tired of wondering and waiting. Hopefully this call would prove once and for all if Tom was alive or not.

And if that didn't do it, the DNA testing would. Of course Matthew and Althea had challenged my petition to exhume Tom's grave. The odds had been in our favor enough to draw a judge whose attitude was, at best, cool towards the MacKinnons. I trusted Justin would be able to work whatever legal magic he'd perfected in his twenty years of practicing law to win the petition. The results of the analysis on the phone recording might help us, regardless of how it turned out. Justin had said the chances I would have to personally present my argument for disinterment were pretty much pegged at one hundred percent. I sent up another silent prayer that he was wrong. I knew Matthew and Althea's lawyers would tear me apart. I was sure they'd paint me as some sick freak faking grief-induced insanity in order to make the truly heartbroken parents suffer the death of their child again.

I braved the rain and wind and wet and reeking hordes on mass transit to get to the office shortly before seven thirty. To my surprise, Doris Roberts and Dev were already there.

Dev unlocked the outer office door and ushered me in with a genuine smile. "Mr. Cooley. I'm surprised to see you already."

"Henry, please. And I'm surprised to be here already." I waved my phone at him. "I got another call this morning as I was getting out of the shower. It was the same as all the others. Just the three words and no response to my voice."

I handed him the device, glad to have it out of my possession for a while. I hadn't realized how much I'd started dreading every noise the thing made until it was in someone else's hands.

"I'll get this to my audio guy first thing," Dev said, still looking at the phone. "I'll have to take the whole phone. The quality will degrade every time we transfer it to another device. Do you mind?"

"Not if it puts an end to this," I answered truthfully.

He nodded. "Good. Would it bother you if I play it?"

I swallowed hard. I didn't really want to hear it again, but I knew it wouldn't hurt me. Not now that I'd somewhat made peace with the probability that it wasn't really Tom calling for aid. "Go ahead."

Dev's fingers slid across the screen several times until he found the application he was looking for. Tom's voice filled the room with the words I'd heard far too many times. Dev studied the air as he listened. When the call, including my screamed response, was over, he sighed. "I'm sorry you're dealing with this, Henry. I'll get this to Scott and we'll have an answer for you as soon as humanly possible. He'll make it his only priority, but it may not be resolved today.

"By the way, why didn't you tell me Tom had been kidnapped as a teenager?"

I stared at Dev, surprised at my surprise. "I, uh, I didn't think about it. I'm surprised you found out about it."

He cocked his head. "It's what I do, Henry."

I held up a hand. "Yes, I know. I didn't mean any offense. Tom didn't like to talk about it. I think we discussed it twice in twenty years. He wouldn't go into details. I don't have much information but I can tell you what he was willing to talk about."

"It's fine. I know enough to know they're not related. How are you coming with the alarm and cameras? Your assistant stopped in with a few questions yesterday."

Was it my imagination or did Dev's cheeks color slightly at the mention of Trevor? "They had it all finished by the time I got home. Turns out Trev's brother owns an alarm company."

"Convenient."

"Unfortunately. I'd rather have gone on not knowing that."

Dev squeezed my shoulder consolingly. "We'll fix this, Henry. You have my promise. If this is Tom, we'll find a way to help him. If not, we'll find out who's behind it and put a stop to it."

I FUMBLED getting the key in the new lock, distracted by Shaun's tale of his bizarre date the night before. As I was leaving the office, he'd surprised me by suggesting that we order in Italian to celebrate the week being half over. That had turned into him meeting me at the Market & Church Street station so we could drive his little two-seater Audi sportster to Bambino's Ristorante for takeaway.

"So then," Shaun continued as we set our dinner down on the kitchen island, "we're leaving the Lookout— *WHAT THE UNHOLY FUCK!"*

We both ducked for cover as strobe lights blinded us and sirens swooped in out of nowhere, dive bombing us like kamikaze sound missiles. "Shit!" I muttered—or screamed, no one would be able to tell the difference—and leapt for the alarm system control panel by the front door. I was three digits into the five-digit code when it dawned on me I could have used the pad by the back door—in the kitchen. By then I was so frazzled I could barely punch in the final two numbers and get the thing to stop. The volume was deafening but the way the sound wove around the room and seemed to attack us was disorienting. It made me want to stop and drop into a fetal position, forget the roll. Finally silence reigned, except for the ringing in my ears.

Seconds later, the phone screeched in my pants pocket, scaring the hell out of me again. I hastily assured the alarm company that I'd simply forgotten about the system and that everything was alright. I struggled for a second to remember the code word—Boston. Once I'd provided it, she strongly suggested I take better care remembering to deactivate the system and said she'd inform the police it was a mistaken occurrence. I thanked her profusely, still trying to catch my breath, and absolutely dreading the pissed off Shaun I was certain to find waiting in the other room.

I came around the corner into the kitchen in time to see Shaun stretching his jaw, trying to combat the residual echo. Without a word, I grabbed the pain reliever bottle from the cabinet and poured out eight. I slid four across the counter to him and turned back to the fridge for a couple of bottles of water.

I knew I was in deep shit. I'd kept everything from him for almost two weeks. He wasn't going to be happy. It was hard to believe it had only been nine days since that first phone call.

I handed Shaun the bottle without making eye contact. I downed the four pills, screwed the cap back on the water, and started digging through the bags to retrieve our dinner.

"So, what?" He started, his clipped, controlled tone telling me just how angry he was. "We're just going to pretend like that didn't happen?"

I sighed and braced my hands against the counter. "That would be kind of impossible, wouldn't it?"

"Yeah. A little."

I met his gaze reluctantly. "Obviously I've had an alarm system installed."

"Really? I hadn't noticed."

I rolled my eyes. "Jesus, Shaun. It's not a big deal." I reached back into the bag but came up empty. Instead of saying anything else, I started slowly folding the thick paper bag. It was nice quality. I wasn't sure what I would use it for, but I certainly wasn't going to throw it away.

"Hank."

The nickname said in that disappointed tone broke me. "Fine! I've been getting calls and there was a break-in the other day. It's not a big deal. I wasn't home—at least I didn't see him."

Shaun looked around the room, noticing the cameras for the first time. "Are those what I think they are?"

I nodded, eyes closed.

"So you have cameras and an alarm system, complete with seizure-inducing strobe lights, that makes you want to fall to the floor and curl into a ball, but it isn't a big deal? You didn't used to lie to me, Hank. What's changed?"

I shoved my hands into my hair as my composure crumbled. I'd been dealing with this alone for nine days. It was freaking me the hell out. At least now I didn't think I was going crazy again—not on my own anyway. That might be a side goal of whoever this stalker son of a bitch was, but he wasn't going to win. Not this time. I released a loud, frustrated sound that sounded strangely like a roar.

"Pour yourself a drink and fix a plate, buddy. This is going to take a while. We might as well be comfortable."

Ten minutes later, Shaun's meal was mostly untouched but he'd refilled his whiskey glass three times, each time adding a little bit more. At the second refill he'd joined me on the couch. I wondered idly if he needed the comfort of proximity like I did.

"I can't believe you kept this from me." He sounded more hurt than angry, which was almost worse.

"I'm sorry. Until the bastard actually stole Tom's jacket, I thought I was losing it again. You don't know how frightening that is, Shaun. Unless you've actually lost touch with your sanity, you have no idea how scary it is to think it's happening in slow motion and there's not a damn thing you can do to stop it."

He conceded the point silently. "I don't understand the phone calls. If it isn't Tom, how did they get his voice? And if it is Tom, where the hell is he? Why didn't anyone ever contact you or Matthew and Althea for a ransom?"

"Unless they never intended to give him back."

Shaun's sharp intake of breath told me that grisly thought hadn't crossed his mind.

"You have no idea the scenarios that have played through my mind. It's like every single action movie I've ever seen has come back to haunt me. Every time one of the good guys is beaten or tortured or killed, all I can see is it happening to Tom." I took an extra-large drink of my wine. "You said they used dental records to identify Tom after the accident. I don't remember that at all. Matthew says he never saw the comparisons. He said he left it to his attorney. Did you see them?"

Shaun shook his head silently.

"Yeah, I was afraid of that." I swallowed down the lump of emotion in my throat. "I'm going to have his grave exhumed."

Shaun shot to his feet. "You're *what?!* Henry! Be serious here. The chances are next to zero that it's anyone else but Tom in that grave. That was his Jeep—*your* Jeep—that burned in that accident. There was only one person in it. Who else could it be?"

I shrugged, almost buzzed enough not to care about his opinion. We were talking about digging up my husband. That concept was so bizarre that body-switching seemed almost rational somehow. "How should I know? I don't think like criminal people." I sighed and slumped deeper into the sofa, bone-weary suddenly. "I'm tired, Shaun. I'm tired of worrying about my sanity. I'm tired of being toyed with by whoever's behind these phone calls. And I'm damn sure tired of being a target. I have to know. Either it's Tom in that grave or it isn't."

Shaun drained his drink. "And what if it isn't? Then what?"

"I try to find him." Easy. There was no other answer to that question. I didn't have the slightest idea how to go about doing it, but, I would find him if it was the last thing I did. CJ needed his father back and I needed my husband. No one else—*no one*—had the right to take that away from us.

"And if it is him?"

"I don't know." That was the truly frightening part. If the love of my life was in that grave, I'd have to start creating a life without him. Before that first phone call had raised vague hopes and stirred fears about what he was going through, I'd convinced myself I was ready to start putting my life back together. But those three little words had changed everything. I wasn't ready to move on. I wasn't even sure I had to. Didn't our years together earn me some level of extended grieving time?

Shaun grabbed a bottle of water from under the bar and returned to the couch. "Do you remember anything about the night before you woke up thinking Tom was missing?"

I shook my head. "I don't remember the weekend at all. I've never been quite sure why."

His hand covered mine where it rested on the back of the couch. His fingers fiddled with my wedding ring. "I've always felt guilty about that night. I knew you weren't ready, but for some reason that didn't matter. I didn't know it would trigger a psychotic break. Jesus, if I had known that, I never would have said anything. I would have taken it to the grave, just like I'd planned to do."

His words, coupled with the fact that he seemed to be staring at a spot somewhere above the couch, frightened me. "What are you talking about?"

He swallowed some water and looked at it in disgust, like he'd forgotten he switched from whiskey. "Hank, I was here that Sunday. We spent all day puttering around in the garden. I changed the oil in your Jeep. We had dinner. I even let you convince me to drink wine with you." He smiled faintly. "You were in such a happy mood. We made dinner together—I know." He chuckled at the shocked look I gave him. "We actually shared a kitchen for something other than sorting takeaway boxes. It was nice. And then...." His voice trailed off and he turned to stare out the window.

"Then what?"

"And then my perfect movie turned into a nightmare." He turned back to me, a faint smile playing at his lips. He squeezed my fingers before removing his hand from atop mine. His gaze turned to the coffee table. "We reached for the last cookie at the same time. You turned and laughed at me. Our faces were only a few inches apart. I didn't think about it, I just reacted. I kissed you."

My heart stopped.

"You kissed me back. It was everything I'd imagined. You tasted so good, like chocolate and wine." He blinked and seemed to come out of his reverie. He cleared his throat and sat up straighter on the couch. "And then it was over. You pulled back and freaked out—kind of like you're doing now. Breathe, Hank. Breathe."

I concentrated on creating a flow of oxygen in and out of my lungs and stared at my best friend. It was like I'd never really seen him before. "Why would you kiss me?"

His brief chuckle was mournful. "That's almost the exact question you asked me that night."

I waited but he didn't seem inclined to continue. "And what was your answer?" I prodded gently.

His gaze caught mine and drilled deep. "Because I've been in love with you for years, Hank. Since before Tom. But as soon as you met him, I knew I didn't stand a chance. So I concentrated on being your best friend. I *am* your best friend. Nothing will ever change that." He swallowed hard. "I loved Tom. He was a great guy and a perfect husband to you and an amazing dad to CJ. I never would have said a word if he hadn't died." He huffed a laugh. "And if you wake up in the morning in another psychotic break, I swear to all that is holy, I will never mention it again."

I wanted to laugh or cry or smack him upside the head, but all I could do was stare into his eyes. Truth and pain fought for dominance in them. I didn't know what to do or say. I'd long ago convinced myself Shaun was straight—aggressively so. This new, bisexual Shaun would take some getting used to. That part I could deal with fine. It was the part about him being in love with me that I didn't know how to handle. It was just one more out of control boomerang waiting to catch me unaware when it zinged back at me.

"I—I never knew," was all I could croak out.

He smiled sadly. "You weren't meant to. Not ever." He sighed and reached for his water bottle again, taking another dissatisfying swig. "I tried to find someone else," he said as he walked to the bar. "I dated and dated, but no one came close to having the spark you have. None of them lit up—*Jesus*, this is so freaking corny. None of them lit up my life like you do."

"I've never known you to date men. Why didn't I ever meet any of them?"

He looked at me over his shoulder. "Are you kidding? I couldn't bring them around you, Hank."

"Why not?"

"Because all they'd have to do is take one look at me looking at you and the jig would be up. They'd know they could never be you."

My mind spun like a merry-go-round. Round and round it went with no sign of stopping. "Shaun."

He laughed, his back still to me. "That's what you said last time too. It's okay, Hank. I know you don't feel the same way. You never did. And I know it's too soon after Tom's death—hell, if he even *is* dead.

"You've got me spinning in circles here. I don't know what to do or say. I don't know if my friend is dead and haunting you or if he's been kidnapped. I don't even understand how or why someone would be stalking you. So what do I do? I confess my deepest secret." I watched him slug back half a rocks glass of whiskey. He refilled it and turned to come back. "Ah, fuck it!" he spat, grabbing the bottle by the neck and bringing it with him.

"I can leave if you want," he slurred. "I can drown my sorrows better at home anyway. Maybe I can call Kelly and pretend he's you again." He winced. "Sorry, you probably didn't want to hear that."

I was watching a train wreck on repeat. "Is this what you did that night? Drink yourself into a stupor?"

"Ha. No, that was all you, big boy. I stood guard until you puked, then I put you to bed and went home. I figured once you puked, you were safe from alcohol poisoning, but I didn't think you'd want to find me on your couch in the morning. Now I wish I would have stayed. I wonder if anything would have been different."

"I don't know," I answered honestly. I sighed and watched him watch me. I loved him. I always had loved him. There had been a time, early in our friendship, when I'd definitely wanted to take him to bed. But I'd never been in love with him. Perhaps if Tom hadn't come into my life that would have happened. But Tom did come. And now he was gone.

Could I love Shaun in the way he wanted? Honestly, I didn't even know how he would want me to love him. It would be very different from being with Tom, that much was sure. I needed time and distance to make any decisions. I needed to know for sure if Tom was dead or not. And then I needed to strangle the little bastard who'd stolen his jacket. And then, maybe, hopefully, my life could stop spinning the fuck out of control for just two minutes so I could figure out what to do about Shaun.

"I can't deal with this right now."

"I know."

"It's not a rejection. I just have too many balls in the air to know where to turn next. You said it yourself, we don't even know if Tom's really gone."

"I know."

"And you should stop drinking for the night."

"I know." He drained his glass and poured more.

Was he even listening to me? "And I'm the greatest human being on the planet, now or ever."

"Don't I fuckin' know it." He stuck out his tongue at me.

I smiled. "I'm done for the night. This is all too much. You are not to leave. Take CJ's bed. It's clean and freshly laundered." I got up from the couch and went to stand beside his chair, needing to give him a reassuring gesture, but not sure what it should be.

He tangled our fingers together. "You're a good man, Charlie Brown."

"So are you, Shaun O'Malley. So are you." I squeezed his fingers and walked away.

SEVEN

Trevor closed the office door behind him and sat on the edge of the chair in front of my desk. "So I just had a weird phone call."

I glanced up and frowned, dragging my mind from the expense sheets on the computer. Something was hinky with them, I just couldn't quite see what yet. Wait. "A phone call?" My heart slammed in my chest. "Like a Tom phone call?"

"No, no, no. Sorry, I didn't even think about that." He scooted back in the chair and shot me a judgmental glare. "Starla just called to say she'd cancelled Shaun's trip to Hawaii and I should do the same for you."

I sighed and rocked back in my chair. "I see."

Thursday morning had been awkward. Neither of us were morning people. And for damn sure neither of us were morning-after people. Shaun had tried to sneak out of the house before I awoke, but the sounds of his furtive movements had yanked me out of troubled dreams. I had the baseball bat in hand before I remembered I wasn't supposed to be alone in the house.

We'd met at the bedroom doors, which faced each other. I swallowed hard as he struggled to pull his shirt over his head. He still had an incredible physique, all smooth skin in hard planes and tight abs. I hadn't stopped to appreciate his body for twenty years, but I could immediately see why he still had no trouble getting women—and men, apparently—into his bed.

He'd stared at me, mouth agape, when his head popped through the opening in the fabric. "I didn't mean to wake you."

I shrugged and covered a yawn. “It’s okay. Take a shower before you go. I’ll make coffee.”

“That’s not necessary.”

I moved past him toward the kitchen. “You’ll feel better.”

“Hank. Stop.”

I turned in time to see him grimace.

“I can’t forget that I told you. And you can’t deal with remembering that I told you. So I’m going to go.” He met my eyes for half a second before looking away again. “You take a few days, figure out what you need to figure out. Then call me. We’ll go from there. But right now, I can’t do this. I can’t pretend everything’s normal when it’s the farthest fucking thing from normal.”

Before I could say anything to refute his logic, he patted me on the shoulder and walked out of the house. Possibly forever.

“Boss?”

Trevor’s voice brought me out of the memory. I glanced at him. “That’s probably a good idea.”

Trevor’s eyes boggled. “He told you!”

“Told me what? You mean you knew? Wait, what are you talking about?”

“He did!” Trevor’s face turned sympathetic. “What did you say? Did you let him down easy?”

“I didn’t have to,” I answered reluctantly. “He did that himself.” I jammed my hands through my hair. “I don’t know what to do, Trev. He says it started in college. Have I been leading him on that long? Have I ever given him hope that we could be together?”

“Don’t be silly. You don’t get to take responsibility for Shaun's feelings. They’re his own. He’s a big boy. He knew what he was getting into by maintaining his friendship with you. That was more important to him than losing you altogether.”

“How do you know all this?”

This time Trevor looked uncomfortable. “We may have dated a few times a couple of years ago.”

I gawped at him. "Well I didn't see that one coming. Are there any more secrets people would like to share with me?"

He shrugged. "Sorry. I didn't think it was something you'd want to know. As soon as I figured out that he was in love with you, I broke it off. I promised him I'd never tell you. There wasn't any reason to. You were happily married to Tom."

I rubbed my forehead. "Well I guess I appreciate the honesty now. I'm sorry it didn't work out for you two."

He waved away my words. "He was fun, but it wasn't meant to be." He held up a finger and tapped the portable telephone device in his ear and got up to leave the room. "Henry Cooley's office," he said as he closed the door behind him.

I considered his words as I pretended to read emails. If I hadn't been able to detect Shaun's level of feelings in twenty-plus years, did that mean he was really good at hiding them, or was I just a really bad friend? I could be overly self-involved at times, but that was giving him far too little credit. In all those years, he'd never once dropped a clue that he was emotionally drawn to men, let alone sexually interested in them.

I frowned at the screen. He'd gotten most of what he wanted—he was the person I loved the most in the world after Tom and CJ. I wasn't sure my feelings for him would ever evolve into something romantic, but those were thoughts for another day. I decided I'd take his advice and give us each the weekend to nurse our wounds. Then I'd call him on Monday and give him hell for cancelling a vacation he'd coerced me into in the first place. My shoulders felt lighter just from putting that madness to rest in my brain.

I AWOKE with a jerk and immediately fell off the bed. "Ouch. Mother*fucker!*" I covered my ears with my hands as I rolled to my knees and tried to stand up, despite the almost physical force of the blaring alarm keeping me pinned to the floor.

I struggled to my feet with the help of the nightstand and stumbled into the living room where the damn strobe lights made everything freaky as shit. I blinked rapidly, but that only increased the effect of the strobes. I darted back to bedroom and grabbed CJ's baseball bat from beneath the bed. I slipped my cell phone into the pocket of my sleep pants, knowing the alarm company would be calling momentarily.

Stumbling through the living room with all the grace of, well, something very much devoid of any, I was finally able to clear the strobes and cancel the cacophony. Through the ringing in my ears, I could hear my cell chirping away.

"Cooley," I barked into it out of habit.

"Mr. Cooley, we have a report of a breach of your system at the back door. Are you safe?"

"Yes, I—I think so." I shook away the after-effects of the alarm and headed for the kitchen—where the back door stood wide open. "Shit! Someone really broke in!" Even though the whole world had just exploded in a freak show of sound and light, I was actually surprised to see it hadn't been just a misfire in the system.

"Mr. Cooley, the police have been notified and are on the way. We suggest you confine yourself to your safe place until they arrive and make sure the intruder is gone."

Whatever. I went to the door and pushed it closed. "No, no, that's okay. It's been raining all day. I don't see any wet prints on the tiles."

"Uhm."

"Yeah, I know. You're doing your job and I'm supposed to cooperate. Don't worry. I'm fine. I'll wait for the police on the front porch." I pulled the back door open to confirm what I thought I could make out through the ringing in my ears. "I can hear them already. Thank you for calling."

"Thank you for using our services, Mr. Cooley. If we can be of further service, please feel free to call. Also remember to reset your system once the police have been there."

"I'll do that. Thank you." I wanted nothing more than to tell her to go to hell and that I wasn't waking up like that ever again. But the fact that I had woken up to a blaze of light and sound proved I needed to use the thing. I ended the call and left the phone on the counter in the kitchen.

In the living room, I'd just pulled open the front door when three uniformed officers with guns drawn came through the front gate. I dropped the baseball bat. It met the wood of the front step with a wet clatter. I immediately put my hands up so they wouldn't mistake the bare-chested, pajama-clad, middle-aged dude for a burglar.

"Are you okay, Henry?"

I recognized Mary Beth's voice and smiled. "I'm fine. They tried to come in through the back door. The alarm scared them away." Immediately two officers peeled away in opposite directions to check the rear of the property.

As soon as I said the words, the reality of the situation coursed through my body. Someone had tried to get into my home while I was sleeping. Someone *had* gotten into the house! The back door had been wide open! If that alarm hadn't gone off, would he have murdered me in my sleep? Or would he have wakened me, just to torture me before he killed me?

Mary Beth grabbed me by the elbow. "Henry, you're shaking. Let's go back inside."

I nodded dumbly and let her lead me into the living room. I collapsed into one of the chairs and she perched on the edge of the couch in front of me. I didn't miss that it was a reversal of the positions we'd been in last time she was here. At least this time it wasn't because Shaun had called her to cover his ass. Or mine. Or whatever.

"Can you tell me what happened?"

I blinked at her, almost surprised she was real. "I—the alarm woke me up. I fell out of bed and turned it off. The alarm, not the bed." I frowned. "Am I making sense?"

She grinned and continued making notes in her small flip-top notebook. "You're doing just fine, Henry. What else can you tell me?"

"Uh, I turned off the alarm. Then the lady said he was at the back door, so I went to check."

"What lady, Henry? The alarm company lady?"

"Yeah. She called."

"Okay, good. And what did you find at the back door?"

"It was standing open. But there weren't any footprints inside, so I knew the noise had scared him off." I swallowed hard. "Jesus, this is really happening, isn't it?"

"I'm afraid so." She said it kindly, as though she'd had a lot of practice with people not quite believing the experience they'd just been through.

The other two officers, another woman and a man, both young and handsome in their uniforms, came in through the front door.

Mary Beth stood and offered introductions. "This is Officers Jane Ramirez and my partner, Tony Shipley."

They both nodded.

"We have tracks in mud. I'm guessing we'll be able to get good prints from them. Maybe from the back door, too," Officer Shipley said. "You should know those probably won't do much good, depending on how many people come in and out of here and how infrequently they're cleaned." He shuddered as if the thought of all those unclean doorknobs repulsed him.

I looked at Mary Beth. "I'd better call Dev."

EIGHT

"You look like death."

I gave Trevor a baleful glare and continued into my office. "Thank you."

He followed, as usual. "Are you okay, Henry?"

I fell into my chair and stared up at him. "No, not really. On the bright side, your brother's alarm system works perfectly. It scared off the intruder I had at 4 a.m. Saturday morning."

He gasped. "Are you serious? Wow. I'm so glad we got it installed then. What happened? Are you okay?"

"I'm fine. I'm just exhausted waiting for something to happen. There haven't been any more attempts on the house and I haven't had another phone call. Not from Tom. Not from Dev. Not from Shaun. Not from the police. I spent the weekend trying to distract myself from everything." I grimaced. "It didn't work as well as I'd hoped."

I tapped the button to wake my computer, trying and failing to work up excitement about what could be waiting in my email inbox. Maybe Ossi had figured out another way to screw the company even further over the weekend.

"Are you still on the outs with Shaun?"

I blew air between my lips. "I'm not on the outs with Shaun. I'm just not quite...ready to see him yet. It's weird."

Trevor tsked. "It's your personal life, so it's none of my business. But, if you wanted my advice—"

"I don't."

"—I'd tell you he's still the same guy you've known forever. He's your best friend before anything else. It's only awkward if you let it be." He made a little bow. "I'm done now."

I tried to hide a smile. "Good. I was going to have to give you more work."

As usual he batted away my words like the idle threats they were. "You and I both know that wouldn't make any difference."

I laughed for the first time that morning. "You're right. I do know it. Now get out of here. One of us has work to do, even if you don't."

I made shooing motions until the door closed behind him. As much of a pain in the ass as he was, he was also the biggest reason I came to work every day.

I typed my password in the required login box, but instead of immediately opening the email program, I opened Word. I'd just typed the salutation when Trevor's disembodied voice sounded from the desk phone.

"Dev needs to see you when you get a minute. They've found something on the recording."

My heart jumped. "Tell him I'll be there in ten minutes."

"Will do."

I turned back to the document and finished typing my resignation letter, effective Friday.

I'd had it. I needed a vacation and a new vocation. Shaun was right about that at least. I had more than enough money to live comfortably for the rest of my life. I didn't need to put up with Ossi Aaltonen's shit anymore.

I printed the document and added my signature, feeling pretty damn pleased with myself. I stuffed it in an envelope from my desk and headed for the door.

I dropped the envelope on Trevor's desk with a sense of satisfaction. My world might be spinning out in front of my very eyes, but I was damn sure taking the first step in regaining control of it. "Make sure Yolanda in Human Resources gets this as soon as possible, please."

Trevor's wide-eyed gaze locked with mine. "You know you're taking me wherever you go, don't you?"

"I don't know what I'm doing next, Trev."

"Doesn't matter. I'm going with you."

I laughed. "Get to work on your own, then, kid. We have a new life to explore."

"About fucking time!" His ecstatic grin was enough to brighten my entire day.

DORIS SHOWED me to Dev's office, though I could have found it on my own. I decided she must be the busybody type, like Mildred or Millicent or whatever her name was on *Remington Steele*.

Dev rose as soon as I walked in, a half grin spreading his lips. "Henry, thanks for coming so quickly."

I strode across the room and shook his outstretched hand. "I'm hoping you have good news." I was feeling strangely loose, almost giddy. Signing my resignation letter had made me feel twenty years younger. Being here with Dev gave me hope that the weirdness of the last few weeks was almost over. I didn't know how I wanted it to end, I just knew I wanted it over.

That wasn't entirely true. I'd have given anything for Tom to be alive, but I hadn't convinced myself that was possible.

"I do. I do," Dev said, dragging my attention away from my thoughts. "Let's go talk to Scott, our audio specialist. I don't want to get anything wrong." He came around the desk and gestured for me to precede him out the door.

We turned left down the hall, walking past three offices in which casually dressed employees worked diligently on their computers. I almost laughed as inspiration struck. "You wouldn't have a couple of open positions, would you, Dev?"

He shot me a startled look. "Employment positions?" He grinned. "Are you thinking about giving up the life of luxury way up in the tower?"

I laughed. "First, it's never been that luxurious. Second, it's already done. I gave my letter of resignation to Trevor to send to HR before I came down here. He's working up his right now."

Dev whistled lowly. "You work quickly, don't you?"

"It's been coming for at least five years. I've hated my job since Aaltonen bought the company. It's pretty sad."

He paused in front of a closed door and rapped his knuckles against it three times. "Let me see what we're in the market for and I'll get back to you."

I shook my head and smiled. "I was really only kidding. I doubt I'm cut out for the detective gig."

He chuckled. "You never know."

The door opened behind him to reveal a wiry youth with wildly curling fire-engine red hair and glasses sucking on the straw of a juice box. I almost laughed. This kid wasn't at all what I had been expecting, but the juice box was a nice touch.

"Boss, boss, come in. I assume this is Henry?" He extended a hand that I shook before he swiftly led us into the room. He removed some tech magazines from the two chairs that weren't in front of a computer and gestured for us to sit. The nervous energy pumping through my body dictated that I remain standing. Dev followed my lead.

The large room was a maze of technology. I counted at least six different work stations, each with a desktop, laptop, and what looked like a tablet. Headphones hung from the upper cabinets at each station, ensuring, I supposed, that no one's work bled over into another person's ears. Three glass booths occupied the width of the far wall. They, too, were packed with tech. We three were the only people in the room, which seemed a bit odd for all the money on display.

Scott fiddled with headphone plugins, his movements quick but sure. I was sure he wasn't nervous about Dev being there, he was just one of those people who couldn't sit still without fidgeting, which made his career choice somewhat baffling.

He handed Dev and me headsets, keeping one for himself. "Okay, first we'll listen to the audio as we would hear it. Then I'll show you what it really is."

I glanced at Dev. He nodded and donned his headphone. I decided to follow his lead, slipping the large cups over my ears. Immediately I could tell they were the noise-cancelling variety, but much better than the ones I had on my computer at home.

Scott spoke into a microphone attached to his headset, his voice coming through my speakers. "Here we go." He pressed a key on his keyboard and my ears immediately filled with sound.

"Henry. Help me."

I shivered at the sound of Tom's voice reverberating in my head. It was so much more intimate than a phone call. I could almost swear I felt him standing behind me, speaking into my ear. My eyes stung as tears threatened. I fought them back and sank heavily into the chair beside me.

Dev's hand on my shoulder startled me. "I'm sorry, Henry. I didn't even think how that would sound to you."

I shook my head and swallowed hard. "No, it's okay. It just caught me off guard. I'm fine. Let's keep going."

Scott watched, his eyes darting between us. "Are you sure?" he asked.

"Yes." I cleared my throat. "I need to know what's going on. Keep going."

He grinned, obviously pleased that he could show off the fruits of his labor. "Okay, this time I want you to watch the monitor as I play it again."

I nodded. Scott hit the keyboard again.

"Henry. Help me."

I gasped as the graph on the monitor showed an enormous spike between the two sentences. I jumped up and pointed at it. "What does that mean? It means something, right?"

Scott smiled widely. "Yep. It sure does. It means a splice. Those two sentences weren't originally spoken together. That is not a live call. It's a recording. Actually two recordings—"

"We get that, Scott," Dev laughed.

"Right, of course. But that's not all!" He bounced on the balls of his feet like a little kid getting his favorite treat. "This time I'm going to filter out everything but the background noise. Whoever did this was pretty good. He just isn't as good as I am."

I nodded the go ahead. My headphones filled with white noise for a second before I heard "—ista?" followed by "—ome to Coffee to—"

I gasped. "Oh my god!" I turned wide eyes to Dev. He grinned widely and held his hand up for Scott to high five.

"Well done, Scott!" he said.

"Yeah—yes! Great job." I sank back into the chair and pulled the headphones off. I handed them to Scott and steepled my hands over my mouth, trying to arrange in my brain what I'd just heard.

Someone at Coffee to the People had recorded Tom in conversation, spliced a few words together, and used that to terrorize me. Tom wasn't alive after all. I hadn't been ignoring his pleas for help because he hadn't been the one to make them. I swallowed hard and bent over as the tears finally fell.

I barely heard Scott excuse himself, but I felt Dev's hand on my shoulder. "You didn't do anything wrong, Henry. It's okay to feel relief."

It was almost like losing Tom a third time. As impossible as it had seemed to my logical mind, and as much as I had resisted, as long as those phone calls kept coming, I could hold out some hope that it had all been a series of misunderstandings. I could allow myself to hope that the love of my life was still out there somewhere. The truth was I had hoped Scott would say the call was genuine. Instead it was almost the final proof that Tom was really gone.

I allowed myself a few minutes to grieve before forcing the pieces of me back together. When Dev was sure I was ready to proceed, he left to find the man who'd so excitedly doused my last hopes.

Scott followed Dev back in the room, his more sedate movements telling me how uncomfortable and sad he felt for me. Studying the tapes may have been a game of 'gotcha' to him, but now he realized exactly how much they changed my life.

"I'm sorry, Henry," he offered as he sat at his computer.

"Thank you, Scott. I really appreciate your hard work. I'd still be going through hell if it weren't for you." I smiled tremulously at him, hoping he understood that I truly was grateful.

He nodded. "There's only one more thing. The video from your security cameras show the person trying to break into your house. They caught a glimpse of his face. Some noise in the distance must have startled him because it's the only time he looks up." He turned to the computer and typed away. Moments later a video played on his monitor. I almost missed the split second or two the bastard's face flashed toward the camera. It didn't matter, though, because I couldn't recognize him.

"I was able to enhance those few frames," Scott continued, typing away again. This time a still photo filled the screen. I shook my head at the first one. It was no help. The second wasn't either. But the third one was a dead-on shot of the son of a bitch's face.

"Motherfucker. I know him." I wanted to beat the living shit out of him now that I knew who he was. I never would have guessed. "I can't believe it."

"Video doesn't lie," Scott offered hastily.

"No, I know." I patted his shoulder. "I just meant I would have sworn on my life he wasn't involved."

"We were also able to match him to the shoe pattern the police captured," Dev said. "They're a limited-quantity sports star brand. Only seventeen stores in town carry them. Three of them sold shoes in his size. And one of those sales happened to have his name on the credit card used to pay for them."

I felt the rage rising. "We gotcha, you sick son of a bitch." I turned to Dev. "Let's go get him."

He chuckled. "Slow down, Lone Ranger. We aren't the police. We can't just go put him under citizen's arrest."

I sighed, pissed off that we couldn't just go shove the evidence in his face and demand an explanation. "Right. So we need to show all this to the cops."

Dev grinned. "Already done. I knew you'd want to be part of taking the bastard down, so your friend Mary Beth and I worked out a scenario." He winked. "I'll fill you in on the way."

KRIS, LINC, and a new guy were behind the counter when Dev and I walked into Coffee to the People. I spotted Mary Beth and her partner, Shipley, having a sandwich and coffee at a table near the front door. I winked at her as I walked by. She nodded slightly, a smile playing at her lips.

Kris greeted me enthusiastically as usual but was too busy taking orders to break away for another hug. I was glad of that. I felt awkward enough as it was. Linc waved and continued turning coffee into foam or whatever he was doing. The new guy looked around like he was missing something.

Dev and I took positions in Kris' line waiting patiently for our turn to order. I broke habit and ordered an iced chai tea and Dev ordered an avocado BLT on wheat and an iced white mocha. I whispered to Kris a request that Linc bring our order to the table when they were ready. She acquiesced without question or concern, which only made me feel worse.

I hated that Kris was going to be hurt by what was about to go down, but I couldn't do anything about it. I supposed we could have taken him outside or tried to catch him at his apartment, but neither Dev nor I had that sort of patience. And the SFPD knew exactly where he was at the moment, so why would they wait until he may or may not be home?

"Stop thinking," Dev said from across the small table.

"I can't help it. I'm disappointed and confused."

"And angry," he supplied helpfully.

I nodded. "That too."

A few minutes later, Linc shuffled up to the table, sporting a happy smile and a small tray laden with our orders.

"You're trying something new today, Henry. I asked Kris twice just to make sure."

I smiled up at him. "I thought I would live on the edge for a change."

"Careful you don't fall off," he said with a laugh, placing Dev's sandwich in front of him.

"Do you get your hand stuck in that rip in the lining of the left arm, Linc? Tom always did, but he'd never let me get it fixed."

He frowned. "What?"

I nodded encouragingly. "You know, in the jacket you stole from my house."

He backed away a step. "I don't know what you're talking about, Henry. You've got the wrong guy." He smiled but his eyes darted to the front door.

"Okay," I said placatingly. "I just wondered, ya know, since we have you on tape wearing it when you broke into my house the other night."

Linc's eyes widened. Before I could blink, he'd dropped the tray and bolted for the door. He made it three yards before Officer Shipley's well-place foot sent Linc crashing to the ground.

"Oops," Shipley mumbled, dropping down to a knee and quickly cuffed Linc, who struggled against the restraints.

"Do you have anything in your pockets that will hurt me?" the big cop asked. "Any knives, needles, or other sharp objects? Any drugs?"

"Get off me!" Linc yelled, squirming on the floor.

"What's going on?!" Kris' panicked cry echoed through the shop.

"Linc Stafford, you're under arrest for harassment, breaking and entering, and felony theft," Mary Beth said. She recited the *Miranda* warning, to which Linc's only reply was a grunt.

Kris looked at me in astonishment. I could only offer a shrug and a sympathetic half smile.

Shipley frisked Linc, pulling a cell phone out of his jeans pocket. He handed it to Mary Beth who handed it to Dev who thumbed through it until he found what he was looking for. He pressed a button.

"Henry. Help me."

"He killed him!" Linc shouted. "He killed Tom, I know he did!"

I opened my mouth but Dev's quick shake of the head made me shut it again.

"He killed him." Linc was crying now, as if the reality of Tom's death had hit him anew. "I loved him and he killed him." He twisted around to glare at me. "And now you have to die too."

Mary Beth gave a slow clap. "Congratulations, genius. Now you're under arrest for stalking and terroristic threats. Anything else you'd like to say?"

Kris gasped beside me, her hand flying to cover her open mouth.

"He's been calling me for two weeks, playing that recording," I told her.

"Oh my god, Henry, I'm so sorry!" She looked like she was about to burst into tears.

I pulled her into a hug as Mary Beth and Shipley took Linc away.

"That is one bad barista," Dev said with a straight face.

EPILOGUE

"So what are you working on now?" Shaun asked as he put the turkey in the pull-out freezer.

I grinned over the bag of groceries I was putting away. CJ would arrive for Thanksgiving in less than four hours. It would be the first time I'd seen him since he checked on me after my return from Crazytown. It had been a long few months. I missed my boy. "It's a pre-divorce case again. Husband number one is pretty sure husband number two is off-shoring a lot of their net worth before number two files for divorce so he can marry his nineteen-year-old model boyfriend."

Shaun laughed. "Sounds like a lot more fun than anything you did at Excellere."

"It is! I'm loving it. Who knew forensic accounting could be so much fun?"

The last three months had been a whirlwind of change. Immediately after I left Excellere for the last time, Shaun whisked me away to Hawaii, where we spent nine glorious days relaxing in the sun and surf. I hadn't felt so young or free since college.

We'd stayed up late every night, talking, drinking, and giggling like school girls over shared memories and new experiences. It had been one of those nights, about three days into the vacation, that I'd summoned the nerve to kiss him.

It was a stupid thing to do. We'd both enjoyed it too much until the guilt kicked in. I couldn't lead him on, not when I still didn't have the DNA confirmation that Tom truly was in that grave. If there was any possibility that he was still alive, then we were still married. I'd never cheated on him before and I never would. I could see the pain in Shaun's eyes when I explained why we had to stop, but there was also understanding and hope.

As time healed the wound, I was increasingly certain that the DNA results would show my husband lay beneath our tree. It was only Linc's parlor tricks and the fact that no one but Matthew's lawyer had seen the dental comparisons that had kept me from believing Tom was gone. It hurt to contemplate life without him, but it was starting to seem like a less monumental task.

Part of that was starting the new job with Dev—and Doris, which actually was her name. Trevor was thrilled to be able to flirt with Dev all day, every day. I wasn't so sure they were only flirting. Neither of them would ever admit to it in the office, but my newly-learned detective's instincts told me they were fucking like bunnies every chance they got.

I tossed Shaun the bags of frozen green beans and dark cherries which he batted out of the air and into the freezer before nudging it shut with his knee. He'd called his mother for the amazing stuffing recipe, which he was going to make from scratch tomorrow. Nothing like a trial run on the day of. I needed to bake a cherry pie for CJ tonight. The kid hated pumpkin-flavored anything, which was a sure sign he was adopted. His father and I both loved pumpkin pie, but only once a year, and only two slices each—with inches and inches of whipped cream on them. "Shouldn't we be thawing the turkey overnight?"

He crossed his eyes. "I don't know. I've never made the turkey. Eating it is as domestic as I've ever been around one."

I laughed. "You're a dork." I was so grateful that we were back. Our friendship was as strong as it had ever been. If the new sexual tinge to the teasing occasionally caught me by surprise, it wasn't unwelcome. It just had to wait.

He pulled the freezer back open and searched the bird for directions. "Did you put all the Hawaii photos on the tablet so CJ can see what you were up to for a week?"

"Yes, dear. Although I skipped the ones where you kept mooning me. I don't need my kid to see your bare ass." I folded up the empty bags and stowed them in the cabinet.

"But it's my best side!" he protested with feigned hurt.

I groaned and reached around him to grab a bottle of water from the fridge.

He traced a knuckle down my cheek. "Are you saying you like my pretty face?"

"I'm saying you might not have a best side."

"Harsh, dude!" He snatched the bottle from me, spun on his heel, and marched into the living room.

"Hey!"

"You don't deserve water after that comment!" he shouted over his shoulder.

I laughed and grabbed another bottle. I'd just cracked open the lid when my cell rang. I grabbed it and answered with my last name as usual.

"Hey, it's Justin."

I braced myself. "What's up?"

"You'd better sit down for this, Henry."

I swallowed hard and looked into the living room where Shaun sat on the couch, thumbing through a magazine, blissfully unaware that our lives were about to change forever, one way or the other. Ice cold fear ricocheted through my body. "Tell me," I whispered.

"The DNA test results are back. We don't know who's buried in Tom's grave, but it isn't Tom."

To be continued...

AUTHOR'S NOTE

Some of you may remember that I started Vanished as a book my Dad could read—a sample of my writing that didn't have any on-page or implied sex. When he died, I didn't intend to continue the story, but enough people asked me for more, that I finally gave in. I had more in my head anyway, why not write it down? Of course, nothing you just read was in my head at the time.

Because I hadn't planned to continue the story, I used the name of a real-life coffee shop in San Francisco. *Coffee to the People is real. The people I wrote about in it are not. There is no Linc in reality.* Do not assume you'll be stalked or harassed if you go there. I've heard it's a pretty awesome place.

VANISHED 3

DEDICATION

For my three sisters.
Thank you for allowing me to survive my childhood. I think. Honestly, thanks for forty-plus years of constant support. I appreciate it more than you know.
I love you.

ACKNOWLEDGEMENTS

Most of you know *Vanished* was a labor of love for my father. Sadly, he passed before I finished the first draft. I've had a love/hate relationship with this series since then. It will always be special because of its attachment to him; and it will always be especially difficult for the same reason.

I adore Henry and the boys. I'm so pleased that you do too. This is the end of their journey (at least as far as I know). I hope I've given you a satisfying conclusion. Thank you so much for sticking in there with me these last fifteen months.

As always, a tremendous thank you to my beta readers. I asked a lot in a short period of time and you all came through brilliantly. This book wouldn't be half as good without you.

ACKNOWLEDGMENTS

ONE

I nudged Shaun with my hip, urging him out of the way, as I bent to pull an apple pie out of the oven. Thanksgiving had been such a rousing success with just the three of us, me, Shaun, and CJ, that we'd decided to up the ante a bit by inviting my boss Blaine Deveraux and Trevor Jourdan, my personal assistant turned colleague, to celebrate Christmas Eve with us.

I had started to invite Tom's best friend, Jamie and his wife, Katie, but I hadn't heard from them since the day I called to apologize to Jamie for calling him from my seat on the express train to Crazytown. He hadn't known I'd misplaced reality; for him, his best friend had died months earlier, so he'd shown no patience when, in my delirium, I'd called to ask if he'd heard from Tom. He'd been on the way to the hospital with a very pregnant wife in the throes of labor, so I couldn't blame him for blowing me off then. Katie had given birth to their son Chadwick James, Jr, that evening. I hadn't been asked to be his godfather, as Tom and I had with their older daughter, Maya. The rejection smarted, but I understood. Jamie was Tom's friend, as Shaun was mine. Looking back, I could see that he'd always kept me at a polite distance.

I shook off the lingering disappointment about that failed friendship and concentrated on happier thoughts. CJ was due to arrive from LA any minute. I set the pie on the cooling rack and picked up my glass of wine.

I was excited to see my boy, but I was also nervous as hell. We had a lot to discuss. A month earlier I'd only had three hours between Justin's phone call and CJ's early arrival. I'd barely been able to wrap my mind around the news about the body in Tom's grave; I certainly hadn't had a chance to decide how to tell CJ about it. When he'd gotten to the house, he'd been as happy as one could expect him to be while confronting his first Thanksgiving without one of his dads.

I'd struggled with the idea of sharing Justin's update with him, but in the end, I just couldn't do it. CJ's happiness was my first concern. How could I possibly strip away the little bit of peace he'd been able to find in the last seven months? It was bad enough he'd had to deal with my excursion to Crazytown. To tell him that his dad might not be dead—but that we didn't know for sure—seemed cruel and unnecessary.

At that point, we hadn't known anything other than that the dental records for Tom and whoever was in that grave didn't match—not by a long shot, as it turned out. Tom had all of his teeth. Whoever occupied his grave had veneers and several implants.

We didn't know much more now. Getting DNA from a burnt corpse and matching it with the national databases was a slow, agonizing process. It made me wish the instant results those television shows were always portraying weren't mere works of fiction.

Dev was keeping me well away from the case, which didn't lessen my frustration. He and his best investigator, Shelby Haynes, were working it as hard as they could, but there was little to go on at the moment. Dev assured me that the whole thing would burst wide open as soon as we identified the occupant of Tom's grave.

I hoped with all my heart and soul that my husband was alive, but I was terrified to believe it. I wasn't sure I could survive learning—again—that he was dead. How many times could I lose him in one lifetime? The first time had literally driven me beyond the brink of insanity. The second time I'd been able to handle better, but a third time? No. Not until we were old and gray and praying for death. He had to be alive so we could spoil grandchildren together like we'd talked about so many times.

The terrifying thought of which brought me back to CJ. The little bastard had better not be making me a grandfather any time soon. His grandfather had said he was more circumspect in his sexual encounters than Tom and I had been, but I didn't really know what that meant. I wasn't sure I wanted to either. Who CJ chose to bed was none of my business. He'd never come out to Tom and I as favoring either sex. He'd done the usual hetero boy stuff in high school, but so had we. He was also an artist, with a creative brain that amazed me as often as it made me proud. His sexuality didn't matter to me one way or another. I only hoped he could find a love as strong as the one his father and I shared. If he did, he'd be an incredibly lucky man.

"Have you decided whether to tell him or not?"

I shot Shaun a dirty look. "No. Either way I go, it's the wrong decision."

He cocked his dark head. "Really?"

"Yes." I sipped more wine. "If I don't tell him, then I've been keeping secrets from him. If I do tell him and we don't find Tom alive, I've put him through hell all over again for nothing."

Shaun popped a small radish in his mouth and chewed thoughtfully. "But if you do find Tom alive, won't you want him to be prepared for that eventuality ahead of time?"

I took a deep breath and exhaled slowly. "At that point, I don't think he'd care if he knew it was a possibility. He'd just be so excited to see his dad again that nothing else would matter. I just don't want to hurt him. He's been through enough."

"He's a strong kid, Hank. He'll be fine either way."

"I know. But I'm his dad. I'm supposed to protect him, not test his strength."

A clatter and clunk from the front door sent Shaun diving for the alarm keypad to disarm it before the whole world of light and sound crashed down on us. Peace and love flooded through me as I heard my kid call out, "Dad? I'm home."

I raced to the front door, too excited to see him to pretend otherwise. As he straightened from setting his duffle bag on the floor, I burst out laughing and pulled him into a hug. He'd shaved his blond hair close to the scalp, leaving a 3-inch tall Mohawk dyed in red and green stripes. "Your grandmother is going to have kittens."

I felt his body shake with laughter as he returned my tight hug. "Don't worry, I brought a beanie. She'll never see it."

I pulled back and held him at arm's length to get a good look at him. Damn, he was a good-looking kid, even with red and green hair. His brown eyes sparkled with mischief, his skin glowed with youth and good health. He'd been hitting the gym more since going to LA, so I knew his clothes hid a fit, muscular body. "I don't know how it's possible, but you look more like your dad every day."

CJ grinned. "I'll take that compliment. Pops was pretty hot for an old guy."

I cuffed the back of his head playfully. "Watch it, mister. You're not too big for me to turn over my knee quite yet."

He laughed. "Love you, too, Dad." Movement behind me caught his attention. "Uncle Shaun!" he shouted and ran to wrap my best friend in a tight hug.

I watched with twin pangs of sadness and anger as they hugged and tussled good-naturedly. Our boy was growing into his own man and Tom was missing it. Whoever took him away from us would pay dearly.

THE LIGHTS on the tree twinkled away in the darkened living room, mocking me with their festive charm. The tree was only there because Shaun had ambushed me with it. I'd completely forgotten about decorating. If CJ hadn't been coming home, the house would still look like it felt on a daily basis without Tom—cold and empty. Instead, Shaun had made me drag the boxes out of the garage and help him put everything together.

He'd made up stories for some of the uglier decorations Tom and I had kept from our poor college student days. I'd laughed as Shaun had given them voices and histories. According to him, the Santa in the sleigh had stolen the wife and reindeer of the Santa who hung by the top of his hat, and the snow globe had been the scene of the crime. It was a ribald tale, full of sex and shotguns and naughty lists.

He'd held me as I'd cried when it was all over and the realization had started to sink in that Tom was going to miss this holiday with me and our son. Grief shadowed me, a constant companion growing darker as Christmas grew nearer and Tom seemed farther away than ever.

I nursed a glass of wine, waiting for CJ to emerge from his shower. Shaun had shooed me out of the kitchen minutes earlier, claiming it was his turn to clean up. I wasn't about to argue with him. I was sure the fact that he had a creepy fascination with my dishwasher had something to do with his enthusiasm to tidy up.

It was now or never. Either I told CJ about his dad now, or I waited until we knew for certain what had happened on that cold, snowy February day. I still didn't know which tack to take.

Listening to CJ and Shaun razz each other over dinner had only served to reinforce my resentment of Tom's absence. While I'd been too stunned by the news to sort out my emotions during the Thanksgiving holiday, a month on, I had filed and refiled them enough to know two things: I loved my husband more now than the day he'd disappeared, and I would move heaven and earth to find him and whoever did this to my family.

There wasn't a single possibility this was an accident. Whoever this man in Tom's grave was, he'd been driving my husband's Jeep—without Tom in it. That led to several possibilities.

Tom could have been killed or severely wounded in a carjacking. If he'd suffered head trauma, there was a possibility he was wandering around anywhere in the one hundred eighty-six miles between San Francisco and Truckee, Nevada, without any memories of who he was. If he'd been killed, then his body was out there somewhere, waiting for me to bring him home.

He could have picked up a hitchhiker. We'd done it once before, early in our relationship, when he'd been traveling from LA to his parents' vineyard. A rare monsoon-style rain had come out of nowhere, intent on drowning everything in its path. We'd stopped to pick up a kid about our age who'd been trying to get from Los Olivos to Pismo Beach. We were young and dumb and invincible. The kid had been almost comically thankful that we'd stopped. He'd counted twenty-six cars that had passed him without even slowing after the rains began. We'd dropped him at his girlfriend's house in Pismo without incident. I wondered whatever happened to that kid. Had he and his girl gotten married and lived happily ever after? Regardless, I didn't truly believe my older, wiser husband would pick up a hitchhiker, especially not while he was alone.

A distant possibility was that the person who'd been killed in Tom's Jeep was also his kidnapper. Perhaps he'd stashed Tom somewhere and had used the Jeep to go to some payphone to make his ransom demands known. Were there still payphones out in the boonies? If that was the case, it was likely Tom had died a slow, miserable death waiting for someone to come back. I couldn't bear to think about that possibility. It was too horrible to allow into my mind.

"Dad?"

I swung my gaze away from the tree to find CJ standing just inside the room, bare except for the towel wrapped securely around his waist. Droplets of water glistened on his chest and rippled stomach. My little boy was a man. Sometimes I forgot. I smiled at his near-nakedness. It was another trait he'd picked up from his father. The fewer clothes Tom could wear at any given time, the happier he was. I, on the other hand, was much more modest. "What's up, naked boy?"

He grinned. "Just making sure you're alright. You looked a million miles away."

"I've got about that many things on my mind. Why don't you put on some clothes and come join me? I need to talk to you about something."

His forehead creased with a frown. "Are you okay?"

"I'm right as rain, son." Physically, anyway.

He moved further into the room, resting a knee on the arm of the couch. "You've seemed a lot happier since you quit Excellere, but today's different, isn't it? Is it just because you're missing Pops?"

I swallowed hard to clear the lump of emotion from my throat. "You're a good kid, you know that? I miss your dad like crazy every day, but today is harder."

He smiled faintly. "He loved Christmas."

"It was his favorite holiday after your homecoming day."

He rolled his eyes. "That's not a holiday."

"It is around here. You're never going to convince us otherwise."

He smiled again. I saw the light dance off the extra water in his eyes. "You know I love you, right?"

"Of course I do. And Pops knew it too."

He nodded and slid his knee off the couch. "Let me get dressed. I'll be right back."

In the few minutes it took CJ to throw on sweats and a hoodie, Shaun emerged from the kitchen with a glass of eggnog for himself and CJ and a new glass of wine for me.

CJ thanked his uncle and sipped the eggy concoction greedily. He grimaced, confirming my suspicion that Shaun had enhanced it a bit. The two of them sat on the couch, gazing at the tree with matching contentment.

Seeing CJ in the gear that he'd favored so heavily in high school reminded me of how young he really was. He had been forced to mature at an early age, due to a biological mother who was too deep into her addiction to be saved, and an unknown sperm-donor father. By the time he'd come to us, he'd been such a strong kid already, determined that no one would find his weaknesses. It had taken a few months to win him over, but once he'd decided we were worth the effort, the amount of love the kid had been able to give and receive had blown Tom and me away.

We'd tried our best to make sure he never questioned our loyalty to or love for him. He'd lost a mother and one of his fathers, helped bring the other one back from the brink, and he was still a teenager for a few more months. I was so incredibly proud of him, which made hurting him like this even worse.

I smiled again at the audacity of his red and green-striped Mohawk. Even his rebellion was tame in comparison to some. He could have grown his hair out and gelled it into 8-inch spikes, but he hadn't. That wasn't him. He wasn't trying to cause a scene or get people to gawk at him; he simply wanted to celebrate his favorite holiday in a festive way.

I took a final, long sip of my wine and set it on the table beside my chair. Shaun caught my eye and excused himself to the kitchen. He had insisted on being nearby while I spilled the beans, just in case one or both of us needed another shoulder to cry on. I wanted to go sit with my son on the couch, but my fear of crowding him kept me rooted. "Ceej, I need to tell you something, but I'm not really sure how to do it."

He grinned at me. "Yia-yia always tells me to cut to the chase."

I rolled my eyes. "That's because your grandmother has the patience of a gnat."

"I thought that was the attention span of a gnat."

Was it? "I guess it is." I grabbed the wine again. This was more difficult than I'd expected. I couldn't force my tongue to create the words.

"Dad, what's wrong?"

I swallowed and stared into the blood-red liquid so I wouldn't have to watch the pain spread across my son's face. "You remember how Linc went a little off the deep end?"

I heard CJ shift on the couch. "He's not bothering you again, is he? Did they let him out on bail?"

I shook my head. "No, there's a pretty good chance he'll go away for a long time. I'm not convinced that's the right solution, but it's out of my hands now." I looked into my son's concerned brown eyes. "CJ, the person killed in your dad's Jeep wasn't him. We don't know who he was yet, but we're trying to find out."

"Wait. What?"

I swallowed hard, pushing the rest of the information out. "That means that whoever's in your dad's grave isn't him either. We had him exhumed and the—"

"Stop!" CJ launched to his feet, his hands trying to dig into his almost non-existent hair. "Dad, Pops is dead. We've been through this.

We went to the funeral. We mourned. You forgot and then Uncle Shaun made you remember again. Do you remember that?"

I cringed with shame. Of course his first thought would be that I'd taken the bullet train to Crazytown again. It made far more sense than the truth, or what little we knew of it. I rose from the chair and went to him. I put a hand on each of his shoulders to steady him. "It's true, Ceej. I remember everything. When Linc started stalking me, I contacted your grandfather. He hadn't looked at the dental comparisons between the body in the Jeep and your dad. He'd left that up to Hugh Lowe, who, as it turns out, didn't bother. They're not the same, son."

He started shaking his head in denial before I'd finished. His eyes filled before he squeezed them shut. "Don't. Dad, please. I can't take any more of this. Not now. Not tonight. Not when he should be here with us."

My own tears spilled over then, hot and heavy, as I pulled my son into a tight hug. "I'm so sorry," I whispered into his ear. "I miss him too."

The steel bands of his arms tightened around me as he released a keening wail over my shoulder. His tears fell, soaking the collar of my sweater. I didn't know if he'd cried for his loss since the time he'd come home to help me deal with the reality of Tom's death in July. It was probably good for him to get that poison out of his system, but was he continuing to grieve for no reason?

We had a glimmer of hope. It was possible Tom was still alive out there somewhere. If he was, we would find him or I would die trying. Those were the only options.

Two more strong arms surrounded us and Shaun's forehead nudged my temple. The relief I felt at his touch told me how badly this had gone. CJ didn't believe it. Hell, some mornings I didn't believe it either, and I'd seen all the tests.

"Is it true?" CJ whispered to Shaun, who nodded that it was. CJ broke away from both of us and crossed the room, a sudden rage flaring in his eyes. "What the hell is going on here?" He let out a frustrated growl that I could tell he'd barely kept from being a shout. "Is Pops dead or not?"

Shaun's hand on my forearm kept me from going to my son. "The simple truth," he said, "is that we don't know yet."

CJ's jaw dropped a bit before he closed and clenched it reflexively. "Fabulous."

"I know this is a lot to take in."

"Ya think? Let's break this down, shall we? First father number one dies. Then father number two goes insane because he doesn't remember that inconvenient little fact about father number one. Then a freaking stalker calls father number two and threatens to kill him because said stalker thinks father number two killed father number one to keep him away from said freaking stalker! Now father number two might not have been insane after all because father number one might not be dead. Well son number one is fed up to here—" he gestured wildly above his head "—with the whole damn thing! Jesus Christ, why can't anything in this family be simple?" He narrowed his eyes at Shaun. "You do know favorite uncle can't become father number three if father number one is still alive, right?"

TWO

Shaun recoiled like he'd been slapped at the same time I shouted, "CJ!"

He immediately put his hands up in surrender. "I'm sorry. I'm sorry. That was uncalled for. You've done nothing but try to help."

Shaun crossed to the bar. I watched his back muscles flex and flare under his long-sleeved Henley as he poured himself a glass of bourbon. I didn't have to see the glass to know it was more than his usual two fingers worth. He slammed half of it while CJ and I watched in silence.

I didn't expect him to retaliate at the kid, but I couldn't help wondering what was going through his mind. CJ might have been taking a shot in the dark with his last accusation, but it hit uncomfortably close to the truth, especially for someone who had been so carefully guarding his feelings for twenty-plus years.

Instead of saying anything, Shaun handed the glass to CJ. "Drink," he ordered.

CJ glanced at me for permission. I shrugged, interested to see where this would go. I knew better than to think it would be his first encounter with alcohol—or even second, considering Shaun had spiked their eggnog earlier. He'd had his first drunk with his high school football buddies. His father had made sure he'd sweated through his first hangover by cutting the front and back lawns with a manual push reel mower in the hot September sun.

CJ threw the bourbon back like water and I cringed, worried for his liver. He was a responsible kid, but he didn't flinch or suck in air like he would have done if he was unfamiliar with the deep burn of whiskey.

Shaun took the now-empty glass back, refilled it, and took a reasonable sip. "Do you have anything else to say right now or are you ready to listen?"

CJ's gaze dropped to the floor. "No, sir. I'm sorry. I didn't mean to be a jackass."

Shaun shrugged and pulled the kid in for a one-armed hug. "It happens to the best of us, some more than the rest. This is a fucked up situation. You're entitled to be confused and to lash out. Just remember that your dad and I aren't the enemy."

CJ swallowed hard and nodded. "I know."

Shaun kissed CJ's temple and pushed him toward the couch. "You know I couldn't love you more if you were my own kid—and that's saying something, given that I went to considerable lengths to make sure that would never happen."

The alarmed look CJ sent him as he reflexively covered his genital area caused his uncle and me to laugh. Typical Shaun. Diffusing the tension.

"Snip, snip." Shaun made the scissors motion with his free hand.

"Dude. There are some things I never need to know," CJ protested, sitting gingerly on the couch as if he'd just undergone the procedure.

Shaun laughed again as he led us back to the chairs facing the couch. The room had been rearranged a bit to accommodate the tree, but I'd made sure to keep a conversation area so it wouldn't be weird when there was more than just me in the house.

I sat in the chair next to Shaun's, picked up my wine again, took a grateful swallow. I was more than willing to allow Shaun to lead the discussion. It appeared my son was more willing to listen to him than to me. Perhaps because Shaun hadn't lost his sanity. Perhaps because Shaun had never lied to him. Perhaps just because Shaun wasn't his parental unit. At that point, it didn't matter why. I was just glad CJ had gotten past his denial stage so quickly—at least the beginnings of it. We still had a long way to go.

Shaun set his drink on the table between us and leaned forward, elbows on his knees. He rubbed his hands together, making sure he had CJ's undivided attention. "Are you ready to listen to this? If you're not, that's okay. We can wait until after Christmas, but your dad feels strongly that you know everything we know at this point."

CJ's Adam's apple bobbed with his swallow and his gaze bounced between me and his uncle. "I-I don't know. That's my honest answer. I'm afraid to hear what you're going to say, but Dad obviously thinks it's important that I hear it."

"Honestly, you've already heard the worst part." Shaun shrugged. "There are details that might help it all make sense in your head, but if it's too much to deal with right now, just say so and we'll wait."

CJ sighed and pointed at the bourbon beside Shaun. "Give me the rest of that and you can tell me anything you want."

"Deal." Shaun chuckled and passed him the glass.

CJ took a bracing breath and swallowed the rest of the whiskey in one gulp. "Hit me," he said, putting the glass on the table and then leaning back into the corner of the couch.

Shaun glanced my way. I nodded, giving him permission to continue. "Long story short, we don't know who is buried in your dad's grave, but we do know it isn't him. We don't know where he is or why that other person was in the Jeep instead of him. We're working on that. Your dad—Henry—was able to provide some hair from Tom's brush from which the lab was able to get a DNA profile. It doesn't match the person in the grave, just like Tom's dental records don't."

"But why didn't anyone catch this when it happened?"

Shaun looked at me. This one was on me, so it was my responsibility to answer. "Do you remember when they told us about the condition of the body in the Jeep?" I continued at CJ's nod. "The local authorities said they wouldn't release the body without confirming an identity. The only way to do that was through dental records, so I had Dr. Markley turn your dad's latest x-rays over to Matthew. He had Hugh go all the way out to Truckee to verify the comparisons. Except apparently he didn't bother to actually compare anything, he just signed off that they matched. We're still working on that part too."

Dev hadn't been able to pin anyone down on the exact sequence of events, but the way the local authorities had handled the identification process seemed somewhere between inept and unethical. I'd overheard Dev scream into the phone that John Doe hadn't been the first person to die out there since the Donner Party, but based on their handling of the situation, their methods hadn't improved any since then.

CJ grabbed his neglected glass of eggnog and took a swig. Judging by his expression, it wasn't exactly the most pleasant thing he'd swallowed that day, but the delay was enough to let him formulate his next question. "So what you're saying is that Pops is out there somewhere, but we don't know if he's alive or dead. Not only that, but there's been some stranger buried in his grave for the last ten months and grandpop's lawyer knew it?"

"Well there's no evidence to suggest Hugh knew John Doe wasn't Tom."

Shaun frowned. "There's certainly evidence he didn't give a damn one way or another."

I tipped a finger at him. "Now that I can't argue with."

CJ rubbed a hand over his forehead. "This is like a bad movie. This doesn't happen in real life, does it?"

"I'm sorry, son." I knew exactly how he felt. I'd been living in that incredulity for months. I could pinpoint to the day when my life had turned into a soap opera, I just didn't know why, or who was pulling the strings, although it was growing increasingly clear that some sick bastard was.

"It's not your fault, Dad. I know you'd rather have Pops here." He sighed, went for a drink of the eggnog, and thought better of it with a cringe. "So what do we do now?"

"You don't do anything. Go about your life as normally as possible—"

He scoffed. "I don't even know if I can recognize the definition of that word right now."

"I know," I empathized. "Dev, my boss, is working on it with his best investigator. They'll figure it out soon. He swears the whole thing will come tumbling down as soon as we figure out who the driver of the Jeep was."

CJ frowned. "Poor bastard. I know it's a horrible thing to say, but I'm glad Pops didn't really go out like that. He deserves a lot better." He slapped his hands down on his knees and gave an almost feral fake smile. "I've heard about all I can handle right now. I'm going to go blow some shit up online and try to put this out of my mind. Do either of you want to join me?" Shaun and I declined wordlessly. "I guess until someone proves otherwise, I'll just pretend he's on a business trip. He better bring me something."

I laughed and rose to pull him into a hug as he stood. "All he needs to bring home is himself."

"Damn right," he whispered into my shoulder.

"WELL THAT went about as well as it could have."

I turned from staring at the closed door to CJ's room and walked into my best friend's waiting arms. "Thank you for being here. I have a feeling it could have gone very differently if you weren't around to vouch for my sanity."

Shaun squeezed me tighter. "I did no such thing. I'll tell everyone I know you're nuttier than a fruitcake, you just happen to be right about this one thing."

I smacked his ass since that was about all I could reach. "You're a jackass, but I love you anyway."

He pressed a kiss to my temple. "I know you do. You're a good dad, Henry. You shouldn't second-guess yourself all the time. You've raised one hell of a kid."

I pulled away in search of my wine. I desperately needed the rest of the bottle after that conversation. "I didn't do it alone. He was always closer to Tom than me. They had that artsy thing in common, so it didn't bother me." I drained the last of the liquid from the glass and headed for the kitchen for more. "I'm sorry about that 'favorite uncle' crack, by the way."

I heard Shaun laugh as he followed me. "Yeah, that caught me by surprise. I haven't decided if he was just lashing out because I was standing there or because he's figured out something I don't care if he figures out I'm bisexual, but I definitely don't want him to know anything else."

"That probably wouldn't be a good idea," I agreed. I concentrated on pouring the wine so I wouldn't have to think about Shaun's deeper feelings for me or CJ figuring them out. Instead, I mentioned the thought that had been niggling at the back of my brain all night. "I'm worried about him going to see his grandparents tomorrow."

"How so?"

I stoppered the bottle and took a long swallow from the glass before turning to answer him. "It's bound to be an emotionally raw experience for all of them, since they'll all know Tom might be alive." I'd not informed Matthew of the Medical Examiner's findings until after Thanksgiving, not to spare him and Althea the emotional turmoil, but because I hadn't been able to process the information myself.

Shaun pulled a face that might have meant anything from I worried too much to who cared what Matthew and Althea felt. "It'll be good for him to be with them. They're a stabilizing influence on him, regardless of how unstable they really are."

I chuckled. "Isn't that strange? They've always hated everything about me, but they love CJ as much as they're capable of. Don't get me wrong, I'm glad; it just seems odd that they've never once tried to turn him against me—to my knowledge, anyway."

"People are weird about their grandchildren." He laughed. "You're barking up the wrong tree if you're looking for a philosophical or psychological discussion of the grandparent-grandchild dynamic. Mine were dead before I was old enough to remember them."

I drained the wine, relieved to finally feel the start of the buzz I'd been chasing all night. "Are you sure you don't want to spend the night? We have a big day tomorrow."

Shaun grimaced. "As much as I love you, I don't love sleeping on your couch. And I don't think it would be a good idea for us to share a bed, especially since CJ is right next door."

I grinned. "I dunno. He might be the only thing that would keep you honest."

Shaun's eyes narrowed. "You're kind of a jackass, you know that?"

"What did I say?"

He walked around the island to stand centimeters from me. I could feel the heat of his body colliding with mine. He trapped me in place with a hand on the counter on either side of me. His voice dropped to a husky whisper that sent chills racing along my spine as he dipped to nudge the side of my neck with his nose. "I've wanted you for twenty years, but I've kept my hands off you all that time out of respect for Tom and your relationship. I don't think you give me enough credit for my self-restraint."

I swallowed hard, blood rushing to my groin as my nerves practically cried out to be touched. The couple of make out sessions we'd shared in Hawaii flashed in my memory, reminding me how wonderful his bare skin felt on mine. I reached for his chest just as he moved away. He'd left my head spinning so much I wasn't sure if I was going to pull him closer or push him away. I wanted to do both at the same time.

His breath came in short bursts, much like mine, as he pressed his forehead against mine. "We'll find out soon what happened to Tom. Until then, we're nothing more than best friends. But the instant it becomes clear you're a single man, you're mine. Do you understand?"

I nodded as much as I could with our heads joined like that. I couldn't find my voice. Hell, I could barely find enough breath.

"Good," he whispered. He stepped back, flashed a cocky grin, and patted my cheek. "Have a good night, Henry. I'll see you bright and early in the morning."

I stood rooted in the spot until I heard him close the front door behind him. I let out a deep breath and turned to punch the code into the alarm system. We were playing a very dangerous game. There was definitely an attraction there that I hadn't been aware of before he'd confessed his feelings for me months ago, but technically, I was still a married man. Until someone offered me irrefutable proof that Tom had departed this life, nothing could ever happen between me and Shaun, as much as we both sometimes wanted it.

In those weak moments alone in the dark when I was most honest with myself, I could admit, at least inside my brain, that at least some of the attraction I felt for Shaun was simple loneliness. It had been a long ten months since Tom's possible-not-death. But that didn't account for all of my feelings. I'd loved Shaun as a best friend for twenty years. It was only natural that if I were to fall in love with anyone after Tom's death, it would be Shaun. There was something to be said for the kind of comfort that many years of friendship would bring with it.

Then the guilt would rush in, reminding me that my husband perhaps wasn't quite as dead as he was supposed to be. Did thinking about being physical or having a relationship with Shaun only if Tom was gone constitute cheating? I knew without question that Tom would say no. If I believed he was dead, then he would expect me to get on with my life, including finding someone to love. Even if I had tumbled into bed with someone else—anyone else—before finding out Tom was alive, he would forgive me. I wouldn't do it, though, because despite everyone's best efforts to the contrary, I'd never truly believed he was gone. Maybe that was what had caused my psychotic break in July—knowing in my soul that he was alive, despite all the evidence to the contrary. Back then there hadn't been any available indications to support my theory.

Now that there was, the choice was even easier.

THREE

I'd expected at least some awkwardness between Shaun and me after the previous evening's encounter, but he'd surprised me again by acting as if it had never happened. I supposed he'd become a master at hiding his feelings after twenty years.

We worked side by side preparing the day's dishes, talking about anything and everything, but never once touching on the elephant in the room that apparently only I could see. After a couple of hours of tiptoeing around him, I'd made the conscious choice to let it go. If he wasn't bothered by it, then I shouldn't be either.

The afternoon turned to early evening long before I expected it to, leaving us just enough time to shower and change clothes before the guests arrived. Shaun used the bathroom off CJ's room, somehow getting in, out, and primped before I'd even completely dried off.

He brought me a glass of wine as I slid into a pair of dress slacks. "You're as slow as any woman I've ever dated."

"Unlike some of you, I don't roll out of bed looking photo-shoot ready."

He struck a pose. "Shaun O'Malley gave good face," he intoned in the tempo of Madonna's "Vogue."

I grabbed the shirt I'd laid out from atop the bed. "You're a mess. It's no wonder you're single. And how did I ever think you were straight?"

He laughed. "You didn't want to think anything else, that's how. And I didn't want you to either." He checked his watch. "CJ's late getting back. I expected him long before everyone else."

I glanced at the bedside alarm clock and frowned. At just after six-thirty, it had been dark for a little more than an hour and a half. Although my son didn't share my phobia of the bridges leading into and out of the City, they always caused me concern when he crossed them after dark. "He didn't call to say he was leaving, did he." It wasn't really a question; I hadn't noticed the lack of phone call until that moment.

"Nope." Shaun undid the top button on my shirt and smoothed the material over my shoulders. "Relax, Dad. I'm sure he's okay. I just thought he'd be home sooner. How interesting can he find the old codgers anyway?"

Good question. "They're his grandparents and he loves them," I said, using the same monotone I'd always used with Tom to show my compliance. "He should be home any minute."

Shaun grinned. "I can't wait to get my first look at this Dev character. Trevor practically drools whenever his name's mentioned."

I laughed, checked my hair one more time in the mirror above the chest of drawers, and led the way into the living room. "It wouldn't surprise me if they're sleeping together. Trev's had the hots for him since long before we went to work there."

"Speaking of which, have I told you lately how proud of you I am for quitting Excellere?"

I grinned at him. "I think you told me at least three times a day when we were in Hawaii. I figured it still stood."

He nodded once. "It damn sure does. You were miserable there, Hank."

"I didn't realize how bad it was until I left. Even submitting my resignation wasn't as fulfilling as walking out the door for the last time. I must have left a thousand pounds of mental baggage at that threshold."

CJ chose that moment to stumble through the front door, weighed down by gift bags dangling from both arms. From first appearances, his grandparents had spoiled him with Christmas gifts yet again. "Dad, I'm home," he shouted, then immediately looked contrite when he saw us standing only ten feet away. "Sorry. Should have looked, I guess. Can you help me with these or the door, please? I'm terrified that alarm is going to go off again."

I laughed at the honest fear in his voice. He'd accidentally set it off once during his Thanksgiving weekend and had been paranoid about doing it again. "At least I don't have to worry about you becoming a cat burglar," I teased him, easing a couple of bags off his left arm.

He stuck his tongue out at me, pushed the door closed, and leaned against it with a giant sigh. "I'm so glad to be home. You haven't gone off the rails again, have you?"

I turned a shocked look at him. "Uh, not that I'm aware of."

"Good." He pushed off the door with a look of relief. "I don't think I could handle any more surprises this week." He placed his two bags next to the two I'd set beside the couch and dove into one of them. "All this is from Grandpa except the one thing Yia-yia gave me. You're not going to believe it." He pulled a bright red book from the bag and handed it to me.

I stared at the leather-bound, gold-filigreed volume in my hands for several minutes before its meaning soaked into my brain. It was a very lovely version of The Orthodox Study Bible, which was the last thing I would have expected to come from Althea. She'd turned her back on her family's religion shortly after they'd been exiled from Greece. I couldn't imagine what would bring her back to it after all this time—not only bring her back, but to try to recruit my very logically atheist son into the flock.

I remembered to close my mouth before looking up at CJ. I had no idea what to say, so I pulled out the most non-committal dad comment I could find in my brain. "It's very pretty. I'm sure you'll find it comforting."

CJ gaped at me. "You don't expect me to read it, do you? I haven't touched one of those books since I was a teenager—"

"You're still a teenager."

"Since I was in middle school, okay?" He took the book back and turned it over in his hands, examining it like he expected it to suddenly transform into something that would make sense in his world. He shook his head and sighed. "Yia-yia has jumped back into the Church with both feet. She told me it was time I learned about the Heaven's Avenging Army and that I needed to turn my life over to Christ so we could all be in heaven together."

I looked at Shaun for guidance, but he only shrugged. "I-I'm surprised, son. I don't know what else to say. I hope you were respectful of her beliefs."

"I was too shocked to be anything else. I just followed her lead. She taught me how to cross myself, Dad. Did you know that the position of your fingers—and how many you use—matters? It's insanity."

"How was your grandfather with all this?"

CJ carefully returned the book to the bag he'd retrieved it from. I took that as a sign of good parenting. Some kids might have tossed it aside with distaste. My son knew better than to show such disrespect to a relic of someone's religion, whether or not he believed the same thing. "He said she's been this way for months and it's only getting worse. I saw some of it at Thanksgiving, but she wasn't actively trying to recruit me then, so I let it go. You know how some people slide in and out of religious phases? She did that a few times when I was growing up, but this is much farther than she's ever gone before.

"I thought it might be her way of coping with Pop's death, but Grandpa said she was moving that way months before. Did you know she actually had a chapel built onto the house?"

"Wow." I couldn't have been more surprised if he'd said she'd built a brothel. Althea had her quirks, and she'd always been afraid for Tom's immortal soul because of his sexuality, but I'd never expected her to go from occasionally observant to zealot.

CJ picked up his bags. "I feel like I need a shower now. I know that's probably mean, but I can still smell the incense on my clothes. Oh that's another thing! She had a priest come to the vineyard to perform the service so we wouldn't have to go into town."

I could read the confusion in his eyes. The poor boy's world just wouldn't stop tilting on him. And I couldn't do a thing to stop it.

"Go grab a shower. Dev and Trev should be here soon."

"Dev and Trev?" Shaun snorted.

I laughed. "I hadn't even noticed how that sounds. Let's just hope they don't decide to be a couple. That's almost painfully cute."

"Almost?"

CJ moved past us both, disappearing into his room without another word.

"He's shaken," Shaun said.

"I would be too. It's weird."

"Could it be an age thing? She's not getting any younger, and now her only child is—well, might be—dead. She could be confronting her mortality for the first time or something."

I looked toward CJ's room, wishing I had all the answers for both of us. It was difficult seeing my child in an emotional minefield. It seemed like no matter where we'd stepped in the last few months, one thing after another had blown up in our faces. "I don't know. I'm not even sure it matters yet. Unless she starts more actively trying to recruit CJ into the faith, I'm going to leave it alone. She's entitled to her beliefs, but she's not allowed to push those onto my son." I squeezed the back of my neck, hoping to stop the headache before it started. "It suddenly feels like the uneasy truce we worked out for Tom's sake all those years ago is about to be broken. I don't want to be the one to do it, but I will if I have to."

I WATCHED with a certain amusement as Shaun soaked in every move Dev made. He'd barely taken his eyes off the man since he and Trevor had arrived almost twenty minutes earlier. He'd also barely spoken, despite the number of times the others had attempted to draw him into the conversation. If I hadn't known better, I would have thought my best friend was besotted with my boss. That wouldn't be the worst thing to ever happen, but it was beyond strange to see.

Shaun had very carefully cultivated the man about town image, leading me to believe he had multiple women at his disposal at all times. That much was probably true, but he'd skipped the part about how he also had multiple men available. Until he'd confessed his decades-long love for me in August, it had never occurred to me that he was bisexual. And I had certainly never had even a blip of a thought that he felt that way about me.

I found myself living in a strange new world. The only thing that hadn't changed since February was my address. After the drama with Linc and the stalking, I'd given that serious thought too. It had taken a while to feel safe in my own home again, something that hadn't ever been a concern before.

I nudged Shaun's elbow unobtrusively and motioned for him to meet me in the kitchen. It was time to bring out the meal, plus I couldn't wait to hear what he thought of Dev. Moments later he came through the doorway carrying an empty tray of snack food.

"Are you finally going to feed me? I'm starving."

I laughed. "Funny, it looked to me like you were devouring Dev with your eyes."

"Shut up." He put the tray on the counter next to the sink and reached into the cabinet above him. He pulled out a glass serving dish and busily filled it with the green beans that had been keeping warm on the stovetop, all the while keeping his back to me.

"So," I tried again. "What do you think of him?"

He shrugged. "He seems like an interesting guy. I can see why you like working for him."

"Uh huh." It took every bit of my strength to keep from laughing. He wasn't very good at feigning indifference. I'd seen him like this with women before, but never over a man. It reminded me of what it was like when I'd just come out and every man seemed like a possibility. Of course he hadn't just come out. "Listen, how do you want to play this with CJ? We should have talked about this earlier."

He turned to me this time, confusion in his eyes. "What do you mean?"

"I mean, you and Trevor have a history. You're making cow eyes at Dev."

He huffed and yanked open a drawer. "I am not. Shut up."

I laughed. "Fine. You're not acting the least bit strange. We'll go with that. The thing is, the only one in that room who doesn't know you're bisexual is CJ."

"Oh." He frowned into the drawer, grabbed a spoon for the green beans, and slammed it shut with a flick of his hips. "Are you saying I should come out to him?"

"I'm not saying anything. That's your decision to make."

"It sounds like you think it's already been made."

This wasn't going the way I'd expected, but then conversations with Shaun rarely did when he was being obstinate. I donned mitts and pulled the turkey from the oven, placing it on the island. "I'm sorry if that's the way it sounded. I'm not—" I sighed and tried again. "You're the only one out there with a secret to keep, Shaun. That's all I'm saying. I would hate for someone to let it slip because we're all so comfortable with being out that we don't even think about it anymore." I dug around in the same drawer Shaun had just closed for utensils to pull the stupid bird out of its pan.

"Are you going to let it slip?" he asked, moving mashed potatoes into a serving dish.

"I don't think so, no." I heaved the bird onto the platter, thankful the legs hadn't fallen apart on me like they had last Christmas.

"So you think this Dev might? Because Trevor knows to keep his mouth shut about me. I'm still surprised he told you about us."

"I don't think he intended to, but somehow he could tell that you'd told me. Shit. I still need to make gravy."

He chuckled. "You start hauling things out to the table. I'll do the gravy. It'll only take a minute. Maybe you should send CJ in so I can come out to him before dinner starts."

I spun to look at him. "Are you serious?"

He grinned. "The only person I've been hiding it from is you, Hank. Well, your little family." He frowned. "Sometimes I think Tom knew, but we never discussed it. I think it was one of those things we both knew the other knew and we knew better than to talk about it because it wouldn't change anything but it could change everything."

I blinked as the words flew by. "That was way too much knowing."

He laughed. "I might as well tell the kid. It'll only take a minute. I'm sure he'll be fine with it. It's not like he's never met an LGBT person before. By the way, any confirmation on which letter he claims?"

I shook my head. "Not yet. I probably shouldn't, but I'm assuming he's straight. Goodness knows there are remarkably few of them in our lives."

He grinned. "Look where you live, dipshit."

"Myths and stereotypes!" I picked up the platter with the turkey. "Are you sure you want to do this?"

"Of course. Send in the clown—I mean, the kid."

"Right, because the clown is already in here." I showed him my tongue to prove I was joking and carried the turkey out to the special table we'd set up in a corner of the living room. Tom and I had agreed years ago that confining holiday meals to the eat-in kitchen had seemed wrong on every level, so we'd never done it. Each holiday we'd hosted, we'd set up a table near the fireplace, just to up the cozy factor.

"CJ, your uncle would like your assistance in the kitchen," I announced as I set down the platter. He didn't bother to question or protest; he simply excused himself and left the room. I moved to the bar to give Dev and Trevor some more time alone. "Who needs a fresh drink?" I asked.

Both of them readily agreed, bringing me their nearly empty glasses. I fixed Dev another Crown and Coke and poured Trevor more wine. I'd been a good boy most of the day, so I grabbed some for me too.

"So what do you think of Shaun?" I asked Dev, trying to keep the grin from my lips.

He shrugged. "He's quieter than I expected."

"He's nervous," I explained.

"He's in fucking lust," Trevor countered. "He's been licking Dev up and down with his eyes since we walked in the door."

"Whoa, son. Calm down." I was surprised by the conviction in Trevor's voice. I couldn't tell if he was annoyed, jealous, or amused, but he was absolutely sure of his statement.

"We're taking him home tonight. I hope that's okay with you." His expression told me he didn't particularly care if it was okay with me or not; he was going to do it.

"Smooth, Trev," Dev said, coloring slightly.

He shrugged. "What? We're all grown-ups. Henry knows Shaun and I have a history. And he knew I lusted after you for months before we left Excellere."

"Yes, but he didn't have confirmation we're sleeping together until just now."

"Oh. Oops." Trevor gazed into his wine glass. "Maybe I should switch to something else. After this glass," he clarified, moving it out of my reach. "I don't usually drink. I'll blame my loose tongue on that. Besides, it's just casual. It's not like we're getting married tomorrow."

"Trev," Dev warned.

"What?"

"Drink more, talk less."

I laughed at the expression on Trevor's face. "We're almost ready to eat. It'll help to get some food in him."

"I'm being embarrassing, aren't I?" Trevor seemed to deflate. "I'm sorry. This is why I don't drink. I seem to lose the filter between my brain and my mouth."

"We're all friends here, Trev. Don't worry about it. But if you hit on my kid, you're going to hit the bricks."

Trevor laughed. "Please. He's way too young and way too straight."

"How old is he?" Dev asked.

"Nineteen, old man," I said with obvious irony, considering he had to be at least ten years younger than me. "That warning goes for you too."

"He seems remarkably put together for nineteen. Good job, Dad."

"He's always been mature for his age," I said. "I'm just hoping he doesn't have his midlife crisis at twenty-one."

Dev shook his head. “Nah. I don’t see it. The striped hair notwithstanding.”

I laughed. “We always encouraged him to express himself in any way that didn’t involve ink or piercings. Everything else is temporary so it can be undone. He does have the same tattoo his dad and I do to symbolize our family. We let him get that on his eighteenth birthday.”

CJ returned to the room, carrying the dish of mashed potatoes. “Uncle Shaun says you all should get comfortable at the table. We’ll finish bringing everything in and then we’ll eat.” He flashed a huge, untroubled smile as he put the potatoes on the table and disappeared into the kitchen again.

His world had just tilted in another direction and he hadn’t even been fazed. I sent a silent promise to him that I’d put us on a new, non-tilting path very soon. All we had to do was find out what had happened to his other dad. Not a problem.

FOUR

The Monday after Christmas dragged as only the Mondays following holidays did. In the three days between, CJ and I had talked about Shaun's bisexuality, which hadn't come as a surprise to him; his grandmother's return to the Old Faith, which caused him concern; and his plans for the next semester, which were remarkably simple: study smart, not hard. I could see the questions about his dad's fate swimming behind his eyes, but he hadn't voiced them. It hurt to see him in the same limbo I was in, but I still thought my decision to tell him was the best one. It might mean that we'd have to grieve for Tom again, but there was also the possibility that we could get him back. And that trumped any other concerns I had.

I looked up as Dev knocked on the open door to my small office. Because of the sensitive nature of the business, each of the associates had his own private office. This one was a lot smaller than the one I'd had at Excellere, but it came with considerably less stress, so the trade-off was in my favor. "What's up?" I asked, minimizing the spreadsheet I'd been working on.

"Justin's here. He has some news."

I leapt to my feet, dislodging stacks of paper from my lap. I couldn't have cared less about them. "What is it?" My pulse pounded so loudly in my ears I could barely hear the answer.

"He has an ID."

Stupidly, I collapsed back into the chair. "Oh my god." I hadn't really thought it would happen. I knew there was a possibility that whoever had occupied Tom's grave hadn't been registered in any of the DNA databases. It was actually more probable that he wasn't. I swallowed and looked back at Dev. "Where is he?"

"He's in my office. Come on."

I nodded, rose to my feet, and followed Dev unsteadily down the hall. This was it. This was another confirmation that I wasn't crazy. Even after seeing the dental records, that thought had niggled at the back of my brain. I had to question everything since Tom's accident. Nothing was as it seemed. Life and death themselves had been turned upside down. Why not sanity?

Justin stood in the middle of Dev's office, a broad grin stretched across his handsome face, as he talked with Shelby Haynes, Dev's top detective, and the man who was working the case with him.

"Gentlemen," Dev said as we entered.

Handshakes and pleasantries exchanged, we all took places at the small conference table in the corner. I reminded myself to breathe several times as Justin dug the file out of his briefcase.

He slid on a pair of reading glasses, apologizing for aging as he did so, and cleared his throat. "Alright, let's cut right to the chase before Henry passes out."

I tried to smile but I was concentrating too hard on regulating my breathing.

Justin passed a folder to each of us. I stopped mine as it slid across the table at me, but I couldn't bring myself to open it quite yet. Instead I listened as Justin explained the contents.

"As you can see from the report, the DNA match is 99.97 percent, which is as close as it gets in the real world. Our subject, Ioannis Berglund, was a known con man, with several convictions to his credit."

I quit listening, allowing my disappointment to swallow me. I'd hoped I'd recognize the name. I'd hoped the whole thing would unravel with the identity of the person who'd occupied my husband's grave, but that wasn't to be.

The photograph almost flopped out of its paperclip as I opened the folder. I stared at it in disbelief. The smirk almost completely changed his face, the pleasant expression I was used to erased by contempt.

"Henry?"

My gaze jerked to Dev's as he called my name again. "I know him." I swallowed around the excitement. "His name isn't whatever Justin just said. At least, that's not how I knew him. He's Jack Berg. He was an intern at Hardwick."

"Tom's firm?"

"Yes!" I didn't know what it meant, but it was a concrete link to Tom's life, which was more than we'd had before. "They were sort of casual friends. Tom was always trying to help people better themselves."

"Like Linc," Shelby said.

"Exactly like Linc. He'd had a tough childhood, so Tom did what he could to encourage him to pursue his dreams of being an architect. If I remember right, this guy was very similar. He'd gotten a late start at his career because he'd spent some time in prison in his early twenties." Snippets of Tom's conversations about Jack Berg floated through my brain, but none of them set off any alarms.

"Is there any reason Tom would invite Jack to join your vacation without telling you?"

I shook my head. "I can't think of one. They weren't that close and it wasn't that sort of vacation. We were celebrating Valentine's Day."

"But Shaun was there." Shelby frowned. The dynamics of our friendship seemed to cause him trouble.

"Shaun's always there. He's my best friend and CJ's favorite uncle. We usually spend a week or so together as a family every year."

"Would Tom have tried to set up Shaun with this Jack?" Dev asked.

"To my knowledge, Tom didn't know Shaun is bisexual, so I would have to say no."

Dev leaned back in his chair. I could practically see the fireworks show in his brain as his synapses fired away. "What else do we know about this Jack person, Justin?"

"He was thirty-eight, lived in Daly City, and had a wife."

"Bank accounts? Medical and phone records?"

Justin pulled more reports from his briefcase, one for each of us again. "I pulled his bank records from most recent activity to a year prior to his death. Nothing jumped out at me. There aren't any large deposits. Medical records are scant but clear; it looks like he spent a lot of time without insurance, even when he was on the straight and narrow. I'm still waiting for his phone logs."

I flipped right to the banking section, something I knew a little bit about. "Why were you looking for large deposits?" I asked Justin.

"To see if he was paid to do something to Tom."

My gaze jerked to his. How could I forget what we were really doing here? This Jack Berg slash Ioannis Berglund wasn't just any John Doe. He was the crispy corpse found in my husband's Jeep and passed off as him. "If he was smart, there wouldn't be a large deposit. Banks are required to report cash deposits above a certain amount to the IRS. Lots of people know that, especially those with criminal backgrounds." I quickly scanned the entries, looking for anything unusual. "He would most likely deposit a safe amount several times to avoid detection."

"I was just looking for a big number," Justin admitted.

"Understood," I answered, thoroughly engrossed with the numbers. Holy shit! Once is an entry. Twice is a coincidence. Three times is a pattern. This was a gift from the gods. "Right there!" I spun the report around so Dev and Shelby could see what I was pointing to. "Look here. He made cash deposits of eight thousand dollars every other week eight times!" I pounded the paper with my finger. "The motherfucker was getting paid for something."

Adrenalin and rage surged through my veins. We wouldn't win a conviction in court on evidence this sketchy, but it was enough to convince me that we were on the right path. Berg was on someone's secret payroll for something—my guess was that something involved my husband.

The questions remained. Who paid him? What were they paying him for? And where was Tom? I didn't even give a damn why anymore, I just wanted Tom home where he belonged. The "who" I would deal with on my own when we got Tom back.

Dev nodded decisively. "Right, good job, Justin and Henry. We have a new place to start looking. Shelby, this is now top priority. Delegate your other cases. Justin, get those phone records to us as soon as you can." He rose from the table, signaling the end of the meeting. The others followed his lead and exited the room with promises to keep each other informed.

I turned my attention back to the photograph, picking it up to examine more closely. It was a typical mug shot. The man in the picture was a few years younger than the one I'd met, but there was no mistaking him. I started as a hand fell heavily on my shoulder.

"We'll get him, Henry. It's what we do."

I nodded. Dev's reassurances were nice to hear, but they didn't ease the emptiness in my heart. Tom was still missing, possibly dead. Probably dead. As much as I wanted to believe this new information meant we would find Tom alive, a damn long time had passed since his disappearance. With each new day, the chances of finding him alive diminished considerably.

TREVOR JAMMED the clip into the grip of his pistol, grinning like a lunatic the entire time. "Can you believe we get to do this as part of our job? Man, this is so much better than Excellere!"

I laughed and loaded my own clip. "I still can't get used to seeing you with a weapon in your hand. It's a little disconcerting."

"Why?"

"My mild-mannered assistant is turning into a bad ass. I'm having trouble reconciling the two."

He threw me a look. "Honey, I was always a bad ass. I'm just a bad ass with a gun now." He grinned. "Are you ready to blow some shit up or do you want to stand around here jawing some more?"

"By all means, let's blow some shit up." I turned back to the target and adjusted my ear coverings. Within seconds, Trevor was firing at his paper target. I laughed again and joined in.

It was exciting learning to care for and shoot a weapon. I was careful not to call my Glock a gun, having that refrain from some military movie echoing in my head: "This is my weapon, this is my gun. One is for fighting, one is for fun." I'd never entertained the idea of learning to shoot before joining Deveraux, but it was definitely a side benefit. It drained a certain amount of aggression and frustration, especially seeing my improvement from the first time Dev had brought me to the range. Now all my shots found the paper, most of them even in the vicinity of the kill zone.

Trevor was better, the little shit. That first time he'd acted like a scared princess until he fired for the first time. Then it was like he'd channeled Rambo or something.

I fired the last round and pressed the button to bring the target to me. Trevor already had his pulled off the hanger and was practically dancing with glee. I held mine up next to his and winced at how much closer his grouping was than mine. I definitely needed work, but I was getting there.

"We kick ass!" He shouted to be heard over the ear protection we both still wore and held his hand up for a high five.

I humored him with a mid-air slap and pulled the heavy protection off my ears. "You kick ass. I'm still learning high kicks."

He laughed. "You're so much better than when we started. You'll get there. Just imagine Tom's parents down there."

"Why didn't I think of that?" I asked with a laugh. It probably wasn't a good idea to think of shooting an actual person, but if I ever had to pull my weapon, chances were good that's what I'd be doing. Maybe the kid was onto something after all.

"I heard you got some good intel this morning."

"We did. We now know the name of the person in Tom's grave. Dev and Shelby were going to pay his widow a visit to let her know we'd found him. She put out a missing person's report in March, so it shouldn't come as a huge surprise, but I feel bad for her. I know what it's like to get that kind of information." My heart squeezed at the memory, the pain as fresh as if it had just happened.

Trevor's hand on my shoulder brought me out of the moment. "It's not your fault, Henry. Thanks to you, she's going to have closure. It might not be the news she wanted to hear, but it's got to be better than not knowing."

My gaze cut to his. "So I'm trading her hell for mine? I get to be the one not knowing what happened to my husband now, Trevor. She can finally grieve, knowing without a doubt that her husband is dead. But what about me? Am I ever going to know for sure?"

"You'll know. Dev will make sure of it." He sighed. "I know you want to find Tom alive more than anything, but I can see your hope fading. You can't let it. You have to fight for him."

I choked on the truth of his statement as I gathered my belongings. I had been losing hope, even with the new information. "Ten months is a long time," I said, walking away.

I hadn't given in to my emotions in front of anyone in a long time, I wasn't about to do it again then. I couldn't deny that it was getting harder to imagine finding Tom alive. I was having trouble picturing his face already. The face I had loved for more than twenty years. What if that meant my love for him was dying too? What if we found him alive and I found I wasn't in love with him anymore? The longer it took to find him, the greater that possibility. It scared the hell out of me. But how could I tell anyone that? I shoved down the feelings of disloyalty and blinked the tears from my eyes.

I needed to be proactive instead of wallowing in self-pity. Something had to change and it was up to me to make it happen. Shelby and Dev might be developing new leads by talking to Berg's widow, but I needed some of my own.

I threw my stuff in the company car and dug out my phone. "Justin," I said as soon as I heard his voice, "I need you to send me Berg's phone records directly."

"I'm still waiting on them. The phone company is notoriously difficult to get information from unless you're the government."

Dammit. The stress I'd just worked out on the firing range suddenly reappeared in my shoulders. "Fine. Get them to me as soon as you can. I need some answers, man. We're running out of time."

"I know, Henry. I'm doing my best here. I'll call and light a fire under their asses."

FIVE

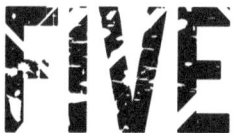

I'm so glad it's Friday," Trevor lamented from the passenger seat eleven days later. "It's only the second week of the year and I'm already exhausted."

I risked a quick glance over to find him staring out the side window. "Maybe you can use your new influence with Dev to convince him we should have an extra-long weekend."

I maneuvered into the left-turn lane and stopped behind the old jalopy already waiting for the light to turn.

"I don't know what influence you mean," Trevor protested without much conviction.

"No, of course not. You don't have any sway over him at all."

I saw his grin out the corner of my eye. "I might sway over him once in a while, but that's about it."

I held up my hand in a stop gesture. "Too much information."

"Actually, I think we need to trade information."

I glanced at him again. "What do you mean?"

"Have you talked to Shaun since Christmas?"

In the two weeks since the holiday, Shaun and I had barely touched base. He was busy with his year-end financial stuff and I was silently celebrating not having anything to do with retail for the first time in memory. "Not really, why?"

"Because he totally bailed on us that night."

"Really?" I hid my smile at the offense in his voice.

"Really. One minute we were having a super hot three-way make out session on the couch. The next minute, he was practically flying out the door."

"Huh." The light turned green. I followed the old car around the corner and accelerated down the street. "I don't know what to tell you. He hasn't said anything about it." That in itself was strange. Shaun was always full of tales of his sexual conquests, although not with other men. That was something he still shielded from me, for the most part. It was sort of cute in its own way. It was like he didn't want me to think he was as much of a slut with men as he was with women, so that I'd know his feelings for me were real.

"Henry, I think we're being followed."

The anxiety in Trevor's voice brought me out of my thoughts. Instinctively, I glanced in the rearview mirror. "What? By who?"

"That black SUV two cars back. You see it?"

"I do. What makes you think he's following us?"

"He's been two vehicles behind us for ten minutes."

I shrugged off his concern. "It's probably just someone from the firm keeping tabs on the trainees."

"Could be. Take the next right. I want to see if he follows us."

"If I take the next right, I won't know where we are."

"Henry. After you do that, take the next left, then the next, then we'll be right back at this street. You really don't drive much, do you?"

I laughed. "No. I don't like it. Tom always drove us around the City on the rare occasion we'd actually take the Jeep."

"Turn. Now!"

Impulsively, I took the corner, as much to prove to him that he was paranoid as to see if he was or not. My eyes darted between the street ahead and the rearview mirror, waiting to see if Trevor was right.

He was. "Shit! He turned too! He really is following us."

"You should call Dev and see if he has someone checking on us." I wasn't willing to panic yet. There had to be a logical reason for the SUV to be back there, aside from random traffic patterns.

"Good idea," he answered, already digging for his cell phone.

At the next corner, I hooked a left and accelerated aggressively, just in case Trevor's paranoia was real. In the rearview mirror, the SUV followed, keeping pace with us. Shit.

The light ahead of us turned amber in plenty of time for me to stop. Instead, I gunned the engine. "Hang on." I closed my eyes and prayed to Tom we'd make it through the juncture unscathed.

"Jesus Christ!" Trevor yelled as we bounced through the intersection, horns honking angrily on all sides of us.

Trevor's terrified voice forced my eyes open again. We were safely on the other side of the crossing, going well over the speed limit down a residential street. I looked in the rearview before letting up on the accelerator. Thankfully the black SUV was stuck at the light, unable to make it across traffic.

I swallowed hard, adrenalin surging through my veins, and took a squealing hard right turn onto the next street. "Fuck me," I said aloud, exhaling a pent up breath. I returned the car to normal speed, hoping we'd lost our tail.

I laughed nervously. I'd never done something like that before. It was liberating as well as scary as hell. I knew if I took my hands from the steering wheel they'd be a shaking mess.

Trevor turned around in his seat, staring out the back window for any sign of our pursuer. Two blocks down, I quickly took another right turn, hoping to confuse him if he was still looking for us.

I slid into an empty parking spot—a miracle in this town—and took a deep breath. I straightened my arms, forcing myself back into the seat and looked over at my passenger. He was still turned around in his seat, his normally tanned face pale from the experience. I laughed. "Holy hell, that was kind of exciting. Beats the hell out of staring at numbers all day!"

His expression told me he was sure I'd finally lost my damn mind. "That wasn't exciting! It was scary."

"What did Dev say? Was it one of his guys?"

"Oh!" Trev looked around for his phone. "I didn't get a chance to talk to him. I dropped my phone reaching for the 'oh shit' handle back at the corner." He laughed unsteadily and turned back around in his seat. "Let's not do that again without warning, okay?"

"I told you to hang on!"

He reached to the floor and picked up his phone. I could hear a tinny version of Dev's voice coming from the speaker. "Yeah, I'm here. Sorry about that. I dropped the phone." He turned to look behind us again. "Listen, do you have someone following us?" Trevor shook his head at me, conveying Dev's answer.

I frowned. We'd probably imagined the pursuit anyway. Why would anyone be tailing us? We were just errand boys at this point. We had thousands of hours of training to complete before we could even think about applying for our PI licenses. It was true the Zuckerman divorce was getting uglier by the minute, but the old bastard wouldn't know which agents from the firm were working on kicking his ass.

I looked in the side mirror in time to see the black SUV slowly turn the corner onto our street. The passenger window slid down, revealing the business end of a semi-automatic rifle.

The next few seconds were like running through water, slow motion with resistance. "Get down!" I shouted. I turned and tackled Trevor to the floor, shielding him with my body. I vaguely registered his phone flying into the back seat. Noise like a fireworks show on steroids exploded around us for what seemed like hours. Glass rained down sharp shards and tiny bits in a never-ending torrent.

Sudden silence set time to normal speed again.

Pieces of glass continued to fall occasionally, but I reluctantly sat back up, looking out all three exposed directions before signaling to Trevor to get off the floor. His wide, panicked eyes told me I hadn't imagined the whole thing. We really had been shot at.

Sound came roaring back to my ears. I forced open the driver door and puked onto the street.

I WINCED as the paramedic applied more salve to the cuts on my back. The safety glass in the car's windows hadn't stood a chance against assault from a rifle. Several chunks of all sizes had lodged in my back, the force of the explosion making them sharp missiles. My favorite dress shirt was a sticky, bloody, torn mess.

The scene was something out of a movie. Blue and red lights flashed everywhere as police marched around the area, demanding answers from any witnesses, photographing the three cars that had been destroyed in the drive-by. Windows had been blown out of two businesses behind us. Thankfully no one inside them had been injured. I would have felt terrible if I'd led the lunatic to this spot and caused someone's pain or death.

Dev had arrived nearly the same time as the paramedics. I still couldn't figure out how he'd managed to get all the way across town in that amount of time. He stood by as Trevor and I gave our separate statements to the police. We'd only been able to tell them the assailants were white males driving a black SUV. Neither of us had thought to concentrate on the make and model of the vehicle or to get its tag number. Getting that information wasn't ingrained in us yet, even though we'd each watched enough cop shows over the years to know better.

"Hank! Thank god!" Shaun's hands were on my face almost before I registered his voice. I took one look into his horrified green eyes and nearly collapsed in relief. "I was so fucking worried when Dev called," he confessed, moving around to sit beside me on the gurney inside the ambulance. "Are you okay? Do we need to get you to the hospital? Why haven't they taken you there yet?"

I used what little energy I had left to chuckle at him. "I'm fine, just a few scratches from the glass." I closed my eyes, leaned against him, and let the exhaustion take over. "Someone shot at us, Shaun. Can you believe that? I mean they literally tried to gun us down in the street. That's so crazy."

He caressed my hair and kissed the top of my head. "I heard that. I'm so glad you're okay. He is, right?"

"Just a few cuts and scrapes," the paramedic answered. "He'll be fine. He'll need to have his bandages changed again later today. Will someone be around to do that?"

"I will. Just tell me what to do."

I zoned out as the paramedic gave him instructions. I absorbed the warmth from Shaun's body, focusing on the strength of his presence. I'd almost made my son an orphan. Well not me, but the idiot who'd fired a goddamn machine gun at me and my friend. Because why? What had we done to warrant that? Who would have wanted us taken out?

I sat bolt upright and turned to Shaun. My gaze drilled into his, making sure he took my words seriously. "This didn't have anything to do with the Zuckerman divorce. This is about Tom. Someone knows we're onto them and they're trying to stop us."

"You don't know that, Hank."

I nodded fiercely. "I do. I can feel it. Zuckerman doesn't have anything to gain by killing two trainee investigators. But whoever took Tom sure as hell has something to gain by killing me." I scrambled for the door. "I have to tell Dev."

Shaun grabbed my hand and pulled me back. "He took Trevor home. You can tell him on Monday."

I yanked against his grip. "Monday is too late. Someone's trying to stop me from finding Tom. That has to mean we're close."

Shaun climbed out of the ambulance after me, accepting the remains of my shirt from the paramedic. "Let me take you home. You can call Dev on the way."

I agreed without a word, already reaching into my pocket for the phone. We had the son of a bitch riled up. We needed to apply pressure now so he would expose himself. I didn't have a clue how to do it, but I was damn sure Dev and Shelby did.

I LAY FACE down on the bed, stiff and sore and not afraid to whine about it. The cuts from where the glass had imbedded itself into my back hurt like hell. Whatever painkiller the paramedic's salve had in it had worn off hours ago.

The bedside lamp provided the only illumination in the room, a clue that I'd slept at some point. Between the excitement of the drive-by and the realization that whoever had paid Tom's kidnappers—because there was no other explanation anymore—had tried to kill me, my adrenalin was shot by the time Shaun had got me home. He'd put me to bed, despite my protests that I could lie on the couch just as comfortably, plus the living room had the television.

"Hello, sleeping beauty."

I turned my head toward his voice and groaned when the action pulled on one of the deeper cuts.

"I heard the freight train snoring stop, so I thought I'd come check on you. How're you doing?"

"I'm fine," I whined.

He laughed. "Yeah, you sound like it." He moved into my field of vision and knelt by the bed.

"I don't snore."

"Of course not."

"I don't," I insisted.

"I never said you did."

"You just did!"

Shaun stroked my hair. "You must have been hearing things. I'd never level such an ugly charge at you."

"You're a jackass."

He grinned. "But you love me, so that's all that matters. Do you want me to get you a painkiller or something? Maybe a nice warm bath would draw out some of the soreness."

I narrowed my one open eye at him. "You just want to get me naked again."

"Guilty as charged, but it's still a good idea."

"It is, actually," I admitted.

"Good. I'll start the water and grab you a pain pill. I'll be back in a few minutes."

"I'm not mixing a bath with a pain pill. Are you trying to kill me too?"

"I won't let anything happen to you, Hank. I'll stay in there and talk with you while you soak."

"Naked."

"Well I was planning to keep my clothes on, but if you insist."

I chuckled and then groaned when that hurt. "Stop. Go start the water. You keep your clothes on. I'll take a bath. Then you can put new bandages on me and then I'll take a pain pill. Or three."

He rose to his feet, a cocky smile on his lips. "Who knew you were such a whiner? A guy fires a few bullets at you and you act like it's the end of the world."

I rolled onto my side and gave him the bird. "Let's see how you feel when it happens to you. Frankly I'm surprised some pissed off husband hasn't already taken potshots at you."

He waved my words away. "That old scene? I've gotten very good at duck and cover."

I slowly moved to an upright position. "See, I can't tell if you're telling the truth or lying to my face. Has that ever happened to you?"

He scowled. "I don't play with married women. Or married men. You should know me better than that."

I stretched cautiously, feeling the cuts pull and recede. "I'm glad to know that at least one thing about you hasn't changed."

"The most important thing won't ever change. I'll always be your best friend."

I smiled at the sentimentality of that statement. It was a truth that I'd based my world around as much as I had my marriage to Tom. They were as constant as the stars in the sky and I was forever grateful for both of them. "I don't hear the water running yet."

"You see? This is what I get for trying to help your sorry ass." He moved into the bathroom, still grumbling. "I should just leave you on your own, but no. I'm a nice guy."

"You are a nice guy," I called over the sound of the water.

"I know it! No one appreciates the nice guys."

Trevor's confession slipped into my brain. "So, mister nice guy, what happened on Christmas?"

He leaned against the bathroom doorjamb, the puzzlement evident in his expression. "What do you mean? I was here all day."

"And after that?"

His eyes dropped to the floor as he pushed off the wall and headed for the exit. "I went to Dev's for a nightcap, then I went home. No fuss, no muss."

"But there was supposed to be fuss and muss, wasn't there?"

He stopped just inside the door, his back still to me. "Is there a specific question you would like an answer to, Hank?"

"Yes," I admitted with a grin he couldn't see. "Why didn't you sleep with them?"

"Because I'm not a whore. I hadn't even met Dev until that day. Why should I fall into bed with him—them?"

"I have no reasons for or against. I'm just curious."

"Well, meow mix, go find a ball of yarn before your questions kill you." He walked out of the room.

I laughed. Oh there was something going on in Shaun O'Malley's brain that I definitely needed to know about. He would spill, it would just take me convincing him it was his idea. In the meantime, I'd just have to wait. I hated waiting.

SIX

The ten days after the shooting were a bust. I couldn't make it through a complete sleep cycle without waking screaming from a nightmare. They all started out differently, but they always ended with someone shooting me. Or Tom. Or CJ. Sleeping pills had only made the dreams more vivid. I'd spent a considerable amount of time staring at the walls and ceiling. I avoided television because of the violence on what seemed like every single program. I couldn't string together enough concentration to read a book. I was too afraid of accidentally becoming an alcoholic to seek too much refuge in wine.

I'd convinced Shaun to go home early Saturday afternoon after the attempt on my life. I was grateful for his tender loving care, but I didn't want him around while my brain tried to process the fact that someone had tried to kill me and Trevor. I didn't need him thinking I was sliding into Insanityville again. Dev insisted Trevor and I take the week off to heal and rest. It didn't help. I might have healed, but I was anything but rested.

I was exhausted and snappish when I returned to work. I was coherent enough to know it, so I avoided as many people as I could, even Dev and Trevor. I closed myself in my office and worked on tracing Adrien Zuckerman's financial crimes. The bastard was a wizard at hiding things. I was just lucky I was better at finding them. It was going to give me perverse pleasure to nail his ass to the wall and make sure his husband got everything he was entitled to. Marriages were meant to last a lifetime, not until the next hot twink with daddy issues came along.

I jumped at the sound of the incoming message from Doris. I hadn't realized how quiet it was until it wasn't. I pressed the button on the phone. "Yes, Doris?"

"Justin is here to see you. Shall I send him back?"

My heart leapt. "Please do." I sent a prayer to the universe that it was good news. At this point, anything that didn't point to Tom's death was good news, so it shouldn't be hard to fulfill that request.

I walked around the desk and opened the door just as Justin strolled up, a grin on his face and a file in his hand. "Good news?" I asked.

His grin widened. "That depends on who you are, I guess." He entered the office and held up the file. "Mr. Berglund's phone records."

I snatched the file out of his hand and was already skimming the pages as I walked back behind the desk. I vaguely noticed Justin make himself comfortable in one of the chairs. Thanks to the fact that I usually stared at numbers all day every day, I was quick to pick out repeated patterns on the pages. I flipped through them impatiently. "He calls four numbers over and over. One is Tom's cell. Another is Hardwick's main line."

"Yep."

"This one," I said, spreading the file on the desk and pointing at a specific line, "looks familiar too, but I can't place it." I didn't have many phone numbers memorized anymore. The invention of the contacts feature on cellular phones had canceled that need. I'd probably seen a number sequence similar to it earlier in the day looking through the Zuckerman accounts.

I turned my focus to Justin. "Why was he calling Tom so often? I know they were friendly, but this number of calls would indicate they were a lot closer than that."

He shrugged. "I can't be sure. There aren't any saved voice mails. We're still waiting on text messages. I have no idea what they talked about, just that it happened pretty often."

I sank into my chair, confusion clouding my thoughts. The man Tom had known as Jack Berg had taken a considerable amount of money from some unknown person. He'd somehow ingratiated himself into Tom's work life enough that they talked several times a day, every day. And then he'd died in Tom's Jeep the very day that Tom had disappeared.

All that pointed to only one conclusion: Berglund had been paid to grow close to Tom and then...what? Kill him? Kidnap him? Or was that just the result of a job poorly done? Was he supposed to get information from Tom about a project? Had Tom figured out he was being used and confronted Berg? Was that why Berg had killed him?

That couldn't be it. It didn't add up. If he'd killed Tom, why hadn't he done it in the city? Why was he in an accident in Tom's vehicle so close to Squaw Valley, where Tom, CJ, Shaun, and I were supposed to spend Valentine's Day? Had he hitched a ride with Tom and asked to be dropped off at some mysterious location along the way? Then where was Tom?

I was missing huge pieces of the puzzle and it was pissing me off. Nothing made sense. Tom being the target of some kill or kidnap conspiracy made no damn sense to begin with. He wasn't involved in anything illegal or even high-adventure. He was an architect, for Pete's sake! Yes, he was in charge of skyscrapers, but who gave a damn? He hadn't designed the Burj Khalifa or anything remotely close to that. His tallest construction was the Elizabeth International Center, an eight hundred foot, sixty-five story business and residential tower in Toronto.

"You're getting distracted."

I sighed and rocked back in my chair, staring at the world's ugliest ceiling. Acoustic sound tiles. Yuck. "Nothing makes sense. Have you ever seen the scars in the earth the wagon trains made by going over the same ground again and again? I feel like I have those in my brain from going over and over what we know about Tom's disappearance. I can't figure it out. We're missing the who and the why. Not to mention the where and the how. So far, all we have is the what the fuck."

Justin chuckled. "I'm sorry. I don't mean to laugh. I know it's not funny. We're talking about your husband. I don't know how you've coped so well so far. I'd be a huge mess if this were happening to my Betty."

"I'm faking it until I can make it."

He pointed to the file again. "Go back to that number that looked familiar."

My gaze locked on his. "Do you know who it is?"

"I know who all of them are."

I jerked forward to the desk. "Why the hell didn't you say something then?" I picked up the file in one hand the desk phone in the other. The company's telephone system automatically disguised our number, so I dialed without question. As always, it took a long time to connect. I held my breath through three rings, my hopes and the tension in my shoulders rising with each one. Finally, in the middle of the fourth ring, the voicemail system picked up.

"You have reached the voicemail of Althea MacKinnon. Please leave a message and Mrs. MacKinnon will ring you back."

JUSTIN SLAMMED me against the wall but it barely registered. My heartbeat thundered in my head. Althea. Althea was the cause of all this! My only thought was how much I would enjoy ripping her limb from limb until she told me where Tom was.

"Henry, stop!" Justin shouted as I struggled against his hold. "Dev! Shelby!"

Justin's forearm to my neck cutting off the oxygen supply finally caught my attention. I tried to pry my way out of his grip, but he was too damn strong.

The elephantine sound of men running down the hallway competed with the pulse of blood in my head. In seconds, Dev, Shelby, and several others appeared in the doorway. "What the hell's going on here?" Dev shouted.

Justin pinned me against the wall again and addressed the others over his shoulder. "We found out who was paying Berglund. Henry's freaking out."

"Get back to work, everyone," Dev said to the rest of the crowd that had assembled in the hallway. "There's nothing else to see here."

I was gaining ground in my attempts to get away from him. I just needed to—

"I can't hold him much longer, Deveraux! Get in here and help me!"

Shelby's big body smashed into us both, forcing out what little air was left in my lungs. Dev entered the office, closing the door behind him. Justin slipped out from between me and Shelby, leaving the former Marine to keep me in place. Even as angry as I was, I knew fighting him was a losing proposition. The man could incapacitate me before I could blink. I put my hands up in the surrender position and glared at Justin. Fucking traitor.

"Who is it?" Dev asked in a remarkably calm voice. He leaned against the door, cutting off my last chance of escape.

"It's Althea," I croaked, swallowing hard to lubricate my abused trachea.

Shelby slowly relieved some of his weight from me, the question in his eyes. At my nod, he patted my chest and took two steps back.

"What?" Dev asked.

Justin cast me a wary glare before explaining. "Berglund and Althea MacKinnon exchanged a series of phone calls several times over the six-month period before Tom's death. I haven't been able to establish for certain that the money Berglund deposited in the bank came from her, but it's a pretty damn good guess. There's no reason those two would have known each other, much less had that close a relationship unless he was working for her. Nothing in his background shows that he could have known the MacKinnons before he started working at Hardwick."

"Well I'll be fucked."

"Shelby," Dev warned.

"Sorry, boss."

Dev pushed off the wall and came to stand in front of me. "And what were you going to do, hotshot? Drive out to the vineyard and confront her?"

"You're goddamn right!" I shouted, not giving a damn that he was my boss. The woman had tried for more than twenty years to make my life hell. Somehow she'd found a way to make it a living nightmare by taking away my husband—her own damn son! There wasn't a question in my mind now that Tom was alive. Althea might be a fucked up bitch, but she didn't have it in her blackened excuse for a heart to kill her own child. He was out there. Somewhere. I just had to force her to tell me where. If she wouldn't come clean, I wouldn't have the slightest compunction against beating the answers out of her. It was the least she deserved after what she'd put my family through.

"Well that's just about the stupidest thing I've ever heard you say."

Wait. "What?"

"You have no proof, Henry. You have nothing but a set of phone calls. How do we even know it was Althea making them? Who else has access to her phone? Could it have been Matthew? One of the maids? Maybe Berglund was having an affair with her personal secretary. Even if it was her, what if she was only paying Berglund to get Tom to cheat on you?"

I shook my head. "No. No, that's not possible. It's her!"

"Where is your proof? You have to have proof before you go in there half-cocked, slinging accusations around like you're her judge, jury, and executioner."

"It's her, goddammit! I know it is! She's never wanted Tom and me together. She finally figured out how to get him away from me and she paid Berglund to do it!"

Dev shrugged. "Yeah, maybe so. Or maybe Tom got tired of his life and decided to start over somewhere else. Or maybe Berglund killed him because he was gay. The point is, we don't know anything yet. And even if we did, we still don't know where Tom is. If you go out to Villa Dimitri and confront her, you're tipping our hand before we have anything in it to nail her with. You think she wouldn't just leave the country on her private jet as soon as you walked out the door?"

I slumped against the wall, the fire inside me successfully dashed by his words. He was right. If I thought about it logically, I knew we didn't have enough to tie events together, much less enough to force a confession out of Althea. I'd put up with her making Tom's and my life difficult for decades. I could wait a few more days to exact my revenge.

"So what do we do? How do we prove that she paid Berglund to do whatever the hell he did with my husband?"

"That, my friend, is where you team up with our little buddy Casper."

"Casper?" I frowned in confusion.

Dev tossed me a grin before turning to the other two. "Great job, Justin. If we need anything else, we'll let you know. It's time for your Officer of the Court ears to leave the building."

Justin laughed. "You don't have to tell me twice and I didn't hear it the first time." He crossed the room and offered his hand. "I'm sorry, old friend. I didn't mean to upset you, but I'm glad we were able to find something to set you in a direction."

I shook his hand and pulled him into a hug. "You're a good friend, Justin. I'm sorry I lost my mind there for a second. Thank you for everything."

"My pleasure, buddy. If you need anything else, you know my number." With that, he slipped out of the room, firmly latching the door behind him.

"Casper?" I queried Dev impatiently.

"As in the friendly ghost. He's a hacker. Brilliant kid. He'll get you into every account the woman has, personal or business, and all you have to do is find the transaction that ties her to Berglund. While you're doing that, he'll get into her phone and email accounts and see if there are any other traces of contact between her and Berglund. He'll be able to find and reconstitute supposedly-deleted files." He patted my shoulder. "If she's responsible, we'll get her. I told you at the outset that we'd find out what happened to Tom. We will. It's what we do. But you have to play by my rules. You can't make any moves without me approving them first. We only have one chance at this. If we fuck it up, Althea's gone for good, along with any chance of locating Tom. Do you understand?"

I nodded.

"Aloud."

"I understand, Dev. I won't do anything without your prior approval."

"Excellent."

I looked between Dev and Shelby, feeling the exhaustion creeping in along with the headache. "So, where do we begin?"

"It's funny you should ask," Shelby said, planting himself in one of the chairs in front of my desk. "Something's been bothering me about this case from the get-go, but I wasn't able to figure it out until a few days ago."

Dev sat in the chair next to Shelby, so I moved around to reclaim my place behind the desk. "What is it?"

"What the hell was Berglund doing so close to Squaw Valley?"

"I've been wondering that too!" I exclaimed, thankful someone else had found the location of the crash questionable.

"Shelby has been looking into the area around the crash. A friend of his from Reno went up there for us and poked around a little bit."

I nodded. "And? Did he find anything?"

"Well, we were just getting to that part of the story when you flipped out and we had to run down here to save your ass." Dev grinned.

Shelby stood. "I'll go get the maps and be right back."

"Maps?" I asked as the detective exited the office.

"Shelby's old school. He likes paper maps. The bigger, the better. They're spread all over my conference table."

I looked around my office. "I don't have that kind of space."

"I know. And Shelby will remember that about half way back here. And then he'll be pissed when he has to ask us to go back to my office."

"So...why don't we just go there now and save him the trouble?"

"Aw, you're no fun."

"You're trying to screw with him?"

"Oh hell yeah. It's my favorite pastime."

I shook my head. "Let's, just this one time, let it go, huh?" I reached into the desk drawer and pulled out the bottle of ibuprofen. I swallowed four of the pills while Dev debated.

"Fine. We'll do it your way," he said, buttoning his suit jacket as he rose. "Next time you have to let me piss him off."

"He's a Marine. Why would you want to piss him off?"

I'd swear Dev's smile contained a touch of insanity. "It's fun."

SHELBY SMILED from his spot on the other side of the conference table when we entered Dev's office. "You thought I'd fall for that again?" he asked in a rueful tone.

Dev laughed. "I was hoping, but Henry spoiled the party."

"Thank you for that, Henry." Shelby chuckled. "Your boss likes to get me riled up for the fun of it."

"So I've heard." I approached the table, anxious to get on with things. It took every ounce of my self-control not to ditch the meeting and drive out to the vineyard to confront Althea. I understood Dev's reasons for waiting, but it didn't change the fact that I had already judged her guilty in my mind. She'd paid Jack Berg—or Ioannis Berglund, whatever his name was—to do something to Tom. She had spent actual money to destroy my family. I would make sure she burned in hell for that.

Maps and large photos covered the majority of the table's surface. They showed the area between Oakland and Truckee in varying scales, from only several square miles to the entire one hundred eighty-mile distance. "What are we looking at here?" I asked impatiently. Whatever it was would be a needle in a haystack on an extreme level.

"I told you I've been wondering why Berglund was so close to Squaw Valley when he was killed. It didn't originally seem like anything out of the ordinary since that's where Tom was headed. But then I wondered where and when Tom had gotten out of the vehicle, assuming he was in it to begin with. Scott is working on finding traffic camera footage of the vehicle that day. With any luck, that will help us determine whether or not the two of them left town together."

"Okay, so then what's all this?"

"This is the route we expect Tom would have taken to get to you, essentially I-80 from here to there."

I sighed. "Shelby, I'm sorry, but I'm not picking up what you're dropping. Can you be more specific, please?"

He chuckled. "Along this route are several places where Berglund could have exited the highway. The question is, where would he have gotten off to stash Tom. Now that we know Tom's mother was behind his disappearance—"

"Technically that's still unproven," Dev interrupted.

"It is," Shelby agreed, "but it makes sense as the only reason she and Berglund would have been in contact." He held his hands up to forestall Dev's arguments. "I know, I know. You can come up with seven hundred other reasons. Those aren't important to us right now. We're looking for a place that Tom's mom would want Berglund to drop her son."

Dev frowned. "Okay, fine. Does this change what you were trying to tell me earlier?"

"Not really. It's the same concept, just with a name behind the money."

"Shelby. Please." I squeezed my temples.

"Right. So, along the way here, there are about a thousand empty cabins. Most of them are hidden from the satellites by trees. How many people do you know would be playing around in the mountains in February?"

"I don't have any rugged-type friends, so not very many," I admitted. It felt strangely like a failure of manhood to confess that to a Marine. The man had endured untold hardships fighting for my freedom through several tours of duty in Iraq and Afghanistan. I was incredibly grateful for his sacrifice, but my idea of roughing it was a hotel without room service.

He nodded as if expecting the answer. "Most people have mountain cabins for summer recreation. They want to escape the hustle and bustle of city life, but they don't actually want to deal with the harsh realities of winter in the mountains."

"I can understand that." Just the thought of being trapped in the mountains during a blizzard made me feel cold. Considering Truckee was only a few miles from Donner Pass, that feeling was intensified with the heebie jeebies.

"My theory is that Berglund dropped off Tom at a cabin somewhere between Oakland and Truckee. Where, I don't know. Why, I don't know. My first thought was that it would be a nice, out of the way place to keep him until a ransom could be arranged, but a) none was ever asked for, and b) now we know—presume, for Dev's benefit—that Althea was paying him to do something else with Tom."

"But what?" My frustration level grew as my headache intensified. This seemed to be an enormous waste of time. There were thousands of square miles of mountains with tens of thousands of acres of farmland between the two points. It would take months to search that much area, even if we could find all of the cabins.

"You said Althea has never liked the fact that Tom was gay, right?"

I shrugged. "Neither one of his parents were happy about it."

"Did they ever try to do anything about it?"

"Aside from trying to make our lives miserable? No. They didn't cut Tom off or anything like that. They just made it clear to him and to me how much they hated me and our relationship."

Dev snapped his fingers. "There's a reparative therapy camp out in the mountains near Nevada City."

"Actually there are three between here and there," Shelby said. I must have shot him a look, because he smiled slightly. "It's information from a case I worked last year. I don't keep track of ex-gay camps for fun."

I dismissed the idea out of hand. "It doesn't matter anyway. That's too crazy, even for Althea."

"Are you sure?" Dev asked. "You're pretty sure she paid someone to do something to her son. Why wouldn't it be to deliver him to a straight camp?"

My heart dropped through the floor. I fumbled for a chair as my knees gave way. "Why would she do that now? I could understand it when we were first dating, but it's been over twenty years."

"Maybe she's confronting her own mortality. She is getting older."

I gasped as the pieces fell into place. "Oh my god, that's it." I jumped to my feet. "She's always been a believer, but nothing radical. I didn't think it was related at the time, but CJ said she had a chapel built onto the house. She's diving into that religion headfirst. If she's turned into a capital-b Believer, then she's capable of anything, even forcibly committing Tom to a conversion camp. He can't be with her in heaven if he's living an unrepentant sinner's life on earth—and she definitely believes homosexuality is a sin. She always has."

"How much do you suppose Matthew knows about all this?" Dev asked.

"I don't have any idea. CJ said he was pretty bewildered by Althea's new enthusiasm for the Church, but he was mainly playing along to get along." I forced all the fragments of thoughts from my head and concentrated on Matthew and his personality for a moment. "No, I can't believe he'd have anything to do with that. He definitely didn't know that wasn't Tom's body in his grave. He was a mess when he found out Tom had died. Althea was stoic, but I chalked that up to her personality. You know, don't let the peasants know they've upset you and all that. But Matthew? He couldn't contain his grief like she did."

"Well if we're right, she knew that wasn't Tom, so she wasn't grieving. She only had to act the part to a degree."

I wanted to punch something. Or someone. The mists around Tom's disappearance were starting to lift, but I wasn't liking what I was discovering. "How do we find out if he's there? I doubt they'll admit it if we flat-out ask them."

"I have a plan," Shelby said, much to my surprise. "Give me two days to get more information." He pulled his phone out of his pocket as he walked out of the office without so much as a wave.

"This is crazy," I said to Dev.

"Is it any crazier than someone else being in your husband's grave?"

I opened and closed my mouth, unable to come up with a response.

"Go home, Henry. Take the rest of the day for yourself, but do not go confront Althea. I'm trusting you."

For the first time since Justin showed up with Berglund's phone records, the truth of the new information seemed to be settling into my heart. Thoughts slowly whirled around my brain, dragged down by the thought of Althea intentionally harming Tom and ruining my family. "No, I won't. I think I need some sleep so I can cope with this."

Dev squeezed my shoulder lightly. "That's a great idea. Let me have one of the boys drive you home so you don't have to deal with public transit."

I nodded, heading for the door, already anticipating the nap I would take as soon as I got home. "That would be great, thanks."

I TUGGED at his lower lip with my teeth, pulling a groan from deep within him. He writhed on the bed, flexing his hips to take more of me. We moved in a slow, almost lazy fashion, making love the way we had a million times before. I stared into Tom's unfocused, half-closed green eyes, loving that I could still make him feel so much after so many years, so many times. I still loved the caress of his skin against mine, loved the heat of being inside him.

His thighs squeezed my hips, urging me to move. I resisted, keeping him on the edge, holding his release just out of reach. Instead, I gripped the length of his erection between us, pulling on his heated skin, giving the twist that he loved so much over the glans. He gasped, throwing his head back, and bucking his hips upward at the sensation. He tightened around me and I drove into him then, short rabbit thrusts aimed at his prostate. I spilled into him, rising just enough to watch his orgasm shoot through and out of him. His release painted his chest and stomach in stripes of white. I scooped some onto my fingers and glazed his swollen lips with it. His tongue shot out to get more. His eyes locked with mine, his expression equal parts teasing and sated, as he ran the tip of his tongue around his lips. I dove for them like he knew I would, kissing him with a breathless passion.

I jerked awake to find the room empty and cool in the late-afternoon light. Both hands were stuffed into my boxer briefs and wrapped around my leaking dick. I gave it a small tug as reality settled heavily on my shoulders. No matter how vivid the dream had been, Tom wasn't here. I was alone again in my lonely bed. I closed my eyes, picturing the scene again. Emotions flooded over me: peace, contentment, satisfaction. I struggled to recall the taste of Tom's cum on my tongue, the feel of his mouth on mine. I tugged my throbbing erection. If Tom couldn't be here physically to help me, I was certainly going to use the memory of an erotic dream to find some physical pleasure.

Lately it had seemed that my masturbation had been less about finding pleasure in my body and more about the physical need for release. I didn't jerk off to enjoy myself; I did it because my body required it.

But this was different. The lingering effects of the dream felt like an almost silent promise that I would find Tom again, that neither of us would be lonely anymore. I'd had trouble picturing Tom's face in my waking hours, but in sleep, the sight, taste, and touch of him appeared easily. I pulled on my dick again, imagining the warm, wet heat of Tom's mouth. A moan escaped my lips as I pulled again, sending a finger to explore my perineum.

Our sex life had always been good, even if it had changed in frequency and mood over the years. What hadn't left us was the ability and need to make each other feel special. Unlike when we were silly kids just getting together, we were no longer mostly out for our own nut. We grew into generous squirrels, more often handing out the first nut to the other before taking our own.

I rolled my eyes at the invasion of thought squirrels and tugged harder on my cock. Whereas Tom preferred to have me concentrate on the head of his erection when I was jerking him off, I paid more attention to my shaft, only grazing the glans, saving that particular stimulation for last.

I shifted onto my side to grab the lube from the nightstand and swore loudly and with conviction when the doorbell rang. With one last sorrowful glance at my straining erection, I swung my legs off the bed and sat up.

It would be Shaun. It had to be Shaun. No one else would be rude enough to interrupt my "alone time." Hell, no one else ever came to visit.

I grabbed my dress shirt from where I'd dropped it on the floor and pushed my arms through the sleeves. I didn't bother buttoning it, nor did I stop to put on jeans or shorts. I didn't have anything to hide from Shaun. I wandered through the semi-darkened living room to pull open the front door.

Lingering memories of Tom kept me from remembering my still-hard dick was only covered by a thin layer of cotton boxer briefs until Shaun's quick scan of me stopped there, probably focusing on the wet spot. He swallowed hard and shouldered past me into the foyer. "You should put that thing away before I take it as an invitation," he said with a voice so strained I laughed aloud.

"You've seen me naked a million times," I said, closing the door and rearming the alarm. I fastened the bottom few buttons on my shirt to cover his so-called invitation.

"Yeah, but I haven't seen you hard in a long time. There's a difference."

"Oh is th—wait, when did you see me hard?"

Shaun flushed and headed for the kitchen. "All the time when you and Tom started dating. Can we change the subject please?" He disappeared from view, but the desperation in his voice made it through the walls. "Would you go put on something decent?"

I laughed. "Don't tell me you've been spanking to twenty-year-old memories of me in the buff?"

"Hank." His voice held a warning I couldn't possibly heed.

"Shaun," I echoed. I knew I shouldn't be such a tease, but I couldn't help it. Well, I could, I just didn't want to. If I allowed my mind to wander from the moment, it was bound to come up with thoughts that would ruin my mood. I sat in the chair that was slightly angled toward the kitchen doorway, throwing my leg across the low armrest, and pulling my shirt up slightly. I squeezed the base of my dick to plump it back up so he would get the full effect of the package when he came back in the room. At this stage of the game, any attention I paid to it was bound to cause it to sit up and take notice.

He came around the corner taking a pull from a bottle of water and promptly spewed it all over the floor. "You're such a jackass!" he shouted before disappearing into the kitchen again. "What are you, twelve? Put some damn clothes on!"

I laughed and covered up. "Did that look like a twelve-year-old's dick?"

"I meant mentally, asshole," he groused. He glared as he came back into my line of sight clutching a wad of paper towels.

"You know you would have done the same thing." I tried to stifle my laughter, but he looked so appalled and offended that I couldn't stop it. I would have never guessed Shaun O'Malley had a prudish bone in his body.

He cleaned the water from the hardwood floor without looking up. "If you don't put some pants on, I'm leaving."

His tone finally caught my attention. "Shaun, I-"

He cut me off, enunciating each word like a separate sentence. "Put some pants on or I'm leaving."

Without another word, I dashed to the bedroom. I pulled a pair of jeans from the dresser drawer and slid them on. Remorse dampened my spirits. I'd always teased Shaun a bit, but never so overtly as I had done since he'd confessed his feelings to me those months ago. It wasn't that I disbelieved him, it was that I needed to keep myself distracted from opening to the possibility that I could feel the same way. No matter how much I might want to, I couldn't allow myself to take those emotions seriously until we knew if Tom was alive.

But I'd allowed my defense mechanism to belittle my best friend. For that I felt shame. I pointed to my image in the mirror. "Get your shit together, Cooley. You're so close. Don't go fucking things up now."

I padded barefoot back into the living room. Shaun gazed out the window next to the Christmas tree I still hadn't taken down, the set of his shoulders betraying his tension. "I'm sorry," I offered quietly. I hoped he heard the sincerity in my voice.

He shrugged and brought the water bottle to his mouth to drain the last of its contents. "What more can I expect from someone who still has his Christmas tree up on the nineteenth of January?"

It was the closest I would ever get to forgiven. "I've been waiting for you to take it down since you insisted we put it up."

He shook his head and shot me a disgusted expression over his shoulder. "Go get the boxes, lazy ass. At the rate you're going, it'll still be up at Easter."

"Labor Day," I agreed with a faux-chastened sigh.

He gestured to the garage with his empty bottle. "Go. You can tell me all about your news while we take the delicate things off the tree. We'll see how many you manage to not to break."

And like a shotgun blast to the chest, the knowledge I'd tried so hard to keep from my brain came rushing back. "Do you already know?"

He nodded.

"Trevor?"

Shaun nodded again. "And Dev. They both called. Separately. They're worried about you."

I huffed. "Don't worry about me. Worry about Althea. I'm gonna skin a bitch alive."

"Oh I know it."

I was getting wound up. "She's going to rue the day she heard the name Henry Cooley."

"Preachin' to the choir, baby."

Damn right. Crazy bitch. "I'm going to chop off her extremities one by one until she knows the pain I've been living with the last year."

"Forget *Boxing Helena*, this'll be Boxing Althea."

The image of a limbless Althea trying to hold court was almost amusing. "I'm going to make damn sure all her little society friends know what a fucked up bitch she is, paying some freak to kidnap or kill her own kid!"

"That's a whole new entry in Page Six."

Ha! Try saving that face, bitch. "It is!" I locked eyes with Shaun, which deflated all my bluster like a balloon. "I'm really scared, Shaun," I whispered.

"I know," he whispered back. He crossed the room and pulled me into a hug. It was one of those times I was glad he was three inches taller than me. I felt safe for the first time in a long time. "We'll get through this," he said.

I squeezed him back. "Thank you for being here for me through all this crazy shit. I don't know where I'd be without you."

"You'd be locked the hell up in some loony bin, that's where you'd be." He tugged on my earlobe. "Still not sure you don't belong there, but I've got you now."

"I'm not crazy."

He chuckled. "And prisons are full of innocents."

I smacked his back. "Now who's being a jackass?"

He shrugged and pulled away. "I just didn't want you getting tear stains on my cashmere sweater. Now go get your boxes. We have a tree to take down."

If I hadn't quashed the impulse as soon as I felt it, I would have given him a quick kiss. Instead, I hustled into the garage to collect my thoughts along with the boxes.

SEVEN

"You're all out of your minds. This will never work. And it's too dangerous besides!" Shelby had just presented his plan for infiltrating an ex-gay ranch near Nevada City. In two days he'd narrowed it down to one—the Heaven's Avenging Army Ranch. Because none of the other prospective sites had events scheduled until late February, he'd come up with a "plan" that consisted of Trevor taking part in a Quest for Masculinity retreat that was already planned for the last weekend of the month, a mere nine days away. Once Trevor was accepted as part of the group, he was supposed to poke around and find Tom. All without back up or any way to signal for help if—when—something went wrong.

Another twist I didn't particularly care for was that Shelby was to accompany Trevor to the ranch posing as Trev's homophobic father. It was hoped that if Shelby threw enough of a bitch fit about having a faggot son, those in charge of the shadier parts of the conversion therapy might attempt to persuade him to put Trevor through their program, thereby giving Trevor a better chance to find Tom. Even if that didn't work, if Shelby gave a memorable enough performance, he might create some sympathy among the staff, and would then have easier access to the ranch itself.

"Henry, if this is the quickest way to find Tom, we have to do it," Trevor said.

"If this is the best way, then let me do it. Tom's my husband. There's no need to put anyone else at risk."

Dev shook his head. "If we're right and Tom's there, the staff has probably been given your photo—or your description at the very least—and they'll be looking for you. Putting you in there could cause them to do something rash."

A shiver ran down my spine at the thought of Althea's faceless minions causing Tom harm. "Okay, that might be a valid point." I jammed my hands through my hair in frustration. The whole thing was nothing but one gigantic clusterfuck. "Why don't we have Liam do it? He's fully trained and more than capable."

"Liam's too straight," Trevor declared. "There's no way anyone would believe he's questioning his sexuality."

"What about Brian or David?"

"Henry, stop," Trevor pleaded.

"I'm not putting you in harm's way on a whim!"

Trevor left his chair to kneel in front of mine. He took my hands in his and looked at me with pleading blue eyes. "Shelby and Dev will make sure nothing will happen to me. This really is the best plan. All I have to do is confirm that Tom is being held there and I can call in reinforcements to get us both out."

"Trevor, this isn't what you signed up for. I can't ask you do to this."

"You're not. I'm volunteering."

"You've been drafted." I shot a censorious look at Shelby. What kind of Marine would come up with this train wreck of a plan?

"That's not true. It wouldn't make sense for anyone else to do it. I'm still within the age range those vultures like to prey on the most, and I'm gay. I can play confused and angry about my sexuality. Hell, all I have to do is remember what it was like in school. And with Shelby there playing the disapproving dad, it'll be a piece of cake." He grinned. "You've been out of high school longer than I've been alive. It would be more of a stretch for you."

I narrowed my eyes at him. "You're either calling me old or questioning my acting abilities, neither of which is helping your case."

He laughed. "I'm just pointing out the obvious. It'll be easier for me. I have a dog in this fight now too. Someone shot at us, probably on

Althea's orders. Hush, Dev." He turned a smile at our glowering boss before focusing on me again. "I want to do this, Henry. I want to do it for you and Tom and CJ. Please let me help."

I exhaled forcibly. I didn't have a viable alternative, but that didn't mean I liked the proposal on the table. "It's against my better judgment to say yes, but I have a feeling you're going to do it no matter what I say, am I right?"

He smiled and climbed to his feet. "You're absolutely right."

"It's not as dangerous as it sounds, Henry," Shelby said. "We have nine days before he checks in. We'll go over and over the details until it's flawless. I know Trev has impressed his self-defense coordinator, so he's capable of taking care of himself if necessary."

"Oh that makes me feel better."

Dev scowled. "We're going to equip him with a pair of sneakers that have a secret compartment in the sole. We'll hide a small telephone in there. That way he can get a message to us when he finds Tom or if he needs help."

"A shoe phone?" I said incredulously. "What is this, *Get Smart*?"

Trevor looked confused but the two older men laughed. "It's a bit more advanced than that," Dev answered. "The phone's equipped with a handheld transceiver."

"A what?"

Dev frowned. I was clearly getting on his nerves by questioning his and some ex-Marine's tactical planning abilities. Well shucks. How many fucks did I give about their precious feelings?

"A walkie-talkie," he explained. "We've used them before. It'll be fine. You don't think I'd send one of my own into a situation without a way to extract him, do you?"

I threw my hands up in frustration. "I honestly don't know what to think anymore, Dev! This is all so surreal. Until eleven months ago, I was a CPA going about my life like I was supposed to do. Happy marriage, happy kid, unhappy job. Now I'm sitting here in a private detective's office—*where I work*, for crying out loud—talking about reparative therapy camps and shoe phones! Sometimes I wonder if I'm still in Crazytown, because it sure as hell feels like it."

The intercom buzzed. "Mr. O'Malley is here, Dev," Doris' voice announced.

I breathed a sigh of relief. What perfect timing. I could vent to my best friend about all the wacko shit that had happened since last we'd talked this morning. "I'll be right there," I said in the direction of the phone.

"Actually, he's here for me," Dev said, coloring slightly.

"He—what?"

He shrugged. "We're having lunch."

I snapped my sagging jaw shut to hide the rest of my surprise. "Oh, okay." I glanced at Trevor to find him staring out the window.

"I promise I won't tell him anything that happened today. I know you'll need to vent to him later."

I scoffed. "Did something out of the ordinary happen? Seems like just another day in Soap Opera Town to me."

Dev and Shelby laughed as they pulled on their suit jackets. "Alright, folks, I'll get all the details ironed out and we'll reconvene tomorrow to go through the steps. Is that okay with everyone?" Shelby asked.

We all answered some variation of "fine," and the other two left the room. I turned to Trevor. "Hey, are you okay?"

He plastered a fake smile on his face. "I'm fine. Don't worry about me."

"I do worry about you. You're like another son to me."

He smiled. "That's sweet, Henry, thanks. I'm okay, really. I'm just thinking about getting in character for this mission."

That sentence wasn't one I had ever imagined someone saying to me. "Shaun and Dev having lunch without you is...?"

Trevor shrugged. "It's fine with me. Dev and I aren't seeing each other anymore."

"What? Since when?"

"Since the day after the shooting."

I didn't even try to hide my surprise. That was pretty rotten timing on Dev's part. "That was three weeks ago. Why didn't you tell me?"

"I didn't want to make it a bigger deal than it was. We'd always said it was just casual. And so it was."

"For him," I added.

"Yeah." He looked away, sadness pulling at his features, making him look older than he was. "Such is life, I guess."

I reached over and pulled him into a hug. "I'm sorry, kiddo."

He hugged me back for a moment before pushing away, wiping wetness off his cheek as he did so. "They'll make a handsome couple, don't you think?"

I did, but that answer would only make him feel worse. He and Dev had made a handsome couple too.

"Let's get back to work," Trevor said, moving for the door. "I appreciate your concern, but I'm fine." He directed a tired smile at me as he left the room.

As if Shelby's plan wasn't bad enough to begin with, now we had a heartbroken Trevor playing the main role. If anything went wrong and he got hurt, I would never forgive myself. Which meant I needed to find a new, better idea.

"TALK TO me about your visit to your grandparents," I coaxed my son over the phone later that night.

"What do you want to know? Yia-yia was being weird, Grandpa was normal. We had lunch. Grandpa and I messed around in the winery for a bit. Then we had dinner. Yia-yia did her usual gift scene with the help. Remember how she always gave them an envelope full of cash, a trinket, and a gift certificate to the grocery store? This year she added a Bible to the mix."

"Is that all?" I was still missing the one thing that would link Althea to Berglund. It was a pretty big stretch of my imagination, but I held out hope that CJ might have overheard or seen something that would help connect the dots.

"No. After that, we went to the chapel for a service."

I shuddered at the thought. Neither Tom nor I were believers, but we'd raised CJ to carefully explore any religion that interested him and to make his own choice. We'd been proud when he'd come to the conclusion that organized religion wasn't for him, but we would have loved and respected any choice he made. "Awkward," I suggested.

"You have no idea, Dad. Yia-yia was in her element, but Grandpa and I were creeped out."

"I can't imagine. Did you discuss anything about Pops?"

His deep sigh traveled over the airwaves. "I talked with Grandpa about it a little bit. He blames himself for not making sure Mr. Lowe did his job correctly. He's pretty upset. You know how hard he took Pops' death in the first place."

"I remember. It can't be easy losing your only child. I don't know what I would do if anything ever happened to you."

CJ laughed. "I'm indestructible."

"Uh huh. That's what your father and I thought at your age too. Turns out, we were wrong."

"I know. Don't worry about me. I may do crazy things, but I'm always careful. I'm not ready to leave this life yet."

"Good." My son, the adrenaline junkie. A nineteen-year-old's definition of careful was a world away from a forty-three-year-old's. I'd seen videos his friends had taken of their antics, from cliff diving in Acapulco to jet ski racing on Lake Havasu. He had the heart of an artist and the drive of a maniac.

"You trust me, don't you?"

"Implicitly. But I also know that sometimes the more dangerous something is, the more you're drawn to it."

He chuckled. "I don't have enough art finished to die tragically young yet."

I laughed. "You're twisted. You get that from your father."

"From both of you."

I wished I could reach through the phone and hug him. He was the best thing about my life and it felt like I was losing him a little more each day. Not because he was pulling away, just because he was in Los Angeles and I was in San Francisco. I missed a lot not seeing him every day. "I love you, kiddo."

"I know, Dad. I love you too."

The doorbell rang. I knew immediately who was there. "Listen, your uncle Shaun just showed up, so I have to go," I told him, crossing the room to the front door. "I have one more question first. Did you talk to Yia-yia about Pops?"

"Oh hell no. Grandpa told me to stay wide of that subject, so I didn't bring him up at all. She said prayers for him, asking god to keep him safe in heaven. It's like she's in denial that he might be alive."

Which was exactly the way I would behave if I were trying to deflect suspicion. Or if I knew he wasn't, regardless of whose body was in his grave. I turned off the alarm and pulled the door open to see Shaun already starting to speak. I held my finger to my lips to shush him. He nodded and came into the house without a word. "Was that it? She didn't bring him up to you at all?"

"She only ever mentioned him in the context of being in heaven watching down on us. To be honest, it was really uncomfortable. I mean, we both know he wasn't in that grave, but she won't acknowledge it. To her, his body's in the ground and his soul is in heaven. Does she know something we don't?"

My head snapped up at the question. "Why would you think that?"

"Because she's so determined that he's in heaven."

"She's a mother grieving in her own way. It's probably easier for her not to get her hopes up that he might be alive. It's going to be a long fall for all of us if we find out he isn't."

"I know." His voice sounded small.

"Are you preparing for that?"

"As much as I can, I guess. It's hard not knowing. I really want him back. There's a hole in my life without him."

"I know exactly what you mean, kiddo. Should I have not told you?"

"No, I'm glad you did. I probably would have died of shock if you hadn't told me and he'd turned up alive. This way I can prepare myself for it either way."

"I'm so sorry you have to go through this. I hope you know I'm going to find out who's behind this and I'm going to skin them alive."

He chuckled. "Save some for me, will ya?"

"I will." I watched Shaun pour himself a drink at the bar. "Listen, I have to go. Take care of yourself. Be safe, be careful, all that, okay?"

"You know me."

"That's why I'm reminding you."

He laughed again but didn't acknowledge just how right I was. He didn't need to. We both knew it. "Love you, Dad. Bye."

"Bye, son. Love you too."

"I WONDERED if you'd show up tonight." My tone conveyed more censure than I'd intended, but I didn't try to soften it with words.

Shaun swallowed his mouthful of bourbon and offered a rueful smile. "I figured you'd want an explanation."

"You don't owe me anything." While that was technically true, I couldn't wait to hear what he'd come up with. I didn't care if he wanted to date Dev, but I did care that it hurt Trevor.

He splashed more liquor in his glass. "Well then maybe you can help me figure out what the hell's going on in my head. Because I damn sure can't make sense of it."

That rare confession of insecurity surprised me. "Am I going to need wine for this?"

He chuckled and poured a second glass of bourbon. "Why don't you try something a little stronger?"

I studied him more carefully then. His appearance had deteriorated since Monday. Only two days on, he looked tired and unshaven—haggard, if I had to pick a word. "You look like hell," I said, taking the glass when he offered it.

He raised his drink in a sarcastic salute and wandered over to flop onto the couch. He was still dressed from the office, but his tie hung loose around his neck, and the first three buttons of his dress shirt were undone, offering a glimpse of smooth, tight skin. He tugged off his suit jacket and slung it across the back of the couch.

I sat across from him, wondering what the hell had happened to him in the last few days. This wasn't the man I'd known for twenty-something years. Nothing affected Shaun, ever. Emotions and people routinely bounced off him, leaving little more than a ripple in their wake. He'd mourned Tom with me, but he'd also been a pillar of strength when CJ and I needed him to be. "What's going on with you?" I didn't even try to keep the concern from my voice. He'd already admitted something was bothering him, I only needed him to spill it.

Shaun tossed back half of his bourbon before turning his gaze on me. His green eyes were made more intense by the thick black smudges under them. "I can't get them out of my head. If I'm with Dev, I'm thinking about Trevor. If I'm with Trevor, I'm thinking about Dev. I can't figure out what the hell's happening to me."

I leaned my head back against the chair, completely taken aback by his words. I'd never seen him torn between two women, let alone two men. He simply didn't let anyone close enough to get under his skin that way.

What about me?

As soon as the thought raced through my head I was ashamed of it. As much as I wanted to, I couldn't pretend it hadn't occurred to me. Acknowledging it unsettled me far more than I could ever admit aloud. It meant that somewhere in the depths of my mind, I'd accepted Tom's death as a reality and started entertaining the possibility of Shaun as a romantic partner.

Shaky hands brought the bourbon to my mouth. I tossed back the entire contents of the glass, grateful for the burn that brought me out of my head for a minute. When had I turned into such a selfish prick?

I stalled for time as I tried to concentrate on Shaun's problem and shove mine into a subconscious closet in the sublevels of my brain. "I've never seen you like this."

He raked fingers through his thick coffee-colored hair. "Because I've never been like this." He laid his head back against the couch and stared at the ceiling. "You know me, Hank. I date who and when I want to, and only as long as it's fun. Sex is a fun experience, but it's nothing to get hung up on. I've turned down sex plenty of times for a thousand different reasons, but never because I was afraid I'd get attached."

"Until now?" I asked nervously. As much as the creature on the couch resembled my best friend in the world, nothing coming out of his mouth sounded like the Shaun I knew. The words were accurate, but the emotions and the tone were wrong on every level.

His gaze locked with mine. "Until now." He sat up on the couch, leaning forward until his elbows were on his knees. He rubbed both temples with long fingers. "I turned down a three-way with them because it felt cheap. I can't even make that make sense in my mind, let alone to tell you. You know Trevor and I had a thing a couple of years ago. He's a great guy, awesome in the sack, but he wasn't you, so it didn't go beyond that. I didn't meet Dev until Christmas. He's hot as hell, brilliant, funny in his own way. So why did I decide that sleeping with both of them would be wrong? I've had plenty of threesomes in my life. Hell, you've heard the saying: if two hard dicks are good, three are better. What the hell is wrong with me?"

"Could it be you're developing feelings for them?"

Shaun scoffed. "That's ridiculous. If I was going to fall for someone else, it would have happened before now."

I shrugged, wishing the bourbon bottle wasn't so far away. I desperately needed more alcohol, but I didn't trust this bubble of truth not to burst if I moved to refresh my drink. "Not necessarily. Look, a lot has happened in the last year. Tom died and maybe came back to life. You finally confessed your feelings to me—not once, but twice. I went off the deep end and you helped me back to reality. I had a stalker and you helped keep me together during all that. Then we went on vacation and finally found out that there is some chemistry between us. But then we had to shut it down because Tom might be alive. Maybe all your heart needed to be able to move on from me is to have your feelings validated. Maybe it knows something we don't."

Shaun rolled his eyes. "You're a shitty shrink. You're saying it's going to take two men to fill your spot?"

I grinned. "I hadn't thought of it that way, but now that you mention it, I am pretty awesome." And, surprisingly, the thought of "losing" Shaun to a Dev and Trevor combination didn't hurt in the least.

"And not the least bit conceited," he countered with an exhausted smile.

"You call it conceited, I call it confident."

"You really think it could work?"

I shrugged. "I think you owe it to yourself to find out. Talk to the guys, see if it's something they're open to trying." I snagged his empty glass from his hand and moved to the bar to pour us both generous refreshments. "I will say this: no one else has ever had you this screwed up within a month of meeting them."

I pretended I didn't hear his quiet, "No one but you," even as my heart squeezed with regret.

EIGHT

The weather couldn't have been worse for The Mission, as I'd taken to calling Shelby's disastrous plan in my head. I was still convinced the whole thing would blow up in our faces and that we were simply leading our little lamb, Trevor, to slaughter. My concerns had been overridden by every single person who'd come in contact with the plan, so I kept my mouth shut.

The drive to Nevada City had started off relatively uneventful, with the snow and wind not showing up until we were well clear of Oakland, thankfully. The last thing I needed was to go across that steel contraption of death known as the Bay Bridge in the beginnings of a blizzard.

Both big silver SUVs pulled to a stop in front of a surprisingly modern-looking cabin. I'd been picturing something like Ted Kaczynski's one-room nightmare. Instead, I found myself staring up at a two-story log structure with enough west-facing windows to put beach-front homes to shame. Thanks to Shelby's contacts, lights blazed inside and a chimney along the north wall puffed grey-white smoke up toward the low, snow-filled clouds. The weather had stretched the two-and-a-half-hour trip into three and a half, but The Mission was still a go.

I climbed out of the SUV and into about a foot of fresh snow. I glared at Dev, who just smiled and handed me an armload to take into the house. The last forty miles of the drive had been treacherous. We weren't yet into the steepest parts of the mountains, but there were more elevation changes and corners than I liked to encounter on slick, snow-packed roads. I'd finally given up looking out the windows and watched Captain America: Winter Soldier with Trevor on his tablet.

I didn't even want to think of the ironies of watching that movie as I headed in the snowy mountains on a rescue mission with a former Marine. I was neither Chris Evans nor Sebastian Stan. I was regular guy in weird ass circumstances looking for his husband. People wrote books and movies and soap operas about this stuff, they didn't actually live it. Yet here I was, almost a year after Tom's supposed death, still somehow trapped in the strangest plot twist of my life. All I wanted was to collect Tom and get back to my real life. And to not lose Trevor in the process.

"Let's get all of this unpacked so Shelby can take Trevor to the lodge and get him checked in," Dev instructed all of us.

As difficult as it was to comprehend that this was my real life, I had to remember that for Dev and Shelby, this was old hat. It was just another day away from the office. It was probably pretty tame for Shelby, compared to some of the things he'd seen in the Marines. They were experts. They'd probably carried out much more complicated and risky operations than this. But none of those had put my husband and a good friend at risk. My nerves were so tightly wound I was like a pissed off cobra, ready to strike out at anything, but with no target available, which only compounded the frustration and fear.

The four of us clattered into the massive cabin, stomping wet snow from our shoes as soon as we got inside. The interior was as impressive as the outside promised. The exterior walls were made of massive tree trunks expertly laid atop each other, giving it an impressive rustic vibe. The walls dividing the rooms were the traditional sheetrock painted in earthy hues, keeping all that exposed wood from becoming too oppressive. It would be an incredible place to spend a spring or summer. With the fireplace roaring away in the living room, aided by hidden central heating, it was a welcoming respite from the incoming blizzard outside.

We piled our gear on and around the massive dining table to the left of the front door. Dev tugged Trevor by the hand into what I suspected was a bedroom while Shelby and I went back outside to grab the last of our things. We dawdled a bit without acknowledging that we were giving the other two a bit of privacy. It occurred to me for the first time that Dev might be a bit nervous about putting his boyfriend—or ex-boyfriend or whatever they were to each other at the moment—into harm's way.

I was suddenly hit by a wave of gratitude for all these three men were doing for me and Tom, all without knowing for sure if we were on a wild goose chase. We still hadn't been able to determine if Tom was being held at the Heaven's Avenging Army ranch. We still didn't even know if he was alive. We were operating under some very big assumptions and very little information. But it was now or never with this group. The weekend's Quest for Masculinity retreat was their last public event until May.

"Shelby, I know I may have been a bit difficult lately, but I need you to know how much I appreciate you and Dev and Trevor. I never would have made it this far without your help."

He reached into the back of the SUV for the massive black drone that took up most of the cargo area. "Difficult? You've been a nightmare." He hoisted the drone and flashed a grin. "But it's okay. I understand. I'd be a lot worse if someone had kidnapped my spouse. It's all part of the job, Henry. You're a good guy. We all want to see you get Tom back. I hope this does the trick."

I blinked away the sudden tears. I was sure the big Marine didn't want to see them. "Thank you," I choked out, turning swiftly to avoid eye contact.

An hour later we were all settled into the cabin. We each had our own room, which was a pleasant surprise. With my raw nerves, I was glad I had a place to go if I needed to get away from the others.

Shelby's maps and photographs of the camp ranch had been tacked to a pegboard Dev had hung on the dining room wall. Apparently that area would function as command central. We were going over The Mission one last time before Shelby took Trevor over to check in.

Heaven's Avenging Army Ranch seemed to be a minimally functioning dude ranch, where the guests reclaimed their masculinity by tending to horses and performing ranch-type chores. John Wayne would be proud, I thought with revulsion. Shelby's friend in the area had captured photographs from a drone he sent up to surveil the site. Since Dev had decided to bring the company's newest drone along, we would be able to peek in on the goings-on occasionally, making sure Trevor was as safe as he could be in the lion's den.

Shelby pointed to the photographs of the ranch house. From the air it was shaped like a deformed tuning fork. There was the general U-shape, but the long tail addition coming off the body wasn't centered on the structure. Only the main part of the building was two-story. The extensions were all one level. "Like we talked about a few days ago, the latest blueprints we were able to dig up are out of date. They don't show this addition here. I'm convinced that's where they're keeping Tom."

"Why?" I asked.

"Because unless the rest of the house has been extensively remodeled from these blueprints, there simply isn't another area that would provide the amount of privacy needed to keep someone away from the weekend guests." He frowned but indulged me once again. "The two short wings here that face the back of the property, towards the barns, are group dining and recreational areas. The main body of the building contains the kitchen, a living room, and bathrooms on the main floor. The upstairs is dedicated to sleeping rooms." He tapped the oddly-positioned addition. "This area is far enough away from the main rooms to provide privacy without drawing a lot of undue attention."

"I'm sorry," I apologized. "I know we've gone over this a hundred times in the last few days, but I keep feeling like we're missing something."

Trevor slung an arm over my shoulder. "Don't worry so much, Henry. Shelby and Dev have studied this front, back, and upside down. It's going to be fine. I'm going to be fine. If all goes according to plan, we'll have Tom out of there in time for Sunday brunch."

"Yeah, well, you just make sure you don't do anything to freak these guys out. If they're really carrying out conversion therapy with electroshock torture, they won't think twice about hurting you."

"I'll be on my best behavior." He grinned impishly.

I knew his "best behavior" and it wasn't at all good, but I wasn't going to argue anymore. We'd come too far for it to do any good now. I just had to trust that the guys knew what they were doing. I threw my hands up and shoved back from the table. "Okay, let's get to it then."

"Thank Cher!" Trevor exclaimed, a true testament to how relieved he was.

"Tell me one more time, from the top," Dev instructed him.

Trevor sighed. "Shelby takes me to check in. He throws a huge fit about how no son of his will be queer and that I'm a gigantic disgrace. He'll throw in some code words about the Bible, blah blah blah. Once I'm checked in, I'll try to take a look around. I'll call you as soon as I've done that.

"Then I make nicey-nicey with the scary Christians and try to find out about Tom, all without mentioning his name or anything about sticking electrodes underneath fingernails—although I can't promise not to mention flaming hot pokers up their asses." He smiled sweetly. "Once I've located Tom or have confirmation that he's there, I'll call you back and we'll figure out how the hell to get him out of there."

Dev nodded. "Aside from the flaming hot pokers, great job. Let's just pray it's that easy."

I choked on my water and coughed. "Can we not?"

Trevor and Shelby laughed and even Dev grinned. Seeing them all with their senses of humor intact actually helped loosen the coils of tension in my shoulders. Maybe we weren't destined to screw this up completely. Maybe we were reaching the end of my long nightmare.

DEV CLAPPED me on the shoulder as we stood on the porch of the cabin watching the SUV's taillights as it slowly disappeared down the long driveway. Shelby was finally taking Trevor to check in at Heaven's

Avenging Army Ranch. It was only two o'clock in the afternoon, but the heavy snow falling and the occasional bursts of wind ensured it would be dark much too soon. I blew warm air into my cupped hands as Shelby finally reached the main road and turned out of sight.

"It'll be alright," Dev said.

"I know. Trevor's a big boy. He can handle himself. I only wish we knew more about the people working at the place. I mean, I know they can't be good people or they wouldn't do what they're doing, but are they delusional folks who truly think they're doing good work, or are they animals who get off on inflicting pain and punishment? Because those are two very different worlds."

He ushered me back inside the warm cabin before answering my question. "For what it's worth, the few people we've been able to find who have gone through the process here say it wasn't pain for the sake of pain. They weren't waterboarded or beaten or anything that horrific. They've been known to employ ice baths and electric shock, but not to the genitals, which is a huge 'Thank Cher,' as Trevor would say."

I laughed and followed Dev into the kitchen, which was a spacious room separated from the living room by a breakfast bar-slash-prep station. The black stainless steel appliances shimmered in the light, reflecting the deep cherry wood of the cabinets. The speckled black granite countertops finished off the room, giving it a comfortable, homey feel that made me want to spend time in there. "That's at least a little comfort."

Dev set about warming milk for hot cocoa on the gas cooktop so I took two mugs from the cabinet, spooning in the chocolate powder.

"What are the chances this isn't an exercise in frustration, Dev? I mean, I can't help thinking we're chasing shadows. We don't even know if Althea has ever heard of this place, let alone that she would actually conceive of or consent to putting Tom through something like this. I know she's a spiteful bitch, but in all the time I've known her, she's never acted against Tom's best interests."

Dev stirred the milk slowly. "There's something I haven't told you."

My stomach clenched at the words. "You know something? What do you know?"

"Casper found a connection."

I gasped. "What?"

Dev killed the fire under the pan and turned to pour the milk into the mugs, and returned the empty pan to a cool burner on the cooktop, concentrating on that job before answering my questions. By the time he was finished, I was ready to strangle him. "He found two separate fifty thousand dollar deposits in their Sacramento bank that he traced back to one of Althea's personal accounts."

I slammed my fist down on the counter in rage. Even if she hadn't intended the money to be used against Tom, she knew damn good and well that the Heaven's Avenging Army organization would use it to torture some other confused gay man. Regardless of her long-held convictions about the evils of homosexuality, Althea was not someone I would have believed would finance such horror. "Dammit!"

"There's more."

My gaze locked with Dev's. He seemed deeply uncomfortable but still confident in his information. "What is it? Why haven't you told me already?"

"I've been trying to keep you from going off the deep end and confronting your mother-in-law. Casper found a seventy-five thousand dollar cash withdrawal from another of her personal accounts dated about three days before Berglund's first big deposit."

His words hit like a shotgun blast to the stomach. Short of a video of Althea handing over the cash, this was as much of a smoking gun as we could ask for. The room tilted sharply. I leaned heavily against the cabinet to keep my balance as I fought to keep my breakfast from coming back up. "It's true then," I whispered through a tight throat. "Althea's behind all of it. Goddamn her! Goddamn her to hell!"

I swept my mug across the counter, sending it shattering to the floor. It was a poor substitute for wrapping my hands around Althea goddamn MacKinnon's throat and watching the life drain from her eyes. I curled into a ball against the cabinets, roiling from the emotional trauma.

What had she done with Tom? How was I going to explain this to CJ? How could I keep my son from knowing what a monster his grandmother was? How would I stop myself from killing her in cold blood? Would we ever have enough solid evidence to take to the courts? My eyes remained dry as all those thoughts and more flashed through my brain, but my soul wept for the pain this horrid woman had inflicted on her son and was about to subject my own son to.

Slowly the ache receded, replaced by a steely determination to save my husband and to take the bitch down in the process. Althea would pay. One way or another, she would know the hell I'd been living for the last eleven months. And I would make sure it was multiplied a thousand times for her.

Taking a deep, shuddering breath, I stood again. That was the last time, I vowed to myself. The last time Althea got the better of me. From that moment on, seeing her punished for what she'd done to Tom and my family was my primary reason for living. She thought she could use her millions and her religion to ruin my family. Let her god help her now because he was the only force that could stop me. Vengeance is mine, sayeth the faggot.

I cleaned up the spilled milk and ceramic shards. The simple but familiar process somehow soothing my nerves. Afterward, I found Dev in the living room tinkering with the camera on the bottom of the huge four-propeller drone. The thing had to have had a wingspan of five feet with a bulbous camera section underneath the rectangular center. I didn't want to know what it cost, but I'd seen five others of various sizes, shapes, and colors when I had accompanied Shelby to sign this one out.

"It's impressive," I complimented Dev, sitting in a chair near him.

"It better be," he agreed with a laugh. "These things aren't cheap. They'll pay for themselves in the long run, but most of them are a bitch and a half to learn to fly. Not this one," he said, unconsciously stroking the drone. "She's a dream. She's loaded with stabilizing features and systems I can't even understand. She almost flies herself. But that's why only Shelby and I know how to use them right now. I'll buy a couple of cheap ones in the spring. Everyone can learn on them before we bring out these bad boys."

"How long can they stay in the air?"

"They vary. This one we had designed to stay aloft for at least an hour, depending on the weather. She also has the longest range, so we don't have to get too close to the ranch to use it. With some of the others, we'd have to be at the gates to be able to keep in contact."

That startled me. I hadn't anticipated leaving the cabin. "We have to leave here to use this?"

Dev nodded. "Unfortunately. We have to be within two miles of her, and HAA is four miles away by road. We'll be able to stay out of sight and on the land that belongs to this cabin, but we'll have to practically be on the property line." He grinned. "Don't worry. I'll keep you safe."

I rolled my eyes. "I'm not worried, I'm just surprised. I thought you'd have the latest and greatest."

"Oh we do. And the biggest and baddest. We're still waiting for the technology to catch up to what we want." He checked his watch. "Trevor should be reporting in soon, which means Shelby will be here any minute."

"Good. The sooner he checks in, the sooner we can get him the hell out of there. I still don't like this." I held up a hand to forestall his argument. "I know, I know. It's the best option we had with the information we have. That doesn't mean I can't be nervous for him. He's like another son to me."

Dev cleared his throat, put the drone aside, and crossed to stand before the fireplace. He adjusted a log, causing the waning flames to jump to life again. "Speaking of which," he said, dusting off his hands, "I feel like I need to come clean with you about something."

I kept my face blank but laughed inside, having more than an inkling about what his confession would be. "Go ahead."

Dev chewed on one side of his full bottom lip. "You knew Trevor and I were dating, right?"

This time I did laugh aloud. "The blind and deaf in Singapore knew, Dev."

He chuckled. "I guess I had that coming. We weren't very subtle. The thing is, we're trying something new, and that sort of concerns you."

"You're grown men. You don't need my permission to pursue your lives."

"Not normally, no," he agreed. "The thing is, we're—that is, Trevor and I—we—we're seeing Shaun. I mean the three of us are try—we're all dating each other. As a three—uhm, I don't know what to call it. A triad, maybe? It's so confusing."

"And how do you feel about that?"

He ducked his head, but not before I saw the splash of color on his cheeks. "I don't like the explaining it part, but the rest of it's great. I mean, so far everything's good. We're still very new to it. It's barely been a week, to be honest." He laughed. "We don't have the slightest idea what the hell we're doing. All we know is that it feels right. Trevor and I weren't quite working. But Shaun and I, when we were together we both felt like we were missing Trevor. You know they had a thing before, right?"

"I do."

"Yeah, well, so we figured if we all felt that something was missing when we were coupled off, why shouldn't we try it with all of us." He smiled shyly. "It's complicated as hell, but I really think we could make a go of it if we keep our heads on straight."

"So to speak."

He flipped me off but laughed. "Yes, so to speak. No wonder Shaun says you're a jackass."

I laughed. "He's had twenty years to learn how to bring out the best in me." I pushed to my feet and crossed to stand in front of Dev. I offered him my hand. "As long as all three of you are in this because you want to be, you have my full support."

He shook my hand, looking as if a thousand pounds had been lifted from his shoulders. "Thank you, Henry. I've been worried you wouldn't approve or that it would drive a wedge between us at work."

"Listen, I've lived long enough to know that love and happiness come in many different forms. If the three of you are happy and you think you can all find love together, then far be it from me to stand in your way.

"Being without Tom this last year has been the most difficult time of my life, but I wouldn't trade a single one of the years we had to eliminate this one. If anything, it's taught me to appreciate him more than I did before he vanished. So go for it. Be good and kind to each other." I grinned. "I don't envy you though. One man is hard enough to deal with, I don't know how you'll manage two—especially if one of them is Shaun O'Malley!"

"Are you trying to scare me?"

"Maybe just a little." I chuckled at his stricken expression. "He's worth it, Dev. They both are. You have my blessing, if that's what you were asking for."

He let out a breath. "I guess it was. Thank you."

"You're welcome. Listen, I'm going to go make sure the phone Trevor will call is on. I'd hate to miss him because we were too busy talking about him." I turned, took two steps, and tossed the word bomb over my shoulder. "The sex must be incredible."

Dev groaned. "There isn't any!"

I whipped around to face him. "What?"

He gestured helplessly. "Shaun said we should wait until we know each other better before we jump into the sack. Can you believe that? I supposedly have two boyfriends but I can't have sex with either of them!"

I picked my jaw up from the floor. "Shaun O'Malley said that?"

TREVOR MADE brief contact Friday night shortly after Shelby returned from HAA. He claimed both staff and fellow Questers were friendly and happy. He thought we might have made a mistake, but he hadn't had a chance to look around the lodge at the time. Dev told him to keep alert but to play their games as long as he didn't feel they would lead to harm. We needed to keep the bad guys off guard as long as possible.

As soon as Trevor had hung up, I'd pled exhaustion and retired to the bedroom to call CJ. I'd needed to touch base with my son, to hear his normal voice from a normal world—if Los Angeles could be called that, even on a good day—and hear his normal teasing. Dev's confirmation that Althea was behind Tom's disappearance had set my top spinning more than I had anticipated. Hearing CJ's voice grounded me and gave me the courage and determination to continue down this path. My boy needed his father as much as I needed my husband. All of us needed his grandmother behind bars or in the dirt where she could never hurt any of us again.

Saturday morning dawned bright, crisp, and cold. Fourteen inches of snow had fallen in the last twenty-four hours, but it appeared the worst was over. I was the first one in the common areas, so I started coffee, then bundled up and shoveled off the front deck and the sidewalk down to the driveway. The wind chilled my face, but the work warmed my body and awakened muscles I'd forgotten I had. By the time I was finished, I was energized and almost happy—as long as I could keep the real reason we were there out of my brain.

Dev met me at the door with a cup of coffee and a smile. I discarded scarf, coat, and boots, and thanked him before taking that first soul-nourishing sip.

"Thanks for taking care of that. I wasn't really looking forward to it," he admitted.

"It was actually fun. I haven't shoveled snow in years. When we got that snow back in 2011, Tom didn't even have time to take the broom to it before it melted."

Dev's eyes lit up. "I remember that. We stayed up all night to see it."

I groaned. "Of course you did. What were you, twelve?"

He laughed. "It wasn't that long ago. I'd just turned twenty-six. Snow in San Francisco is a rare sight. We couldn't just sleep through it!"

"Of course not. That would be silly." I winked to show I was kidding and drank more of the coffee, appreciating the spreading warmth within me.

"Good morning, boys," Shelby said, coming around the corner from his bedroom. "Trevor just made contact again. He was able to look around a little bit last night after lights out. The addition we've been worried about is blocked from the rest of the house. It's only accessible through a keypad."

Dev clicked his tongue against his teeth. "That's not helpful. I'll have to call Casper and see if he thinks it's feasible to hack into their alarm system from here and disable that pad. Shelby, you'll have to do that dirty work."

"That's way beyond my skill set; but if Casper walks me through it, we should be fine. Oh, Trevor also said they've had breakfast already and are about to start on chores. He's been assigned to hay the horses. He's freaking out a little bit. Apparently he's never seen a horse in person before."

"What?"

"You're kidding!"

Dev and I expressed our disbelief at the same time, causing all three of us to crack up. Dev shook his head. "The poor guy's going to have to dig deep to find his masculinity around those big, scary beasts."

"There are all kinds of masculinity," I chided him good naturedly.

"Exactly," Shelby agreed before walking into the kitchen. "Not liking horses doesn't make you any less of a man."

Dev and I exchanged glances. By the size of the smile lighting his face I knew Shelby would regret that comment for a very long time.

Before he could tip his hand by bursting into laughter, Dev nudged me. "Come on, let's go get that big bird in the air. Maybe we'll get to see Trevor."

I perked up like a puppy. "Really? We can see it right away? We don't have to download the camera footage or anything?"

"Hell no," he said, walking into the dining room. "How do you think I navigate the thing? The camera has a real-time feed to the controller, but it also records everything. This one is actually a mapping camera, which is why I brought it. It'll create topological maps on the computer."

"I don't know what good that is, but it sounds impressive."

Dev sat to pull on his snow boots. "It'll come in handy for a lot of things, but the first one that comes to mind is another missing persons case. If we believe the bad guys have killed the victim instead of holding them for ransom, we'll be able survey the ground where we think they buried the body. The mapping program will show any recent disturbances of the earth, especially if we can compare the images to Google Maps or if we've already surveyed the area."

I stared at him in disbelief. "Well that's not disturbing at all, says the husband of a missing person."

Dev grimaced. "Sorry. I didn't mean—"

"Is that why you brought it? Do you think they killed Tom?"

"No, no, no. Slow down." He exhaled heavily. "I need to pay more attention to what I'm saying. No, I don't think they killed Tom. I believe he's in that weird addition. But yes, I am going to use the mapping feature while we use the drone. It doesn't have anything to do with Tom; I just need more practice with that feature."

"Slick," Shelby opined sarcastically from his end of the table.

"Shut up, Mr. Ed," Dev clipped, getting up from the table and grabbing the drone's massive case. "Have you ever driven a snowmobile, Henry?"

I hadn't, but I was a quick study. Within fifteen minutes Dev and I were zipping along across massive snowdrifts. Under any other circumstances, it could have been fun, a word I never would have associated with me and snow. Soon enough we approached a fence line, the border of the property that belonged to the cabin. Dev slowed his machine to a crawl and surveyed the area for a spot he liked. Twenty yards further up the hill, we killed the motors and Dev started to unpack the massive drone.

I watched in silence, trying to commit his movements to memory so it wouldn't be so foreign when I had to eventually learn how to assemble and operate the thing. He lost me long before he set the bird on the seat of the snow mobile and started fiddling with the controller. Eventually the four propellers sputtered to life and the beast soared into the air.

"Come watch," Dev instructed.

I stepped up behind him, captivated by the footage the drone's camera beamed back to the eight-inch display attached to the controller. Dev maneuvered the machine expertly, over trees and off toward the HAA ranch.

Within minutes, the buildings came into view. "This is so cool," I enthused, momentarily forgetting why I was seeing the thing in action. People moved around between the stable and the ranch house. I couldn't determine which if any of them were Trevor until Dev had the camera zoom in on a hesitantly-moving figure near the outbuilding. "There he is!" I pointed to Trevor and heard Dev laugh.

"He sure is. Looks like we know one person who didn't ask for a pony when he was a little boy."

I chuckled and smacked his shoulder. "Don't be a jerk. That's my job. How can you get so close without them hearing the drone?"

"We're actually not as close as it looks. The drone is several thousand feet above them. They probably won't ever hear it because of its altitude. The engines aren't that loud."

We watched as another young man approached Trevor. They spoke for a moment before disappearing into the stable. I was relieved to be able to see with my own eyes that he was safe and sound.

"Let's look around. I'll show you where I think they're keeping Tom."

I stepped away. "No. I don't want to see that."

Dev glanced up from the controller. "It's just an addition to the house, Henry. It's not like I'm going to fly in and show you a torture room."

"I know. I'm being stupid. I just don't want to think about it. We're this close to getting him back. Let me concentrate on that instead."

"Henry, stop. You're being emotional when you need to be professional. If we have to physically extract him, you're going to need to have this information to guide you."

"Physically—" Oh. Of all the scenarios that had played through my mind, participating in storming the ranch house had not been one of them. That was incredibly naïve on my part. Perhaps I should rethink my new career choice. Whose life was I living? I took and released a deep breath, bracing for what I was about to learn. I moved back behind Dev. "Okay, let's do it."

He smiled over his shoulder. "Good call. Alright, here we go."

DESPITE CASPER and Shelby's best efforts, they weren't able to find a way to access whatever alarm system HAA were using. They determined it wasn't hooked up to dial out so it wasn't housed on any computer system. It was simply designed to go off when triggered.

Trevor didn't have any new information about the secure addition or Tom when he checked in Saturday evening. He didn't feel safe enough to talk long, but he mentioned he'd talked to one of the counselors about possibly undergoing a more, as he called it, beneficial therapy program to help him stay on the straight path. The counselor had been receptive to his questions and promised to get him more information before he checked out Sunday morning.

Which he should be doing at any moment. I prodded the bacon strips sizzling in the skillet and pondered what little information we'd gathered at a great cost of time and money. The Mission had been an abject failure. The only thing I could tell we knew now that we didn't know Thursday was that the suspect area of the ranch house was blocked from the rest of the house by a door and secured by a keypad lock. Trevor had seen no sign nor heard any mention of anything that we could trace back to Tom being there. It was as if the people running the place were as clueless as we were.

Maybe Tom wasn't there. Maybe he was being held at another of HAA's facilities. Maybe I was chasing my tail and would never, ever catch it. The only thing I could think to do next was confront Althea and politely compel her to tell us where Tom was. And if that didn't work, to peel her like a banana until she started talking.

I blamed the Morena Baccarin version of the television series *V* for my apparent fascination with flaying Althea alive. Baccarin's character,

Anna, had favored that method of torture. The absolute horror of it had lodged itself in my brain. Now it didn't seem so bad. In theory.

I fished the bacon slices from the skillet and lay them on a paper towel-draped plate to drain. I cracked a dozen eggs into the bacon grease, hoping the other guys liked them fried. I'd already made a huge stack of pancakes. Cooking breakfast was the only useful thing I could think of doing to keep my mind occupied until Shelby returned with Trevor.

I was more than a little depressed at the lack of progress the weekend had brought. In a few hours we would return to San Francisco empty handed. I hadn't actually thought it would end with Tom back in my arms, but I'd allowed myself the luxury of hoping something would give.

It hadn't.

Somehow that made everything worse. I almost wished I could go back to the time before I'd awakened in Crazytown thinking my husband had vanished into thin air. At least then I was sure Tom was dead and my life made sense. Instead I was stuck in a cabin in the mountains with a retired Rambo, a younger Magnum PI, and a gay Ryan Gosling. Who and what that made me, besides the stupid sap who had hired them all, I didn't know.

I scooped the fried eggs onto another plate and carried them and the bacon to the table. Around them I arranged the butter and syrup containers and the plate of pancakes. I set four places, then stood back to wait. It wouldn't be long before the guys came in the front door. Dev was in his bedroom on the phone, probably with Shaun.

I hoped those three boys made a go of their experiment. They all deserved to be happy. It shouldn't surprise anyone who knew them that it would take an unconventional arrangement to satisfy all of them. I couldn't imagine what the three of them—

"Henry! Dev!" The door burst open with Trevor running in and screaming at the top of his lungs. He skidded to a halt, looking around for us.

"What is it?" I asked, my heart dropping to my feet. He looked like a wild man, his blond hair askew, blue eyes blazing, cheeks bright red with excitement and the cold.

He rushed over to me breathless, gripping my forearms. "Holy shit, Henry—!"

"What's going on?" Dev raced into the dining room. His socked feet slid across the hardwood floor, sending him crashing into the wall. He recovered with bruised grace, hurrying over to grab ahold of his boyfriend.

Trevor's gaze bounced between me and Dev for a moment as he found his voice. Then his outpouring of words broke land-speed records. "I didn't think we'd gotten anything and I was so depressed this morning I couldn't stand it. So I went wandering around to kill time and I came across Jimmy and Lloyd talking in the kitchen. They didn't know I was there, so they don't know I know, but I do! I heard them with my own ears!"

"Trevor. Get to the point."

He bounced on the balls of his feet. "They're moving him first thing tomorrow! That's what Lloyd said. He got orders this morning to have 'the little prince' ready to travel at first light."

"'The little prince?'" I echoed.

Trevor nodded frantically. "That's what he called him. He didn't say a name, but who else could it be but Tom? And we almost missed it! If I hadn't gotten all depressed and started moping, I never would have heard that much." His eyes grew huge as he gasped. "They could have moved him and we never would have found him! Oh thank Cher!"

"Hey, yeah, no worries. I got your stuff," Shelby interrupted with gruff, good-natured affection as he dropped Trevor's duffle bag beside the table. "I see he dropped his bomb."

"He did," Dev admitted, pulling Trevor into a hug. "My little spy. Excellent job."

Trevor beamed up at him and moved in for a kiss.

I stepped away and went over to the other side of the dining room where Shelby was pulling off his snow boots. I collapsed into the chair at the end of the table, numb from tip to toes. I understood Trevor's words, but I couldn't believe I'd heard them correctly. Was it possible that we were almost at an end to this? Was I really about to get Tom back? "Talk to me," I urged Shelby.

He grinned and laced up the sneakers he wore indoors. "Don't get your hopes up, Henry. We don't know for sure they were talking about Tom. We don't know anything yet."

I jammed my hands through my hair. It was a wonder I had any left at the rate I'd been doing that. "I'm so sick to death of those five words."

Shelby squeezed my forearm. "I understand. But look at it this way, tomorrow we'll know something. We're going to stop them before they move him. Even if they aren't talking about Tom, we'll stop them. And then we'll get them to talk before we let them go."

Instead of making me feel hopeful, this new revelation only made me feel empty. I could feel the blackness of depression rolling into my being but I didn't have the strength to stop it. There wasn't any point. Tomorrow would be the same as today, which was the same as yesterday, one more fruitless search for that one clue, that one tidbit of information that would lead me to Tom. Except none of them ever did. Even knitted together they didn't create a full picture. We don't know anything yet. I felt like that sentence was tattooed on my forehead because it was all anyone ever said to me.

I stood. "Get yourselves some breakfast, guys. Great job, Trevor. Thank you for putting yourself on the line for me. I don't have words to tell you how much I appreciate it. If you'll excuse me, I'm going to lie down for a bit."

I left them to their excited squawking and fled to the privacy of my bedroom. I reclined on the bed, picked up the phone, and opened the app CJ had installed for me. He'd uploaded a couple hundred photos of our little family, starting from when Tom and I first started dating. I scrolled through them slowly, realizing again just how much I missed being his barista. The tears came with our wedding pictures. The love and joy and excitement that filled us all spilled from our eyes on those photographs. I allowed myself to embrace the loneliness, to feel the ache of arms that would never again hold the man I'd loved for half my life.

Eventually I slept.

NINE

The next morning Trevor shook me awake an hour before dawn. We needed to pack up, go over the plan to intercept the "the little prince's" transport, and decide what to do afterward. I was groggy and cranky from too much sleep. I'd been out for nearly twenty hours, a marathon session I hadn't done since right after Shaun forced me to remember Tom's supposed death.

I sat at the dining table with my first precious cup of coffee, watching as Shelby drew lines with his finger on an aerial photograph of the entrance to the HAA ranch. From high above the main road, their driveway looked like the outline of a weather balloon. It was a mile from the road to the ranch, but it split off about a quarter of a mile from the road. The other three-quarters was a long loop. Drivers could approach the ranch house from either the left or the right, but they'd go around and converge again before getting to the county road. From there, they could choose to go left or right. Like many roads in the foothills and the mountains, this particular road doubled back on itself like the shoulder of a coat hanger until it connected back to the road it had split from.

"Dev and Henry, you two will set up here," Shelby said, pointing to a spot on the county road. If the folks from HAA turned left, we'd get them. "Trevor and I will be here," he continued, showing a spot in the other direction. "Either way, we've got them. The question is if they'll stop and surrender peacefully."

"I'm inclined to say yes," Dev said. "They haven't shown any signs of aggression yet and we haven't found any connections between them and any of the gun- and bomb-happy Christian extremists."

"I agree. Just the same, we'll all wear our Kevlar."

"We brought Kevlar?" Trevor asked excitedly.

"Of course we brought Kevlar." Dev grinned and put a finger to his lips in a shushing motion.

"And be prepared to take cover," Shelby continued, clearly irritated by the interruption. "We'll block the road and approach them civilly. If they mean Tom no harm, they may hand him over without a struggle."

I laughed bitterly. "Althea has paid these guys way too much money for them to just hand him over without some sort of struggle. Believe me, this bitch isn't someone you want to cross. I'd wager she made that crystal clear to them."

"That's a good point," Dev conceded. "Henry and Trevor, I want you two to act as back up. You'll approach the car from the passenger side, but only after Shelby or I have made initial contact. You'll stay at least three paces farther from the vehicle than we do unless we tell you otherwise. I don't want to put you two in any more danger than we have to, but Shelby and I can't do it alone."

"Understood, boss," Trevor grinned. It amazed me how easily Trevor could turn off the lust-struck act in favor of professionalism. I wasn't sure I'd have been able to pull that off at his age.

Shelby passed out mics and receivers. "Okay, boys, let's get packed up, suited up, and get out there. We don't want to miss them because we dawdled here."

Dev and Trevor disappeared into their bedroom to gather their gear. I was about to follow when Shelby's hand on my shoulder stopped me.

"Henry, I know you're feeling helpless and hopeless right now, but I want you to know we will complete this mission. If not today, then tomorrow or the next day. As far as I'm concerned, Tom is a man left behind. That is unacceptable to this United States Marine. You have my word that we will bring him home to you and your son."

Tears sprang to my eyes. "Thank you," I answered thickly. "I appreciate everything you've done so far."

Shelby nodded, turned on his heel and went out the door.

I stared after him for a minute before returning to my room to pack. Shelby had just proved I was surrounded by incredible people. He didn't have to take this personally. He'd never met Tom. He was assigned to the case by Dev, who didn't know Tom either. The fact that they'd each separately expressed their determination to find and retrieve Tom touched me more than I could ever tell them. It was almost enough to reignite my hope that we would eventually find him.

Almost.

HALF AN hour later Dev positioned the SUV across the road at the position he and Shelby had agreed to earlier. I was more amused than alarmed that he'd put me on the bloody side. Even after three cups of coffee I struggled to shake off the melancholy that had overtaken me while I cooked breakfast the previous morning. I fully expected to end the day in jail, arrested for unlawfully detaining my fellow citizens at gunpoint. Wouldn't that make CJ proud.

"I hope you're going to reimburse me for bail when this all goes tits up," I teased him.

He grinned. "I hope you're going to add a nice bonus to that check you write me when we bring your husband home today."

I grimaced. "If that happens, you can count on it."

He climbed out of the vehicle. "It'll happen. If not today, then soon. Trust me. Come around this side of the truck. I don't want you inside when they come around the curve."

I exited the SUV and walked around to stand beside him, leaning against the engine compartment. "Did you guys call Shaun last night and let him know Trevor made it out of Hell House safely?"

Dev chuckled as he took a swig of his coffee. "We did. He was very happy to hear from us. Apparently he's a bit of a worrier?"

"He can be," I agreed. "I'm actually surprised he isn't here."

Dev's eyes widened in acknowledgment. "I thought he was going to hide in the truck when I told him he couldn't come. Although I guess I could have let him come. He would have been good emotional support for you. I was just thinking of this as business."

"No, you were right to keep him away. I need to have some sort of separation from the case where he's concerned. I need to be able to vent to him if something goes wrong. Like this weekend. If he was here, I wouldn't have anyone to yell at but you."

Dev paused mid-chuckle, cocking his head to hear better. "Do you hear that?"

I looked around stupidly, like I could hear with my eyes. But my ears didn't detect anything out of the usual either. "I don't hear anything."

"Shh." He dove into the SUV, emerging with a pair of binoculars in a case. He freed them and instantly put them to use, scanning the skies in all directions. "Dammit. I can't see anything for the fucking trees." He scooted me out of the way, then climbed up on the roof of the SUV, using the tire as a step. "Come up here, please, Henry."

Confused, I clamored atop the vehicle, much less gracefully than he had done, but I wasn't about to tell anyone and he wasn't watching. I stood beside him on the roof, trying to figure out what he was looking for. Suddenly I heard what sounded like—

"A helicopter?" I asked in dismay.

"Yep." Dev continued spinning circles trying to find the source of the sound.

"You don't think...?"

"I damn well do think," he answered curtly. "If I could just find the goddamn thing I'd know for sure." He hit the mic on his collar. "Shelby do you hear that?"

"The copter?" Shelby's disembodied voice sounded in my ear, throwing me mentally off-balance for a second. "Roger that. I can't see it yet."

"Me neither. That tells me it's a huge mother."

"Yep. Definitely long-range, probably four or five rotors."

"What are you talking about?" I asked impatiently.

"The more and larger the rotors, the more noise they make," Dev explained without stopping his search of the sky. "The more noise they make, the longer you can hear them before you can actually see them."

That new information made me wonder why they were used in warfare. Wasn't the objective usually to surprise the enemy?

"There you are, you massive bitch," Dev cooed. "Oh she's a beauty." He handed me the binoculars. "See her?"

It took a few seconds to find the helicopter in the limited vision of the binoculars, but as soon as I did, I slammed the glasses against Dev's stomach and proceeded to lose my breakfast over the side of the SUV.

"It's Althea," I gasped around the burn in my throat.

"What?"

When I was sure I wasn't going to hurl again, I straightened up and pointed in the general direction of the helicopter. "That's the vineyard logo on the side of that thing."

"Fuck! They aren't using the roads at all!" Dev jumped down. "Shelby! Get that bird in the air now! They're evacuating him by helo!"

"Roger that."

"Get in the truck, Henry. We're gonna go get your man."

TEN

Dev drove like a man possessed, barking out orders to Shelby and Trevor as we went. The roads still had plenty of snow on them, so I was grateful the seatbelt and the "oh shit" handle kept me in my seat as Dev sent the SUV bursting through drift after drift. We almost missed the turn off to the ranch, but he somehow recovered in time, hurtling us down the driveway as he kept peering at the sky, watching as the helicopter drew closer. We would beat it, but it would be a close call.

As he drove, he opened the console between us, throwing its contents haphazardly into the back seat. When he got to the bottom, he slid a panel out of the way, revealing another compartment with a keypad lock. He typed it in twice only to be rejected each time.

"Goddammit! Henry, type in six three seven two. I can't do that and drive at the same time."

I quickly typed in the code, triggering the unlock mechanism which popped the lid open slightly. Dev's reached in and pulled out a 9mm Glock 19. He handed it to me and then retrieved a thirty-three round clip and tossed it on my lap. "Get ready," he said gruffly as he dug in the compartment to arm himself.

"I don't know what we're going to run into, but we're going to do this as safely as we can. Whatever you do, do not shoot first."

I'd been so caught up in staying in my seat that I hadn't had time to comprehend exactly what we were doing, much less formulate a plan to shoot anyone. My heart raced wildly, first from Dev's crazy driving, second from the realization that I might be only a few minutes from laying my eyes on my husband for the first time in almost a year.

"It's my birthday," I said stupidly as the thought registered for the first time all morning.

"Happy birthday. Hang on," he said through gritted teeth.

I looked up just in time to brace against the dashboard and gasp before Dev sent the SUV barreling through the ranch's unmanned iron rail pipe gate. "Shit!" I yelled as the fork in the road appeared almost out of nowhere. Dev cranked the wheel to the right but the SUV didn't respond for several yards. Finally the tires gripped, sending us surging down the driveway.

About half a mile on, Dev cranked the wheel to the right and we were suddenly off-roading, bouncing along the uneven ground through foot-deep snow. He seemed to have a plan, but I wasn't going to break his concentration to ask what it was. Obviously he didn't want to announce our presence to the ranch personnel by remaining on the driveway.

A few hundred yard into the forest he skidded to a stop. "We get out here," he said, stuffing his Glock into an inside pocket in his coat. "We'll watch from the edge of the tree line. As soon as we see Tom we'll have to act."

"Act how?" I asked, climbing out of the SUV.

"That depends on what we see."

Great. That was as clear as mud.

I followed Dev as he ran through the forest to the edge of the ranch's cleared area. I tried to recall the aerial view from Saturday to figure out where we were, but I couldn't be sure. All I knew was that we were on the south side, with the main house to our left and the stable to the right. There was plenty of open ground between the two for a helicopter to land, even one as huge as Althea's.

We had the element of surprise on our side, but that was about it. With all the noise the helicopter was making, the HAA employees would never hear us, which meant Tom wouldn't be able to either. We couldn't yell for him to come to us or to hit the deck before shooting started. I hoped Dev had a good plan. I didn't see any way around rushing them physically when Tom finally appeared.

"The helo is on the ground," Shelby's disembodied voice said in my ear, scaring the bejesus out of me. I'd forgotten we were still connected.

"Roger," Dev answered.

We hunkered down a yard away from the clearing. The spot Dev chose gave us an easy view of the entire operation. Even from about a hundred yards away, the house was much larger than the photos had made it seem. The helicopter's rotor wash tossed loose snow into the air, obscuring it from view. Three staff members went about their morning chores around the stable, but there was no movement at the house yet.

"What's the plan, boss?" Trevor asked in my ear.

"Looks like they'll be bringing Tom out any second," Dev said. "How far away are you?"

"Just passed the gate. Very subtle, by the way." Trevor's chuckle calmed my fraying nerves.

Dev grinned slightly but didn't take his eyes off the scene in front of us. "Didn't have much choice. It didn't open when I said please," he said into the mic. "Why aren't they turning off the helo?" he asked rhetorically. "That snow is going to blind them."

Two staff members emerged from the house—with Tom between them. Even from a distance, he looked awful. "*Tom*," I whispered, unable to believe I was really seeing him. His hair was too long and disheveled and his clothes hung on his thinner frame. His hands were cuffed in front of him, allowing his captors to guide him by his elbows.

I blinked away a flood of tears threatening to blind me. I lunged forward, only to be blocked by Dev's strong body.

"Don't. Not yet," Dev whispered harshly, pulling me down.

I struggled against him, desperate to get to Tom. My eyes could see him. My brain understood the puffs of steam escaping his mouth were his breaths. But my heart wouldn't believe he was real until I touched him.

Dev roughly pinned me down in the snow. His gaze swung between me and the two brutes slowly marching Tom towards the helicopter. He growled quietly into my ear. "You have a job to do first, Henry. You can be Tom's husband when it's done, but not until then, okay? We have to get him out of here."

I took a deep breath and tried to rein in my swirling and swelling emotions. *Tom was alive!* Really and truly alive. "I'm here. I'm here." I didn't know if I was talking to Tom or to Dev, but it didn't matter. Dev understood now and Tom would soon. After all this time, almost an entire damn year, I could see the love of my life alive and breathing only a football field distance away from me.

Dev drew his Glock from inside his coat and chambered a round. "Remember not to shoot unless you have to. Shelby, make sure that bird never leaves the ground," he ordered, inching toward the clearing.

I nodded and got to my feet, retrieving my own weapon from my coat pocket. My emotions faded into the background, replaced by a calm sense of purpose. We had a mission to complete. I could fall apart after we got Tom somewhere safe, but not before.

The two goons had made it about a third of the way to the helo with Tom between them. He wasn't resisting, but he wasn't leading their charge either.

A loud bang rang out, followed by a massive boom. Sparks showered and smoke billowed from the tail rotor of the helicopter.

"Now!" Dev yelled, sprinting towards the commotion as fast as he could in the foot-deep snow. I followed, cursing the snow for slowing me down.

The engine noise immediately ceased, leaving only the sound of the spinning top rotors as they slowed to a halt.

Tom and his two captors had stopped, perhaps stunned by the sudden death of the helo. I took off at a run after Dev.

"Don't fucking move!" he shouted.

The three men turned. One of the goons reached under his coat.

Pop.

The goon staggered two paces and fell onto his back in the snow, moaning in agony.

It barely registered that Dev had shot the guy before I saw the other three emerge from the stable at a run.

"Stop! Don't move!" I yelled at them, training my weapon on the one in the middle. They skidded to a halt, throwing their arms in the air.

"Don't shoot!" one of the yelled.

"Get on the ground! Face down, hands behind your head!" I demanded. All three of them quickly complied, no doubt confused as hell. It wasn't every day armed men infiltrated a Christian dude ranch.

Meanwhile Dev was still yelling at the other captor to release Tom and get on the ground.

Instead of complying, the freak shoved Tom into the snow and let out a roar as he charged Dev.

Another gunshot rang out and the man crumpled to the ground, screaming like a banshee.

"Shelby, call 911. Tell them we have at least two GSW's. We'll need police and paramedics."

"Roger that."

"Nice flying, by the way," Dev complimented Shelby.

"Thank you. It was a little heartbreaking."

Dev moved so he could cover everyone, so I pocketed my weapon and ran to Tom. I dropped into the snow beside him, reaching out with shaky hands to cup his face. "It's really you." His skin felt warm against mine. For the first time I believed he was real and alive. His image blurred. I furiously blinked away the tears of joy and concern.

"Barista," he whispered and gifted me with the most beautiful smile I'd ever seen.

I kissed him then, wrapping my arms around him and pulling him close. His familiar taste and scent refilled my soul.

With a ferocious roar of the engine, Trevor's SUV burst into the yard, coming to a bouncing stop between us and Dev. Trevor bounded out and ran to me and Tom.

"You got him! Oh thank Cher!" Trevor practically glowed with delight.

I felt only relief at having Tom in my arms again. I wouldn't be happy until we got him home—or at least safely away from here.

"Don't move, dammit!" Dev shouted.

I quickly kissed Tom again and scrambled to my feet. "Get him out of here," I ordered Trevor. I retrieved my weapon, sprinting around the front of the SUV.

While I concentrated on Tom, Dev had grouped the two wounded men with the other three. It didn't take a trained eye to know they'd planned to charge Dev and were pissed that they'd missed their opportunity.

It annoyed me that these freaks weren't cooperating. Because of them I couldn't see Tom anymore, which pissed me off and scared me at the same time. I'd just got him back. I didn't want to take my eyes off him yet.

One of the unwounded men lunged forward. Dev fired a warning shot into the snow a foot in front of the charging fool. He stopped short, throwing his hands in the air and stepping back in line with his brothers.

I swung to the left when the back door of the helicopter slid noisily open.

Althea.

In my excitement to finally have Tom back I'd almost forgotten about his mother. My plans and priorities immediately changed. I trained my weapon on her and approached the disabled aircraft, heedless of anyone else in the area. "Get out of the helicopter, you fucking cunt!"

She didn't move except to slowly smile. Demonic bitch.

"Henry, stop." Dev's hand clamped onto my shoulder.

I shrugged him off. "Get Tom the hell out of here. Get him somewhere safe. I'm not leaving until this bitch is either dead or in police custody."

"You won't shoot me." It wasn't a taunt. She genuinely didn't believe I had it in me to shoot someone. She was wrong. After the hell she'd put my family through, I would shoot her as a full-time job.

"You have no idea what I could do to you," I snarled, anticipating the myriad options open to me. *Try me, bitch. Just try me.*

"Hey!" the pilot yelled from his seat. "Can I get out? I'm unarmed. Please don't shoot me."

"You worthless coward," Althea spat, though to me or to the pilot, I wasn't sure.

"Climb out slowly and get your ass over there with the rest of them," I instructed the pilot, keeping my weapon trained on the door.

"Henry!" Trevor yelled. "I've got Tom in the SUV. I'm taking him to the Grass Valley hospital. It's the closest one."

"Good," I said, not taking my eyes off Althea as the pilot clumsily jogged over to Dev's group. "Tell him I love him and I'll be there soon."

"Gotcha!"

"Pick up Shelby on your way out of here," Dev shouted.

"Already on it, boss," Trevor answered.

The doors slammed shut behind me and the engine roared to life. Snow flew in all directions as Trevor bolted the scene with my husband, safe at last.

"Dev, round up these other pieces of shit and take them into the stable or the house. It's time for Mommie Dearest and me to have a come to Jesus meeting."

ALTHEA AND I exchanged death glares silently while Dev corralled the HAA staff members and the pilot into the stable. The two Dev had shot protested weakly until he threatened to finish the job.

I moved closer so my monster-in-law and I could talk quietly. Plus the proximity would help my aim. I took in the well-appointed leather interior of the helicopter, knowing by the blue and white stripes everywhere that it had been custom-made to her standards. It was such a shame she'd never get to use it again.

"Why did you do it, Althea?"

"I have nothing to say to you."

"You tried to ruin my family. You pretended my husband was dead. What would possess you to be so cruel?"

She stared arrogantly over my head, as if I were literally beneath her. She always dressed well, but today she was decked out in Princess Diana chic. Her white and gold sailor-inspired dress suit shimmered in the early morning light. Her hair, which was too black to be natural at her age, was mostly covered by a brilliant white turban adorned with a grotesque brooch also in blue and white, the Greek national colors.

"Tell me why you did this!" I shouted, my temper about to get the best of me. I could handle her condescension, but I wouldn't tolerate her silence. I deserved answers. We all did.

She turned her gaze to me then, her expression registering nothing but disgust.

I fired a shot into the electronics above her head. She screamed and ducked as sparks showered down around her.

"You'd better start talking, bitch." I growled through gritted teeth, aiming my pistol at her again.

"I had to save his immortal soul!" she shouted, still cowering beside her seat.

"Oh give me a fucking break!"

"He was living a life of sin! It's all your fault! You ruined my son!" She was warming to her topic now. I could tell she had wanted to say this to me for decades. "Before you came along he was a good, God-fearing boy. He never would have turned to homosexuality if you hadn't corrupted him!"

I scoffed. "Believe me, honey, your son was sucking dick long before he met me."

She held up a hand. "I won't hear your lies! God knows the truth!"

"Then god knows he loved every minute of it."

"Shut up!"

Oh no. It was my turn to inflict some pain. "Your son—my husband—lives for my dick in his ass. He begs me to pound him harder and harder. He screams my name in pleasure."

"That's not true! The devil speaks through you!" She covered her ears with her hands and started loudly babbling some prayer or another in Greek.

I was about to take another shot at the helo when Dev's hand on my arm stopped me.

"You'd better put the weapon away, man. The police are almost here. They will shoot you if they find you holding her at gunpoint."

"I should just kill her now." I wanted to. If there was a deity up there watching, he had to feel how much I wanted to put a bullet between that bitch's eyes. Who knew what kind of torture Tom had gone through. Even if I had him back physically, I couldn't be sure he was the same man who'd been taken from me. The thought that we might have rescued a stranger was enough to turn my stomach.

Dev wrested the Glock from my grip and walked away to the helicopter. He drew a pair of handcuffs from his back jeans pocket and secured Althea to her plush leather seat.

"The others are tied up in a stall." He grinned. "Who knew there'd be so much rope handy in a stable?"

I offered him a semblance of a smile and jammed my hands into my hair. I felt relief, frustration, elation, and aimlessness pour through me. "I need a minute," I said, turning away and walking toward the forest. We had Tom back. He was safe and alive. How much worse for wear I didn't know, but that didn't matter as much as the safe-and-alive part.

But now, after almost seven months after I'd waken up in Crazytown and very nearly a year after Tom's disappearance, I felt like Gooch after she'd "live, live, lived!" I had to find out what to do now.

ELEVEN

After hours of seemingly endless questioning by the police, they finally allowed Dev and me to leave the ranch. There would be consequences to our actions, but law enforcement was much more interested in the kidnapping and unlawful imprisonment issues than with a couple of well-placed but ultimately harmless bullets from Dev's Glock.

The late afternoon sun reflected off the snow, adding confusion to my emotionally mixed state. I was overjoyed that we'd found Tom alive and well. I was eager to see him again, but the day had exhausted me physically and emotionally to the point of struggling to stay awake.

I settled back in cushiony leather seat, dropping my head back on the rest. I looked over at Dev, who was silently concentrating on negotiating the snow-packed road. Peace surged through my body. I couldn't keep the smile from my lips. "We found him."

Dev glanced at me, smiling widely. "We did. I told you we would."

My eyelids drooped. I didn't mind. It was easier to pull up the Tom's image that way. I should call CJ, but that would have to wait until I'd talked to the doctors. I needed to make sure Tom was healthy—or at least not permanently damaged by whatever those animals had done to him—before I made my son's day. I didn't want to lie when I said we'd found him alive and well. If the kiss we'd shared was any indication, he would be fine.

What seemed like only a second later, I awoke to Dev shaking my shoulder. "We're here, Henry. Wake up."

The day had significantly darkened. Red and blue lights swept over the white building Dev had parked next to. Over his shoulder I saw the portico emblazoned with a bright red, backlit EMERGENCY sign. My heartbeat kicked up at the thought of Tom having a heart attack or a stroke on the way here.

Dev must have seen the instant panic in my eyes. "Don't worry. They brought him here out of precaution. We don't know what they did to him. Trevor called while you slept. They've already seen the doctor. Tom's mostly fine."

I swallowed hard. "Mostly?"

Dev shrugged. "He's a little dehydrated and vitamin D-deficient, but otherwise he's good. They're going to keep him overnight for observation."

I hadn't realized how worried I was until I heard Dev's words. Pressure equal to my body weight instantly lifted from my shoulders. I didn't even mind the extended stay. If the doctors thought it was a good idea, I wasn't about to argue. Once I'd heard the same thing from the doctor, I would be able to call CJ. Or maybe I'd let Tom call him. I smiled at the thought of reuniting those two.

I blinked away the water and exited the SUV. "Let's go see my man."

Dev clapped me on the shoulder and walked with me inside.

Once we'd asked for Tom MacKinnon, our presence created a muted buzz among the hospital staff. It seemed most, if not all, of them had heard some version of what happened, and they all wanted to get a glimpse of the kidnapped dude's husband.

Within minutes I faced the door to my husband's room. Dev stood behind me for emotional support. I was suddenly nervous. Our brief reunion at the ranch had been only long enough for each of us to know the other was there. As soon as I walked through the door I would come face to face with my greatest fears: whatever they'd done to Tom in the last year. In the best case scenario, there would be little to no lasting emotional or physical damage. I couldn't bring myself to think what the worst case could look like.

Casting one last glance over my shoulder at Dev, I pushed open the door. I'd imagined Tom half-awake or completely asleep in his bed, connected to umpteen machines. Instead, he sat with one mostly-bare leg dangling off the side while he and Trevor played cards on the bed table. Aside from the hospital gown and the IV-tube trailing into his left arm, he looked haggard but healthy.

They both looked up at the sound of the door. Out of the corner of my eye, I saw Trevor get up from his spot on the bed, but my whole attention was focused on the warm, broad smile on my husband's lips.

"Hi," I said, suddenly overcome with shyness.

"Hi," he answered, holding out a hand to me.

I stepped forward to take it, letting him pull me into a hug. He buried his face in my neck and drew a deep breath.

"I never thought I'd see you again," he whispered, his voice laden with tears.

Unable to speak around the lump of emotion in my throat, I tightened my arms around him and buried my fingers in the hair at the nape of his neck. He was too thin and his hair too long, but he was alive and warm next to me. Nothing else mattered.

"They told me you were dead," I whispered, breaking into sobs. "I didn't want to believe it."

"I'm so sorry." He pulled back and cupped my face. He brushed away my tears and studied my face for a long time. He'd never been more beautiful than he was at that moment, even with his eyes filled with the battle between the torment of what he'd been through and his love for me. "I love you," he whispered, pulling me in for a kiss.

I fell into the taste of him, relishing the privilege I'd been too long without. There was an anguish and desperation to our kiss that had never been there before, but as it went on, as one kiss turned to two and to three, promise and hope replaced the heartbreak.

I BRUSHED Tom's overlong bangs back from his face and trailed a finger down his jawline. It was all I could do to believe I was really touching him. He was truly alive, warm flesh and blood right before my very eyes, sharing the other half of his tiny hospital bed.

"What happened?" I asked, almost afraid to hear the answer. I didn't know what he'd been through, didn't know if it would upset him to talk about it, but I had to try.

His gaze shifted over my shoulder, as if the answers were there. I imagined he was reliving the experience for the millionth time. "I don't remember. Jack Berg from work heard I was going to meet you at Squaw Valley. He asked if I could give him a lift to Citrus Heights—something about his wife having just moved there for a job. The last thing I remember was pulling over because he was about to get carsick. Then I woke up in that godforsaken place."

"We think he was hired to kidnap you."

Tom's eyes closed and he shook his head slightly. "That makes sense, if I can say that about any of it. I'm just glad it's over now and that you found me."

"We almost didn't. We were packing up and getting ready to leave yesterday. If Trevor hadn't overheard them saying they were moving you at first light, we would have been long gone. And so would you. We got very lucky."

He shivered. "God knows what they would have done to me then."

I swallowed hard. I desperately didn't want to know the answer to the question, but I had to know. "Did they torture you?"

Eyes still closed, he gave a small nod. "Not at first. Mother must have given them strict instructions that I wasn't to be harmed. But after my second or third escape attempt, they weren't interested in being kind."

My heart squeezed with pain. "I'm so sorry. I should have looked for you sooner. I should have known something was wrong."

Tom's clear green gaze met mine. For a man who'd just been talking about being tortured, his eyes showed a remarkable peace. "It's not your fault. I'm sure they made it as realistic as possible."

"I should have known." I shouldn't have let them convince me I was wrong when my heart didn't believe he was gone. I should have fought harder. I should have hired Dev a year ago.

Tom's big hand cupped my cheek. His palm was softer now. The calluses he'd built up had worn away during his captivity. I longed for the day in the near future when they came back. "I'm here now. That's what matters. If you hadn't believed, I would still be with them."

I nodded even though I wasn't finished beating myself up. I didn't know if I ever would be. We'd lost a year because of his mother's deceit and my unquestioning compliance with it. I'd take it out on myself when I was alone, never when he was around. He deserved my full attention and love for the rest of our lives. "When did you find out your mother was involved?"

He laughed harshly. "That would be after my second escape attempt. I don't know how long I'd been there then, but I managed to make it to the road before they caught me. I think it scared the hell out of them. She was there the next morning."

Fucking bitch. I hated her with the burning passion of a thousand suns. "Did she tell you why?"

"She feared for my immortal soul, of course. We were sinners in the eyes of god, et cetera. She didn't tell me the real truth until not that long ago."

"What is that?" Knowing Althea, whatever she'd told him were more lies.

"She has a brain tumor. She showed me the MRI on her tablet. She's only got a few more months."

"What?"

He tried a smile but it fell flat. "That's why she did it. She wanted to make sure I was right with god, as she put it, before she passed away so that we could all be together in Eternity."

This was rich, even for Althea. "You've got to be kidding."

"I wish I was. She kept talking about this house she'd built in Dubai and how we would go live there as soon as I accepted that being gay was a sinful and destructive lifestyle. She had it all worked out. She even had some Greek woman picked out for me to marry. She wanted a biological grandchild before she died."

I blinked at him repeatedly. My mind had stopped absorbing his words somewhere around Dubai.

He laughed harshly. "She's batshit crazy."

My rage at Althea had turned to pity as he talked, but it resurfaced as anger again. "How could a mother do this to her own child? It's inhuman."

"I've convinced myself it's the tumor. I know you two never liked each other, but she was a good mother when I was growing up. I don't know this woman."

I did. I'd seen glimpses of her for twenty years, I just didn't know it then. But I wasn't going to force Tom to see it. He'd been through enough. If he had to blame her actions on a brain tumor, then that was good enough for me. He'd lost so much I wasn't about to force him to give up more.

"I love you," I said. That was what it all came down to. After everything we'd been through, that was the one thing no one had been able to take away from us. He kissed me and, for a moment, we were home again.

I reached into my pocket and retrieved my phone. "There's someone who's dying to hear your voice," I told him. I speed dialed CJ.

He answered on the third ring. "Hey, Dad, what's up?" Tom's eyes lit up at the sound of our son's voice.

"Are you driving or doing something otherwise dangerous?"

His warm chuckle filled my heart. "Nope. Sitting here sketching out a new project. What's up?"

"Good. There's someone who'd like to say hello to you." I pushed the speakerphone button and nodded to Tom.

"Hello, son."

A stunned silence filled the room for a moment before CJ's tentative voice asked, "Pop?"

"It's me, CJ," Tom said, tears streaming down his face.

"*Omigod, Pop!*" Hearing CJ come apart over the phone broke my heart, but at least this time they were tears of joy. "You're alive. You're really alive."

TWELVE

Without opening my eyes, I slid my arm across the sheet to find...only more cool sheet. Not again! I sat bolt upright in bed, scanning the room for signs of Tom. The panic didn't recede until I heard him whistling lightly in another room. I fell back against the pillow, panting in relief. It had been almost a week since we rescued Tom from his mother's evil clutches. Every night since then he'd awakened me with nightmares. He'd only talk about some of them, probably the ones that affected him the least. His mental health had worried us both enough that we'd arranged for counseling for both of us. I needed to understand how to react to him when he acted out, if he acted out, as much as he needed to purge himself of the horror.

Despite or perhaps because of those nightmares, every morning I'd awakened alone and panicked. He had always been an early riser, but I was about to put a stop to that.

"New house rule," I shouted. "You can't get out of bed before I'm awake."

He chuckled as he came through the door, clad only in a pair of my boxers, carrying a tray. "How would I make you breakfast in bed then?"

I scooted up to rest against the headboard, drinking in the sight I would never tire of seeing. My husband. The love of my life was back where he belonged, alive and well in our home. He was thinner and paler from his confinement, but he had never looked better to me.

I swallowed down a lump of emotion and flashed a smile. "Well when you put it that way, maybe we can compromise."

He chuckled and positioned the tray over my lap, leaning in to drop a lingering kiss on my lips. I wanted to reach out, pull him back into bed, and never let him out of my sight. Instead, I savored the familiar feel of his lips against mine, the sweet, maple syrup taste on his tongue, and the earthy, masculine scent of his skin. It had been a near thing that I would never be able to enjoy those simple pleasures again. I planned to take full advantage of our second chance.

He pulled back with a mournful sound. His closed eyes told me he, too, was treasuring the moment. He perched on the edge of the bed and brought a strawberry slice to my lips.

I took it eagerly, my gaze locked with his green one. I had missed those eyes with their flecks of gold and brown. They were so expressive, giving away almost every thought in his head.

"To what do I owe this treat?" I asked, more to break the spell of the moment than because I cared about the explanation. I wouldn't ever object to being served breakfast in bed.

"It's the one-year anniversary of the very premature announcement of my unfortunate death."

"That's not funny."

He grimaced and tried to make it better. "But it's the six-day anniversary of my resurrection!"

"Alright, Lazarus, can we just have breakfast and not think about that for a minute?"

"I was thinking more along the lines of Prometheus."

"Does that make me your Hercules for slaying the eagle?"

He leaned in to kiss me again. "You've always been my hero, barista. Enjoy your French toast, I'm going to take a shower." He stopped to look around the room. "And, uhm, maybe we could go shopping today? Since you gave away all my clothes, I mean."

He didn't say it to be cruel, nor was there any malice in his words. It was simply a fact. I'd given away his clothes after Shaun reminded me of his supposed death. I smoothed the worry lines from his forehead with my thumb. "If the Hell Hounds aren't at the front door this morning, I would love to go shopping with you."

The press, having been alerted to a shooting at the HAA ranch, had been unrelenting once they'd stumbled upon the rest of the story. Our landline was turned off, the television and radio were unplugged for good measure, and my cell number had been changed twice in less than a week. Eager reporters had camped out on the street outside the house, aiming their cameras at our windows. One enterprising young prick had been caught by Shelby going through the trash. Our neighbors were less than pleased, but they were very understanding.

Dev acted as our spokesperson, issuing a statement that we had nothing to say and requesting privacy, which only seemed to make them hungrier for the juicy details. And it was a juicy story—one the district attorney was playing for maximum publicity. *Multi-millionaire mother has son kidnapped and imprisoned for a year in pray away the gay camp.* It had all the makings of a really horrible movie.

What no one seemed to care about was that there were real people involved. Real, regular human beings with emotions that could be hurt by the trash they chose make up and broadcast, print, and whatever the hell else they did.

It tore my heart out that I wasn't able to protect CJ from them. Matthew, who had been blindsided by Althea's machinations, had doubled CJ's security detail and offered to provide us with one too. We'd declined since Dev and company had our backs.

As the only other person we knew near Tom's six-foot-three height, Dev had brought over some of his own casual clothing. The shirts fit alright, but the jeans were a little too snug around the thigh, even after Tom's twenty-pound weight loss. He'd never been a label whore so since he couldn't remember the exact style and size that he preferred, he'd been limited to track pants and shorts. As much as we both hated it, he would have to venture out and buy his own stuff.

"I didn't see them when I peeked out earlier," he said, getting to his feet. "Maybe we're off the hook."

"They'll come back when your mother's arraigned. And once the trial starts. And probably at random times before, between, and after." I cut a piece of the French toast he'd made just for me and peered up at him. "How much do you love this house? Maybe we should consider moving?"

He shook his head. "Hell no. I dreamed about coming home to this place every night for almost a year. No one is driving me out of it."

I grabbed his hand and kissed the back of it. "I love you, you know."

He gave me that same smile that had stopped and then captured my heart twenty-plus years ago, the smile I had been craving since he'd vanished. "If I didn't know that, I wouldn't have made it through the last year. Knowing I had you and CJ to come home to gave me the courage to keep fighting."

Tears welled up in my eyes. I put the tray aside. "Forget breakfast. I want to spend more time with you. Let's go get naked and wet."

"Ew, Dad, gross," CJ intoned from the doorway.

I laughed and tossed a pillow at him. "That wasn't intended for little ears."

"There's nothing little about my ears," he huffed, chucking the pillow at Tom. "I suggest you keep that in mind while you're carrying on in the shower." He stepped into the room and made grabby hands. "I'll guard your breakfast while you do that."

"I left yours in the oven," Tom said, hurling the pillow back to me.

CJ grinned widely. "Great! I'll guard that too!"

CJ had been waiting for us when we'd returned from Grass Valley. The three of us had immediately engaged in a prolonged hug and cry session. I finally understood the meaning of the word cathartic. Clinging to each other in the living room had gone a long way to promote healing.

"Don't forget the boys will be here in a couple of hours," I reminded my men, handing CJ the breakfast tray. I briefly mourned the loss of Tom's fantastic French toast, but consoled myself with the thought of tapping his even more fantastic ass.

"I remember," CJ said, picking up a piece of toast and eating it like the heathen we had tried to train out of him. He grinned when he saw I'd noticed. "It's good! I'm starving!"

"Uh huh," I said, trying not to roll my eyes, considering all the times I'd verbally smacked him down for doing just that. "Go eat that in the kitchen. Your dad and I have a date with the shower."

He shrugged and turned to go, still chomping on the toast. "Don't forget the lube."

This time the pillow hit him in the back of the head. He laughed and closed the door behind him.

"I'VE NEVER been happier for you," Shaun said quietly, pulling me into a hug. "You and Tom have a second chance a lot of people would give their eye-teeth to get."

He had accompanied me into the kitchen to retrieve more snacks for the assembled masses, his two boyfriends, my husband, and my son. Six grown men ate and drank a lot more than I was used to. I would have to adjust my shopping habits if things worked out the way I hoped they would.

"I know. I'm so grateful." I squeezed him tight and stepped back, holding him by the shoulders. "Thank you for always being there for me, for always putting my needs ahead of yours. I'm sorry for being such a jackass sometimes."

He grinned. "Hey, if you weren't a jackass sometimes, I would think you were pod-Henry."

I shook my head. "We've really got to make you start watching movies from this century. If you hadn't made me watch that when we were kids, I wouldn't have a clue what you meant."

He laughed. "If it makes you feel any better, I just made Trevor and Dev watch it with me last night." The rush of color to his cheeks surprised the hell out of me. "Well, part of it anyway."

My eyes widened. "So you did it? You finally caved?"

My sex-loving friend had been putting off sleeping with his two new boyfriends, declaring that they needed time to get to know one another before they added that complication to an already complex situation. I'd been stunned when he'd made the decision, considering how important sex was to him. Perhaps that was why I shouldn't have been so taken aback. Shaun enjoyed recreational sex a lot. Knowing that he was falling in love with not only one man but two had shaken him. From the moment he surrendered to the fact that he was in a triad relationship, his days of marauding the City for sex partners would be over. Sex between the three of them would have a deeper meaning, creating a connection he'd never allowed before.

He wouldn't meet my eyes, but he nodded. "I did—we did."

"And?"

He scratched behind his ear nervously. "It was...awkward at first. So many knees and elbows to put in the wrong places. We figured it out eventually."

"Uh huh...and?"

His gaze locked with mine. "It was everything I hoped and feared it would be." He blew out a long breath. "If I wasn't sure before, I am now. They're what I've been missing."

I laughed and hugged him again. "I'm so thrilled for you, my friend. You deserve all the happiness in the world." I pulled back and playfully tapped his cheek three times. "Go figure it would take two men to satisfy you, ya stubborn bastard."

"Aw, babe, don't be that way," he teased. "You should look at it like it took two men to fill the place I'd been saving for you."

I tilted my head and pretended to think about it. "Huh. I really am pretty awesome, aren't I?"

"You are," he agreed, rolling his eyes.

"*DAD!* Are you coming back in here or what?"

I groaned. "You buy 'em books and you buy 'em books, but they never learn *not to yell in the house!*" I answered, each word a bit louder than the previous one.

"Yeah, yeah," CJ answered, appearing in the doorway. "We kinda need you out here."

Shaun clapped me on the back and turned me in that direction. "Come on, old man. Let's see what the emergency is."

I could already see the blackout drapes had been pulled over the sheers, darkening the living room considerably, regardless of the lamps and candles blazing away.

As soon as I stepped into the room they all started singing the Happy Birthday song in five different pitches and at five different speeds. I laughed and moved over to Tom, threading our fingers together. Love filled my heart, pushing tears into my eyes. These were my guys, my safe harbor against the storms of life. They'd seen me at my worst and at my best and they were still here. There wasn't a thing I wouldn't do for any of them.

They included Tom when the lyrics called for names, a nice touch since his birthday had occurred a month earlier, while he was still being held captive by his mother's goons. I turned and gave my husband a lingering kiss, discreetly wiping the wetness from his cheeks.

CJ and Trevor bent over two medium-sized white boxes on the coffee table, pulling off the tops to reveal two cakes, one decorated with my name and one with Tom's. I swallowed down emotion as I watched my son deftly light a single candle on each cake.

"Pops, we wanted to celebrate your birthday today because having you back with us where you belong is sort of a rebirth." CJ smirked. "That doesn't mean you can start saying you're young again or anything. You still have to be forty-four."

"Aw, shucks," Tom responded with a laugh.

"And Dad, since your birthday was the day that everything went down, it kind of got skipped. Sorry about that."

"That's fine," I said, gazing between my husband and son. "I got your father back. That's the best gift I could have asked for."

"I know. That's why I didn't get you anything," CJ said with a grin. He lifted Tom's cake and held it out to him. "Make a wish, Pops."

Tom swallowed and wiped away a stray tear. "Being home with you and your dad means my wish has already come true."

"Dammit, you're not supposed to say stuff like that when I have a German chocolate cake in my hands," CJ said, quickly putting it back down. He took the three steps to the chair Tom sat in and knelt in front of it, pulling his father into a long, tight hug.

We'd never been known for sparing affection, but in the last week there had been a lot more spontaneous outpourings of emotion as we all adjusted to our new normal. Tom, CJ, and I shared an unshakable love, so I knew our little family would pull through this madness just fine.

Judging by the way Trevor took ahold of both of his men's hands, I had every confidence they would make it too.

I knelt beside my husband's chair and joined him and our son in their hug, so grateful my family was whole again.

EPILOGUE

A YEAR LATER

I collapsed on top of Tom, sweaty, winded, and drained in all the best ways. His lips found mine, pulling me into a long, deep kiss. He tasted of wine and chocolate and sex. My skin tingled from my orgasm. He gripped my ass, urging me back into a rhythm. I eagerly complied, diving into his kiss. He thrust hard and deep, more and again, until he broke the kiss with a shout. I tightened around him as he emptied hot into me, dragging a strangled groan from him.

I nudged his ear with my nose. "Happy Valentine's Day, my love," I whispered.

He chuckled breathlessly. "Happy Valentine's, barista."

I slid off of him and curled up against him with my head on his heaving chest. I didn't want to stop touching him. I dragged my fingertips from his navel to his nipple and back again, loving the way his abs contracted at my teasing touch.

It had been a long year, filled with utter destruction and slow, careful rebuilding. We'd both undergone counseling, although Tom's was much more intensive and devastating than mine. For a time I'd feared the process would tear us apart, but the communication skills we'd practiced well for the previous twenty years had served us well. We'd worked through the hard times with talk and tears.

We had just conquered our most difficult time when Althea's trial started. It took six painful weeks to convict his mother of a litany of charges, including kidnapping, unlawful imprisonment, and conspiracy to commission murder. She hadn't paid enough for her crimes though. She'd only been in prison seven weeks when the brain tumor claimed her life. I'd kept a careful watch over her corpse, just to make sure it was her they put in the ground.

Dev and Shelby had tracked down the thugs who'd taken shots at Trevor and me. They'd been happy to roll over on Althea in exchange for a lighter sentence regarding the drugs they were carrying when the police picked them up.

I'd thought the shooting had been the only attempt on my life, but I was wrong. The idiots had confessed to mistakenly blowing up a house down the block, hitting Four One Four instead of Four Four Four. I remembered the explosion. It had been the first week of December, about two weeks after we'd discovered that Tom wasn't in his grave. The neighbors had been told it was a gas leak. We hadn't been told the fire department suspected foul play.

If Althea's minions hadn't successfully robbed Tom and me of a year of our lives together, their incompetence would have been hilarious. One of them got himself killed, the other two couldn't find the right house, nor could they hit one six-foot male with a semi-automatic rifle. Instead of being amused, however, I was enraged again at each revelation.

On days I was being generous, I could count two good things that came out of the most hellacious year of our lives. Matthew, who had been appalled by Althea's treachery, had grown closer to accepting me in Tom's life. He'd dropped the passive aggressive bullshit and started treating me like a real human being.

And then there was Shaun and his boys. If Tom hadn't vanished, I never would have hired Dev or left Excellere. Which means Shaun, Dev, and Trevor never would have gotten together. And they were so disgustingly cute together.

"Stop thinking."

I smiled into his chest. "You always tell me that."

"And I'm always right." He ruffled my hair. "Let's go shower. We have to meet the guys in a little bit."

"I was just thinking about them," I confessed.

"I'm glad Shaun found them. He was unhappy for a lot of years."

I rested my chin on his pec so I could look into my husband's beautiful green eyes. "How did I never notice that? I just thought he was happy playing around. Does that make me a bad friend?"

"He showed you what he wanted you to know. I think if either of you had forced the subject, it would have ruined your friendship instead of bringing you closer. You both had too much to lose."

"And then I had nothing."

"I wouldn't say that, but you'd taken a blow. I know I would be lost if I didn't have me."

I smacked his chest. "You're a jerk."

He laughed and rolled to pin me beneath him. He'd regained about half the weight he'd lost at the ranch and it had all come back as muscle. He was sexier than he'd ever been, not just physically, but emotionally too. He bent to gift me with a slow burning kiss, one that made my toes curl and gave me goosebumps. "I am the luckiest man alive to have been loved by you all these years," he said. "I've never known a better husband, father, or lover. I want to spend the rest of my life and all of eternity with you, barista. Will you marry me again?"

Tears rolled into my ears as I swallowed hard. "Yes," I whispered.

He smiled and when he kissed me again, the whole world vanished.

The End

AUTHOR'S THANKS

If you enjoyed this book, please consider leaving a rating and/or review at Goodreads, Amazon, or your ebook retailer. Ratings and reviews help bring an author's work to new audiences. Thank you!

ABOUT THE AUTHOR

Carter Quinn was born and raised in a very small Western Kansas town where cattle vastly outnumber humans. He came out in 1992, when doing so was still considered an act of rebellion. He discovered M/M in 2010 and started writing again after a fifteen year break. Now he's told Corporate America to kiss his books. Carter again lives in cattle country, entirely too far from his beloved Colorado Avalanche..

You can find Carter here:

carterquinnbooks.com
carterquinnbooks@gmail.com
facebook.com/CarterQuinn
goodreads.com/author/show/5607272.Carter_Quinn
On Twitter: @Carter_Quinn

Also by Carter Quinn:

Out of the Blackness (Avery #1)
Into the Light (Avery #2)

The Way Back (Kansas #1)
Fire & Rain (Kansas #2)

The Bridge

Coming Soon:

Ashes to Embers
Behind the Mask